SECRETS TO THE GRAVE

Also by Tami Hoag

Deeper Than the Dead
The Alibi Man
Prior Bad Acts
Kill the Messenger
Dark Horse
Dust to Dust
Ashes to Ashes
A Thin Dark Line
Guilty as Sin
Night Sins
Dark Paradise
Cry Wolf
Still Waters
Lucky's Lady
Sarah's Sin
Magic

TAMI HOAG

SECRETS TO THE GRAVE

First published in 2010 by Orion Books,
an imprint of The Orion Publishing Group Ltd
Orion House, 5 Upper Saint Martin's Lane
London WC2H 9EA

First published in Great Britain in 2010 by Orion Books

An Hachette UK Company

1 3 5 7 9 10 8 6 4 2

A CIP catalogue record for this book is
available from the British Library.

ISBN (Hardback) 978 0 7528 9894 0
ISBN (Export Trade Paperback) 978 0 7528 9895 7

Printed in Great Britain by Clays Ltd, St Ives plc

The Orion Publishing Group's policy is to use papers that are natural,
renewable and recyclable products and made from wood grown in sustainable
forests. The logging and manufacturing processes are expected to
conform to the environmental regulations of the country of origin.

www.orionbooks.co.uk

*With thanks and appreciation to Brian Tart, Ben Sevier,
and all the team at Dutton.*

Thanks for understanding what I do and how I do it.

AUTHOR'S NOTE

1986. Ronald Reagan was in his second term as president. On January 28, the space shuttle *Challenger* disintegrated seventy-three seconds after its launch, killing all seven astronauts aboard, including teacher Christa McAuliffe. *Out of Africa* won the Oscar for best picture. A mishandled safety test at the Chernobyl Nuclear Power Plant in the Ukranian SSR, Soviet Union, killed more than 4,000 people and caused 350,000 to be forcibly resettled away from the area. The New York Mets won the World Series, defeating the Boston Red Sox in seven games. The Bangles had a number one worldwide hit with "Walk Like an Egyptian."

It was a year of big hair, big shoulder pads, and spandex.

In 1986, DNA science was still in its infancy with regards to law enforcement and had yet to be presented as evidence in a court of law. Investigators with foresight were holding on to evidence obtained at crime scenes and from crime victims, waiting for the science to advance enough to help them convict killers and rapists.

In 1986, California's organization for Court Appointed Special Advocates—CalCASA—was still a year away. Local CASA programs (which provide advocates for children to assist them in dealing with the courts and foster care system) existed but were still relatively few and far between.

In 1986, AIDS was only just becoming widely known as a killer of near epidemic proportions worldwide, and the gay community was under fire. In 1986, it was still considered scandalous for single women to become pregnant and to raise the child on their own. My, how times have changed.

At the end of 1986, I made the decision to put my best effort into becoming a published author the following year. My first book would be published in 1988, and I would purchase my first desktop computer—with black-and-white monitor—with my advance from that book.

When I sat down to the first book of this series, *Deeper Than the Dead,* it never occurred to me that I would be transporting readers to a simpler time. Nineteen eighty-five didn't seem all that long ago to me. Then, one night at work an infomercial came on my television—for *Greatest Hits of the Eighties.* As I listened to the sampling of songs, smiling at the memories they evoked, I suddenly came to a shocking realization: Oh, my God, I've become nostalgic! I'm *old*!!

Once I finally accepted that stunning truth, I embraced my trip back in time while also gaining a renewed appreciation for the technology available to law enforcement—and to the rest of us—today.

SECRETS TO THE GRAVE

1

November 1986

The house stood by itself back off the road in a field of dried golden grass, half hidden by spreading oaks. An amalgam of styles—part Spanish, part ranch—the once-white stucco building was weathered in a way that made it seem a part of the natural surroundings, as if it had grown up out of the earth and belonged there as much as any of the hundred-year-old trees.

The scene was a plein air painting, soft and impressionistic: the golden grass, the dark trees, bruise-purple mountains in the background, and the whisper-blue sky strewn with long, thin, pink-tinted clouds; the small white house with its old tile roof. On the other side of the mountains the sun had begun its descent toward the ocean. Here, the day seemed to have paused to admire its own perfection. Stillness held the landscape enraptured.

Nothing gave away a hint of what lay within the house.

The driveway was a path of dirt and crushed rock with grass and weeds sprouted up the middle like the mane of a wild pony. Falling-down fences the color of driftwood created the lane between two overgrown pastures that had once been home to cattle and horses.

A vintage Woody station wagon well past its glory days was parked at a casual angle near an open shed full of rusted farm equipment. An old Radio Flyer red wagon had been abandoned near the front porch with an orange tabby cat sitting in it, waiting for a ride. On the porch two kittens played peekaboo among overgrown pots of parched geraniums and kitchen herbs. One propped herself up on the screen door and peered into the house, then squeaked and leapt and dashed away, tail straight up in the air.

Inside the house nothing moved but flies.

A horrible still life had been staged on the Saltillo tile kitchen floor.

A woman lay dead, her hair spreading out around her head like a dark cloud. Her skin was the color of milk. Her lips had been painted as red as a rose—as red as her blood must have been as it drained from the wounds carved into her flesh.

She lay discarded like a life-size broken doll—made up, torn up, and cast aside, her brown eyes cloudy and lifeless.

Beside her lay a smaller doll—her child—head resting on her shoulder, face streaked with the last of her mother's life's blood.

The flies buzzed. The wall clock ticked above the sink.

The telephone receiver dangled near the floor, stenciled with small bloody fingerprints. The last words spoken into it were a whisper still hanging in the air: "*My daddy hurt my mommy . . .*"

2

"The victim is Marissa Fordham, twenty-eight, single mom. An artist."

Sheriff's detective Tony Mendez rattled off the facts as if unaffected by what he had seen inside the house. Nothing could have been further from the truth. In fact, shortly after he arrived at the scene, he had had to excuse himself from the kitchen to vomit under a tree in the backyard.

He had been second on the scene, the property being on his side of town. The first responder—a young deputy—had puked under the same tree. Mendez had never seen so much blood. The smell of it was still like a fist lodged at the back of his throat. Every time he closed his eyes he saw the victims in freeze-frame shots from a horror movie.

His stomach rolled.

"You said there were two vics."

Vince Leone, forty-nine, former special agent with the FBI's legendary Behavioral Sciences Unit, former Chicago homicide detective. Leone had been his mentor during his course at the FBI's National Academy—a training program for law enforcement agencies around the country and around the globe. In fact, Leone had come to Oak Knoll more than a year past in part to work a serial-killer case, in part to try to recruit Mendez to the Bureau.

The case was ongoing. Neither of them had left.

Leone had just arrived on the scene. They drifted slowly away from his car toward the house, both of them taking in the cool, eucalyptus-scented air.

"The woman's four-year-old daughter," Mendez said. "She had a faint pulse. She's on her way to the hospital. I wouldn't expect her to make it."

Leone muttered an expletive under his breath.

He was an imposing man. Six foot three with a mane of wavy salt-and-pepper hair. A thick mustache drew the eye away from the small, shiny scar marking the entrance wound of the bullet that should have ended his life. Instead, the thing remained in his head, inoperable because of its precarious location.

"I hate when it's a kid," he said.

"Yeah. What did a four-year-old do to deserve that?"

"Witness."

"She knew the killer."

"Or he's just one mean bastard."

"I'd say he has that covered," Mendez said.

They went through the little gate to the yard and followed the rock path around the side of the house, past an old concrete fountain that gurgled soothingly despite the occasion.

"Who called it in?"

"A friend who happened to drop by."

Leone stopped and looked at him. "It's the crack of freaking dawn."

To be precise, 7:29 A.M. The sun was barely up.

"Yeah," Mendez said. "Wait until you meet him. Odd guy."

"Odd how?"

"Looks-like-a-suspect odd. Who drops in on a neighbor at six in the morning?"

"Is he here?"

"He's with Bill."

Bill Hicks, sheriff's detective, Mendez's partner. Hicks had a way of putting people at ease.

"Is Cal coming?" Leone asked.

Cal Dixon, county sheriff, Mendez's boss.

"On his way."

"I don't want to step on toes here."

Leone was not on the SO payroll, but he was too good a resource not to call. Studying the country's worst serial killers for more than a decade, he had seen just about every atrocity one human being could inflict on another. More important, he could discern much from the scene that could point them in a direction in the search for the perpetrator.

"I spoke with him," Mendez said. "He agreed."

"Good."

They paused at the kitchen door. Mendez pointed at the tree.

"The official puke zone. In case you need it."

"Good to know."

The scene struck him almost as hard going in this time as it had the first time. The contrasts, he decided—and the smell. Visually, the contrasts rocked him. The kitchen was like something from another era: old-fashioned painted cupboards, a cast-iron farmhouse sink, checked curtains, appliances that had to have been from the fifties.

It was the kind of kitchen that should have had June Cleaver or Aunt Bea in it. Instead, crime-scene techs bustled around like so many cooks, dusting this, photographing that, all working around the bloating, discolored body of a murdered woman on the blood-drenched Mexican tile floor.

Leone took in the tableau with a dark frown and his hands on his hips.

"She's been dead awhile."

"A couple of days, I'd say."

"Maggots already," Leone commented. "Has she been moved?"

"No. I didn't let the paramedics touch her. There was no question she was dead."

The victim's throat had been cut so viciously she was nearly decapitated. Someone had painted her lips red with her own blood.

"And the little girl was where?"

"Laying with her head on her mother's left shoulder. I moved her when I felt her pulse," Mendez said.

"And what had been done to her? Was she stabbed?"

"I couldn't tell. She was covered in blood. I couldn't tell if it was hers or her mother's. Looked to me like she might have been strangled, though. There were bloody finger marks on her throat."

Leone took a handkerchief out of his pocket to hold over his mouth and nose as he moved closer to the body on the floor. He was careful not to step in the blood. He squatted down for a different angle.

The woman's breasts had been cut off. There was no sign of them anywhere in the room. The killer had to have taken them with him when he left. A macabre souvenir. The gaping wounds were alive with fly larvae.

She lay spread-eagle, faceup, staring at the ceiling. She was naked. Wounds slashed her arms, her legs, her torso. She had been stabbed so many times in the lower abdomen, the area looked like a lump of ground meat, crawling now with maggots.

The blade of a butcher's knife protruded from her vagina.

Leone arched a brow. "That makes a statement."

"Have you ever seen that before?" Mendez asked.

"I've seen the blade inserted. Never like this. What do you make of it?"

Leone looked up at him, ever the mentor. He sure as hell had an opinion. The man was a legend. He probably had already begun to build the profile of the killer in his head. By the time they broke for coffee he would have decided the perp had a stutter and walked with a limp.

He wanted Mendez to think for himself, read the scene in front of him, call on cases he had studied and things he had been taught at the National Academy and in the field.

"I think maybe the statement is about her more than it is about her killer," Mendez said.

Leone nodded. "It would seem so."

He stood up, took a step back, crossed his arms. His gaze slowly scanned the room, taking in every detail. Outside the house an engine died, a car door slammed.

"He didn't bring the knife with him," he said, pointing to a wooden block of knives on the counter. "The big one is missing."

"That's a lot of overkill for a crime of opportunity," Mendez said.

Leone hummed a low note. "Any signs of a robbery?"

"I made a quick pass through the house. There's no sign of forced entry. A couple of rooms have been tossed, but I don't know why. There's some expensive-looking jewelry on her dresser. It doesn't look like anything in the way of electronics was taken."

"Drugs?"

"No paraphernalia. The house is too clean for a junkie. I don't make it for drugs. It doesn't feel that way."

"No," Leone agreed. "This was personal. No question. We're looking at maybe thirty or forty stab wounds."

The screen door opened and Cal Dixon stepped into the scene. Dixon was fifty-four, silver-haired, and fit. His uniform always looked freshly pressed. He turned his piercing blue eyes first to the victim, then to Leone and Mendez. His expression was grim and washed pale.

"What the hell is the world coming to?"

"First murder in a year, boss," Mendez said, as if that were a bright spot in their lives.

Dixon came over to stand with them, hands jammed at his waist. He pointedly did not look down at what remained of Marissa Fordham.

"Dispatch had a nine-one-one call yesterday," he said. "Early morning. A child's voice saying that daddy had hurt mommy. That was it. No address. No name. The phone went dead and that was that.

"The supervisor came to me, but what could I do? I can't have every house in the area searched on the off chance there might have been a crime committed."

"I read Orange County has the enhanced nine-one-one system," Mendez said. "All the info comes up on the screen with the call. Name and address."

"That costs big bucks," Dixon said. "I've filled out the paperwork for a grant, but who knows how long that will take."

Once again, progress progressed at a painful crawl toward Oak Knoll, California. Mendez kept abreast of the latest technology being developed for law enforcement, yet tantalizingly out of reach—particularly for smaller agencies. They didn't have the budget or the clout.

He glanced down at the corpse of Marissa Fordham, two days into the decaying process, smelling like an open sewer on a hot summer day. "Too late for her."

3

Vince excused himself from the kitchen, made a beeline for the designated tree, and threw up. He had looked at every kind of horror during his career with the Bureau. His life's work was the study of murderers. He had spent three years traveling the country from one maximum-security prison to the next, interviewing men who had committed some of the most horrific crimes in the history of mankind as the Bureau gathered information and ammunition to aid in the hunt of human predators. He had stood over crime scenes, one bloodier and more depraved than the next. He'd seen so many bodies in so many states of decay, he had learned long ago not to attach that visual to any emotion other than disgust for the crime.

It wasn't the visual that got to him.

It was the bullet in his head.

He'd been living with it now for a year and a half, and had grown familiar with the tricks it liked to play on him. The pain ebbed and flowed. Sometimes it was like a thunderstorm contained in his skull. Sometimes it was a dragon sleeping just under the surface.

There were no medical texts in which a list could be found of side effects to having a .22 caliber bullet in one's head. Seeing as the great majority of people didn't survive the experience of being shot at nearly point-blank range, anecdotal information was hard to come by. Vince's own doctors usually had only one thing to say when he would tell them about his symptoms: huh.

One of the stranger side effects was the sudden heightening of senses. Sometimes his vision would become so acute, color so saturated, the light so bright, his eyeballs would ache. Sometimes the smallest sounds would be so amplified in his head he would cringe. Sometimes—now—his sense of smell became so sensitive, every molecule of scent seemed swollen, so full he could literally taste them.

It wasn't the visual that got to him today. It was the smell.

Like any dead creature, the body of Marissa Fordham had begun its inglorious process of decomposition. Nature was without mercy or modesty. There were no exceptions to the rules. The business of death was dealt with in a no-nonsense, practical matter. Once the heart ceased to pump blood, systems shut down and chemical changes began the process of reducing the highest being on the food chain to food for other creatures.

It didn't take long. Especially in the warm weather they'd been experiencing. Absent a soul, the eyes glaze over and flatten, the skin loses color, the body's temperature begins to drop. As if summoned, the blowflies come, laying their eggs in the wounds and orifices. A couple of hours after the last breath, rigor mortis begins in the jaw and neck, slowly spreading through the body. Bacteria rampaging through the abdomen cause gases to form, causing bloating, and the smell begins to gain strength.

It was the smell that got him today.

Vince dug a pack of Doublemint gum out of his pocket, unwrapped two sticks, and began to chew the taste of vomit out of his mouth.

He felt a little weak, a little dizzy. He had no time for either. To clear his head he thought about his bride of five months burrowing under the covers of their bed as he had dressed to leave for this crime scene. A warm sense of calm washed over him and he smiled a little at what a lucky son of a bitch he really was.

"You want to talk to the neighbor?"

Mendez had come out the kitchen door. He took a deep breath of the cool morning air, clearing his head of the stench of violent death. The yard around the house was scattered with pots of geraniums and marigolds and garden herbs. Vince took a deep breath of his own.

Mid-thirties, sharp and ambitious, Mendez had been a good candidate for the Bureau. That had been half of Vince's goal when he had first come to Oak Knoll to help with the See-No-Evil murders the year before—to recruit Mendez. With some further education and experience, he would have made it to the Investigative Support Unit—the field side of Behavioral Sciences. He had shown a strong interest and talent for the job during his time at the National Academy. But See-No-Evil had consumed the young detective—as it had Vince. Mendez was still working it, trying to help the DA build as tight a case as possible against the man who had murdered at least three local women—and in Vince's opinion, probably more.

"Yeah, sure," he said. "Where is he?"

They went around to the front of the house where Bill Hicks sat on a porch bench, forearms resting on his thighs as he talked to the man who had called in the crime. Tall, lanky, red-haired, Hicks was a cowboy in his free time. He was good in an interview, had an easygoing way about him that helped take the edge off in an otherwise tense situation.

Hicks looked up and allowed himself a lazy smile. "Hey, Vince. Good to see you. How's married life?"

Vince took a seat on an old painted metal chair. "Great. How you doing, Bill?"

"No complaints." Hicks tipped his head in the direction of the neighbor. "Vince, this is Mr. Zahn. Mr. Zahn, unfortunately, made the discovery this morning."

Vince reached out to the man sitting beside Hicks on the bench. Zahn stared at his hand for a moment before looking up. His face was strangely blank.

"I'm sorry," he said in a hushed, breathy voice. He clasped his hands together on his lap but couldn't keep them still, wringing one over the other again and again. "I don't shake hands. I'm . . . a . . . I have a problem with that. I'm terribly sorry."

Zahn was maybe in his late thirties or early forties, but prematurely gray. His hair stood out around his head like a soft cloud. His face was long and narrow with sharp angles, his eyes wide, pale, translucent green, and vacant in the way of someone looking inward at a terrible memory.

"My condolences on your loss," Vince offered softly. "I assume Ms. Fordham was a friend—you stopping by so early and all."

"Yes," Zahn said. "Marissa and I were friends."

"Why so early?" Mendez asked. He stood, leaning back against a post, his arms crossed.

Too blunt, Vince thought. This was where his protégé lacked finesse. Zahn was already nervous. He almost flinched at the tone of the detective's voice.

"I wasn't doing anything wrong," Zahn said. "Marissa is always up early. She likes the early light."

"You've been friends for a long time?" Vince asked.

"As long as she's been here. As long as I've been here. Four years?" he asked, as if Vince would know.

"Maybe you can help us then, Mr. Zahn," Vince suggested. "What can you tell us about Ms. Fordham? Was she married? Divorced?"

"Single. She was single."

"What about her little girl?"

"Haley. Please tell me Haley isn't dead," Zahn pleaded. "I couldn't stand it if Haley was injured or dead."

"She's been taken to the hospital," Vince assured him. "She isn't dead."

"Oh my God. Thank God."

"What about Haley's father? Is he ever around?"

"I don't know him. I don't know who he is. Marissa was very private."

"Do you know if she has any family in the area?"

"Oh, no." He shook his head. "They were estranged. She never spoke of them."

"Do you know where she was from?"

"The East Coast, I think. From a good family, I'm sure."

"Mr. Zahn—"

"Call me Zander, please. *Alex-zander.* I've always gone by Zander. That's what people call me. Please call me that."

"All right. Zander. I'm Vince. This is Tony," he said, hooking a thumb in the direction of Mendez. "You already know Bill."

"Vince and Tony," Zahn murmured, wringing his hands. "Vince and Tony."

"Do you know if Ms. Fordham was having trouble with anyone?" Mendez asked. "Had anyone been bothering her lately? Was she afraid of anyone?"

"Marissa was never afraid. She didn't believe in fear. She embraced life. Every day. She had the most courageous spirit I've ever known."

When he spoke of his deceased friend Zahn's face took on a beatific, rapturous glow, as if he had seen an angel.

"Do you know of anyone who might have posed a threat to her?" Mendez asked.

"Detractors of her art," Zahn said. "Detractors of her art threatened her creativity."

"I meant more of a physical threat," Mendez corrected himself.

Points for patience on that one, Vince thought. Zahn couldn't seem to give a straight answer. The guy was socially off, his manner of speaking peculiar and often repetitive. He didn't like to make eye contact, but once he made it, he went into a stare. A fascinating study if they hadn't needed answers to jump-start a murder investigation.

Zahn looked away. "No," he said, but Vince thought he didn't mean it.

"Marissa was an artist?" Vince asked.

"Oh, yes. You didn't know her? She was quite well-known. I'm surprised you didn't know *of* her."

"I'm new to the area," Vince explained.

Zahn nodded. "Quite well-known. She was."

"What do you do for a living, Zander?"

He seemed to think about his answer before saying, "I'm an artist as well. My life is my art."

"You like the early morning light too," Vince said, smiling like an old friend.

"Yes. I also meditate. I meditate very early. And then I come to see Marissa and Haley. We drink mimosas. Not Haley, of course," he hastened to add. "Marissa is an excellent mother."

"But this morning no mimosas," Vince said. "Tell us your story, Zander. How you came here, what you saw along the way."

"My story," Zahn said, rolling the concept around in his labyrinth mind. He liked it. "I meditated until five twenty-three and then I walked here."

"Where do you live?" Mendez asked.

"Over the hill. Off Dyer Canyon Road."

"That's a long walk."

"I enjoy walking."

"Did you see anything out of the ordinary as you approached the house?" Mendez asked.

"Not at all. It was quite dark."

"What happened when you got here?"

"I went to the kitchen door. It was open, as always. I called out to Marissa. There was no coffee on. I couldn't smell the coffee, but something else . . . And then I saw them."

Zahn stood up so abruptly they all startled.

"I'm finished telling my story now. I can't tell this story," he said, agitated, rubbing his palms hard against his thighs, as if trying to wipe off something greasy. "I'll be leaving now. I have to go. This is very disturbing. I'm so disturbed by this."

Vince rose slowly from his chair and put a hand out toward Zahn, as if to steady him, but very careful not to touch him.

"It's all right, Zander. You've had a terrible shock," he said quietly. "Someone here can drive you home. We'll talk more another time."

"I'm very disturbed," Zahn said. "I would prefer to walk, thank you. Good-bye."

They watched him cross the yard on his way to the path he had come on. He walked very quickly, his arms straight down at his sides as if bound to him.

"He's disturbed," Vince said.

Mendez rolled his eyes. "I'll say."

4

"I hate this fucking place. Everybody here is a fucking nut job."

Anne ignored the profanity designed to get a rise out of her. Dennis Farman was a disturbed little boy. He stared at her now as she sat across from him at the white Melamine table in the visitor's room. He was a slightly odd-looking boy with his shock of red-orange hair and ears set a little too low on his head. His small blue eyes held either anger or emptiness, depending on his mood. Seldom anything in between.

He was twelve now. Anne had met him at the start of the school year in 1985 when she had been teaching fifth grade at Oak Knoll Elementary.

She had known from the first day Dennis would be trouble. She had been forewarned by his fourth-grade teacher. Having been held back in the third grade, Dennis was a little bigger than the rest of the boys in her class, and he had the look of a bully—which he was. But she'd had no idea at the time just how disturbed Dennis Farman was.

"Are you hating anyone in particular today?"

He jutted his chin out at her. "Yeah. You."

"Why do you hate me?" she asked evenly. "I'm the only person who comes here to see you."

"You get to leave," he said, fidgeting on his chair. "I don't. I have to stay here with the freaks."

"I'm sorry about that."

"Why?" he asked bluntly. "You think I'm a freak."

"I never said that."

Anne never considered herself naïve. She had firsthand knowledge that not every child grew up in an ideal environment. But no one had suspected the horror Dennis's life had been. He had been physically and emotionally abused, and had been made an orphan a year ago by the murder of his mother and the suicide of his father, a deputy sheriff.

Just hours before his father's suicide, Dennis had stabbed a classmate, a little boy who had been his only friend. The boy, Cody Roache, had survived. It remained to be seen if Dennis would survive to live any kind of life.

Vince said no. In his experience, children as broken as Dennis Farman were beyond fixing. Anne wanted to hope that wasn't true.

Maybe she was a little naïve after all.

Hopeful, she preferred to call it.

The judicial system didn't know what to do with Dennis. He was considered to be too young to go to a juvenile facility, let alone prison, even though he was guilty of assault at the very least, and a case could certainly have been made for attempted murder. He had no relatives willing to take responsibility for him. No families in the foster care system would take him.

The temporary solution had been to house him in the county mental hospital. Partly her fault, Anne thought. She had been the one fighting to keep him out of the juvenile system by arguing that he was sick and needed help.

She had quit teaching to finish her degree in child psychology in part because of Dennis Farman. She had taken the training course to become a court-appointed special advocate for children specifically because of Dennis. Someone had to act as his voice in the court system and try to explain to him what was going on.

Troubled as he was, guilty as he was, he was still a little boy lost with no one in his corner. Anne had stood up and taken the job.

It wasn't that she wanted the job. It wasn't that she held any affection for Dennis Farman, personally. He was inherently unlikeable. The crime he had committed was shocking and terrible. It wasn't even that she believed he could be salvaged or saved. She simply couldn't stand by and watch a child be cut adrift for the rest of his life.

Vince wasn't particularly happy about it. He worried she would only be disappointed at the futility of her battle and would, in the end, be heartbroken. Since her husband was one of the world's leading experts on the criminal mind, it was difficult to argue with him on the subject. Anne had known only one homicidal child.

There was no doubt Dennis exhibited classic signs of being a sociopath with no ability to empathize with others. He was filled with rage at the rough hand life had dealt him. Anne suspected he had attacked Cody to make someone else hurt as much as he did. And to further complicate and twist his profile, Dennis had been harboring dark, sexually tinted fantasies for a long time—especially troubling in a child so young.

"You think I'm a freak. I know you do. Everybody does. Everybody hates me."

"I don't hate you, Dennis. Nobody hates you. Everybody hates what you did to Cody."

He scowled and looked down at the table, pretending to draw on it with his thumb. Anne wondered what he was imagining. She would never forget the day she had discovered Dennis's notebook masterpiece depicting naked women with knives in their chests. It was the first time she had ever really understood the concept of a person's blood running cold.

"He didn't die," Dennis said. "What's the big deal?"

"How would you feel if he had died?"

He shrugged with a nonchalance that would have been stunning if they had never had this conversation before. "Why did you do it, Dennis?" she asked.

Dennis rolled his eyes. "You keep asking me that. I keep telling you: just because. I just wanted to see what it felt like."

She had never asked him to describe what it had felt like to plunge a knife into the stomach of his only friend. "Have you done your homework?" she asked.

"Why should I?" he challenged. "What are you gonna do to me if I don't? Put me in jail? Put me in the loony bin?"

"I'm not going to do anything to you. But you would be helping yourself if you did it. Do you want to repeat the fifth grade when you get out of here?"

She had taken it upon herself to tutor him. No one else was interested in the job.

"I'm never getting out of here," he said. "Or I'll go to prison. Prison might be cool."

"Why do you say that?"

"Because there's killers in there."

Anne sat for a moment with her chin in her hand. This was like a chess game. How did she know she was making the right move? She felt way out of her league.

"You think killers are cool?" she asked. "Why?"

Now there was something like excitement in his eyes. Anne's stomach twisted.

"Because," he said, "if they don't like somebody, they just kill them. Then they never have to see them again."

What should she say to that? That killing is wrong? Who would he like to kill? She tried never to take the bait with him, thinking he mostly said these things for the shock value. What if she was wrong? For a moment she felt like she was drowning.

Dennis was watching her from the corner of his eye as he turned and sat sideways on his chair.

"I would kill Tommy Crane," he said.

Anne didn't react. It was no surprise. In fact, it was nothing he hadn't said before.

"I know you don't like Tommy," she said. "You think he has a perfect life, but he doesn't, Dennis. His father is going to go to prison."

"Yeah. He's a killer. That's so cool."

So was yours, Anne was tempted to say. What would he do? Would he react? Would that crack the hard shell? Would he break down and cry?

Tommy Crane had been the object of Dennis's jealousy and bullying. Outwardly, Tommy had appeared to have the perfect family. His father was a well-respected dentist with an office on Oak Knoll's trendy—and expensive—pedestrian plaza. His mother was a real estate agent. They had lived in a beautiful home, in a beautiful neighborhood. But Tommy's life had not been beautiful.

Tommy's father was sitting in jail awaiting trial, suspected of being the See-No-Evil killer, though he had yet to be charged with any of the murders. He would first stand trial for assault and the attempted murder . . . of Anne Navarre Leone.

"Tommy doesn't live here anymore," was all she said.

She rose from her plastic chair, grabbing her purse.

"I have to step outside for a minute," she said. "When I come back in, I want to see your math homework. If you haven't done it, you're going to sit here until you do."

The boy looked up at her, a little bit shocked by her sudden steely attitude.

"I'm trying to help you, Dennis," she said. "You need to do your part."

5

Anne walked out of the room and down the hall, past a man in his pajamas talking to the fire alarm. She walked past the nurses' station without exchanging glances with the staff she had come to know well. She needed to be alone, even if only in her head. The too-familiar pressure was building in her chest. She couldn't get a good breath. She remembered the feeling of a hand around her throat.

She buzzed herself out the security door.

The day was sunny and quickly turning hot. Another day in paradise. Anne had grown up in Oak Knoll, far enough north and west of Los Angeles to escape the city's uglier vices. Most of the time. She had left to attend UCLA, despite the fact that her father had been a professor at the highly respected private college in Oak Knoll—or, perhaps, because of it. She hadn't planned on coming back, but life had had other plans for her.

She sat down on a concrete bench along the front of the building and rested her head in her hands as the emotions rocked through her. Post-traumatic stress syndrome: Not just for war veterans. Victims of violent crime suffered the same way.

The memories flashed strobelike through her mind: hands around her throat, choking her; fists punching her; feet kicking her, breaking her ribs, collapsing a lung.

Even a year after her abduction and attempted murder, the first and strongest feeling that assaulted her when she thought of what had happened was fear. Raw, primal fear. Then anger—rage, in fact. Then a profound sense of loss.

Her therapist told her to let the emotion come like a wave and wash over her, not to fight against it. The sooner she accepted the feelings, the sooner she could let go of them.

Easier said than done. The fear of drowning in that wave was strong; the sense of losing control, overwhelming; the swell of anger for what she had lost, crushing.

She tried again to take a deep breath. She felt like there were bands of steel tight around her chest.

"Hey, beautiful," a deep, familiar voice said. A big hand brushed over her hair and rested on her shoulder. She leaned into him as he sat down next to her, turned her face toward him, her head instinctively finding the perfect spot against his shoulder.

"You look a lot like my wife," he said softly, wrapping his arms around her. "Only my wife is always happy. I make sure of it."

Her breath hitched in her throat as she looked up at him. "H-how did you know I n-needed you?"

He brushed a tear from her cheek with his thumb. "Well, I like to think you need me every minute of every day," he said, his dark eyes shining.

Anne sniffed and managed a little smile. "I do."

He leaned down and kissed her softly on the lips.

To people who didn't know them, Anne supposed they seemed an unlikely couple. Vince, forty-nine, more than a little world-wise and world-weary, a man who had dedicated his life to understanding evil. And Anne herself, twenty-nine, a former fifth-grade teacher who had dedicated her life to understanding children.

Yet they made perfect sense to her. Even as a child, Anne had been mature beyond her years. She had never been interested in young men. Vince was mature, strong, full of integrity, a man who knew his own mind. A man who had no interest in wasting his second chance at life.

"Tough morning with the demon child?" he asked.

"Don't say I told you so."

Vince shook his head. "I know you have to try. I get it. I don't like it, but I get it."

"Thank you."

"You want to talk about it?"

She shook her head. "Same old, same old. Dennis said something . . . I just needed a moment. I'll be fine."

He brushed her dark hair back. "Tough cookie."

"When I have to be."

"The point is, you don't have to be."

"I know," she acknowledged and deftly changed the subject. "What did Tony call you out on so early?"

"A homicide," he said, getting what Anne called his cop eyes—an expression that gave away nothing.

"I know that," she said with a hint of irritation. "Was it something bad?"

Stupid question. Nobody called Vince Leone for a bar brawl that ended with one idiot breaking the skull of another idiot. He got calls in the middle of night from detectives in Budapest, FBI agents in New York, law enforcement agencies all over the world, to consult on only the most grisly, psychologically twisted cases. If Tony Mendez called before dawn, he had a big reason.

"Do you know a woman named Marissa Fordham?"

"No," Anne said, "but the name is familiar."

"She was an artist."

Anne thought about it. "Oh, right. She did a poster for the Thomas Center last year. It was gorgeous."

Marissa Fordham was dead, she realized. She would never know the woman. There would be no more beautiful artwork to help raise money for charities.

"What happened?"

"Found dead in her home by a neighbor. She and her daughter. The little girl is at Mercy General."

"How old?"

"Four."

"Oh my God. What—"

She started to ask the question then caught herself. Did she really want to know what some sick bastard might have done to a four-year-old child?

"It was a bad scene," Vince conceded. He brushed her hair back again. "I needed to see you as much as you needed to see me. I knew you'd be here."

"Was it a random thing, or do you think it was someone who knew her?"

Anne wasn't sure which was worse, really. A random crime put everyone into a state of panic. Better if the killer was someone who had a problem with the victim. Unless that someone turned out to be somebody like Peter Crane. The serial killer next door.

"It seemed personal," Vince said.

So had Peter Crane's first murder . . . until he committed another, and another.

"I'm on my way to the hospital to see about the little girl," he said. "I just wanted to stop and see you first."

To check on her. The victim wasn't the only one to suffer the after-effects of crime. What had happened to her had left its mark on Vince, as well. He had shown up at her house within an hour of her abduction. If only he had gotten there earlier. If only he had figured out the puzzle sooner. He was one of the top men in his field in the entire world. How could he not have prevented it from happening?

All these thoughts had plagued him in the year since. As a result, he kept close tabs on her, made sure he knew where she was going and whom she was seeing. He still didn't like having her out of his sight.

They were both damaged. Fortunately, they had each other to confide in and support as they worked through the aftermath. Not all victims were so lucky to have that shared understanding with someone close to them.

Anne slipped her arms around her husband and hugged him tight for a moment. Vince held her and kissed the top of her head.

"I should go back inside," she said. "I'm adding to Dennis's abandonment issues."

"I have to get on with it too."

Neither of them moved.

"What's the rest of your day?" Vince asked.

"I have a class at one thirty, then an appointment with the ADA. I'm meeting Franny for a glass of wine at Piazza Fontana. I'll be home by six thirty."

"Me too, then," he said. He brushed his lips across the shell of her ear. "And after dinner, I am going to make such sweet love to you, Mrs. Leone . . . Remember that the next time you start to feel a little tense."

Anne smiled up at him. "Do you know how much I love you?"

He shook his head, a grin tugging up one corner of his mouth. "I think you'll have to show me later."

"That's a promise."

Vince walked her back to the front door of the hospital and kissed her good-bye. Anne watched him walk back to his car, then went back inside, ready to face Dennis Farman for Round Two.

6

Mendez was on his fifth cup of coffee by the time the hearse crept down the long driveway with the body of Marissa Fordham inside. It was after ten. He had been on the scene more than three hours.

Dixon had overseen the processing, asking for extra photographs, video of every room of the house. It wasn't his habit to take over a scene, but for something like this there was no question. He had worked homicide for the LA County Sheriff's Office for years. He had run more homicides than Mendez hoped to ever see.

The struggle between victim and perpetrator appeared to have started in Marissa Fordham's bedroom, where lamps had been toppled, furniture shoved around and tipped over. Dresser drawers had been pulled open, the contents vomited out onto the floor.

A large bloodstain dyed the flowered sheets of the bed. Cast-off blood stippled the ceiling, indicating the viciousness of the stabbing.

Some of the dresser contents had fallen on top of blood streaked on the floor.

"He came back and looked for something," Dixon muttered, directing the deputy with the camera to get a close shot.

"Hell of a vicious attack for a robbery," Bill Hicks commented.

"He killed her first," Mendez said. "Anything that happened next was an afterthought. He took too much time with the body for the murder not to have been his priority."

"And he left the jewelry," Dixon said, pointing at some expensive-looking pieces casually strewn across the top of the dresser. "He was looking for something in particular."

"I wonder if he found it," Hicks said.

"I don't know, but he cleaned himself up before he looked for it.

There's no blood on the stuff that came out of the drawers. He washed up before he looked."

"That's cold, man," Mendez said. "The little girl was laying in there half dead while he was cleaning up, having a look around."

"He probably thought she was dead. No witness, no hurry to leave."

Dixon gave the directive to clean out all the drain traps in the bathrooms and kitchen, in case they might yield some trace evidence that might later be matched to a suspect.

Mendez believed someday the DNA markers of convicted felons would be stored in a giant database available to law enforcement agencies all over the country. They would have only to run DNA on a hair left behind at the scene, a drop of the killer's blood, a piece of skin, and a search of the database would give them the name of their perp.

Unfortunately, it was 1986 and that day was still a long way off. For now, they would collect evidence and hang on to it, hoping they would be able to match it to a suspect when they had one.

Somehow, the victim had made it out of the bedroom. The trail of blood and overturned chairs and lamps was easy to follow.

Mendez couldn't help but picture it in his mind: Marissa Fordham, bleeding profusely as she tried to get away. Her hands had been covered in blood, as if she had tried desperately to stem the gushing from her wounds. Her heart would have been pounding. She would have been choking on panic.

Where had her child been during all of this? Had the little girl seen it happen? Had she been roused from her own bed by the commotion? Had she stumbled, sleepy eyed, out of her own bedroom to witness her mother fighting for her life?

Hell of a thing for a little kid to have to see.

At last check with the hospital, the child was still alive.

What kind of witness would she make?

The 911 operator had reported the call to Dixon. *"My daddy hurt my mommy."*

If it was that simple, they had only to go in search of the child's father. Maybe Zander Zahn didn't know who that was, but someone would. Women didn't keep secrets like that. Marissa Fordham would have confided in a girlfriend. They just had to find out who her friends were.

The deputy who had been first on the scene came in through the kitchen door, looking to Mendez.

"There's a woman here who had an appointment with the victim."

Mendez followed him outside and around to the front yard of the little ranch house.

The local media had come to camp out shortly after Vince had gotten there. A TV news van had arrived from Santa Barbara before nine. Bad news traveled fast.

The deputies had kept them at a respectful distance down at the end of the driveway. A lone blue Chrysler minivan had been allowed to pass. The woman sitting behind the wheel stared at Mendez now as he approached her door.

Sara Morgan.

He recognized her instantly. The cornflower blue eyes, the tousled mermaid's mane of blond hair. Her daughter, Wendy, had been one of four children to stumble upon the body of murder victim Lisa Warwick the year before.

She watched him approach, her expression guarded. Her window was open. He guessed she probably wanted to close it, turn the car around, and leave.

"Mrs. Morgan."

She remained in the car. "What's going on? Has something happened? Is Marissa here? Is she all right?"

"You had an appointment with Ms. Fordham?" he asked. "What kind of an appointment?"

"Where is Marissa?" she demanded, annoyed and frightened. "You can answer my question first, Detective."

"Ms. Fordham is deceased," he said bluntly, and watched the color drain from her face.

"Was there an accident?" she asked in a thin voice, her hands clenching and unclenching on the steering wheel. "Did she have an accident?"

"No, ma'am," Mendez said.

Sara Morgan looked past him toward the house, murmuring, "Oh my God. Oh God."

Tears magnified her eyes.

"I'm sorry, ma'am," Mendez said.

"What about Haley? Where's Haley?"

"She's been taken to the hospital."

"Oh my God." Two big crystalline tears spilled over her lashes and rolled down her cheeks. She had begun to tremble.

"How did you know Ms. Fordham?" Mendez asked. "Were you friends?"

"I can't believe this is happening," she murmured, her focus still on the house.

"The deputy told me you had an appointment. What kind of appointment?"

"What?" she asked, coming back to him as if she were a little startled to see him, to hear him speak.

"Your appointment was for what?"

"Marissa is—was—teaching me to paint on silk," she said, struggling with the change of verb tense as if it were something surprising and bitter in her mouth. "She's an extraordinary artist. Was."

"You teach art, don't you?" Mendez asked.

She shook her head dismissively. "Community Ed. It's nothing. Marissa . . . Oh my God. She's dead. Why would somebody do that? Who could have done that?"

"How well did you know her?" Mendez asked.

Sara Morgan shrugged. "I don't know. We were friends—friendly—casual friends."

"Do you know if she was seeing anyone?"

"No. I wouldn't know that. We never talked about anything like that."

"You don't know anything about the little girl's father?"

She seemed annoyed he would ask. "No, of course not.

"I would really like just to leave now, Detective," she said. "I'm sure I can't help you. I would like just to go home. This is very . . . I don't even know what to say."

Mendez ignored what Sara Morgan wanted. "I didn't see a studio in the house. Where did she do her work?"

"The studio is in the old barn."

"Would you show me?"

"It's right there. Behind the house. You don't need me," she argued.

"You might be able to tell if something is missing."

"Missing?" she asked. "You think someone came to rob her? You think she was killed because someone wanted to steal her art?" she said, becoming more agitated. "That's crazy."

"Can you think of another reason someone would want her dead?"

"Of course not!" she snapped, slapping the steering wheel in frustration. She had gauze around her hand and blue Smurf Band-Aids on three fingers. "How could I possibly know that?"

Several more tears squeezed over the edges of her lashes. Mendez took in her reactions, feeling bad for her. She had just lost a friend. He couldn't blame her for being upset.

"Can you show me the studio, please?" he asked again.

She wanted to say no, but in the end turned her car off, resigned. Mendez opened her door for her.

They walked together beneath the pepper trees toward the barn. Sara Morgan was in bib overalls streaked with paint, splotches of yellow, swipes of red. It wasn't hard to imagine her with paint on her hands, on her chin, on the tip of her pert nose. And it would look good on her, he thought. Even though the morning had turned warm, she hugged herself hard, as if she were freezing and trying to stop the shivers.

"What happened to your hands?" he asked, noting that the fingers on her right hand sported a couple of Smurf Band-Aids as well.

"I'm working on a multimedia piece that includes wire and metal as part of it," she said. "It's difficult to work with, but I don't like to wear gloves."

"Suffering for your art?"

She made a little sound that might have been impatience or sarcastic humor.

"How is Wendy doing?"

She frowned down at the ground and her old Keds tennis shoes. "She's having a hard time. She still has nightmares about finding that body in the park and about Dennis Farman trying to hurt her. She misses Tommy. She thinks you should be looking for him."

"We are," he said. "Trying to, anyway. We just don't have a clue where to look. Janet Crane hasn't contacted anyone—or the relatives aren't talking if she has. There's no trail to follow. We just don't have anything to work with."

"I guess if I found out my husband was a serial killer I would take my child and disappear too."

The big sliding door that led into Marissa Fordham's barn/studio stood open by a couple of feet. The space had been converted to a large work area at one end, and a gallery at the other. The morning sun poured in through a wall of windows, bathing everything in buttery yellow light.

"Oh, no," Sara Morgan said, as they stepped inside. "No, no, no . . ."

It should have been a beautiful space. It probably had been a beautiful space filled with Marissa Fordham's extraordinary art—all of which had been torn and ruined, slashed and broken. Paintings, sculpture—all of it now nothing but debris, the detritus of a murderer's rage.

Sara Morgan put her hands to her face and started to cry, mourning not only the loss of the woman she had known, but the loss of the beauty Marissa Fordham's soul had expressed in her art. She slipped inside the door, careful not to step on anything, and squatted down and reached out toward a small impressionistic painting cut almost in two. A small dark-haired child in a field of yellow flowers.

Mendez gently put his hand on her shoulder. "Please don't touch anything, ma'am. This is a crime scene now."

7

"I don't understand why someone would do that. Any of it," Sara Morgan said quietly. She sounded defeated, worn-out.

Mendez walked with her away from the barn as the crime-scene team moved in. There were more photographs to be taken, more fingerprints to search for. She went to an old rickety-looking park bench situated under an oak tree and stared at it.

"Can we sit?" she asked. "Is this a crime scene too?"

"It's all right. Have a seat."

The bench under the tree seemed a small, untouched oasis between the carnage in the house and the carnage in the barn. An old washtub had been planted with fuchsia, and delicate purple lobelia spilled over the sides. A folk art fairy suspended from a branch smiled as she reached a magic wand over the wild growth.

Sara Morgan reached out and touched the sparkling gold end of the wand, no doubt wishing for a transformation of the day and the terrible things that it had brought with it.

Do over.

"I'm sorry you're going to be dragged into this for a while," Mendez said, taking the opposite end of the bench. He sat with his forearms on his thighs, feeling the hours press down on him as the last blast of caffeine subsided.

Sara Morgan said nothing. She sat looking down at her bandaged hands in her lap. Blood had begun to seep through the gauze.

"Can you tell me who some of her friends were?" he asked. "People we should talk to?"

"The Acorn Gallery sells a lot of her work. The people there would know her well." She continued to look down into her cupped hands as if she could see visions there, pictures of Marissa Fordham and the people she knew.

"She has this weird neighbor," she said. "He's seriously creepy. A couple of times he just showed up while I was here working with Marissa. She would say hello to him and he would just hang around, looking at her. He never had much to say. He would just hang out for a while, and then he would leave."

"Did Ms. Fordham seem afraid of him?"

"No. I was afraid of him," she admitted. "That's strange—don't you think? That he would just—just—*loiter* like that, like some kind of—I don't know—pervert or something."

"But it didn't bother Marissa?"

"No. When I would say something about it, she would just shrug it off. 'That's just Zander,' she would say. 'He's harmless,' she would say. 'He's odd, but he's a friend,' she would say."

She looked at him hard, looking for an answer he couldn't give her. "What if he wasn't harmless?"

"We've already spoken with Mr. Zahn," he said.

She sat up a little at that. "And? Didn't you think he was weird?"

"Do you know any of her other friends?"

"That's really annoying, you know," she snapped, brushing a rope of unruly waves back behind one ear. "You never answer a question."

He conceded with a hint of a sheepish smile tipping up one side of his mustache. "Goes with the job. Sorry."

Sara Morgan sighed. "She worked with Jane Thomas, designing the fund-raising poster for the women's center. Gina Kemmer. Gina owns Girl—it's a boutique on Via Verde near the college. I don't really know her more than to say hello, but I've seen them together a lot. And she has a patron—*patroness*. Milo Bordain supports her work. Bruce Bordain's wife."

Mendez jotted the names down in his notebook. Bruce Bordain, the parking lot king of Southern California, was a big shot not only in Oak Knoll, but all the way south to Los Angeles. He had made his money first buying up and managing parking lots, then expanding into the construction of multimillion-dollar, multilevel parking structures. He owned some high-end car dealerships just for fun, and sat on the boards of McAster College and Mercy General and who knew what else.

His wife was a well-known patron of the arts, instrumental in the organization of the prestigious Oak Knoll Festival of Music, which took place every summer, drawing renowned classical musicians from all over the world.

"And you never knew her to have a boyfriend?" Mendez asked. "An ex-boyfriend? A lover?"

Sara Morgan stared down at the blood soaking through the gauze around her hand. "No."

"She must have had," he pressed. "She had a child. She never talked about the girl's father?"

"Not to me."

"You never asked?"

"It's none of my business. I don't pry into people's lives.

"Can I go home now?" she asked softly.

"Are you all right to drive?" he asked. "I can have a deputy take you home or follow you home."

"No," she said, getting up from the bench. "No offense, Detective Mendez, but I've had more than I ever wanted to do with your office already."

He let her walk herself back to her car, but he watched her the whole way.

8

"The little girl hasn't regained consciousness," Vince announced as he took a seat in what they so aptly called the "war room."

This was the room where Cal Dixon gathered his six full-time detectives to plan their strategy for a major investigation. They had spent a lot of time in this room in the last year. The walls and whiteboards were still covered with photos and information regarding the See-No-Evil cases, which were still being actively worked in preparation for the upcoming trial of Peter Crane.

Dixon was lucky; most larger departments didn't have the luxury of forming their own task force for a murder investigation. Because the crime rate in his jurisdiction was relatively low, Dixon could pull all of his investigators together to tackle a high-profile case as one unit. And Dixon, himself a homicide detective for years with LA County, could turn his administrative duties over to his second in command and spearhead the investigation.

"She was admitted with severe dehydration and hypothermia," Vince went on. "I can confirm she was strangled manually—at least partially."

"What do you mean—partially?" Dixon asked as he organized some papers on the podium.

"The kid is tiny. Any adult could easily have crushed her larynx entirely. But that didn't happen. She also has damage to the insides of her lips where her teeth cut into the flesh, which suggests suffocation. Could be your UNSUB started to choke her and didn't have the stomach for it, then switched to pressing something over her face. Luckily, he only thought he finished the job."

"Sick bastard," Dixon growled, frowning darkly. "I'm glad to have you in on this with us, Vince. I'm talking with the budget director this afternoon to see about cutting you a consulting fee."

"Don't worry about it, Cal. I'm doing fine. What I make consulting makes my salary from the Bureau look like minimum wage. I don't need your money. You guys are always on my priority list, you know that."

Vince had grown to think of Dixon and his people as extended family. He may have initially come to Oak Knoll to work a case, but he had found a home here, a second life, and Anne. Whatever Cal Dixon needed, Vince was happy to oblige.

"I appreciate that," Dixon said.

Mendez took a seat next to Vince. "The attack on Marissa Fordham was over the top. Out-of-control rage. It seems strange to me that didn't just spill over to include the child. It's like he killed the mother, then flipped a switch on the rage."

"He killed the woman with a lot of personal fury," Vince said. "The child was unfortunate collateral damage."

"He had to kill her because she was a witness," Hicks said. "It didn't mean the same thing to him."

"He must have believed the kid could ID him," Dixon said. "The question is, will she ever be able to?"

"So far her brain activity appears to be normal," Vince said. "But there are a lot of factors that could weigh against us. That kind of trauma, that young a child—a kid might block that out for the rest of their life just out of self-preservation."

"If she comes around, do you think Anne might be able to help us with her?" Mendez asked.

Vince's instinctive reaction was to say no. Not because he didn't think his wife was capable of helping. Quite the opposite was true. Anne had a gift with kids. He had encouraged her to go back to school to finish her degree in child psychology. But his first instinct was to protect her. She had been through enough. He didn't want her pulled into another murder investigation.

"Isn't that the job of Child Protective Services?"

"This seems out of their league," Mendez said.

This was a mostly rural county with a lower-than-average crime rate. Oak Knoll, with a population of roughly twenty thousand (not counting college students), was the Big Town. Crime here routinely consisted of small-time drug deals, burglary, the odd assault, a murder now and again.

There was no Oak Knoll Police Department. The city contracted with the sheriff's office for their needs. There was no dedicated homicide division within the SO, but a group of detectives who worked all manner of crimes. County Child Protective Services had no psychologist on staff. They had a small administrative group, two full-time social workers, and a number of volunteers. Anne was one of only two court-appointed special advocates for children in the county.

All of these things would change as more people were enticed north out of the LA sprawl. But for now life in the Oak Knoll environs remained more or less idyllic.

"Technically it's their call," Dixon said. "I've spoken with the director. The protocol would be to try to find a relative. In the absence of a relative, the child would be put into foster care."

"How many people are going to want to bring the only living witness to a violent murder into their home?" Detective Trammell asked.

"Is there any sign of family anywhere?" Mendez asked.

"Not so far," Dixon said. "We didn't find an address book in the house. We didn't find a birth certificate for the child or a social security card for the woman. I want you to start checking around the local banks to see if Marissa Fordham had a safe deposit box somewhere."

"We get the birth certificate, we get the name of the father, we get our number one suspect," Mendez said.

"That might be why you haven't found a birth certificate," Vince suggested. "The neighbor, who was allegedly a close friend, doesn't know who the girl's father is."

"Can you see a woman—or *anyone*—confiding in that guy?" Hicks asked. "There is one strange dude."

"Bill and I walked up that trail Zahn took home," Mendez said. "That's a hike. I find it hard to imagine anybody just strolling over that hill before dawn to say hey."

"I want to know more about this guy," Dixon said. "Who is he? What does he do for a living? Just what kind of a relationship did he have with Marissa Fordham?"

"What's his name?" Detective Hamilton asked.

"Alexander—aka Zander—Zahn. Z-A-H-N," Mendez said.

"He's some kind of genius," Trammell said. "He teaches at the college. Math or physics or philosophy or something."

Everyone turned and looked at him with suspicion.

"How the hell do you know that?" Mendez asked.

Trammell was the kind of guy who could spout sports stats and belch the national anthem. No one would have looked to him for information on physics or philosophy.

Trammell spread his hands. "What? My kid goes there."

"You been robbing banks in your spare time?" Hicks asked.

"He's a smart kid. He got a scholarship."

"Must take after his mother," Detective Campbell suggested.

They all laughed. Their first good laugh of the day. As serious as their business was, it was important to loosen things up when an opportunity presented itself, no matter how small. Otherwise, the gravity of the job would pull them all into a black hole.

"Fuck you guys," Trammell said with good humor.

Dixon steered them back on topic. "Let's get back to Zahn."

"Sara Morgan said Ms. Fordham was perfectly comfortable having him around," Mendez said.

"Sara—Wendy's mother?" Vince asked.

"Yeah. She's an artist too. Marissa Fordham was teaching her some technique for painting on silk, whatever that means. She showed up this morning for her lesson."

Vince cocked half a smile. "My uncle Bobo from the South Side used to have a silk tie with a painting of Wrigley Field on it. If that's coming back, I've got an inside track. Put your orders in now, fellas."

They all chuckled.

"Let's get one for Trammell," Hamilton suggested. "With a picture of Einstein on it."

"Anyway," Mendez said, "Sara said Zahn would sometimes just show up and hang around. He gave her the creeps, but Ms. Fordham didn't seem bothered at all."

"She was comfortable with him," Vince said.

"Apparently."

"I'd like to see him in his natural environment," Vince said. "I'm curious. And I think he definitely knows more than he told us this morning. I'll take Junior here," he said to Dixon, hooking a thumb in the direction of Mendez. "He makes the guy nervous."

"I hear his dates have the same reaction," Trammell said.

"If he didn't always have to read them their rights . . . ," Hicks said.

"I thought it was the handcuffs," Mendez joked.

Dixon cleared his throat. "And do we have any names of friends to start checking out?"

Mendez read off the short list he had gotten from Sara Morgan.

"No boyfriends?" Vince questioned.

"Not that Mrs. Morgan knew of."

"But they were friends."

Mendez shrugged. "She said they never talked about it."

"I've never known a woman who could stop herself from blabbing on and on about what guy she's sleeping with," Trammell said.

"Unless the guy she's seeing belongs to someone else," Vince suggested.

"A married lover?" Dixon said. "Always a possibility—and a motive. Let's talk to the other women on that list and see what we can come up with. It's tough to keep a secret in a town this size—especially a juicy one.

"I know most of you are already working other cases," he went on, consulting his notes, reading glasses perched on the end of his nose. "But I need all of you on this initially. The press is going to have a field day with a gruesome murder in Oak Knoll practically on the anniversary of the See-No-Evil cases. I want to clear this one before they can get up a head of steam."

"We've got a vic with forty stab wounds, her breasts missing, and a knife sticking out of her vagina," Mendez said. "Somehow, I don't think they're going to let this one go."

Dixon turned to Vince. "What are your impressions so far, Vince?"

Vince shrugged. "Obviously, it's a sexual homicide, but what's it about? Rage, yes. Rage over what? She done him wrong? She must have done him *way* wrong.

"Taking the breasts sometimes suggests a kind of envy," he said. "Breasts are symbolic of a woman's beauty, her power."

"Take her breasts, take her power," Mendez said.

"Right. And sometimes removing body parts is about possession, possessing the victim by keeping a part of them."

"Like Ed Gein."

"Like Ed Gein."

The notorious 1950s Butcher of Plainfield. The Wisconsin man had made lampshades and chair seats out of the skin of his victims, and bowls out of their skulls, to name but a few of his atrocities.

"Only Ed not only wanted to keep his female victims with him," Vince said. "He wanted to *be* them. He made himself a 'woman suit' out of the skin and parts of corpses."

"Man, that's disgusting," Hicks said.

"You think that's disgusting. I can tell you about a couple of cannibals and what possessing their victims meant to them."

"Maybe after lunch," someone suggested sarcastically.

"Sometimes the body parts can be strictly a trophy," Vince went on. "We'll hope to God that's not the case, because that would suggest he's a hunter, and hunters don't stop hunting."

"Jesus, that's all we need," Dixon said. "Another serial killer. One was more than enough."

"The odds of you having another serial killer on your hands are about as long as they can get," Vince said. "We're talking about an extremely rare animal, no matter how many of them appear every week on television.

"In my opinion, the attack on Marissa Fordham was personal. That many stab wounds is personal. But that butcher knife looks to have belonged to the victim, which makes this seem more like a crime of opportunity, of the moment. Someone got angry, grabbed that knife and used it. I think the knife protruding from the vagina is the killer making a personal statement about the victim."

"Don't fuck her, she's dangerous?" Trammell asked.

"Exactly."

"All right," Dixon said. "Let's get out there and find out who felt the need to send that message."

9

"How is Mrs. Morgan?" Vince asked as they climbed into the car.

Mendez looked over at him as he stuck the key in the ignition. "Not happy to see me. I can tell you that."

"She went through a lot last year," Vince said. "Anne gets together with her and Wendy every so often. She really wants to maintain that contact with the kids. Wendy has had some trouble coping. She's withdrawn a bit. It's a sad thing."

"Is the husband still in the picture?"

"As far as I know."

"I don't get that." Mendez shook his head. "The guy cheated on her with a woman who ended up dead, lied about it, withheld information from a murder investigation. He's a Class-A prick and she stays with him. What's wrong with women? She's a beautiful, talented lady. She deserves better."

"He's the father of her child," Vince said. "I'm sure Wendy loves her dad. Given the choice, kids want their parents to stay together. Tension in a marriage is a scary thing for a child, but not as scary as losing one of the two most important people in their life."

"You were married before. How did your kids take it?"

Vince made a face. "I was an absentee father most of their lives. My girls already knew what it was like to live without me. Their day-to-day didn't change all that much when I moved out."

"You regret that."

"Hell, yeah. They're my daughters. I love them. I blew it. My ex-wife is a great gal, but she got tired of being a single parent and eventually she found herself another partner. I picked my career over my family."

"But think of everything you've done in your career, man. You were a fucking pioneer. The Behavioral Sciences Unit wouldn't have evolved in the same way without you. Think of the cases you've helped solve, the killers you've helped put behind bars. That's worth a lot."

"It is. I don't discount that," Vince said. "I've made important contributions to the larger world. Unfortunately, those contributions cost me a big price. They cost me my marriage. I missed watching my daughters grow up. But we make our choices and we live with the good and the bad of them. I just know I'm not making the same mistakes twice, that's all."

"Yeah," Mendez groused with good nature, "rub my nose in it, why don't you?"

Vince grinned. He had beaten his protégé to the punch where Anne was concerned—a fact that never ceased to please him. "You snooze you lose, Junior. But don't take it too hard. Maybe we'll name our first-born after you."

"Asshole."

"Ha!"

Their first stop was the administration building at McAster College. The school's campus was beautiful, impeccably maintained, shaded with huge old oak trees. Established in the 1920s, many of the buildings were original, a mix of traditional ivy-covered brick and Spanish Revival stucco.

The administration building would have looked just as at home on the campus of Princeton. Wide front steps led to a grand set of doors.

"What do you think that says?" Mendez pointed up to the inscription carved in stone above the doors.

"If I had absorbed any of the Latin the nuns tried to pound into me in school, I could tell you."

"I think it says, If you have to ask, you can't afford it."

They took the elevator to the third floor and walked down the hall to the president's office. Vince had met McAster's president, Arthur Buckman, nearly a year ago, after the press had finally gotten wind of Vince's role in the See-No-Evil cases. He had been swamped with requests for interviews and speaking engagements.

Still an agent at the time, he had to route all requests through the Bureau. The FBI was not keen on agents grandstanding or freelancing. Most of the requests had been denied. Vince had personally asked several people to hold off, pending his retirement. Arthur Buckman had been one of those.

"Vince!" Buckman greeted him, coming out of his office. A transplanted New Yorker, he was a vertically challenged, balding doughboy in wire-rimmed glasses and a three-piece suit. Always smiling. As the head of one of the top private colleges in the country, he had a lot to smile about.

Vince pumped his hand. "Art. This is Detective Mendez with the sheriff's office. Tony, Arthur Buckman."

Buckman motioned them into an impressive, wood-paneled corner office that boasted a view of the McAster quad, busy now with students crisscrossing from class to class. "You shouldn't be surprised to hear your lectures are already full, Vince. Our psych department is thrilled."

"I'll do my best to live up to expectations," Vince said, taking a seat. The scent of lemon furniture polish went up his nostrils and seemed to stab into the backs of his eyes. Damn bullet.

"What can I do for you gentlemen?" Buckman asked.

"Just a little background on a faculty member," Vince said.

For the first time the president lost his smile. "Has something happened?"

"Alexander Zahn," Mendez said, digging his notebook out of the inside breast pocket of his sport coat.

"Dr. Zahn? Has something happened to him?"

"No, no," Vince assured him, sitting back, squaring an ankle over a knee. The picture of relaxation. "He reported a crime against a neighbor of his this morning. We just want to get a feel for who he is. Someone told us he teaches here."

"Yes. Periodically," Buckman said.

Mendez glanced up at him. "He's not on the faculty?"

The president squinted behind his glasses, pained somehow. "It's . . . complicated . . ."

"We met Dr. Zahn this morning," Vince said. "He's a complicated kind of guy."

"Yes. That's safe to say," Buckman agreed. "Zander is a genuine genius. We're very lucky to have him in any capacity. But he does have certain . . . limitations."

"Some high-functioning offshoot of autism?" Vince asked.

"Good guess."

"And this guy can be a professor?" Mendez said. "Here?"

"He's not intellectually impaired," Vince explained. "He's socially challenged."

Mendez grimaced as he stared down at his notebook. "I'll say."

"Of course, you understand I can't really discuss a faculty member's mental health with you," Buckman said.

"No, of course not," Vince said. "I'm just trying to get some insights on the man. Put some things into context."

"You said something happened to a neighbor of his?"

"A woman he was friends with was murdered," Mendez told him. "Zahn discovered her body."

"Oh my God," Buckman said. "Another woman murdered? Not again. It's not like the others—"

"No, no," Vince assured him. "Unrelated."

"That's not good news either, is it? You don't think Dr. Zahn—?"

"We don't have any reason to think that, sir," Mendez said. "He reported the crime and cooperated fully this morning."

"Thank God." Buckman sighed. "That explains why he hasn't come in today. He was supposed to give a lecture this morning. His assistant reported he wouldn't be able to make it, that he was terribly upset, but that he wouldn't say why."

"Does he do that often?" Vince asked. "Cancel?"

"Sometimes he cancels. Other times he becomes so absorbed in the subject matter he goes on with a lecture for hours over his allotted time. He's difficult, but he's a brilliant mathematician. The students are all aware of his issues, but his classes are always full with a waiting list."

"He has an assistant?" Mendez prompted.

"Rudy Nasser," Buckman said. "Brilliant young man. He has advanced degrees in physics and mathematics from USC. He could have a very good position at any top school in the country. He came up here to work with Dr. Zahn. He's probably one of a handful of people in the world who can truly follow the density of Zahn's reasoning. He probably understands the man better than anyone. You'll want to talk to him."

"Marissa Fordham is dead?"

Mendez went instantly on guard. All he had said was that Dr. Zahn's neighbor had been killed.

"It has to be Marissa," Nasser explained. "She's the only neighbor Dr. Zahn ever visits."

Rudy Nasser sat back against the edge of the desk. The lecture hall had emptied out except for a couple of students still copying notes from the big chalkboard. It looked like Aramaic to Vince. The students—both cute girls—seemed more interested in stealing glances at their teacher than his mathematical concepts.

"Did you know her?" Mendez asked.

Nasser pulled in a deep breath and blew it back out as he processed the information and whatever it meant to him.

"This is bad, man."

In his mid-twenties, he looked like a beatnik with the black goatee and soulful dark eyes, and dressed like a *Miami Vice* drug lord in a slouchy charcoal suit over a black T-shirt and loafers with no socks. He was undoubtedly as socially smooth as his mentor was socially awkward.

"Yes, I knew her," he said. "Dr. Zahn . . ."

He shook his head and left the thought unfinished.

"Dr. Zahn what?"

Nasser shrugged, not wanting to say too much. "Was fond of her. He found her body?"

"Yes," Vince said. "He called nine-one-one."

"He didn't tell me. When he called this morning I knew something had happened. He was so agitated. But he wouldn't tell me."

Vince could see him planning damage control, how to get his eccentric boss away from the fray of a murder investigation.

"How well did you know her?" Mendez asked.

"Well enough to have a conversation. I gave her my number to call if she needed me."

"Needed you to what?"

"To come get Dr. Zahn. He doesn't always know when he's worn out his welcome. When he gets manic he loses all sense of time."

"Does that happen often?" Vince asked, trying to imagine Zahn in a manic state. He had seemed closer to catatonic that morning.

"Not often."

"Recently?"

"A couple of weeks ago."

"How is he during these episodes?" Vince asked.

"Happy," Nasser said. "Euphoric, in fact. Like he's in the throes of some kind of rapture. He becomes animated, can't stop talking about whatever idea has taken hold of him. He's done some of his best work in that state of mind."

"How did Ms. Fordham react when this happened?" Mendez asked. "Was she afraid?"

Nasser shook his head. "No. Marissa took it in stride. She's been his neighbor for several years. She knows Dr. Zahn isn't a violent man. I can't imagine him ever hurting anybody. He doesn't like touching people or having people touch him. I'm sure it never entered Marissa's mind that he might hurt her somehow."

"Were they involved?"

"Sexually?" Nasser laughed, flashing an array of brilliantly white teeth. "No. God, no. Like I said: Dr. Zahn doesn't like touching anyone. If you shake his hand, he'll go open a fresh bar of soap and scrub like a surgeon."

"He's obsessive-compulsive?" Vince said, not surprised to hear it. He thought back to Zahn wringing his hands over and over as they asked him questions.

"To the tenth power."

"What about you, Mr. Nasser?" Mendez asked. "Ms. Fordham was a beautiful woman."

"Yes, she was. But my first obligation is to Dr. Zahn. I would never jeopardize my position with him. The man is fucking brilliant. He has one of the brightest minds of our time."

"And you're one of the few people who can understand it," Vince said.

"I've been a disciple for a long time. I realize how fortunate I am to be working with him."

"What exactly is your role here?" Vince asked.

"Dr. Zahn doesn't like to interact with people," Nasser said.

"That must make it difficult for him to teach."

"That's where I come in," Nasser said. "Mathematics is his world. He's most comfortable with numbers, not people. And he loves trying to open that world to others, but he's socially awkward. I'm here to do the actual interaction with the kids, sort of a liaison, if you will."

"That makes sense."

"And Ms. Fordham?" Mendez asked. "What was your take on her?"

Nasser glanced away and shrugged. "She seemed nice enough. I wasn't a fan of her art. Too sweet, too idyllic for my tastes."

Vince thought of the scene in Marissa Fordham's retro-ranch kitchen. There had been nothing sweet or idyllic about that—except perhaps in the eyes of the person who had wanted her dead.

"We have some additional questions for Dr. Zahn," he said. "Can you give us directions to his house?"

"I'm finished here," Nasser said. "I'll take you."

10

Rudy Nasser led the way out of town in his old black BMW 3 Series convertible. The two-lane road wound through beautiful country quilted by four-rail fences and studded with spreading oak trees. They passed horse ranches and vineyards, and a lavender farm that colored the valley floor purple as far back toward the mountains as the eye could see.

"I'm surprised you let him come along," Mendez said, glancing over at Vince.

"Let's see that dynamic," Vince said. "Let's see how Zahn interacts with someone we can assume he's comfortable with. He might let his guard down more."

"In that case, I'm surprised you let me come along. I make the guy nervous."

"You need to learn patience."

Mendez rolled his eyes. "I know, I know."

"You're like a great fastball pitcher," Vince said. "But you can't just throw fastballs for the whole game. You're going to come up against guys who can belt your best one out of the park. Your arm is going to get tired and you're not going to get them all over the plate. You need a repertoire. You need a change-up. You need a slider. The occasional spitball."

This was one reason Mendez had chosen to remain in Oak Knoll, even though Leone had encouraged him to make the move to the Bureau with an eye to eventually becoming a part of the Investigative Support Unit. He wanted to learn from the best. Vince Leone was the best, and Vince Leone was here.

He slowed and turned the department Taurus onto Dyer Canyon Road, and gave it a little gas to catch up to the quicker BMW.

"What do you make of him?" Vince asked.

"Nasser? He's got it all going on—the smarts, the looks, working his dream job with his hero," he said, grinning. "Kinda like me."

Vince laughed.

"He's a little on the slick side," Mendez commented. "He's sure as hell not like any math teacher I ever had."

"I guess the new math is sexy," Vince said. "My math teachers all had horn-rimmed glasses and thick ankles."

Zander Zahn's home sat behind a high stucco privacy wall. Only the tile roof of the house was visible from where they parked the cars on the shoulder of the road.

"He won't want you going inside the house," Nasser explained. "And he won't like it if you touch anything in the yard."

He keyed in the gate code and the solid wooden gate rolled back.

Mendez had been about to ask why they didn't just drive in, but the reason was obvious. Every inch of Zahn's yard was covered with stuff. Whatever lawn there had been at one time had been removed and replaced with decomposed granite dust, creating a parking lot for all manner of junk—all of it neatly arranged in categories.

Groups of old kitchen chairs. A collection of plant pots organized by size with the smallest in the front row and the largest in the back. Concrete statuary—from gargoyles to lions to replicas of Michelangelo's *David* and the Statue of Liberty.

He seemed to have a special affinity for refrigerators, which were lined up front to back, row after row, like a platoon of soldiers; and for chest-style freezers, rectangular box after rectangular box, like so many rusty white coffins.

"I'll buzz him at the front door," Nasser went on as they followed the narrow path to the house. "Hopefully, he'll agree to come out. Better if the two of you stay a good ten feet back."

He hustled up the steps ahead of them.

Mendez glanced at Leone. "What the fuck?"

"He's a hoarder," Vince said, looking over the collections through a pair of mirrored aviator sunglasses. "Interesting."

"It's part of the obsessive-compulsive disorder?"

"It would seem to be, but there's a lot of conflicting opinions on the subject. For instance, we've already seen that Zahn is a germaphobe, yet hoarding often creates unsanitary conditions. The two seem not to go together, yet here we are."

"When I was in a uniform in Bakersfield, I had a call-out on a possible missing person," Mendez said. "A woman reported her elderly mother missing after not hearing from her for several days. She had gone to the mother's house. No sign of her.

"Me and my partner get there. You can't believe this place. It was like a landfill inside a building—and smelled like one too. You could hardly walk inside. Every window was blocked. There were mice and rats like something out of a horror movie. Long story short: It took three days and a cadaver dog to find the woman's body. A pile of stuff had fallen on her and buried her alive."

Vince looked around at the yard. "At least Dr. Zahn is tidy."

Contrary to Nasser's instructions, Vince took the step below him and struck a casual stance with his hands in his pants pockets. The breeze flipped his necktie back over his shoulder.

Zahn's voice came out of the squawk box on the wall above the doorbell. "Who are you?"

Nasser answered, "It's me—Rudy."

"Who's with you? Someone is with you. Why would you bring someone here? You know not to bring someone here. Why would you do that?"

"They're detectives, Zander. It's about Marissa. They need to speak to you."

No answer.

Vince leaned past a frowning Nasser and pressed the intercom button himself. "It's Vince Leone, Zander," he said in a pleasant, casual tone. "We spoke earlier this morning at Marissa's house. I'm sorry to bother you, but I've got a couple more questions you might be able to help me with."

"I don't think so, Vince," Zahn said. "I don't think I can help you. I'm terribly upset by all of this."

"I know. So is everyone—especially people who loved Marissa. Imagine what it would mean to her if you could help in any small way to find her killer. You've been such a good friend to her."

No sound came out of the box for moment. Mendez looked from Vince to Nasser and back.

"I do have some good news from the hospital," Vince said. "I went to check on little Haley, and she's going to be fine."

Another moment passed then came the sound of locks being turned on the other side of the front door. Zahn emerged wearing what looked to Mendez like black Chinese pajamas and a pair of clogs.

"Haley?" he said, looking up and just to the right of Leone's head, as if he were seeing a vision in the sky. "Haley is all right? She's going to be all right?"

"I spoke to her doctor."

"Oh my God. Oh thank God," Zahn whispered, wringing his hands absently as he spoke. "Could I see her? Do you think that might be possible—that I could speak to her and see her?"

"You would have to go into the hospital to see her, Zander," Nasser said.

Zahn looked at him sharply.

His assistant shrugged. "Hospitals are full of sick people."

"Haley isn't sick, though," Zahn pointed out. "She's injured. She was injured somehow and her heart is broken. She'll be heartbroken over Marissa. I'm heartbroken."

"They won't want her to have visitors yet," Vince said. "But I'll let you know as soon as they give the go-ahead, Zander. You'll be my first call."

"Thank you, Vince. I will appreciate that because I will want to see her. I—I'm so upset about what happened. Haley will be also."

"I understand," Vince said, nodding, then he glanced around. "Is there somewhere we can just sit down for a few minutes, Zander?"

The idea seemed to startle their odd host.

"I don't want to add to your stress," Vince assured him. "I'm just thinking we could sit down for a few minutes and chat. You knew Marissa so well. You might have some useful insights you may not even be aware of.

"Do you know what I mean, Zander?" he asked. "Sometimes we know things that may not seem significant until put into another context. I'm sure it's the same in mathematics. A number is just a number until you assign it a purpose, right?"

Zahn put his head to one side like a quizzical bird, then slowly began to nod, pleased. "That's a very interesting statement, Vince. I like that. I like that."

His face took on a wondrous expression that made Mendez think the guy had some kind of psychedelic kaleidoscope hallucination going on in his head.

"So many people think of mathematics as being very static and absolute," he said. "But that's so wrong. It's thinking in the abstract that frees the mind to the greatest of possibilities."

He spoke with as much passion and clarity as Mendez had heard out of him. His gaze then became acutely focused on Leone, and he took a step closer to him. "We should talk about this, Vince."

Vince made a comical grimace. "I'm afraid you're already way ahead of me on the subject, Zander. Math was never my forte."

"Because you were undoubtedly taught by people trapped in the pedantic world of what I call 'base academia.' And by *base* I mean 'low' or 'common' as opposed to bas*ic*."

He looked sharply at Nasser again. "Did you hear that, Rudy? Vince's thought? *Contextual* mathematics. This is another verbal approach to help us articulate how we want our students to open their minds to our subject. Don't you agree, Rudy?"

Nasser looked a bit pissed, Mendez thought. Or maybe "jealous" was a better word. His mentor had found favor in someone else. Interesting.

But he covered it well and replied, "It's brilliant. We should use that in orientation."

"Brilliant," Zahn said, tasting the word in his mouth like something buttery and smooth. "And you didn't think you knew that, did you, Vince?"

"No, I didn't," Vince admitted. "See? It's like I said: You may have some piece of knowledge that—unknown to you—could help Marissa."

Zahn didn't seem quite so pleased at having the idea turned around on him, but he couldn't argue with the logic.

"I have chairs," he said. But instead of inviting them into the house, he gestured like a bad public speaker at the collection of chrome and vinyl kitchen chairs lined up in five rows of five on his gravel yard.

As Zahn led the way down the path, Mendez leaned toward Vince and muttered, "Do you think he'll offer us refreshments from one of those refrigerators?"

Leone gave him an elbow.

They sat down in a row like they were going to watch a play. Nasser, Zahn, Vince. Mendez very deliberately picked up an orange chair, pulled it out of line and sat it down facing the others. Zahn looked at him like he was the devil incarnate, but said nothing. Vince watched him, reserving his reaction.

"I'm sorry," Mendez said, ducking his head contritely. "This is embarrassing, but I'm a little hard of hearing, Dr. Zahn. I had an accident when I was nine. Actually . . . my mother struck me in the side of the head. It left me a little deaf. It's been a problem my whole life."

Vince arched an eyebrow.

Zahn studied him for a few seconds, letting his story sink in. "I'm so sorry, Tony. It's difficult to be a child. I was a child once. It was difficult. Haley will find it difficult now. Not for the same reasons, though."

"I'm not looking for people to feel sorry for me or anything," Mendez said. "I'll put the chair back when we're finished. I just didn't want you to think I'm trying to intimidate you. That's not my intent at all."

Zahn nodded and looked down in his lap. He rubbed his hands together, rubbed his palms against his thighs. His legs were thin as rails.

"Of course, Tony. Of course, Tony," he muttered.

"Detective Mendez spoke with another of Marissa's friends," Vince said, then raised his voice to a low boom. "Isn't that right, Detective?"

"Yes," Mendez said, straight-faced. "Sara Morgan."

"Sara, yes. She doesn't like me," Zahn said. "That's all right. I understand. She's very sad, I think."

"Why would you say that, Zander?" he asked, taking Vince's cue to use Zahn's name as if they were old acquaintances.

Zahn gazed off into the distance. "Because that's what I think. I think she's very sad. It's in her eyes. She has beautiful eyes. Don't you think so? Blue like the Aegean Sea. But sad. And frightened. She was frightened of me."

"Why is that?"

"She thinks I might be dangerous, I think."

"That's ridiculous, Zander," Nasser said.

"Not to her," Zahn said. "Her perception is her reality. She doesn't understand who I am. People fear what they don't understand."

"You're world-renowned in your field," Nasser said.

Zahn nodded, looking away from them. "But not in *her context*. Isn't that right, Vince?"

"I suppose so. She doesn't really know you."

"I'm just the strange neighbor," Zahn said. "I am *un*known. People fear the unknown. I fear the unknown. What we don't know *can* hurt us."

He began to rock a little on his red vinyl chair, twisting his hands together, rubbing his palms on his thighs.

Nasser still seemed to feel the need to suck up. "Still," he said, "you would never hurt a woman."

"Oh, but I would," Zahn said candidly, looking at his protégé.

Mendez felt every cop instinct in him come to attention. He cut a glance at Vince, who appeared not to react at all. Leone crossed his legs and picked at the crease in his trousers.

"I have," Zahn said, looking Mendez straight in the eye. "I killed my mother."

11

No one moved, no one breathed

Rudy Nasser looked stunned, completely at a loss for words.

Zander Zahn sat wringing his hands and rubbing his palms against his thighs.

Blood, Mendez thought. He's trying to wipe the blood off his hands.

He had to have been a boy at the time, Mendez reasoned—a juvenile at most. Otherwise he would be doing life somewhere. He sure as hell wouldn't be teaching at McAster College in Oak Knoll, California. He wouldn't be a world-renowned anything. Mendez wondered if Arthur Buckman knew.

"It's difficult to be a child." Zahn repeated exactly what he had said moments before, after he had considered Mendez's cock-and-bull story about being rendered deaf by a blow from his mother. "I was a child once. It was difficult."

"Your mother abused you, Zander?" It was more of a statement than a question from Leone.

"I'm finished telling that story now, Vince," Zahn said calmly. "It's not a story I like to tell."

Then why had he told them at all? Mendez wanted to ask. He wanted to pounce on the opportunity and press for more answers. But Leone was watching him from behind the mirrored lenses of his sunglasses, and Zahn was starting to rock on his chair as memories and old emotions churned inside him. Now was not the time to push.

"I'm sure those memories are upsetting," Mendez said quietly.

Patiently. "I know they are. That had to make it all the more shocking for you to find Marissa the way you did," he said. "All that blood."

"Terrible, terrible," Zahn murmured, rocking, looking off to the side as he rubbed his hands. "So much blood. So much blood."

Mendez wondered which scene he was replaying in his head: the murder of his mother or of Marissa Fordham. What had been the manner of his mother's death? Had he used a knife? Could he have had some kind of mental break or flashback and gone after Marissa Fordham, somehow relating her to his mother, or maybe confusing the two women?

"Did you touch Marissa's body?"

"No, no, no." Zahn wagged his head. "I couldn't. I didn't. I couldn't. I didn't."

If that was true, that explained why he hadn't realized the little girl was still alive. He hadn't touched her, hadn't tried to find a pulse. He couldn't bring himself to touch the blood.

Rudy Nasser stirred at last, his brain racing to catch up to the moment and rescue his mentor.

"This is starting to sound a lot like an interrogation," he said. "Zander, I think you shouldn't say any more until you talk to an attorney."

"Why would he need an attorney?" Vince asked. "We don't consider Zander a suspect."

Nasser stood up, ready to give them the bum's rush out the front gate. "Let's keep it that way."

Leone didn't move. He was sitting a little sideways on his green vinyl chair, leaning against one arm on the chair back. He was a big man and took up a big space, and didn't look like anyone was going to move him until he was good and ready.

"Is that what you want, Zander?" he asked. "Do you want us to leave? Or do you want to help us find who killed Marissa?"

"He doesn't know who killed the woman," Nasser said, getting his back up. "Why aren't you out talking to people who had a reason to kill her? Why aren't you out talking to her boyfriends?"

"You know who they are?" Mendez asked, poising pen against paper.

Nasser backtracked, looking away. "Well . . . I . . ."

"You don't know," Mendez said, his patience slipping away. "You're just shooting your mouth off."

"She didn't buy that place with the proceeds of her art," Nasser came back. "Someone was footing the bills."

"But you don't know who."

Nasser didn't answer.

"Mr. Nasser," Vince said calmly. "If you have something useful to contribute here, then you should say so. If all you want is to cast aspersions on a woman who can't defend herself in order to distract us, then you should shut up."

"She wasn't like that," Zahn said, rocking himself harder. "She wasn't like that."

Nasser closed his eyes. "Zander, for God's sake. She had a child. Who was the father? Where is he?"

"You don't know. You don't know her. You don't know anything."

"You know she wasn't a saint."

Zahn came to his feet suddenly and shoved Nasser backward with all his might, shouting, "YOU DON'T KNOW HER!"

Taken by surprise, Nasser staggered backward, tripped himself, and sat down hard on the crushed stone.

Zahn shook his hands as if they were wet, horrified that he had touched another living being.

"Oh my God. Oh my God," he muttered. "I'm so sorry. So sorry. I have to go now. I have to go. It's time to go."

He turned and ran back to the house as he had run away from Marissa Fordham's house that morning, with his arms straight down at his sides.

Mendez and Vince both got up from their chairs. Mendez glanced from the professor to his protégé struggling to his feet, and back at Leone. "If I had a kid at that college, I'd be asking for my money back."

12

Kathryn Worth might have been a queen in a past life. She had that kind of bearing: straight, proud, regal, with a mane of golden hair swept back from her face. Disapproval was a statement made with an ice-blue stare down her patrician nose—a look that could make grown men cringe and cower.

In this life Kathryn Worth's title was Assistant District Attorney. At forty-two, she had worked hard to achieve a position of prominence in what was still a male-dominated field—and she made no secret of her desire to go higher up the food chain. She was capable, clever, and ruthless, three traits that would take her far in her chosen profession.

All these qualities and her gender had landed her the plum role of lead prosecutor in the matter of State of California v. Peter Crane.

District Attorney Ed Benton, a man who had not prosecuted a case himself in twenty years, had quickly assigned the case to Kathryn Worth, who had an impressive résumé of wins in the courtroom. Appointing a woman to prosecute a heinous crime against a woman had won him praise in the press and in the minds of the broad base of liberal constituents of Oak Knoll.

Anne had no argument with Benton's choice. She found Kathryn Worth to be smart and tough, and by no means intimidated by Peter Crane's big-name defense attorneys.

She entered Worth's office on the second floor of the county courts building and settled into the now-familiar ancient leather chair opposite the desk. As were many of Oak Knoll's prominent buildings, the main county courts building had been constructed in the 1930s and was a gem of Spanish style with a twist of Art Nouveau thrown into the décor. The courtrooms and offices were full of heavy oak furniture in the Stickley mission style. The hallways boasted original Malibu-tile wainscoting and hand-painted borders. It was the kind of solid, substantial place that made a person believe Lady Justice was on his side.

Kathryn Worth smiled at her as she pulled off her oversize reading glasses. "Anne. How are you?"

"Fine, I hope," Anne said. "I guess it depends on what you have to tell me."

Worth made a little shrug, trying to minimize the significance of what she was about to say. "They've filed a motion to try to exclude some evidence. They'll lose, of course."

Anne sat up a little straighter. Her heart beat a little harder. "What evidence?"

"The tube of superglue."

"On what grounds?" she demanded.

"They're claiming it was planted."

"He was going to put it in my eyes!" Anne said, the upset quickly building a head of steam inside her.

She flashed on the image as if it were a scene from a movie: Peter Crane looming over her, holding her down with a knee on her chest, his left hand pressing down on her throat, choking her. He fished for something with his right hand in his jacket pocket and came out with a small tube. The glue.

All of his victims had had their eyes and mouths glued shut.

"I saw it!" she exclaimed. "I knocked it out of his hand!"

"I know. And you'll testify to that."

"Not if they get it thrown out!"

"Anne, calm down," the ADA said quietly. "There's no way they'll get it thrown out."

"There must be some reason they think they can."

"Michael Harrison thinks he could part the Red Sea if he needed to. It's hubris. He's full of shit. It's just another tactic to delay the inevitable."

"And?"

"And what?"

"You're not telling me everything."

Worth scowled. "You would have made a hell of a prosecutor yourself," she muttered. "There are no useable fingerprints on the tube. I can't explain why. Because the tube is small. Because one of the CSIs smudged it when they collected it. Who knows? It doesn't matter."

"It matters to me," Anne said. She was beginning to feel sick to her stomach.

"Anne, you need to keep your eye on the big picture here. There is not a jury in Southern California that is going to acquit Peter Crane of kidnapping and trying to kill you. There's no way. The glue isn't even relevant. It's not important."

"It links him to the murders of Julie Paulson and Lisa Warwick. And to the attempted murder of Karly Vickers."

"He's not going on trial for those murders. He's going on trial for what he did to you. And there is no way he's getting out of it."

"Then why am I so afraid he will?" Anne asked. Tears welled in her eyes. She pressed a hand across her mouth and felt assaulted by her own fear. Anger would follow—anger that she should be made to feel this way, then anger at her own inability to fight the feeling off.

Kathryn Worth leaned her arms on her desk and sighed. "Because that's a part of it, Anne. Peter Crane made you a victim, and that doesn't stop. It doesn't go away."

"Thanks," Anne said. "That's exactly what I wanted to hear."

"I'm not trying to make you feel worse, Anne. I'm not. But I've sat across this desk—and other desks—from a lot of victims. I know how it works."

"I hate it," Anne whispered, her throat tight around a hard lump of despair.

"I know. I know you do. I'm so sorry," Worth said. "Are you still seeing your therapist?"

"Twice a week."

"It takes time. My mother always likes to say time heals all wounds."

"Your mother is full of shit," Anne said bluntly.

Worth nodded. "Yes, she is. The best we can hope for is that the wounds scar over well enough we don't feel them all the time. And we move on. We have to. Otherwise, the bad guys win."

"I know. That's what Vince says too."

"You've got your own in-house expert," Worth pointed out. "You're ahead of the game."

"That's true," Anne said, mustering a little smile. "And I've been going to a victims' group at the Thomas Center. It helps."

"Watching Peter Crane being sentenced to life without parole will help more."

"Absolutely."

"Don't worry about this motion, Anne. I'm not concerned. I just wanted you to hear about it from me instead of seeing it on the evening news."

"I appreciate that, Kathryn."

"How are things otherwise?"

"Good. Well . . . I'm worried about Dennis Farman," she admitted. "I don't know that he's in the right place. He's isolated there. He has no one his own age to interact with."

Worth spread her hands. "He's there or he's in a juvenile facility. Those are the choices. I'm sure I don't have to remind you he knifed a boy his own age. That's not exactly healthy interaction."

Anne sighed. "I know. And I know there are no boys his own age in the juvenile facility. There simply isn't a good answer for him. If Child Services could place him somewhere . . . in a halfway house or something."

"He's a violent offender, Anne," Worth said. "If he was eighteen, you wouldn't be so concerned about finding him anything outside a penitentiary."

"That's the problem, though. He's not eighteen. He's a little boy."

Worth nodded, thoughtful for a moment as she weighed the pros and cons of what she was about to say.

"Let me tell you about 'a little boy' I dealt with when I was prosecuting sex crimes in Riverside," she said. "Brent Batson. When I was prosecuting Batson he was twenty-eight. He was a serial rapist. A vicious, brutal monster. I put him away for three consecutive life sentences. He had raped nineteen women that I knew of. He later told a reporter that he had committed at least twice that many crimes.

"At the time of his first violent offense—a rape—he was twelve years old. He spent all his juvenile life in one program or another with people trying to straighten him out. When he turned eighteen, he celebrated by going out and raping a fourteen-year-old at knifepoint. When he got out of prison for doing that, he celebrated by raping a homeless woman and her ten-year-old daughter."

"You're saying there's no fixing Dennis Farman," Anne said.

"I'm saying the social worker that lost sleep over him when he was twelve will never get that time back," Worth said. "Justice is a tough business, Anne. You won't do yourself any favors by caring too much."

"I know all that," Anne said. "Believe me, if Dennis had one person in his life to sit on his side of the courtroom, I'd be out of there."

"You got him an attorney," Worth pointed out.

"I'm his advocate. And I just can't stand the idea of being twelve and having absolutely no one give a damn about me. Imagine having your whole life stretching out ahead of you, and it's just a long empty road."

"Anne, you need to learn the difference between sympathy and empathy," Worth said. "One makes you a humanitarian. The other will make you miserable."

"I'll remember that," Anne said, rising from her chair, giving the ADA a sheepish smile. "I don't know how successful I'll be adhering to it, but I'll remember it."

13

"That's fucking bizarre, man," Bill Hicks said. "He killed his own mother."

"He says he killed her," Mendez said. "Why would somebody just blurt that out to a couple of cops? I don't care if the guy is some kind of mathematical genius. He's a fucking wack job."

"What did Vince have to say about it?"

Leone had gone on to the college to have another conversation with Arthur Buckman, one the college president was not likely to enjoy. Mendez had grabbed Hicks in the parking lot at the SO. They were on their way to the Thomas Center for Women to speak to Jane Thomas, who was probably not going to be happy to see them, either.

"He thinks it's probably true."

"Does he think Zahn killed Marissa Fordham?"

"He's not leaning that way. He thinks the murder was too messy. Zahn is a freak about touching other people. This killer had to have been covered in blood."

"That many stab wounds, killing in a frenzy like that," Hicks said. "It would be a safe bet the killer would have cut himself at some point. A bloody knife is slippery."

"He could have worn gloves."

"He didn't bring a weapon to the scene, but he brought gloves?" Hicks arched an eyebrow, dubious.

"If he knew the vic, had been to her house, he would know she had knives there. No need to bring his own," Mendez pointed out.

"What are the odds we get blood evidence on the perp out of that mess in the house?"

"Slim to none. We'll send the knife to BFS."

"How about to the FBI?"

The state Bureau of Forensic Sciences lab was good. The Bureau was the best—although it would take weeks to get results.

"If the boss says we can, why not?" Mendez said. "And if we get lucky and get seminal fluid off the body or off the sheets, maybe they get DNA."

Hicks made a face. "What's it good for? A bunch of scientific mumbo-jumbo and mathematical statistics to put a jury to sleep? That is if a prosecutor can ever get it admitted. It hasn't happened yet."

"You wait and see," Mendez said as he slowed the car and turned into the Thomas Center parking area. "Once the gurus get all the bugs worked out, DNA will be the thing."

"If you say so."

"I do."

The Thomas Center for Women had originally been built in the twenties as a private Catholic girls' school, and operated as such into the sixties. Modeled on the style of the old Spanish missions that dotted the length of California, the white stucco buildings and connecting archways formed a large central courtyard. A huge stone fountain gurgled at the center. Beautiful small gardens lined the stone pathways that radiated out from the fountain. Roses the color of fresh salmon were still in bloom. Mexican heather created ribbons of purple beneath them.

Inside the large administration building, the hall was wide and gracious, painted a warm, welcoming ochre yellow. The old Mexican pavers on the floor had been polished to a soft sheen.

The center was a place for women to reinvent themselves. Women from all walks of life who needed and deserved a second chance were welcome here. Homeless women, battered women, women with drug histories and even police records went through the program, which offered shelter, assistance with health care, psychological and job counseling.

It was a remarkable place with a remarkable woman at the head of it.

Mendez and Hicks went to the front desk and asked for Jane Thomas.

She emerged from her office with a look of concern marring her brow. In her early forties, she was a tall and elegant woman. She wore a black-and-white-printed dress that wrapped around her slender frame. Her blond hair had been slicked back into a simple ponytail.

"Detectives," she said, shaking the hand of Hicks and then Mendez. "I would say it's a pleasure to see you again, but I think you'll understand if I reserve judgment."

She had lost a former employee, Lisa Warwick, to the See-No-Evil killer, and had all but lost a client, Karly Vickers. Vickers had survived her ordeal, but had been left deaf and blind.

"We hardly ever show up with good news," Mendez said.

"And today is no different."

"I'm afraid not."

Thomas sighed, resigned. "Let's go into my office."

"How is Ms. Vickers doing?" Hicks asked as they went into the spacious office that looked out on the courtyard garden.

"She's got a long road ahead of her, and it's all uphill. I don't know," she said, shaking her head as she took her seat behind the desk. "She's had two surgeries now to try to repair the damage to her inner ears, without much success. She'll never see again. She can talk to us, but all we can do is answer her by writing on the palm of her hand with a finger.

"She's extremely depressed, and who can blame her? She can't even testify against the man who kidnapped and tortured her—if he ever goes on trial for those crimes—because she can't identify him. She asked us if we knew who he was. Either she never saw him, or he drugged her and she can't remember, or she was too traumatized to remember."

"It's frustrating for us too," Mendez said. "We still have no idea where he held the women. If we could find a location and link it to Peter Crane, we'd be in business."

"He'll go away for a long time for what he did to Anne Leone," Hicks said. "That's something anyway. I don't see how he gets out for twenty-five years. Maybe more."

"I hope so," Jane Thomas said. "But I don't think you gentlemen have come here to talk about Peter Crane, have you?"

"No, ma'am," Mendez said.

"Cal came by earlier and told me about Marissa. I don't even know what to say. How can something like that happen? It's a nightmare."

"Did you know Ms. Fordham well?" Hicks asked.

"I've known Marissa socially since she moved here. Her daughter was just a baby then. She did that remarkable poster for us," she said, pointing to a two-feet-by-three-feet framed print on one wall of her office.

The poster depicted the Thomas Center logo—a stylized woman with her arms raised in victory—against a rich backdrop of magenta and purple, lavender and pink.

"We've raised a lot of money selling the prints," she said.

"Were you friends?" Mendez asked.

"We were friendly. Milo Bordain, who sponsors her, is also a big supporter of the center. We would see each other at dinners and so on. I have a couple of Marissa's paintings at my house. She did some wonderful work in the plein air style."

"Do you know anything about her private life?" Mendez asked.

"Not really. She volunteered some time here as a guest teacher in our art therapy program. She came to fund-raisers. I saw her at gallery parties."

"You didn't know her daughter's father?"

"No. I never heard her speak of him."

"Did you ever see her in the company of a man?"

"At functions from time to time. I saw her with Mark Foster a couple of times. I saw her with Don Quinn a couple of times."

"Don Quinn from Quinn, Morgan?" Mendez asked. Quinn, Morgan and Associates was a local law firm that did a lot of pro bono work for the center. The Morgan of Quinn, Morgan was Steve Morgan, Sara Morgan's husband.

"Who is Mark Foster?" Hicks asked, taking notes.

"Mark Foster is the head of the music department at McAster," she said. "But I didn't get the impression Marissa was serious about anyone. They looked like casual dates. You know, Guest Plus One. She was fun. She liked to laugh. She was a very devoted mother.

"Milo would be able to help you more than I can," she said. She flipped through her Rolodex for Bordain's address and jotted it down on a piece of paper, then handed it across the desk. "She'll be devastated. Marissa was like the daughter she never had."

Mendez took the piece of paper and tucked it inside his little notebook as he rose from his chair. "We'll speak to her. Thank you for your time."

As they started toward the door, Jane Thomas asked, "Marissa's daughter—have you heard anything? Will she be all right?"

She held up a hand before Mendez could draw a breath to answer. "What am I thinking? She witnessed her mother's murder. What could be all right after that?"

14

Don Quinn was a good-looking guy in his late fifties—tan, a mane of silver hair, chiseled features, wide white smile. He could have been an actor on one of the prime-time soaps. He could have been the roving guest star who appeared one night as a deadly doctor on *Murder, She Wrote*, and as an oil tycoon days later on *Dynasty*.

Here in Oak Knoll he played the role of senior partner of a successful law firm.

The John Forsythe smile dropped away when Mendez told him why they were in his office.

"Oh my God," he said, sinking down into his leather executive's desk chair. He aged suddenly as the tan seemingly drained from his face.

"We understand you sometimes saw Ms. Fordham socially," Hicks began.

Quinn didn't respond for several moments as he tried to absorb the shock of the news.

"No offense intended, Mr. Quinn," Mendez said, "but you seem considerably older than Ms. Fordham."

Though he clearly didn't want anyone to think of him as "older," Mendez thought. The man was in great shape, dressed in a black T-shirt under his tan sport coat. Probably the only reason he didn't dye his hair was that it made such a striking contrast to his tan.

Quinn shook off whatever memories had been playing through his mind. "Marissa and I have gone out a few times. Not lately. She was a lovely young woman. Interesting, vivacious. Is there some reason I shouldn't have enjoyed her company?"

"Your wife, maybe?" Mendez said, shooting a pointed look to a framed family photo on the bookshelves behind Don Quinn. Quinn,

Mrs. Quinn—a slightly plump woman his own age, and two good-looking kids—a boy and a girl in their late teens or early twenties. The trendy Quinns posed on a sandy beach, all of them in khaki pants and French blue turtlenecks.

"I'm divorced," Quinn said. "Was it a robbery?"

"No."

"Oh my God. Someone murdered her? Why?"

"We were hoping you might be able to shed some light on that subject for us," Hicks said. "When did you last see her?"

"I saw her at fund-raiser for local school music programs back in September."

"You were together?"

"No. She was with Mark Foster. Marissa and I were friends. We dated off and on. It wasn't serious."

"Do you know if she was serious with Mr. Foster?"

"No," Quinn said dismissively. "Marissa enjoyed the company of men. She was a delightful date. But she only let you get just so close and no closer. I always imagined she'd been hurt badly by someone—presumably Haley's father.

"Haley!" he said, realization dawning. "Oh my God. Where is Haley? Was she . . . ?"

"She was taken to the hospital," Hicks said. "We don't know the extent of injuries at this point."

"Oh, no. That just makes me feel sick."

"So Marissa and Mark Foster were dating?" Mendez asked, steering them back on point.

"They were friends."

"Like you were friends?" Hicks asked.

"Not exactly. Mark occasionally needs a date for a function. Marissa was happy to step in."

"I don't understand," Mendez said.

"I don't think Mark really dates women," Quinn said.

"He's gay?"

He shrugged. "In the closet. That's my impression. He's a nice guy. It's nobody's business."

"But there might be some members on the board of McAster who wouldn't be happy."

"It may be a liberal arts school, but not everyone on the board takes that word 'liberal' to heart," Quinn said. "You know, it wasn't five months ago the Supreme Court ruled homosexual activity between consenting adults in the privacy of a home is not protected by the Constitution. Men like Mark have to be discreet. I think Marissa was his beard."

"And you don't think she was serious about anyone else?" Mendez said.

Quinn shook his head. "No. Marissa was a free spirit. She enjoyed her life. She enjoyed her daughter. She didn't need a man to complete her emotionally."

"What about financially?" Hicks asked. "She has a nice place out there. Had to cost some bucks. Was she that successful as an artist?"

"She did well as an artist, but I don't think she needed the money," Quinn said. "I think she has family money."

"What do you know about her family?"

"East Coast. Rhode Island, I think. She never spoke of them. It seemed to be a sore subject."

"Were you her attorney as well as her friend?" Mendez asked.

"No. Steve helped her set up a trust for her daughter. That's been the extent of her business with us."

"Was he friends with her too?" Mendez asked, wondering why Sara hadn't mentioned the connection earlier. He probably shouldn't have been surprised. She had already had the unflattering light of police scrutiny illuminate the flaws in her marriage. Why invite that again?

Quinn frowned. "He wasn't sleeping with her, if that's what you mean."

"Like he wasn't sleeping with Lisa Warwick?" Mendez challenged.

"You never had any proof he had an affair with Lisa."

"It's not against the law to cheat on your wife," Mendez said, feeling himself get a little hot under the collar. "We're not going to spend taxpayer dollars trying to prove the guy is an adulterer. But it doesn't speak well for his character, does it?"

"Steve is a fine person," Quinn said firmly as he sat back in his expensive leather chair—withdrawing from the interview. "He works hard. He gives back to the community. He's a good father."

"He's just not a good husband," Mendez said. "I guess everybody has their flaws."

"I don't see why we're talking about this, Detective," Quinn said. He propped his elbows on the armrests of the chair and made a tent with his hands—subconsciously putting a physical barrier between them. "Someone murdered Marissa Fordham. It wasn't me, and it wasn't Steve. You should look elsewhere."

"Is he in today?" Mendez asked.

"I believe he's in a meeting with a client."

And if he wasn't, Don Quinn was going to make damn sure he pretended he was. Mendez figured he'd be on the phone to his partner's office the instant he and Hicks stepped out the door.

He glanced at his watch. 4:42. The office would close soon. Steve Morgan would leave and head home—or elsewhere.

Mendez rose from his chair. "Thank you for your time, Mr. Quinn."

"If you think of anything that might be helpful to the investigation, please give us a call," Hicks said, setting a business card on the desk.

"What's with the hard-on for Steve Morgan?" Hicks asked as they walked back to the car parked down the street at a meter.

"The guy rubs me the wrong way," Mendez said. "He's got a beautiful wife, a beautiful daughter, a beautiful home, and he's a fucking dog. There was no doubt in my mind he was sleeping with Lisa Warwick—who ended up murdered. Now he's got a connection to Marissa Fordham—also murdered."

"Peter Crane killed Lisa Warwick," Hicks pointed out.

"I know. I just don't like coincidence."

"You just don't like Steve Morgan."

"No, I don't. Do you?"

"He doesn't mean anything to me one way or the other. He's just another name on the list of people to talk to regarding our victim."

"Then let's," Mendez said as they got in the car.

"You want to wait for him here?" Hicks asked. "Go back and park ourselves in the office?"

"No. I'd say we go park in front of his house, but there's no guarantee he's going home when he leaves here. Let's go around the back and catch him coming out."

They didn't have to wait long.

They had just pulled down the alley when Steve Morgan came out the back door of the Quinn, Morgan offices. He was tall and lanky with a mop of sandy, wavy hair; the kind of guy who would look good with a tennis racket in his hand and a sweater tied around his neck.

Mendez pulled the sedan in directly behind Morgan's black Trans Am, blocking his exit.

"Slipping out early?" he asked as Morgan got out of the car.

If Morgan was annoyed, he did a good job of masking it.

"Detectives. Don just told me about Marissa Fordham. She was a friend of my wife's. I want to break the news to Sara before she sees it on TV."

"She knows," Mendez said. "As it happens, she had an appointment with Ms. Fordham this morning. I've already spoken with her."

Morgan sighed. "Oh God, she must be upset."

"She didn't call you?"

"I've been in and out of the office today. I saw she left a couple of messages, but I haven't had time to call her back."

"She took it pretty hard," Mendez said. "You knew Ms. Fordham as well."

Morgan sat back against his spotless vehicle. "Yes. I knew her. Is this the part where you're going to accuse me of sleeping with her?"

"Were you?" Hicks asked.

"No. I knew Marissa from the Thomas Center. I helped out with the copyright business on the poster she did. And I knew her socially a little bit—charity functions, cocktail parties, like that."

"She dated your partner," Hicks said.

"She dated a few different men. Marissa wasn't interested in being tied down by anyone other than her daughter. She was a terrific mother."

"You put together a trust for her little girl," Mendez said. "Can you tell us who the trustee is?"

"I am. That's not uncommon when people don't have close family—and actually just as common when they do. They want a neutral third party. Relatives can get crazy when there's money involved."

"Are we talking about a lot of money?"

Morgan frowned. "I can't tell you that. It's confidential."

"Your client is dead."

"But her heir is alive, and who knows what relatives might crawl out of the woodwork now," he said. "I can't release the information without a court order or I could end up in front of the ethics committee and/or being sued."

"Let me put it this way, then," Mendez said. "Will the little girl be well taken care of?"

"Yes."

"What about a will?" Hicks asked.

"I asked her about that. She said it was taken care of. I didn't draw it up for her."

"Did she tell you if she had made provisions for the care of her daughter in the event something happened to her?"

"No. Not beyond the trust. But I can't imagine she hadn't. Sara and I took care of that for Wendy before she was even born."

"You're an attorney," Hicks pointed out.

"Yes, but I'm a father first," Morgan said. "Marissa was a mother first—and a single mom at that. I'm sure when you go through her personal documents you'll find everything you're looking for."

"Did she ever mention the little girl's father to you?" Mendez asked.

"Not by name. And only to tell me he wasn't a factor in Haley's life."

Morgan glanced at his watch and frowned. "I don't know what else I can tell you. Does Jane Thomas know about Marissa?"

"Yes. We were there earlier," Hicks said.

"I'd like to get going then—if there's nothing else."

"Not for the moment."

"You know where to find me," Morgan said.

Yeah, Mendez thought as he backed the sedan up to let Steve Morgan out of his parking place, just this side of a murder victim.

15

"Anne Marie! You look like something the cat dragged in!"

"There's nothing like a good friend to brighten a dark day," Anne said, sliding into the booth.

Fran Goodsell had been her best friend from her first day teaching at Oak Knoll Elementary six years ago. Completely irreverent in all the most inappropriate moments, he always found a way to distract her from whatever troubled her.

Sharp-witted and loyal to a fault, he was the fourteenth of fifteen children born to an Irish Catholic family in Boston and had just turned forty in the spring, celebrating with an outrageous costumed fete he called "Franival!"

His phenomenal teaching skills had helped him create an impressive résumé at top private and public schools on the East Coast before he had migrated to California.

Despite the fact that he actually loved his work and was brilliant with children and parents alike, he liked to profess that teaching kindergarten had driven him to drink and to contemplate the mandatory sterilization of most of the population.

"Honestly, darling," he said, casting a disapproving eye at Anne's present state. He was, of course, as always, perfectly preppy with a twist, dressed in khaki pants and not one but two Ralph Lauren Polo shirts—a vibrant blue one over a vibrant orange one—with the collars turned up.

Anne supposed she looked a little worse for wear at the end of this day, even though she had started out feeling smart and together in olive slacks and a lightweight black sweater set. Now her slacks were creased and wilted, and her sweaters seemed to have stretched and grown in the heat of the afternoon.

She had cried off most of her makeup during what she called her "mini-meltdowns" of the day. At some point she had given up on her hair and pulled it back into a ponytail with a brown scrunchie she had found in the bottom of her purse.

"You're not seeing me at my freshest," she said. "I feel like something the cat threw up."

"Are you pregnant?"

"No. And thanks for reminding me."

It was no secret to Franny that she and Vince were anxious to start their family. He made it his life's work to dig out the most private details of her life—and she usually gave them up without too much of a fight because he was in many ways better medicine than her therapist had ever prescribed.

His face softened and he reached across the table to put his hand over hers. "It'll happen, honey. You're just still under a lot of stress."

"I know," she said softly. And pushing thirty. Ticktock.

"For God's sake, you haven't been doing it all that long," Franny said. "And don't forget, we're talking practically uncharted territories down there."

"That isn't true!" Anne protested, finding an embarrassed grin.

"Virgin forest," he said, eyes twinkling. "Thank God you found yourself a lumberjack with a big axe."

"Stop it!" Anne said, giggling as her cheeks burned. "You'll get us thrown out of here."

"You're a lucky girl, Anne Marie. That's all's I'm saying," he said with an extra-thick Long Island accent.

A waitress came by and took Anne's order for a glass of pinot grigio.

Piazza Fontana was the restaurant where she and Vince had had their first unofficial date. He had asked her here on the excuse of wanting to talk about her students who had discovered the body of Lisa Warwick. She had gone, protesting the notion that she was interested in anything other than just that. After dinner he had stolen a kiss when he walked her to her car. Her lips had tingled all night.

The restaurant had become their favorite haunt. Vince, who came from—by his own description—a big, loud Italian family from Chicago, knew good food and wine. Anne loved the ambience of casual elegance—dark wood and white table linens, exposed brick walls, a fountain gurgling in a corner. They dined here at least once a week.

The owner himself, a transplant from Tuscany, brought her a glass of wine and a broad smile.

"Signora Leone! What a pleasure, as always."

"Thank you, Gianni. It's good to see you."

"Where is your husband?" he asked, looking around. "He lets you out of his sight? All the young men will be looking and saying 'Who she is?' "

"I'm here to protect her," Franny announced.

Gianni Farina rolled his eyes comically, patted Franny on the shoulder, and muttered something in Italian.

"No tip for that!" Franny called after him.

Anne laughed and took a sip of her wine as the front door opened and Vince walked in, greeted by no less than three people before he made it past the maitre d' stand. He traded a few lines of Italian with Gianni, an exchange that ended in laughter and a big grin from Vince.

"Are you keeping an eye on my bride, Franny?" he asked as he slid into the booth next to Anne.

"I can't be held responsible for how she looks."

Vince ran a hand back over her hair, his eyes shining as he looked down at her. "She looks beautiful."

"You're in love."

"I am." He leaned down and gave her a sweet little kiss that filled her with a soft, warm glow. "You look tired."

Anne mustered a smile. "Long day. What's your excuse?"

His head was hurting him. He wouldn't say so, but she had learned to read the signs: the tightness around his eyes, the deepening of the lines across his forehead. He needed to lie down. She needed to take care of him.

"The same," he said. "I told Gianni we'd take something home with us."

"And ditch me," Franny complained.

"Three's a crowd," Vince returned.

"Do you have any leads on the case?" Anne asked.

"Some interesting possibilities," Vince said evasively.

"What case?" Franny asked. "Peter Crane?"

Franny was obsessed with the prospect of the Crane trial. The idea that his dentist—the person he allowed to put his hands in his mouth, for God's sake!—was a serial killer. And that Crane had abducted and hurt Anne made him all the more rabid on the subject.

"Somebody murdered Marissa Fordham, the artist," Anne said.

"What?"

"Marissa Fordham," Anne said again. "She did that beautiful poster for the Thomas Center."

"Oh my God!"

"Did you know her?" Vince asked.

"I've met her a few times at social events. She just brought her little girl to school for the pre-kindergarten Halloween party. I liked her. She's a cool lady. We talked about her coming in for a visiting artist day. What happened?"

"She was found dead this morning," Vince said, giving no details away. "We're trying to find out who her friends were in the hopes they might be able to turn the investigation in the right direction."

"People aren't supposed to get murdered here," Franny said, getting angry. "Do we really have to go through this again? This is unbelievable!"

"People who kill other people don't tend to stop and think how it's going to impact the community," Vince said. "They don't stop in the heat of the moment and think *Oh my God, there were all those murders here last year. Maybe I should wait.*"

Franny ignored the edge of sarcasm in Vince's voice. His mind was racing to try to make some kind of sense of a senseless act. "Was it a robbery or something?"

"No."

"Oh my God. Someone just went to her home and killed her? At random?"

"We don't think it was random," Vince said. "In fact, I would say it was very personal with a lot of rage behind it. She managed to piss someone off to the point of no return.

"I remember you once telling me you know everybody worth knowing in Oak Knoll, Franny," he said. "You run in some artsy circles. Have you ever heard anything negative about her?"

Franny looked uncomfortable. Vince sharpened his stare a little.

"She was single, independent, talented, and gorgeous," Franny said. "A lot of not-single, not-independent, not-talented, not-gorgeous women are threatened by that. Surprise, surprise."

"Women worried about someone stealing their husbands."

Franny rolled his eyes. "Like anyone would want them."

"Does anyone in particular jump to mind?"

"No, no. I've heard the odd catty remark, that's all. She's a sexy single mom—she must be a slut. That kind of thing. It's 1986, for God's sake," he said. "Single women have children. Hello: The scarlet letter went out with the poodle skirt.

"What about her daughter?" he asked. "Where is she?"

"In the hospital," Vince said. "Unconscious, the last I heard."

That was the final straw for Franny. Color slashed across his pale cheeks and his eyes all but disappeared behind an angry brows-down squint.

"When you find who did it," he said, "do the world a favor and just shoot him."

"If only life was that simple," Vince said.

"It should be," Franny declared. "Bad people off the planet! Now! More wine for the rest of us!"

He raised his glass in a toast and tossed back the last of his cabernet.

16

Sara walked around her sculpture, trying to concentrate, trying to focus and see the direction she needed to go. Nothing came.

She had a vision a week ago, when she started the project. It was supposed to be about strength and femininity. The metal—the strength—would bend but not break. From the wounded heart would flow feminine beauty in the form of hand-painted silk ribbons.

But as she looked at the piece now, she saw nothing but a mess of twisted wire and steel mesh. *Car Wreck on a Stick*. That was what it looked like.

Anxiety swirled through her. Fragments of the morning kept flashing through her mind like a strobe light. Detective Mendez, grim faced, mustache framing his downturned mouth. Marissa's house. The ruined studio. The ruined art.

"Ms. Fordham is deceased."

Oh my God.

"Ms. Fordham is deceased."

"Oh my God," she whispered, trembling.

In her mind's eye she could see Marissa walking, talking. She used her hands when she spoke as if she were trying to draw a picture to illustrate her point. Vibrant. Animated. Full of life.

"Ms. Fordham is deceased."

She felt nauseous.

She reached out and tried to adjust a piece of the wire mesh, and nicked the tip of a finger. A droplet of blood rounded bright red like the sudden bloom of a flower on a cactus, then rolled off her fingertip to splash like a tear on the heavy canvas drop cloth that covered the garage floor.

They had converted the space above the garage into a studio for her some months ago. But it was no place for a sculpture as tall as this was, made from steel and requiring welding. She had commandeered this far stall of their three-car garage for the project.

Her studio upstairs was a beautifully lit space with plenty of room for painting and crafts projects, and working with the silk, her latest passion. Although in empty moments when her head wasn't full of whatever she was working on, she could never escape the thought that the studio was her consolation prize. It was her payment for not divorcing Steve.

He had been cheating on her with Lisa Warwick, a nurse who had volunteered her time to advocate in family court for women from the Thomas Center. Just as Steve devoted hours and hours of his time— *their time*—to the same cause.

Sara had suspected for a long time, but had never had the courage to confront him. If she had confronted him, she would have then had to confront the reality of the next step. Did they go to counseling? Did she just divorce him? Could she ever trust him again?

The answer to the last one was no. He had never admitted to the affair. To this day, he had never accepted culpability. Typical lawyer. His accomplice was dead. There were no witnesses to testify against him. But Sara knew, and Steve knew she knew. And she got a lovely art studio out of it, but her self-esteem had taken a beating.

She accepted that and lived with it, but she wore that mantle of the betrayed wife like it was made of chain mail and coarse hair. It was heavy and uncomfortable, but she couldn't get out of it. She told herself she did it for Wendy. She hoped that was true. She hoped that was right.

Wendy loved her father. She very much enjoyed being the center of her parents' world. She didn't need to know that her parents' marriage no longer existed in a true sense of the word. At least, that was what they all pretended.

Sara tried again to focus on her work, walked around to see it from a different angle. It didn't look like anything.

She wondered if it would have looked like something to Marissa.

"Ms. Fordham is deceased."

Murdered.

Oh my God.

A car door slammed in the driveway, making her jump. She pressed her bleeding hand to her heart and glanced at her watch. Must be car pool. Wendy coming home. Time to pull herself together. She forced a smile as she turned. It froze and cracked as her husband came into the garage.

"Oh. I thought you were Wendy. You're early."

"I heard some bad news," he said. "About Marissa Fordham."

"Where did you hear it?" she asked stupidly, as if no one else would know by now. As if it were somehow her terrible secret to keep.

"Detective Mendez told me you were there, at her house."

"Marissa and I were supposed to work this morning. I got there and . . . he told me."

"Are you all right?"

"No. Of course not. Are you?"

Steve had known Marissa. As part of his volunteer work for the center he had helped with setting up the copyright on the poster so the proceeds of sales would go directly to the Thomas Center.

She had wondered if that was all her husband had done with Marissa. The curse of the woman scorned: to look at every woman her husband had contact with and wonder if he was sleeping with her too. Marissa was beautiful, headstrong, sexy—a description people had used for Sara what seemed an awfully long time ago . . . How strange that was, she thought now, remembering that she and Marissa were close to the same age.

Her husband shook his head, hands on his hips. He was standing not three feet away from her. There had been a time when they both would have closed that distance and she would have been in his arms.

"No," he said. "It's terrible."

"What's going to happen to Haley?"

"I don't know."

She went to push a chunk of hair out of her eyes and smeared blood across her cheek.

"You're bleeding," Steve said.

Once he would have taken her hand and kissed her wounded finger.

"I cut myself."

"Why don't you wear gloves when you're working on this thing?" he asked, more annoyed than concerned.

Suffering for your art? Mendez had asked her.

She wondered what either of them would think if she told them the physical pain was a relief.

Another car door slammed out on the street, and the opportunity was lost—not that she ever would have taken it. Her daughter was home. Time to put on a happier face.

17

Wendy went to her room as soon as dinner was over and the kitchen was cleaned up. She tended not to hang around downstairs when both her mom and dad were home because they weren't happy and everyone was tense and it sucked. And it was her fault, which sucked even worse.

Her parents stayed together because of her, because that was what she wanted. Only it wasn't. She wanted them to go back in time and be happy the way they used to be—*that* was what she wanted. If she could have time-traveled like Michael J. Fox in *Back to the Future*, she would have gone back and changed so many things.

She would have gone back and made sure that whatever had happened to make her parents fall out of love never happened. She would have gone back to that day last October and made sure she and Tommy didn't take the shortcut through Oakwoods Park, and they never would have found that dead body, and none of what had happened would have happened.

But she couldn't travel back in time. She couldn't fix what was wrong between her mom and dad. And she was too afraid of losing what family life she had to tell them not to try anymore.

Restless and depressed, she wandered around her sunny yellow bedroom with its white wicker furniture and her stuffed animals on the bed. Her Barbies lived in their own little cul-de-sac in the corner in the pink Barbie dream house with the pink Barbie Corvette parked beside it.

Wendy felt like she was in somebody else's room. The room of a stupid happy child who didn't know the things Wendy knew.

She turned her radio on and sat down on the bed. Her newest favorite song was playing—"True Colors," by Cyndi Lauper. She had been crazy for the song "Girls Just Wanna Have Fun." She would always sing along and dance and be ridiculous when the song came on the radio. Her mom had joined in with her sometimes. Tommy had always blushed and practically died of embarrassment when she did it.

Tommy wasn't allowed to listen to popular music because his mother was a bitch. Wendy wasn't actually allowed to use that word, but she used it all the time in her head—and out of earshot of adults. Janet Crane was an evil bitch. She had always been a bitch to Tommy, and then she took him and left, and nobody knew where they were.

Wendy kept hoping she would hear from him, that he would send her a postcard or a letter or something just to let her know he was all right and that he was thinking about her. They had been best friends since the third grade. But more than a year had passed with no word. In her darker moments Wendy wondered if the Evil Bitch might have killed him, just like Tommy's father had killed all those women.

The world was such a dark place. So many bad things happened. It made her feel stupid to have a sunny yellow bedroom.

After everything that had happened with the murders, and Tommy's dad attacking Miss Navarre, and Tommy disappearing, Miss Navarre had tried to get their fifth-grade class interested in something good, something positive.

They had begun to follow the space shuttle program and learn about the astronauts and the scientific experiments they would perform on the next mission. It had been especially fun because one of the astronauts— Christa McAuliffe—was a schoolteacher. They had all been so excited to watch the launch on the twenty-eighth of January. But seventy-three seconds into the flight the space shuttle *Challenger* had exploded, killing everyone on board right before their very eyes.

Weeks later the navy had found the crew compartment in the ocean with the bodies of all seven astronauts still inside. Wendy had had nightmares for weeks about looking inside the capsule and seeing the rotting corpses.

And not long after that a nuclear power plant had a meltdown in the Soviet Union, and killed and poisoned thousands of people and animals and the environment, and now there would be freaks and mutants there like something out of a horror movie—only it was real.

It just seemed like everything in the world was bad and wrong.

Now her mother's friend Marissa was dead. Wendy had known Marissa too, and Marissa's daughter, Haley, was so cute and sweet.

Wendy had begged and begged to babysit for Haley, but her mom thought she was too young and wouldn't let her babysit until she was at least thirteen. Two whole years away.

And her parents wouldn't say exactly what had happened to Marissa, but Wendy knew she had been murdered, because she had heard part of the story on the news.

She didn't know why people did these things. Why had Tommy's father killed those women? Why would anyone kill Marissa? No adult had given her a real answer. They didn't know. Did people just wake up one day and decide they wanted to kill? Did they just get so angry they couldn't stop themselves?

She had especially wondered about that because of Dennis Farman. Dennis was just a kid, like she was a kid, like Cody Roache was a kid. He had always been a bully, had always liked hurting people—maybe because his father had picked on him and hurt him, Miss Navarre had said—but why had he decided that fateful Saturday to bring a knife to the park and stab Cody and try to stab her?

Did he just go crazy? Did people just go crazy? Would she go crazy? Would her dad go crazy? Would a crazy person come in their house one night and kill them just because he felt like it?

Wendy wandered into her bathroom and looked at herself in the mirror, and wondered whether other people wondered these things too or whether she was losing her mind. How did people know if they were going crazy? If they were crazy didn't they probably think they were normal, and everyone else would think they were crazy?

Just to try to do something normal, she brushed her teeth and took the scrunchie out of her hair. She had done her hair that day mostly down but with some messy sections snatched up into an off-center ponytail that looked like a blond fountain coming out the top of her head. She liked to dress like her favorite singers: Madonna, Cyndi Lauper, the girls in the Bangles. Although she didn't put as much effort into it lately as she once had.

Everyone told her she looked just like her mother, which she did. They had the same thick, wavy hair that was all different shades of blond but darker at the roots. They had the same unusual blue eyes. Wendy had grown nearly two inches since fifth grade. In another year or two she would be as tall as her mother.

As she crawled under the covers of her bed she made a vow to herself not to end up as unhappy as her mother.

She snuggled her favorite brown teddy bear and kissed his nose. She was going to grow up to be a famous journalist, and she was never going to get married—until the perfect man came along.

She pressed her cheek to her bear's head and whispered his name as she closed her eyes: "Tommy."

18

On the other side of town, in the county mental health facility, Dennis Farman wondered too, what made people crazy.

He sat on his bed in his room, all alone because there were no other kids in the place, and because people thought he was dangerous and would probably kill a roommate in his sleep. The lights in his room had been turned out for the night, but pale yellow light came in from the hall, and white-blue light came in through the window from the parking lot.

He had none of his own prized possessions here. The pocketknife he had stolen from his dad's dresser—the one he had used to stab Cody—had been taken by the detectives. He had put all of his most treasured things in his backpack that day, including the dried-out head of a rattlesnake he had watched a gardener kill with a spade. He never got his backpack back after they arrested him.

The knife had been the most important thing. He had always pretended that his father had given it to him for his birthday when he was nine. He had made up all kinds of fantasies about his father showing him how to use it, the two of them camping out and using the knife to cut branches and gut fish. The truth was, his father had never given him a present, had never even remembered his birthday.

When Dennis had asked Miss Navarre when he could get his knife back, she had looked at him like he was crazy. Maybe crazy ran in his family. He was locked up in a mental hospital after all.

Dennis had never thought of his father as crazy, just mean. But in the end, everyone said he had to have lost his mind to do what he had done.

People didn't think Dennis knew what all had happened, but he did. He had never told anyone, but he had been right there the night his father had beaten his mother to death. Hiding up in his room, he had heard every slap, every curse, every cry. It hadn't been the first time (so he didn't think his father had gone crazy, just that he was drunk and mean, as he often was) and he hadn't thought his mother would die, but she had.

The rest of what had left him an orphan he had heard in bits and pieces, listening to people when they didn't know it. That was one thing he was really good at.

He had been in a room at the sheriff's office when it happened, on account of everyone making such a stink about him stabbing Cody—*who didn't die*. Some stupid cow from Child Services had been trying to get him to draw pictures of his feelings. What the fuck was that? You couldn't draw a picture of something you couldn't see.

Anyway, his dad had come into the sheriff's office and took the sheriff hostage and threatened to kill him. But in the end he had killed himself.

His dad was a loser. Dennis was glad he was dead. And his mother was a stupid, useless drunk who never did anything for him. All she ever did was yell at him. He didn't need her.

He didn't need anybody.

Nobody liked him anyway. He had never had a real friend. Everybody said Cody had been his friend, but Cody had only been his friend because he was afraid of Dennis and it was smarter for him to be Dennis's friend than not. Stupid little cockroach. Dennis had showed him.

Miss Navarre didn't like him. But she came to see him anyway.

Dennis knew she had married the FBI agent, but he wouldn't call her by her married name. She would always be Miss Navarre to him. She was trying to help him. Nobody else wanted to help him. Everybody else wanted him to go to prison and rot there for the rest of his life. He had heard people say over and over that there was no fixing what was wrong with him.

But Miss Navarre was trying to help him.

Sometimes he dreamed about Miss Navarre.

Sometimes he dreamed about doing things to her. Bad things, dirty things.

Dennis knew all about sex. He used to like to go around at night and look in people's windows. He had seen all kinds of people do all kinds of things to each other: men with women, women with women, men with men. A lot of it was gross, but he got excited anyway.

He had watched Miss Navarre with the FBI guy do it on the back porch of her house. He had never thought of her doing anything like that. She was a teacher. He never thought of teachers having sex or having to go to the bathroom or farting or anything like that. It made him angry that she wasn't as perfect as she pretended to be. She was just a slut, fucking a guy on her back porch.

But she came to see him.

She tried to help him.

She was pretty.

She was a whore.

He closed his eyes and remembered what he had seen, what he had heard, the sounds she had made.

She would come to see him again tomorrow.

He would dream about her tonight.

19

They made love slowly, sweetly, gently. He touched, she sighed. Lips clung, tongues tangled. Her breath caught, he groaned, she gasped. They whispered and murmured, "I love you . . . I need you."

Anne slid her hands over her husband's muscled back. She ran her foot up and down the back of his thick calf. She loved everything about him. She loved making love with him. She loved his strength, the size of him, the warm smoothness of his skin. She loved the way he smelled, the way he tasted, the way he filled her, the way he moved against her, the way he held her.

He was a patient lover, always careful she was ready, always careful that she was satisfied. He made her feel beautiful and powerful and feminine and sexual. He always held her afterward and kissed her hair and whispered how much he loved her, how he would keep her safe and never let anything bad happen to her ever again. And she felt safe and protected and so at home.

Vince tangled his hands in his wife's dark hair. He kissed the graceful curve of her neck where it met her shoulder. He loved everything about her. He loved making love with her. He loved her softness, her delicate places, the heat of her, the smell of her. He loved the way she tasted, the silk glove tightness of her around him, the way she took him inside of her until he filled her.

She was his perfect lover, so open, so giving, unreserved. She made him feel strong and male and animal. Afterward he cradled her in his arms and kissed her hair and told her how much he loved her, and how he would keep her safe. And he felt so blessed and protective and completely at home.

He was one lucky son of a bitch.

He smiled down at Anne, thinking she looked like an angel in the soft light from the lamp on the nightstand. She smiled back, reached up and touched his cheek, her thumb brushing over the flat shiny scar that marked the entrance of the bullet fragment in his head.

He hoped this might have been the perfect moment for her to conceive, but he didn't say it aloud. He knew she was worried about it. She worried that the post-traumatic stress would keep her body in self-protection mode and not allow her to conceive. One worry preyed on another—a vicious circle.

Vince had no doubt at all that they would have a family. He could close his eyes and see Anne round with their child. He could see her smiling down as a dark-haired baby nursed at her breast.

He brushed her hair back and kissed her softly. She kissed him back. Desire began to slowly stir again.

Until his pager went off.

Vince groaned. Anne made a little sound of frustration.

He looked in the window of the pager.

Mendez's phone number plus 911.

He grabbed the phone off the nightstand and dialed.

Mendez answered on the first ring and said, "Haley Fordham is conscious."

"I'm on my way," Vince said.

"Bring Anne."

20

"I heard that," Anne said as Vince got out of bed with no announcement other than that he had to go to the hospital because their witness was awake.

Vince scowled and went into the bathroom. Anne threw the covers back, got out of bed, and followed him.

"Do you think if you just ignore me, I'll lie down and go to sleep?" she asked.

"I don't want you going," he said as he turned the shower faucet on.

"Tony thinks I could be helpful—"

"I don't care what Tony thinks."

Anne's temper boiled up as he basically dismissed her by getting in the shower. She pulled the door open and climbed in after him.

"Don't you dismiss me, Vince Leone," she snapped, blinking hard as water pellets bounced off her husband and into her face.

"Anne," he growled, "I won't have it."

"And since when are you the boss of me?" she demanded to know.

"Since I'm your husband," he said, soaping his chest and arms.

"Ha!" She held up her left hand to show him the diamond he had put on her finger not so many months ago. "This is a ring, not a collar and leash. I'm going."

"I'm not taking you."

"I'll drive myself."

"Not if I get to your car keys before you do."

"I have a spare set hidden."

"I don't. I'll take my keys and your car."

Anne narrowed her eyes in frustration. "Why are you being such an ass?"

"I'm protecting you, damn it," he said. "Could you cooperate, please?"

"Protecting me from what? A four-year-old child who must be scared to death?"

"She's a witness to a murder."

"And a victim herself," Anne pointed out, hastily running a soapy washcloth over herself. "She's been traumatized. She's lost her mother. Has anyone found a relative?"

"No," he said, turning his back to her to rinse the front of him off. "She has no one."

"She'll have someone from Child Services."

"Seriously?" she said, ducking in front of him to rinse herself off. "You think Child Services should foster out a witness to a murder?"

"Well, I sure as hell don't think you should do it."

"I'm only going to see if I can help the little girl through this."

"Uh-huh," he said, unimpressed. "Like you were just going to see if you couldn't help Dennis Farman a little, and now you're his fucking guardian ad litem?"

"Don't you curse at me!" Anne said, leaning up toward him, as if she could hope to make herself big enough to intimidate him.

He leaned down over her, water dripping off his nose and mustache. "I'm going to lock you in a closet in a minute."

Now truly angry, Anne got out of the shower, grabbed a towel and did a half-assed job of drying herself off. The hell if he was going to tell her what she could and couldn't do. And how dare he throw Dennis Farman up in her face? She was only trying to do something good.

She could see him scowling at her via the wall-to-wall mirror over the long vanity.

"Anne," he said, climbing out of the shower and reaching for her arm.

Anne twisted out of his reach and went to her closet to find some clothes to pull on. Underwear, a pair of acid-washed jeans, and a big, slouchy black sweater that wanted to fall off one shoulder. Good enough. She pulled on an old pair of once-white Keds and headed for the door.

"Anne," Vince said again, stepping in front of her, still naked, water droplets glistening in his chest hair.

She looked to the left of his head and past his shoulder, waiting impatiently for him to say what he had to say, then get out of her way.

"Sweetheart," he said, softening his tone. "You've been through so much in the past year. You're still struggling with it. I don't want you getting involved in something that's going to add to your stress level—and mine," he admitted.

He had a good point. He was only trying to protect her, which was very sweet and chivalrous. Still, now her pride was involved, and her feminist tendencies were offended. She wasn't going to let Tony Mendez or Cal Dixon or anyone else think that she had to have her husband's permission to do anything. It was 1986, for God's sake, not 1956.

"I'm going," she declared.

Hands jammed at his waist, Vince heaved a big sigh of absolute frustration. Muscles worked at the back of jaw as if he were trying to choke something down.

"Let me get some clothes on," he said at last. "I'm driving."

Mercy General was a jewel of a small hospital. One of the benefits of being located in an affluent, educated community was the generosity of its residents.

There was no shortage of bequests and contributions rolling in to fund new wings, new equipment, renovations. Mercy General had up-to-date, state-of-the-art everything and attracted top-notch staff from doctors and nurses to administrators.

Haley Fordham lay in a bed in the ICU, a unit Vince and everyone else involved in the See-No-Evil case had come to know well during the time Karly Vickers had been there. The ambient lighting was soft, the walls painted a honey amber color. The feeling was one of being cocooned in glowing warmth. The rooms were fronted by glass so all patients were visible to the staff at the central desk.

But they heard Marissa Fordham's daughter before they saw her. As Vince and Anne stepped off the elevator, they were greeted by the piercing shriek of a terrified small child.

Anne tensed instantly. Vince felt her back go rigid beneath his hand as they headed toward the source of the screaming.

Mendez came to meet them, looking grim.

"What's going on?" Vince asked.

"She woke up screaming and hasn't stopped. The doctor says it could be a sign of brain damage from being asphyxiated."

"Or she could be terrified," Anne said, upset. "Imagine being four years old and waking up in this place, hooked to machines, surrounded by strangers. Poor little thing!"

"Yeah," Mendez agreed. "There's that. Thanks for coming, Anne."

"Of course I would come," she said, cutting Vince a look. "I'm happy to help. Can I go in the room?"

"I'll introduce you to the doctor and Mrs. Bordain," Mendez said, taking her gently by the elbow.

"Mrs. Bordain, Marissa Fordham's sponsor?" Vince asked, separating his protégé from his wife.

"Yes," Mendez said, rolling his eyes as he raised his hands clear of Anne. "Bill and I went to talk to her and tell her the news. She demanded we bring her here to see Haley. She's the girl's scary godmother or something. The kid woke up and started screaming, but Mrs. Bordain is the closest thing we've got to a relative so far."

"She's not exactly having a calming effect," Vince said dryly. Milo Bordain, early- to mid-fifties, tall, blond, dressed to the nines, stood well back from the bed, horrified, one hand pressed to her chest as if to hold her heart in.

Mendez shrugged. "The woman doesn't know what to do. Like I said: The doc thinks the screaming could be a sign of brain damage. We know the girl was strangled unconscious. Who knows how long her brain was deprived of oxygen."

"Did you call Child Services?"

"Yeah," Mendez said, carefully avoiding Vince's stare. "No sign of them."

"Maybe you should call again," he said pointedly.

"Oh, for God's sake," Anne muttered. She pushed past them both and went into the room.

Vince poked Mendez in the chest with a finger, pissed off. "I don't want her involved in this."

Mendez shrugged, feigning innocence. "Then why did you bring her?"

"I ought to kick your ass, Junior."

"Yeah, maybe Bill will hold your walker for you while you try that, Old Man."

"Ha-ha. You're a laugh riot," Vince said sarcastically. He glanced into the room to see his wife reaching out a hand to Haley Fordham. "You're not the one holding her after the nightmares," he said quietly.

Mendez had the grace to look contrite. "Jeez, I'm sorry. I didn't think of that. She seems okay."

"She's not."

"I'll call Child Services."

"You do that."

Mendez went in search of a phone.

Vince stared into the little girl's room, thinking it was already too late.

Anne stood close to the bed, her arms around the sobbing child clinging to her for dear life.

21

Anne walked into the hospital room, Haley Fordham's screams piercing her eardrums. She went straight to the doctor standing at the foot of the bed, a small dark-haired man with a close-cropped beard. He was making notes in the chart, strangely calm, considering the state the child was in.

"Anne Leone," she said, holding out her hand. "I'm a court-appointed special advocate. Detective Mendez asked me to come."

That sounded very official, at least, she thought, even though there was nothing official about it. They were circumventing protocol in about eight different ways. There was no one from Child Services present. Anne had not been assigned to Haley Fordham's case. She hadn't spoken to her supervisor to apprise her of the situation. She didn't know if relatives had been notified. The list went on. But in her heart her only concern was for the terrified child in the bed.

"Dr. Silver," he said, clipping his pen to the chart and shaking her hand.

"Why are you letting her scream like this?" she asked. "Isn't there something you can give her to help her calm down?"

"She's just coming out of a coma. She hasn't responded to anyone. It's as if we aren't here. This sometimes happens with brain injury patients," he explained. "She probably doesn't even realize she's doing it."

Anne looked from the doctor to the child and back. "I'm sorry," she said calmly. "You're an idiot."

She didn't bother to care that Dr. Silver was offended. She didn't bother to introduce herself to the well-dressed older woman standing frozen in shock along the wall. She went alongside the bed to the head of it, where Haley Fordham was curled into a ball, shrieking.

"Haley?" she said softly, reaching her hand out to the little girl. "Haley, sweetheart, you're all right. I know you're scared. You don't need to be afraid, honey. We're all here to help you."

Still screaming, the child looked up at her. Her eyes were entirely bloodred, petechial hemorrhages filling the whites of her eyes around the dark iris and pupils. It was a result of the strangulation, but even knowing that, Anne was startled at the sight.

"It's okay," Anne murmured, brushing the girl's damp dark curls back from her forehead. "It's okay, Haley. You're not alone. I'm here for you."

The screams subsided as the little girl looked up at her. Her breath caught and hiccupped and stuttered in her throat. She was trembling, dressed only in a flimsy hospital gown. White tape held an IV catheter in place in her tiny arm.

The bruises on her throat were purple. Anne felt her own throat tighten. She knew exactly how it felt to be choked, to look up into the face of the person trying to take her life away from her. Had Haley known the person doing that to her? How confused and terrified she must have been.

Her mother had to have been dead by then. No mother would have stood by and allowed someone to harm her child this way, no matter how dire the circumstances. Haley had been all alone with her killer.

"I'm so sorry, sweetheart," she whispered, continuing to stroke the girl's hair. "I'm so sorry."

Slowly Haley came up on her knees and reached her arms out. Her lips moved, but no sound came out. She tried again, croaking out a scratchy sound.

"I can't hear you, honey," Anne said, bending down close.

Haley wrapped her arms around Anne's neck and the word came out in a whisper as the tears began again.

"Mommy."

Anne's heart broke for the little girl. She held her close and rubbed her back and kissed the top of her head, offering as much comfort as she could.

Finally the woman draped in Gucci and reeking of Chanel moved forward.

"Thank God someone has a magic touch," she said softly. "I had no idea what to do. I've never seen anything like that."

"She's terrified," Anne said, irritated that neither this woman nor the doctor seemed to have been able to figure out something so simple.

"She wouldn't even look at us," Bordain said. "It was like she was in her own world."

In her own world where she was watching her mother be butchered and was helpless to escape the killer, Anne thought.

"Did you know Marissa?"

Anne glanced at her. "No. I never met her."

"But Haley went to you," the woman said, bemused.

Milo Bordain, Anne realized, doyenne of Oak Knoll society. Anne had seen her picture in the paper many times—photographs from various charity fund-raisers and the summer music festival. She was a tall, handsome woman in her fifties. Her features were just a couple of steps this side of masculine, but perfectly made up. Marissa Fordham's sponsor, Vince had said.

A woman who had probably spent time with Haley—at least in proximity to her. But not quality time, Anne guessed. She had not one hair out of place, but scraped back against her skull and pulled into a flawless, tight chignon at the base of her skull. She wore a beautifully patterned silk scarf draped artfully around her broad shoulders over the top of her camel-hair blazer, pinned in place with a jewel-encrusted brooch. Chocolate brown kid gloves and a pair of perfectly pressed black slacks completed the picture.

"Mommy!" Haley wailed, burrowing her face into Anne's shoulder.

Anne rocked her and shushed her, and stroked her hair.

"I don't understand," Bordain said, hurt. "I've known Haley since she was a baby. She's like a granddaughter to me. It was like she didn't even recognize me."

Haley's cries were building toward another crescendo.

Anne cut the woman a look. "If you don't mind," she said. "I'm a little busy here."

Offended, Milo Bordain drew herself up to her full height—she had to be six feet tall, if not a little more—and looked down her patrician nose at Anne.

"Do you know who I am?"

"Yes," Anne replied. "I just don't care. This isn't about you."

Bordain left the room without another word. Anne watched her through the glass wall as she marched up to Cal Dixon and Vince to file her grievance.

Later, Anne thought, she might feel a little guilty for being rude to the woman. But for now, she cared only about the child in her arms.

22

It was well past midnight before Mendez climbed into his own car and drove out of the sheriff's office parking lot. He and Hicks had hung around the ICU, hoping for a chance to have Haley Fordham make all their lives easy by simply telling them who had attacked her and killed her mother. No such luck. His clever call to bring Anne in had backfired on him in more ways than one.

Vince was pissed off at him. And once Anne had connected with Marissa Fordham's daughter, there had been no getting near the child.

He should have foreseen that. Anne had been like a tigress with cubs protecting her students who had discovered the body of Lisa Warwick. She wouldn't let anyone—not him, not Vince, not the kids' own parents—push them. She would be no different with Haley Fordham. Her first priority would be the child, not the investigation.

Still, it seemed the smartest way to go—to keep Marissa Fordham's daughter within the law enforcement family, a more controlled environment with the watchful eyes of trained professionals on her. If Child Services fostered her out, they would lose control of her to a certain extent.

Of course, the woman from Child Services who had finally showed up at the hospital had been furious at the breach of protocol, and had demanded a meeting with all concerned parties and a family court judge the next day regarding the placement of Haley Fordham. Dixon himself would go to represent the interests of the SO. Which meant Dixon was pissed off at him too.

All would be forgiven if Anne could get the little girl to tell them what they needed to know. In the meantime, Mendez was feeling restless and anxious for some kind of progress, some small lead, anything that could point them in a direction.

Instead of going home to crash for a few hours, he prowled the empty streets of Oak Knoll, thinking, reviewing the day, making a mental list of the people he needed to speak to the next day.

They had to find out the details of the death of Zander Zahn's mother and what role he had actually played in it. Had he meant he literally murdered his mother with a weapon, or had he been speaking in the abstract? Maybe she died giving birth to him. Or maybe she had committed suicide when he was a child. Children often blamed themselves for things like the suicide of a parent or the divorce of parents.

It had been a damned strange revelation for Zahn to make no matter what the truth was. Why tell homicide detectives he had killed before?

Arthur Buckman had been as shocked at the revelation as Mendez and Vince had been. There was nothing in Zahn's personnel file to indicate he had ever been in prison. If it had happened when Zahn was a juvenile, the records would likely be sealed. A court order would open them.

Zahn seemed to think of Marissa Fordham as some kind of perfect, ethereal creature. But Marissa Fordham had dated a number of men, according to Don Quinn. Zahn might have gotten jealous, might have seen his perfect woman turning into something else before his eyes.

Disappointment and rage could drive people to do terrible things.

He drove down the Morgans' street, parked the car and killed the lights. The landscaping lights were on, casting a soft amber glow. The windows were dark. Steve Morgan's black Trans Am was parked in the driveway.

It was a pretty yellow house with white trim and blue shutters, the kind of house the ideal American family should live in. But despite the fact that they were beautiful, successful people with a beautiful, bright child, the Morgans did not have the ideal family. The perfect picture was skewed and out of focus.

He didn't like Steve Morgan. He had never liked Steve Morgan. The guy was a little too calm in the face of accusation. He had been that way during the investigation of Lisa Warwick's murder.

Morgan had known Lisa Warwick. He had worked closely with her on several family court cases for the Thomas Center. Mendez would have bet the farm Morgan had been sleeping with her, but they had never gotten him to admit to anything. When confronted with their suspicions, Morgan had been as cool as a cucumber. He never blew up, never got nervous, never really reacted.

That wasn't normal. Innocent people are usually quick to react in outrage to a false allegation. Not Morgan.

For a while, Mendez had liked him for See-No-Evil. Steve Morgan had been woven into the stories of those murder victims almost as well as Peter Crane had been. Crane and Morgan were friends and golfing buddies. There had been more than a little speculation that Peter Crane had an accomplice . . .

When they had told Morgan they had semen on the sheets of Lisa Warwick's bed and would be able to get a blood type from it, he hadn't reacted at all. In the analysis of the semen they had discovered the donor was a nonsecretor. His bodily fluids did not contain the antigens of the ABO blood group. They couldn't get a blood type. Had Steve Morgan known that would happen? Was that why he had been so calm?

Lisa Warwick's sheets were still in the property room at the SO. If they could get DNA analysis on the semen. What? The science wasn't as sophisticated as it would eventually become. They would need a blood test or another semen sample from Morgan to get a match. They had no legal reason to compel him to give them samples.

Morgan had known Marissa Fordham, had worked with her on the project for the Thomas Center and on the trust for her daughter. She was a beautiful, sexy, single woman. If he had been tempted before—and succumbed—

True, this murder was different from the others. The See-No-Evil victims had been held somewhere and very systematically tortured. Eyes glued shut, mouth glued shut, eardrums pierced. The wounds had been identical from body to body—very specific cutting wounds of the same length and the same placement. The women had ultimately been strangled to death, each in exactly the same manner.

Marissa Fordham's death had been frenzied, not studied; full of rage, not systematic. But then if Crane had an accomplice, the accomplice was now free to kill however he wanted. Maybe the ritual had been strictly Crane's.

Could he picture Steve Morgan slicing a woman's breasts off?

He thought of Sara Morgan and her reactions that morning. She had been upset. Marissa Fordham had been a friend. He tried to recall her face and her body language when he had asked her if Marissa had a boyfriend or an ex-boyfriend or a lover.

She hadn't looked at him. She had looked down at her hands and said no. It was none of her business. She wasn't one to pry. But they had been friends. Women talked about men—even if only to say they didn't need or want one. Mendez had sisters, his sisters had friends. He was around women enough to know the subject of men was always a hot topic.

He wondered how long Sara Morgan had been friends with Marissa Fordham. Had that friendship begun before or after Fordham had gotten to know Steve Morgan?

Sara didn't look well, he thought. She was thinner than a year ago. Pale. Drawn. There were dark smudges beneath the cornflower blue eyes. She seemed preoccupied, though a murder scene did have that effect on people who weren't cops.

He would go see her in the morning. Just checking on her. How was she doing? After her husband left for work and Wendy had gone to school. He would press her a little bit. See what happened.

He didn't like Steve Morgan . . .

23

The lead story on the local morning TV news was the murder of Marissa Fordham. Immediately following the report was a live interview with Milo Bordain.

"What the fuck?" Mendez demanded, stopping halfway to his seat, coffee in hand.

Dixon's expression said the same thing.

They were gathering in the war room with the first coffee of the day to go over what they had, what they needed, who would do what. Someone had turned on the TV they mostly used to look at video of crime scenes and interviews with suspects.

Mendez looked at Vince, who was shaking his head and pinching the bridge of his nose, pained literally and figuratively.

Bordain looked like she was about to get on a horse and go foxhunting in her brown tweed riding jacket and dark brown gloves. She was making an appeal for any information that might lead to the arrest of Marissa Fordham's killer. She was personally offering a reward of $25,000.

"Who told her she could do that?" Mendez asked, looking at Dixon.

"Don't look at me," the sheriff said. "I specifically told her we would handle everything."

"Did she say anything about a reward last night?" Vince asked.

"She offered to do it," Dixon said. "I told her we'd discuss it and get back to her."

"I guess that shows how much she values your opinion," Hicks said.

"It would never occur to her that she needed permission to do anything," Vince said. "She thinks she's being helpful."

A reward was a tool. If they offered one, when they offered one, what amount was offered, were all decisions that had to be made carefully with many different factors taken into consideration. Too large a reward offered too soon invited the greedy, vindictive people in the county to give up whoever they hated most in their life on the off chance that they might end up collecting some cash. With $25,000 at stake, the phones would be ringing off the hook with leads that would lead nowhere.

"What do you think, Vince?" Dixon asked.

Leone dragged a hand back through his salt-and-pepper mane and heaved a big sigh. He looked like shit—pasty and haggard. It had been a long night. Anne had refused to leave Haley Fordham. Vince had refused to leave Anne. He had spent the night on a chair in the corner of the little girl's room.

Feeling like a heel, Mendez sank down into a chair at the other end of the table from Vince, who spread his hands and shrugged.

"There's nothing you can do about it now," he said. "Put some extra personnel on the phones and be prepared to chase your tails."

"How will this sit with our perp?" Hamilton asked.

"Hard to say. As far as we know, we're not dealing with a habitual predator," Vince said. "A serial killer might take it as a challenge or a chance to gloat. We must be desperate, throwing all that money around. Maybe he should taunt us, play with us, toss us another victim.

"But if Marissa Fordham's murderer was someone known to her, someone who had a grudge against her and lost their mind in the heat of the moment—and that's the way I'm leaning—that person is either going to be quiet and try not to attract attention, or he might come forward and try to insinuate himself into the investigation and be overly helpful in the hopes of keeping tabs on what you've got.

"The thing to be afraid of with that perpetrator is that there's a good chance he's going to get skittish and paranoid, and might strike out at a perceived threat—say, an acquaintance who might know or suspect something."

"A tipster looking for the reward," Dixon said.

"We could have another murder on our hands," Trammell said.

"That's a possibility," Vince agreed. "You'd better hope the perceived threat drops a dime before your UNSUB turns on them.

"With a killer known to the victim, someone who hasn't done this kind of thing before, he's not going to know how to handle the emotions that come with the deed. Friends could see a change in personality.

He may become erratic, short-tempered, depressed. He may alter his appearance—grow a mustache, shave a beard—"

"Like a disguise?" Hicks asked.

"In a way," Vince said. "A disguise to himself. My personal theory on this is that this person literally can't look at himself in the mirror after he's committed the act, so he changes the way he looks. Or sometimes the change is made to look *more* the part. If he's a killer, maybe he should try to look like a badass.

"I know of a case where the perpetrator was a clean-cut college kid with no history of violence. He ended up killing an elderly man during the course of a burglary. Next thing you know, he's moved five hundred miles away and he's suddenly a tattooed skinhead with a bad attitude.

"It depends.

"You might also see him start drinking heavily or start abusing substances. On the flip side of that, there may be a sudden interest in religion."

With a possible profile in mind, they discussed what they had and what they needed. Bank and phone records would be available that morning. Marissa Fordham did not have a safe deposit box at any bank in Oak Knoll.

The autopsy would take place later in the day in Santa Barbara. There was no forensic pathologist in their own county, just an undertaker who served as coroner and was comfortable signing death certificates for deaths by natural causes, but happily stepped back from anything more complex.

Santa Barbara County—which had a larger population—had a sheriff-coroner and a morgue with a forensic pathologist who performed autopsies, a sergeant supervisor, three coroner's investigators, and an administrative assistant. With Oak Knoll growing—and the murder rate rising—a movement was already underway to institute a similar office in their county.

Not that the death of Marissa Fordham was a mystery. Both cause of death and manner of death were obvious. But a forensic pathologist would collect evidence from the body, trace evidence such as hairs and fabric fibers. A rape kit would be performed looking for foreign pubic hairs, semen, signs of sexual assault—after they extracted the butcher's knife from her vagina.

Campbell and Trammell had interviewed Gina Kemmer, Marissa Fordham's friend from the boutique called Girl.

"She freaked out when we gave her the news," Trammell said. "Total meltdown."

"We asked her about the vic's love life," Campbell said. "She said Fordham dated casually, there was no one serious, and she doesn't know who the little girl's father is."

"She's lying," Trammell said. "She's bad at it. She ran to the john right after."

"Bring her in," Dixon said. "We need to have a more serious conversation with her. Vince, maybe you would sit in?"

"Happy to."

"I'll tell her to wear her Depends," Trammell said.

"What about the professor?" Dixon asked. "Do we have any background yet?"

"I made a couple of phone calls, called in a couple of favors," Vince said. "We should hear something later today, tomorrow at the latest. But I think you should also take a closer look at his associate, Nasser. He's very protective of his boss. And he didn't like the victim. He all but accused her of being a whore."

"You think he was jealous?" Hamilton asked. "Like a gay thing?"

"No, not a gay thing. Nasser is a doctor in his own right. He could be teaching at any top university in the country," Vince said. "He chose to come to McAster to be Zahn's underling. Zahn is Nasser's mentor. Nasser is Zahn's protector. He didn't like Zahn's obsession with Marissa Fordham. She was a distraction, the object of Zahn's obsessive-compulsive attention."

"Jeez," Mendez said, half joking. "I just thought the guy was a jerk."

"You don't know everything, Junior," Leone said with an edge in his voice.

"No, I don't."

"Good that you realize that. Remember it next time before you make a bad decision."

Mendez ducked his head.

Dixon went to the whiteboard, marker in hand. "Who were her boyfriends?"

"Don Quinn, Mark Foster," Hicks said.

Campbell glanced at his notes. "Add Roy Thatcher and Bob Copetti."

"I think we should add Steve Morgan to that list," Mendez said. "He knew her, he worked with her, he spent time with her, he cheated on his wife before."

"Nobody has put them together romantically," Hicks pointed out.

"Nobody put him with Lisa Warwick either, but who didn't think he was doing her?" Mendez argued, irritated. "Morgan could have been Peter Crane's accomplice, for all we know. There were a lot of coincidences—"

"No," Vince said.

"Why not?" Mendez challenged. "What about Bittaker and Norris in '79; Bianchi and Buono, the Hillside Stranglers; just last year—Ng and Lake—"

"I'm not saying Crane couldn't have had an accomplice," Vince said. "I'm saying it's not Steve Morgan."

"Why not? They were friends. They played golf—"

"Who was the dominant partner?"

"I don't know," Mendez said. He hadn't thought about it. He should have. Now he was going to take a shot in the dark arguing with a profiling legend who wanted a piece of his hide this morning. "Crane."

"Why?" Vince demanded. "They're both successful professionals, leaders in the community, controlled, careful—"

"Okay," Mendez said, frustrated. "Morgan."

"Crane gave Morgan up," Vince reminded him. "You interviewed him that Saturday afternoon before he took Anne. You asked him if Steve Morgan was having an affair with Lisa Warwick. He said yes.

"First of all, there are no partnerships with two dominant partners," he said. "The egos wouldn't allow it. There is always a dominant partner and one that will claim he just came along for the ride, or that he was coerced. Second, if there ever were partners that smart, one wouldn't give the other one up on a point so unimportant," he went on, happy to teach a lesson at the expense of Mendez's pride. "If one cracks, they both go down. And third, if Morgan and Crane were partners, Morgan likely would have killed Marissa Fordham in the same manner as the See-No-Evil victims in order to cast doubt on Crane's involvement—particularly now with Crane's trial coming up.

"This is an entirely different kind of murder," he concluded.

"Okay," Mendez said on a sigh, sufficiently set down. "So they weren't partners. I still say we should put Steve Morgan on the list."

"Can we get back on point here?" Dixon asked. "Tony, if you find something concrete to link Steve Morgan to Marissa Fordham romantically, we'll pursue it. If not, don't go looking for a harassment suit. The guy's a lawyer, for God's sake."

"Man, the old lion smacked you down," Hicks said, chuckling as they walked to the car.

Mendez scowled. "I suppose I had it coming, but he didn't need to be such an asshole about it."

"Sure he did."

"Thanks, partner," Mendez said sarcastically.

"Well, what are you going to do about it?"

Mendez grinned then and laughed as it sank in. "Work my ass off to prove him wrong."

24

At Anne's insistence, they had scheduled the meeting in a conference room down the hall from the ICU. She had spent the night in her clothes, on the bed with Haley Fordham clinging to her, alternately sleeping then waking up to the little girl's cries and whimpers.

Vince had spent the night in the chair in the corner of the room. She felt guilty for that. He should have been home, in bed, sleeping off his headache.

She worried about him. The doctors didn't have any idea what the long-term effects might be to having a bullet fragmented inside one's head. When the pain came on him suddenly, it always made Anne afraid that some piece of shrapnel was moving inside his brain, doing damage.

He had finally gone home to shower and change around six fifteen and had returned with a change of clothes for her.

He wasn't happy about the decision she had made, but she hadn't seen any alternative. Haley Fordham had likely watched her mother die, had probably witnessed her murder. She had been choked unconscious and left lying against her mother's bloody corpse, left for dead for— what?—two days, Vince had thought.

Trauma didn't begin to describe what this four-year-old child had been through. What she needed now was stability and consistency, and someone who had at least some training in how to help her through the aftermath of her ordeal.

Anne knew she fit the bill in a way no one else would be able to. She had been a victim of a violent crime herself. She knew the kind of fear Haley must have known and would continue to experience.

Haley was asleep and quiet when Anne finally left the room for the meeting. On her way out of the unit she told one of the nurses, "If you need me, come get me."

Knowing what was waiting for her in that conference room, she half hoped for the interruption. This wasn't going to be easy or pleasant, and she wasn't going to have the patience for it.

One of the aftereffects of her ordeal was an extreme intolerance of people's bullshit. Life was too precious to waste time pretending to be diplomatic in the face of overinflated egos.

Anne was the last to arrive to the meeting. On one side of the conference table were Vince and Cal Dixon, who had come to represent the interests of the sheriff's office and the investigation.

On the other side of the table, wearing her perpetual sour expression, sat Maureen Upchurch from Child Protective Services, a woman built like the corner mailbox. A bad home permanent made her look as if she were wearing a wig made out of an apricot poodle.

To the right of Upchurch was Anne's CASA supervisor, Willa Norwood, decked out in one of her vibrant African caftans, her head wrapped in a matching turban. To the left of Upchurch, in all her designer glory, sat Milo Bordain, perfectly coiffed, perfectly made up, perfectly dressed, and pointedly avoiding eye contact with her.

Anne cringed a bit inwardly. She had made a mistake being so short with the woman the night before. Bordain had sponsored Marissa Fordham, had apparently thought of her as a surrogate daughter, had thought of Haley as a granddaughter. Now Marissa was murdered and Haley's future was uncertain. Anne realized she should have been more sympathetic. If she had made it to the meeting sooner, she would have approached Milo Bordain and apologized.

To Bordain's left, at the head of the table sat the Honorable Judge Victor Espinoza from family court. Anne was thankful to see Espinoza would be hearing the issue. He had proven somewhat sympathetic in several matters involving Dennis Farman.

He was a practical man in his fifties with more hair on his upper lip than on his head. He wore a thick black mustache threaded with gray, and polished his bald head with wax every morning in his chambers before court started—or so said his longtime clerk.

Anne nodded in his direction and took a seat next to her husband. She snuck her hand under his on the arm of his chair, and he gave her fingers a reassuring squeeze.

"All right," Judge Espinoza began. "I've got the gist of the situation. The little girl likely witnessed the murder of her mother. No relatives have been located?"

Dixon shook his head. "We've been told Marissa Fordham was from the East Coast, possibly Rhode Island, but that she was estranged from her family. We've contacted the authorities in Rhode Island to see if they might be able to help us. No one seems to know who the little girl's father is, and we have yet to locate a birth certificate."

"I'm as close to family as she has, Your Honor," Bordain said. "Her mother was like a daughter to me. I've known Haley since she was a baby. I'll make sure her every need is taken care of."

"Did Ms. Fordham make any legal arrangements for you to become her daughter's guardian in the event of her death?" Espinoza asked.

"No. We had been talking about that, but Marissa was so young. She just didn't see the need. Of course she expected to outlive me. But if I'm willing to take the child and take care of her and raise her—and I certainly have the means to do so, as you well know—I don't see why this should be an issue."

"It's a matter of law, Mrs. Bordain," Espinoza said. "If there's no document relating the decedent's wishes for you or anyone else to have custody of the minor child, she is essentially—for the time being, anyway—a ward of the state."

"That's ridiculous!"

"That's the law."

"Which means my department should have been notified immediately."

Maureen Upchurch was the kind of person who believed everyone in the world was a potential member of a conspiracy against her. Always aggressive in attitude, defensive by nature, she had a chip on her shoulder the size of Iowa. Her mouth was carved into her doughy face in a permanent frown, and her eyes were perpetually narrowed in suspicion. Anne had run afoul of her from day one of her advocacy for Dennis.

"I alerted you myself, Ms. Upchurch," Dixon said.

"I was on my way to a court date," the woman said defensively. "I couldn't do anything about it then."

"Nevertheless, don't say I didn't call you," Dixon said. "It's hardly the fault of my office or my detectives that you were too busy to deal with the situation."

"The girl was in a coma," Upchurch said. "You *told* me she was in a coma. How was *I* to know she would come out of it so quickly?"

"Everyone in this room knows I am more than qualified to raise this child," Milo Bordain announced, drawing the attention back to herself.

"But Lady Justice is blind, Mrs. Bordain," Espinoza pointed out. "She can't see that you're wearing Armani and driving a Mercedes."

"I knew I liked him," Anne whispered. One side of Vince's mustache twitched.

Bordain was offended by the judge's statement. "It isn't just a matter of money. I practically brought Marissa to this community. I set her up with contacts, gave her a place to live and work. I've done nothing but nurture and support her and her daughter."

"And who called Mrs. Leone into the situation?" the judge asked.

"Detective Mendez," Dixon said.

"Detective Mendez isn't aware of proper protocol?"

"He has a connection to Anne through Vince. He knows Anne has a gift with children. When the little girl came out of the coma, she was extremely agitated. Detective Mendez called Vince, who is consulting with us on this case, and asked if Anne couldn't come with him. He knew personally she could handle the situation."

"Does it really matter now who was called first?" Willa Norwood asked, always the voice of reason. "Can we just get on with it?"

Upchurch glared at her. "Of course it matters, *Willa*. *She* came in here last night and convinced the child she's her *mother*."

"That's absolutely not true," Anne said, her focus more on the judge rather than her accuser. She knew from experience there was no winning an argument with Maureen. The woman was as tough and unyielding as gristle, as unmovable as a city bus.

She was also so red in the face she seemed in danger of having a stroke. "When I got here last night, she was calling you *Mommy*. How do you explain *that*?"

"It's a simple case of transference," Anne said calmly. "Haley's last moments of consciousness before she lapsed into the coma were spent with her mother's dead body. She regained consciousness in totally unfamiliar surroundings, in a room with strangers, hooked to monitors and machines. Who is the first and only person she really wants to see? Her mother—alive."

"And you just *happened* to look like her mother," Upchurch said.

"No, Maureen, I planned that in my mother's womb," Anne snapped. "I knew it would come in handy one day."

There goes the patience, Anne thought. She could feel it sliding through her mental grasp like a very short satin ribbon.

"The girl's mother had dark hair and dark eyes," Dixon said to the judge. "Anne has dark hair and dark eyes. It only makes sense. The poor kid was terrified. She needed someone to be Mommy. Anne was there."

"I *would have* been there if Detective Mendez had called me sooner," Upchurch griped. "It was already too late by the time I got there. And *she* made no effort to put a stop to it."

"What was I supposed to do, Maureen?" Anne asked. "Rip the sobbing child from my arms and tell her I wasn't her mother because someone cut her mother's head off?"

"Oh my God!" Milo Bordain cried out, pressing a gloved hand to her throat. Tears rose up in her eyes.

"Mrs. Leone, did you at any time try to tell the little girl you aren't her mother?" the judge asked.

"No," Anne admitted. "She was terrified and hysterical. My only concern was calming her down. I certainly didn't encourage her. I didn't *tell her* I'm her mother. I just let her call me what she wanted."

"Now the girl has attached to *her*," Upchurch said. "How am I supposed to place her with a family?"

"Maybe you won't have to, Ms. Upchurch," Judge Espinoza said pleasantly.

"She should be placed with *me*," Bordain argued. "She knows *me*."

Upchurch didn't like the judge's tone. "But she's a ward of the state, Your Honor. Her case clearly falls under the auspices of CPS."

"But *I'm* the judge," Espinoza explained calmly. "And what I love about being a judge is that what I say goes."

He turned to Dixon. "What's your position on this, Sheriff?"

Dixon sighed. "Obviously, what's best for the little girl is most important. She's the only witness to a brutal homicide. At this point, we have no idea who the killer is, if he's someone known to the girl, if he's still in the area. The child was strangled and left for dead. If the perpetrator knows she's alive . . ."

"She's potentially still at risk."

"Yes, Your Honor. And, therefore, whoever has custody of her."

"How do you expect to place this child into foster care, Ms. Upchurch?" Espinoza asked. "You'd be putting your foster family at risk."

"There doesn't *need* to be any foster care!" Milo Bordain insisted. No one seemed to be listening to her.

"If you aren't willing to award custody to Mrs. Bordain at this time, I have a foster family willing to take her temporarily. The Bessoms."

Willa Norwood rolled her eyes to look at Upchurch. "Are you serious? The Bessoms already have five foster children and run a day care center. You seriously think that's an environment for this little girl, as psychologically fragile as she is?"

"Being around other children will take her mind off what happened," Upchurch said, as if witnessing a murder and nearly being murdered were no more traumatic than losing a tooth or scraping a knee.

"She'll be lost in the shuffle," Anne said. "How can she get the kind of attention she needs? Is Mrs. Bessom trained in child psychology? Does she have any experience grief-counseling children?"

"A stable environment is just as important as any of that," Upchurch declared. "Mrs. Bessom runs a tight ship. Those kids say 'Yes, ma'am,' and 'No, ma'am.' They toe the line and do their chores—"

"Great," Anne said sarcastically. "Why don't we just send Haley to a military school? They can drill the grief out of her."

Upchurch glared at her. "I don't appreciate your smart mouth."

"And I don't appreciate that, so far, all your concern has been about pissing on fences," Anne shot back.

Milo Bordain stood up, red faced, shouting, *"LISTEN TO ME! I WANT HER WITH ME! SHE SHOULD BE WITH ME!"*

"Mrs. Bordain." Judge Espinoza stood up and tried to put a hand on Milo Bordain's arm in attempt to calm her. She jerked away.

The uncomfortable silence embarrassed her back to her senses. Tears squeezing from her eyes, she sat down and dug a linen handkerchief out of her Hermès bag.

"I'm sorry," she said tersely. "I'm so distraught. I've lost Marissa, now Haley . . . I can't believe this is happening."

"Mrs. Bordain could apply to become a foster parent," Upchurch suggested. "If Mr. and Mrs. Bordain became foster parents, I have the authority to place the child—"

"The circumstances here are extraordinary, Your Honor," Dixon said. "The child needs to be in protective custody with people trained to help her through the nightmare of what happened to her. Both Mrs. and Mr. Leone have degrees in psychology. Anne was a teacher. She dealt with the grief of her students last year—"

"She's not even an employee of the state, Your Honor," Upchurch argued. "She's a *volunteer*. And they're not licensed foster parents. Their home hasn't been screened—"

"Are you kidding me with that?" Anne said. "You're objecting on the basis that I haven't filed the proper paperwork? That you haven't come to my home to see if I have dust bunnies under my bed?"

"There's much more to it than that."

"Yes, there is," Anne said passionately. "There's what's best for Haley. She's a victim of a violent crime. Do you know what that's like, Maureen? Mrs. Bordain? Because I do. I know exactly what that's like.

"I know exactly what it's like to wake up screaming in the night, to be terrified to walk around a corner, or to turn your back even to someone you know, let alone a stranger.

"Do either of you know how that feels? Do you know what it is to suddenly, inexplicably, be filled with so much fear you think you'll choke on it? To break out in a cold sweat in the middle of a crowded room? I do. I've had those experiences. I know exactly what Haley is going to face. I can help this child in ways no one else can."

"Have you thought this all the way through, Anne?" Willa Norwood asked. "You know our policy as advocates is never to take a client to our homes. There's a reason for that. I don't want you to put yourself at risk."

"My husband is a former Chicago police detective and a former agent for the FBI. Our lives are filled with law enforcement personnel. You can't swing a stick at my house without hitting a cop."

"That's not the only kind of risk I'm talking about."

She was talking about the risk of becoming too emotionally involved, Anne knew. She had already chosen to ignore that risk.

The judge turned to Vince. "What about you, Mr. Leone? You've been awfully quiet through all of this. Do you have an opinion to contribute?"

Anne tensed. Vince was against the idea of her fostering Haley Fordham or being attached to this case in any way. He was afraid it would upset her, set her back, put her in danger physically and psychologically.

He looked down at her and said, "Honestly? I have to say . . . there is no one more uniquely qualified to help this child than my wife."

Anne let the air out of her lungs and her chest flooded with warmth. Tears rose up behind her eyes. Still holding her hand, Vince gave her fingers another reassuring squeeze.

Judge Espinoza nodded and placed his palms down on the tabletop, pushing up out of his chair. "Then, as far as I'm concerned, it's all over but the paperwork. Anne will be appointed guardian. When the little girl is released from the hospital, she'll stay with the Leones. We'll revisit the issue if a relative turns up."

25

"Guess who's babysitting on date night?" Vince said.

Mendez grimaced. "I volunteer. I know you're pissed. I don't blame you."

They had met up at the SO and were driving through a beautiful old neighborhood near the college. A pricey part of town, Vince knew. The streets were lined with big mature trees. The houses were a mix of styles and sizes, built mostly between the thirties and forties with excellent craftsmanship. The house he and Anne had settled on was in this neighborhood, just a few blocks away.

Vince sighed. "I'm over it. I'm trying to look at it from a different perspective. It might actually be a good thing for Anne. She's pretty passionate about helping this little girl because they share the experience of having been victims of violent crimes. That might help her as much as it helps the child."

"If that happens, do I get a big pat on the back?"

"Don't get greedy. I could still kick your ass."

"You kind of did that this morning," Mendez pointed out.

Vince laughed. "You think I was hard on you?"

"You made me look like an idiot."

"You did that on your own by not being prepared. You present a case at the Bureau, you had better have those fucking ducks lined up beak to tail."

"So you were just trying to toughen me up," Mendez said, clearly not believing a word of it.

"Hell, no," Vince chuckled. "I was pissed. I wanted to punish you."

"Just so we're clear on that."

Vince dug a prescription bottle out of the pocket of his sport coat and shook out a colorful variety of pills. One for pain, one for nausea, an antidepressant . . .

"You should have seen her take on that horrible woman from CPS," he said, glowing with pride. "She's a tough little mouse. She's got a lot of spunk."

"I wouldn't want to cross her," Mendez said. "She sank her teeth into me a couple of times over her students last year."

"She stands right up to me," Vince said, a sudden wave of love swelling through him.

"You've got a good thing going, man," Mendez said. "Look at all the marriages that fail and fall apart these days. People have no sense of commitment anymore."

"You really think Steve Morgan was having an affair with the vic?" Vince asked.

"Gut feeling."

"You don't like him."

"I'm not crazy about you either, at the moment," Mendez complained.

Vince rolled his eyes. "Get over yourself."

He chose a trio of pills, tossed them back, and washed them down with locally bottled orange cream soda.

"He worked with Lisa Warwick on projects for the Thomas Center," Mendez said. "He had an affair with her. He worked with Marissa Fordham on a project for the center. She was beautiful, sexy, single, liked men . . ."

"Why would he kill her?"

"Say she threatened to tell his wife. What's left of his marriage falls apart, and he loses his daughter."

"What about the wife?" Vince asked, watching his reaction. Confusion.

"What about her?"

"Her good friend was having an affair with her husband," Vince said. "Women aren't that shocked when men cheat on them, but to be betrayed by one of their own . . . That's unforgivable."

Mendez looked at him like he'd lost his mind. "You think Sara could have killed Marissa Fordham?"

"I'm saying if you're looking at one spouse in a love triangle, you need to look at them both. They both lose in a divorce. The husband loses the wife and family. The wife loses a fairy tale—the handsome prince, the castle, the lifestyle . . ."

"That's crazy," Mendez said. "Sara Morgan is just trying to hold herself and her family together. For her to have the kind of rage to do what was done to Marissa Fordham . . . ? No way. Besides, Fordham was found naked."

"So? Maybe she slept naked and was attacked in the middle of the night. Or, let's throw a twist into the story: Maybe she and Mrs. Morgan were more than friends."

Mendez didn't want to hear any of it. Interesting.

"The nine-one-one call," he said. "The little girl said her daddy hurt her mommy."

"People wear disguises."

"The kid would know her own father."

"Why?" Vince challenged. "Nobody else knows who he is."

"Maybe Ms. Kemmer will know," Mendez said, pulling the car to the curb in front of a fanciful Tudor cottage with a wildflower garden filling the front yard.

Dixon had asked them to bring Gina Kemmer in for the interview, but Vince wanted to see her in her own environment. A lot could be learned from a subject's surroundings.

He got out of the car and looked around. Ms. Kemmer was the domestic kind. She loved her home, took pride in it, had literally and figuratively set down roots here.

The garden was an expression of joy, filled with old-fashioned climbing roses and tea roses, tall blue delphinium and pink foxglove, and snapdragons of all colors. Flower boxes under the front windows of the house spilled over with pink geraniums and ivy and blue lobelia.

The car in her driveway, parked in front of the little garage that matched the Tudor house, was a blue 1981 Honda Accord. Gina Kemmer was doing well for herself.

She wouldn't like law enforcement officers coming into her sanctuary— not that anyone did.

She answered the door looking like she'd been knocked around. Her face and her eyes were swollen and red. Battered by grief. The girls working in the boutique on trendy Via Verde had told them their boss had taken the day off because of her friend's death. They had batted their eyelashes at Mendez as they gave him Kemmer's home address and phone number.

"Ms. Kemmer," Mendez said, holding up his shield. "I'm Detective Mendez from the sheriff's office. This is my associate, Mr. Leone."

"We're terribly sorry for your loss, Miss Kemmer," Vince said gently. The kindly uncle act. "I apologize for the intrusion. We know this is a tough time for you."

"I already spoke to detectives yesterday," she said, looking worried. "I answered all their questions."

Vince guessed she was probably around thirty. She was probably a pretty girl when she hadn't been crying for a couple of days.

"Yes, ma'am," Mendez said. "We're just following up."

"Having been Ms. Fordham's best friend," Vince said, "we're hoping you might be able to give us a little more insight into who she was as person."

"Oh."

"May we come in?" Mendez asked.

Gina Kemmer nodded, tears welling up. She was in gray sweatpants and a McAster T-shirt that looked like she had slept in it. But she had made an effort and brushed her blond hair back into a ponytail. The girls from the boutique might have called to tell her the cops were on the way.

She turned away from them and walked back into the house, leaving them to follow.

"I can't believe she's gone," she said, sinking down into an overstuffed chintz-covered chair in her living room. Her hand was shaking as she dabbed a tissue under her eyes. "Murdered. Oh my God. I heard she was stabbed like a hundred times! Is that true?"

She was afraid—like she thought if her friend had been murdered, she was probably next. The one good thing about murder, Vince thought: It generally wasn't contagious.

"She was stabbed, yes," Mendez said.

"You have a lovely home," Vince said, admiring the space, checking for photographs. There were two of Gina Kemmer and Marissa Fordham in frames on the console table behind the sofa—one recent, one not.

"Thank you," she murmured.

"Do you rent or own?"

"Rent."

"Are you the gardener?"

"Yes."

"That's some green thumb you have," Vince said with a smile as he took a seat on the end of the sofa nearest her.

She turned a tiny shy smile and glanced down. "Thank you."

"I'm so sorry you lost your friend," he said sincerely. "We never imagine something like this will happen to someone we know. Murder is something that happens in the newspapers, on television."

"No," she said. "It's like a nightmare, but I'm awake. I can't believe she died that way. What could she possibly have done to deserve that?"

"Nothing," Mendez said. "No one deserves to die like that."

"It's tough," Vince said. "A person dies only once, but the loved ones they leave behind live that loss every day."

Gina nodded, crying a little into her crumpled tissue.

"I'll bet you have a lot of fond memories, though."

"Yes."

She had been looking back at her friendship with Marissa Fordham. Photographs were strewn on the coffee table. Vince picked up one of Gina Kemmer and Marissa and Haley Fordham—probably about two years old at the time—at the beach, laughing and happy, building a sandcastle. He put that one down and picked up an older photo of the two women in bikinis and floppy hats at a different beach.

"How long had you and Marissa been friends, Gina? Is it all right if I call you Gina?"

She nodded.

"Did you and Marissa grow up together?" Mendez asked.

"No," she said, looking at the floor. "We met when we moved here. It seems like a long time ago. It was like that, like we were sisters, like we'd known each other forever."

"That's a special friendship," Vince said. "How did you both end up here?"

"Um, well, I wanted a change of scenery. This is such a nice town."

"It is," Vince said. "It's a beautiful place. I just moved here last year, myself. I love it. Where did you move from?"

"LA."

"The big city."

"Yeah."

"Pollution, traffic. Who needs it? Right?"

She smiled a little, nodding.

"And Marissa came from . . . where?"

"The East Coast."

"Did she ever talk about her family?" Mendez asked. "We're trying to locate her next of kin to notify them."

"No, she never talked about them."

"That's odd, don't you think, Gina? I mean, I talk about my family if only to complain about them. Don't you? I think most people do."

"They had some kind of falling-out," she said.

"Must have been something bad, huh?"

"I guess so."

"It must have been really bad if Marissa wouldn't even tell you, her best friend."

Kemmer said nothing. She had yet to hold eye contact with him for more than a second or two.

"What brought her to Oak Knoll? Why not Santa Barbara? Monterey? San Francisco? All very artsy places. Why Oak Knoll? We're a little off the beaten track."

"She just liked it. She came for the fall art fair. It's very famous, you know. Artists come from all over the country. She came for the art fair, and she loved it here, and she stayed."

"Kind of impulsive."

"That was Marissa."

"When was that?"

"September 1982."

"So Haley was how old then?"

"Um . . . four months. Her birthday is in May."

"Do you by any chance know where Haley was born?"

"No."

"We're trying to find her birth certificate," Mendez said. "Do you have any idea where Marissa would have kept that?"

"No."

"Actually, what we really want is to find Haley's father," Vince said. "Do you know who he is?"

"Marissa never talked about him."

"Never? You were like sisters. She must have said something."

She shook her head.

"Was he from around here?"

"No."

"But she did have a few boyfriends over the years, right?"

"Yes, of course," she said. "Marissa liked men. Men liked Marissa. It worked out for her. Men were drawn to her, fell all over her. They would just give her things—even men she wasn't dating."

Mendez looked up from his note making. "What do you mean *give her things?*"

"Jewelry, clothes, flowers, whatever. Men loved her."

"One didn't," Vince pointed out.

He reached inside his jacket, plucked a Polaroid from his breast pocket and handed it to her. She took it automatically. It was a shot of Marissa Fordham lying dead on the floor of her kitchen, butchered and bloody.

Gina Kemmer shrieked and jumped up out of her chair, flinging the photograph away from her as if it had transformed into a venomous snake.

"Oh my God! Oh my God!" she shouted, scrambling backward, trying to get away from the hideous image. She hit a plant stand with her arm and knocked a huge Boston fern to the floor. The heavy pot broke with the sound of a gunshot and she screamed.

"Someone did that to her, Gina," Vince said.

"Why would you bring that here?!" She looked horrified and, more important, terrified. "Why would you show that to me? Oh my God!"

"Because that's the reality here, Gina," Vince said soberly. "That's the truth. Someone did that to your best friend."

The color went out of her face like water being sucked down a drain. She turned and doubled over and threw up on the fallen fern.

Vince stood up and dug a business card out of his wallet and placed it on top of the photograph on the coffee table.

He put a hand on Gina Kemmer's shoulder as she sat back down on her chair, gagging and sobbing hysterically, shaking hard.

"You're a poor liar, Gina," he said without rancor, almost gently. "Your heart's not in it. It doesn't come to you naturally. But you're scared. You probably made a promise to Marissa. You don't want to break it, but it's a terrible burden. You're shaking under the weight of it.

"You give me a call—night or day—when you want to take that burden off your shoulders and tell me the truth."

26

"That was some hardball you just threw," Mendez said as they walked out to the car.

"She's lying," Vince said. He hadn't gotten any pleasure out of what he had just done to Gina Kemmer, but he knew his shock tactic had a good chance of being effective. "She needs to know she shouldn't do that. The policeman is her friend—if she cooperates."

He climbed into the car on the passenger side, feeling a little light-headed from the drugs he had taken. Mendez slid in behind the wheel.

"Some of those photographs on the table looked older than she claims to have known Marissa Fordham."

"Absolutely," Vince said. "The one beach shot had to be from the seventies, and it had the Santa Monica Pier in the background," he said. "I think coming here from LA is probably the only true statement she made."

"That and being like a sister to the vic," Mendez said. "She's pretty broken up. She'll have nightmares for years from seeing that Polaroid."

Vince did feel a twinge of guilt for that. Gina Kemmer was probably a nice enough young woman. She struck him as someone who just wanted to live a comfortable, simple life. She didn't have the stomach for intrigue and subterfuge, but she was somehow tangled up in this mess just the same.

"Find out everything you can about her life in LA," he said. "I'm willing to bet Marissa Fordham was there at the same time."

"So why the big story about being from the East Coast?"

"I don't know. She probably liked the mystique. Coming to a new community, she could start fresh and be whoever she wanted to be. It's a hell of a lot more interesting to say you come from money in Rhode Island than to say you grew up in Oxnard."

"True," Mendez said. "And if she and Gina have been friends for a long time and moved up here together, Gina for sure knows who Haley's father is."

"And if Daddy killed Mommy, Milo Bordain is willing to pay her twenty-five thou for that information," Vince said. "And if Daddy killed Mommy, and Gina is the only person who knows who Daddy is . . ."

"And Daddy knows Gina could make twenty-five grand to give him up . . . ," Mendez continued the thought. "I'll tell the patrol sergeant to send a prowl car past here every half hour."

"She's our bait for a predator," Vince said. It sounded callous, but would be a much safer situation for Gina Kemmer than if they simply left her to her own devices. "Ask Cal to put an unmarked car on the street. We should keep her in sight."

"We're stretched pretty thin for detectives."

"Then a couple of lucky uniforms get to move up to plainclothes for a while."

"Do we tell Gina we're watching? Give her a little peace of mind?"

"No. Let's see what she does. For all we know, she could lead us straight to our killer. Look into her finances too," Vince suggested. "That's an expensive car and an expensive neighborhood for a girl that age. She has a boutique, it ain't Tiffany's."

"Are you thinking blackmail?"

"Think about what Nasser said yesterday. That he didn't believe Marissa Fordham made enough money from her art to pay for her lifestyle. Maybe nobody knows who Haley's father is because it was profitable for Marissa Fordham to keep that information to herself."

"Maybe Daddy got tired of paying," Mendez said, starting the car. "That's a damn fine motive for a murder."

Vince nodded. "Or two."

Vince parted company with Mendez back at the SO. The detective went inside to set the background check on Gina Kemmer into motion and to see what Marissa Fordham's bank and phone records had revealed.

Vince got behind the wheel of his old Jaguar and drove out of town.

The drive to Marissa Fordham's home was beautiful and tranquil—a stark contrast to what he would experience when he reached her house.

Anne had asked him to go to the house to collect clothes and toys for Haley. He would have gone anyway. The scene had been processed. The CSIs were gone. Once he ran the gauntlet of media being held at bay at the end of the driveway, he would have the murder scene to himself.

The downside of being Vince Leone was that he was easily recognized by crime reporters. He had spent too many years in the spotlight of high-profile cases for the Bureau. Locally, there had been so much coverage of the See-No-Evil murders, and Anne's abduction, people on the streets of Oak Knoll called him by name.

News vans lined the sides of the road as he drew closer to the driveway. Several reporters, bored and lounging beside the vehicles, spotted him and jumped to attention, running toward him.

Vince flashed his ID at the deputy guarding the end of the driveway and was waved past before the hungry newshounds could get to him.

Another deputy sat in his cruiser under the shade of a pepper tree at the top of the driveway. Vince waved to him on his way to the house.

He went in through the front door, ducking under the yellow tape. The house was empty of human life, but he always felt a strange, tense energy in the aftermath of a violent crime. Sometimes he thought it might be the lingering fear and tension of the victim, hanging in the air, entangled with the scents of blood and death. Sometimes he thought perhaps it was the remnants of evil, a dark energy that vibrated in the air like the last tremors of sound from a tuning fork.

The current wisdom and protocol of his colleagues in the FBI's Investigative Support Unit was not to send profilers immediately to the scenes of the crimes they were called to consult on. The procedure was to review all available information on the case at Quantico in their subterranean offices known to the agents as the National Cellar for the Analysis of Violent Crime.

There, removed from the emotion and other influences at the scene of the crime, the entire team could review the case objectively and brainstorm ideas, combining their individual experiences into a dynamic group effort. It was a system that worked very well and allowed them to take on more cases at once. Vince had worked within that structure for years, but it had never really suited him.

After years as a homicide detective, he still liked to walk a scene, see it in three-dimensional reality as opposed to videotape or photographs. He wanted to be aware of everything in the surroundings, including that last, lingering tremor of energy in the aftermath of death.

It was his unique mix of experience and education that had made him the profiler he had become: a homicide cop/FBI field agent with a degree in psychology earned on the side.

He went to Marissa Fordham's bedroom. The sheets and mattress had been taken from the bed to be sent to the state crime lab. Everything else remained as it had been.

She had been attacked here first. Cast-off blood spattered the ceiling from the killer yanking the knife out of her body and over his head only to plunge it down into her again. The ransacking had come later when Marissa had either been dead, or lay dying on the kitchen floor.

Had she been attacked as she lay sleeping or in the aftermath of sex? By an angry lover or a jealous would-be lover? By a stranger or a friend?

In his mind's eye he pictured the scene over and over, each time with a different person in the role of killer. Zahn, Rudy Nasser, the faceless form of Haley's father, Steve Morgan, even Sara Morgan—taking the advice he had given Mendez, unlikely as it was for a woman to murder another woman in such a violent manner. Women usually reserved rage like that for abusive or faithless husbands.

What had been the motivation here? Rage? Jealousy? A flashback to another crime?

Had Haley witnessed this early part of the attack? Had she watched in horror as her mother ran from the room, naked and bleeding with a knife-wielding killer chasing her?

Her bedroom was directly across the hall. It was the room of a fairy princess, frilly and pink. Her mother had covered the walls with a mural of a magical land full of magical creatures. A winged fairy rode on the back of a unicorn. A smiling tabby cat looked down from the branches of a lollipop tree.

Sweet and innocent. Innocence shouldn't end at the age of four, he thought.

He followed the blood trail to the kitchen and stood there, looking from the pool of dried blood on the floor to the blood-streaked telephone on the wall. The little girl had to have climbed onto the chair against the wall and from the chair to the counter to reach the phone.

She had to have made the call either during the attack on her mother or just after, while the killer had been busy searching the house for whatever he had been so desperate to find. Vince could picture him coming back into the room to see little Haley on the phone, could see him grabbing the little girl and choking her, then smothering her, then dropping her seemingly lifeless body like a piece of garbage next to the body of her mother.

If Gina Kemmer didn't come through, that left Haley as the only key to the crime.

Vince recalled the picture from the night before: his wife holding the sobbing child in her arms, trying to console the inconsolable.

Innocence shouldn't end at the age of four. It would have been better for Haley if her mind simply blocked out everything that had happened. But it wouldn't have helped the case. They needed to catch a killer. And the child would be the key.

27

"Maureen Up-*chuck*," Franny said with as much disdain as he could manage and still keep his voice down. "I would call her a stupid cow, but that would be offensive to cows everywhere."

They sat at the far end of Haley's hospital room while the little girl slept quietly. Franny had brought tea and tea cakes from the Mad Hatter tea shop and bakery on Via Verde near the college.

"I had her nephew in my class a few years ago—right before you came back to teach," he went on. "Thank God she, herself, hasn't reproduced. Somebody burn the nest before that can happen!"

Anne chuckled under her breath, appreciative of the distraction from the day's tensions. "You're terrible."

"*I'm* terrible?" he said, incredulous. "She reported *me* to the school board because her nephew was a weenie wagger!"

"Oh my God!" Anne covered her mouth to stifle her laughter. "How was that your fault?"

Franny was delighted, of course. "She claimed it was my 'gay influence' that made him do it. But the kid had a well-documented history of weenie wagging from day care on, and she knew it. He got expelled from Sunday school for whipping it out during the Christmas pageant right in front of the Virgin Mary, for God's sake!

"She was just pissed off at me because I had told her sister her kid was going to grow up to be a pervert flasher if she didn't make him stop it."

"And that made her angry. Go figure," Anne said.

"Yeah. And the next thing I know, here comes Maureen Upchuck like a charging elephant, accusing me of being gay!"

"You *are* gay."

"It's got nothing to do with my teaching abilities. Am I not a stellar teacher?"

"The best in the West."

"Besides, she's the biggest, fattest Lickalottapuss around."

"She's a what?"

Franny rolled his eyes. "You're so out of touch, Anne Marie. What do you call a lesbian dinosaur? A Lick-a-lotta-puss."

"Oh my God!" Anne put her hands over her face to hide her flaming blush.

Franny smiled his eyes into crescents above his apple cheeks. "Made you laugh!"

Anne shook her head, wiping the tears from her eyes. "You're something else, Francis. What would I do without you?"

"Well, you'd be really boring."

"Thanks."

"It's all right. I'm happy to be your spirit guide into modern pop culture."

"I don't know if 'culture' is the right word."

"Anyway, she got me in trouble. She's a bitter, vindictive bitch. She blames all normal-size people for her being as big as the freaking Goodyear blimp," he said. "Like she doesn't buy two dozen doughnuts and a bucket of fried chicken every time she goes into Ralph's. I've seen her."

"Well, she's plenty mad at me," Anne said. "I jumped the chain of command."

"You did what was best for Haley."

"She doesn't see it that way. Neither does Milo Bordain. She had a total meltdown. I do feel bad about that."

"Fuck 'em," Franny said. "What does Vince think about it?"

"He didn't want me to do it, but he backed me up."

"He's just trying to protect you, sweetheart."

"I know."

On the bed, Haley began to stir and whimper. Anne got up and went to her, bending over and brushing the girl's damp hair back from her face.

"You're all right, sweetie," she said quietly.

Haley opened her bloodred eyes and stared up at Anne.

Anne waited for the tears to come, but there were none.

"Do you remember me?"

The swollen, bruised little rosebud mouth pursed for a moment as she tried to decide whether she would answer or not. Anne offered her a sip of water through a straw. She knew from her own experience how her throat had felt after being choked.

Haley sat up and took the drink.

"Do you remember me from last night, honey?" Anne asked again.

The child nodded. "You're the mommy," she said in a scratchy little voice.

"My name is Anne. I'm here to help you and make sure you're all right."

She took that in and thought about it.

"Hi, Haley," Franny said softly, joining Anne at the bedside.

Haley studied him for a moment. "Are you the daddy?"

"No, sweetheart. I'm Mr. Franny. Do you remember? You came to my classroom at the school for the Halloween party."

"I was a kitty," Haley said.

"Yes, you were. I remember. You were a very pretty kitty."

She looked around the room and through the glass wall to the desk where people in hospital scrubs were busy reviewing charts and making notes.

"You're in the hospital," Anne said. "You got hurt and you were brought here so the doctors could make you feel better. Do you remember getting hurt?"

Haley shook her head, eyes cast downward. She picked at the tape that held her IV catheter in place then turned back to Anne. "Where's my mommy?"

Pain squeezed Anne's heart. There was no easy way to do this, but she had decided to give Haley little pieces as she asked for them. There was no point in telling her straight out that she would never see her mother again when she was feeling alone and afraid, surrounded by strangers.

"Your mommy was hurt too."

Anne held her breath, waiting for the next question. *Can I see her? Where is she?*

But Haley Fordham didn't ask. She sat quietly, eyebrows lowered as she thought it over. When she looked up at Anne, she had moved on to other needs.

"My throat hurts. Can I have Jell-O?"

"I'll go ask," Franny said. "I'll bet you can. The Jell-O is very good here. Isn't it, Anne?"

"Excellent Jell-O."

Franny went out the door as Vince got off the elevator, laden down with a couple of duffel bags. He came into the room, eyebrows raised at the sight of Haley sitting up in bed.

"This is a good sign," he said.

Haley looked up at him. "Are you the daddy?"

"I'm Vince," he said, bending down to her level. "And you're Haley. And I have something I think you're going to be very happy to see."

From out of one of the duffel bags he pulled a floppy-eared, much-loved velveteen rabbit.

The little girl's face lit up. "Honey-Bunny!"

Vince handed her the toy and looked at Anne. "Has she said anything?"

"She doesn't remember getting hurt."

"Did you ask—"

"I'm not going to push," she warned.

"I know. I know. I was hoping for what the attorneys call an excited utterance."

"Hmm. No. No excited utterances," she said as he deposited the duffel bags on one of the chairs and helped himself to a Russian tea cake on the tray. "Will you be in trouble for taking evidence from a crime scene?"

"The CSIs already took everything they thought might be significant. Thank God the rabbit didn't look suspicious," he said, nodding at Haley, who had curled up with her old friend and was looking decidedly sleepy again, a thumb inching toward her mouth.

"She's so precious," Anne said quietly. "I feel so bad for her."

"I was twenty-three when I lost my mother," she said. "I was devastated, but at least I have a lot of memories to look back on. She was there for every significant event of my life: my first day of school, Brownies, school plays, my first date, the first breakup, going off to college.

"Haley won't have that. I can't imagine being that young, that small and vulnerable, and not having anyone."

Vince slipped his arms around her and kissed the top of her head. "She has you."

"For now."

Anne gave a long sigh, leaning into her husband's solid warmth. She watched the little girl's eyes flutter closed, her impossibly long eyelashes curling against her cheek, and marveled at how quickly she had become attached to Haley Fordham. She would have to be careful not to pass the point of no return. Their paths were crossing now for a reason, and they would eventually go their separate ways—after they had finished helping each other.

She was already dreading that day.

A deputy came to the door and knocked hesitantly on the glass.

"Mr. Leone? I have a message from Detective Mendez. He said to tell you we found the breasts."

28

The two orbs of flesh in the box had ceased to resemble breasts. The skin was turning black and slimy, and was slipping off in places. The nipples had shriveled and hardened like old raisins. The fatty tissue had become gelatinous. The smell was horrific.

"The mailman brought this?" Mendez asked. "What the hell did he think was in it? Rotten fish?"

Milo Bordain nearly gagged. She sat on an old bent-willow settee on the porch of her sprawling ranch house. She didn't seem nearly as formidable after losing her lunch in the rosebushes.

Her face was pale and waxy, and she was sweating, despite the chill coming on now as the sun slipped behind the mountains at the backside of the ranch.

The box sat on a footstool a few feet away. Mendez crouched down to examine the postmark.

"Lompoc," he said. "Mailed on Monday."

It was now Wednesday. The pathologist had estimated Marissa Fordham's death as having taken place sometime on Sunday.

"I guess we can add severed body parts to the list of things that should be thrown out after three days," he said to Hicks.

"Fish, houseguests, and rotting human flesh," Hicks said.

Mendez glanced back at Mrs. Bordain to be sure she was out of earshot. She had gone to the far end of the long porch to be sick again.

The average citizen didn't appreciate cop humor. Not that there was anything funny about the situation. It was just a way of releasing the tension that built doing a sometimes-grim job.

"No return address," he said, standing.

"Why send them to her?"

"She supported Marissa Fordham."

"Our killer is a demented art critic?"

Mendez shrugged. "Everybody's got something to say."

The sheriff's car pulled up the driveway and Dixon got out.

"We're not good enough for the grand dame?" Mendez asked as their boss joined them.

"That's right," Dixon said. "Only the top of the food chain for Mrs. Bordain."

"I wouldn't mention food to her right now," Mendez said. "She's pretty shaken up."

"The box was sent from Lompoc," Hicks said. "No return address."

Dixon's face twisted as he leaned over the box for a look. "Glad I'm not the one taking that to Santa Barbara for the pathologist."

"Don't look at me," Mendez said. "I just bought this jacket. I'm not spending an hour in a car with that smell."

"Relax. I can't spare you for running errands," Dixon said as a pair of crime-scene techs came onto the porch.

"The box is evidence," he told them. "The contents have to go to the morgue in Santa Barbara. The pathologist is expecting you."

"Cal, thank you for coming."

Milo Bordain had collected herself. She came as far as the front door, staying well back from the view and the smell of the box. The pastiness had passed out of her system along with her stomach contents. Ashen best described her now. She was still visibly shaking.

"I'm sorry you're having to deal with this, Mrs. Bordain," Dixon said. "You saw the mailman leave the box?"

"He brought it to the door along with the rest of my mail. I sat down here to open it." She closed her eyes and shook her head at the memory. "Oh my God. It was . . . I've never seen . . ."

"You should sit down, ma'am," Mendez suggested.

"No, no. I can't stay out here with that box," she said, waving a hand. "I can't stand it. That's part of Marissa. Someone did that to her. It's sick!"

She turned and went into the house. Dixon followed her. Hicks and Mendez followed.

"I feel ill," Bordain said. "I have to make some tea."

They followed her through a great room that looked like something out of *Bonanza* to a huge kitchen outfitted with commercial appliances. She went about the business of filling a teakettle and putting it on the stove to heat. When she turned around and saw Mendez and Hicks, one eyebrow sketched upward in disapproval.

"I thought we would talk about this privately, Cal," she said to the sheriff.

"Detective Mendez is my lead investigator on the case. Detective Hicks is his partner."

"I thought you were handling the case personally."

"It has my full focus, but an investigation like this is always a team effort."

She didn't seem to like that answer. She wanted the sheriff's undivided attention.

"This is quite a place you have, Mrs. Bordain," Hicks said. "Is it a working ranch?"

"Yes. We raise exotic cattle—Highland cattle. And of course we have a few horses—pure Spanish Andalusians—and some interesting types of chickens."

Even the animals on her ranch had designer labels.

She was dressed to go riding in tan jodhpurs and tall boots, and a butter-soft suede jacket that probably would have cost Mendez two weeks' pay. A beautifully patterned silk scarf was wound around her throat into an elaborate cravat inside the open collar of her crisp white blouse. She wore kid gloves so thin and fine she didn't bother taking them off.

The boots didn't look like they had ever seen the inside of a barn or stepped into a stirrup.

"Do you know anyone in Lompoc, Mrs. Bordain?" he asked.

"No."

Lompoc didn't have the right zip code for the Bordains, who had a mansion in posh Montecito on the coast adjacent to Santa Barbara, and a condo on the Wilshire Corridor in Los Angeles.

"The box was postmarked Lompoc."

A city roughly the same size as Oak Knoll, Lompoc was north and west of Santa Barbara. Its biggest claim to fame in Mendez's book was the federal penitentiary.

"You'll get fingerprints from the box, won't you?" Bordain asked.

"If we're lucky," he said. "Mrs. Bordain, do you have any idea why the killer would send that box to you?"

"No! My God! Of course not! I don't understand any of this! Why would anyone kill Marissa? She was like a daughter to me. And why send that—that *thing* to *me*?"

"Maybe that *is* why," Mendez said. "She was like a daughter to you. Could someone have been jealous of her or angry that you supported her?"

"I suppose so," she said. "I get a lot of requests from people who want someone to pay their way for something."

"You get letters?"

"Yes. I have one of Bruce's secretaries deal with them."

"We'll need to see those letters, if possible," Dixon said. "In case somebody's holding a grudge."

The kettle whistled and she jumped as if she'd been shot. Hands shaking, she made her tea with a teabag, and the scent of peppermint filled the air on a cloud of steam. The cup rattled against the saucer as she took it to the kitchen table and sat down.

"This is such a nightmare," she said. "I'd just gotten back from the meeting about Haley when the mail came. I was already upset. I'm filing the paperwork to become her foster parent. That woman from Child Protective Services is coming tomorrow to see the house. Haley should be with people she knows, people who care about her.

"What must she be thinking?" she said. "She has to be terrified, surrounded by strangers. Has she said anything about what happened?"

"Not so far," Dixon said. "She was unconscious for some time. She may never remember anything."

Bordain sighed. "I hope so, for her sake. Poor little thing."

"If she remembers and can give us a name or a clue," Mendez said, "we can catch Ms. Fordham's killer. Isn't that what you want?"

"Of course, but Haley is only four years old. Would she have to testify in court? Is a four-year-old child considered a credible witness?"

"I had a case in LA County years ago," Dixon said. "A triple homicide—a mother and two children. The only person left alive was a twenty-two-month-old baby.

"The killers let him live because they didn't think he was able to talk," he said. "Turned out they were wrong. He was perfectly able to speak, he just didn't speak to strangers.

"He had heard their names. He had seen the whole thing go down. He didn't testify in court. We had to corroborate what he told us through a third party. But that baby solved the crime. Haley could do the same thing."

"And be traumatized all over again," Bordain said. "She'll never be normal. People will always look at her as the girl whose mother was murdered, the girl who was left for dead. She'll have to live with this for the rest of her life."

"Anne Leone will help her through it," Dixon said.

Bordain frowned. "I don't like that woman. She's very bossy and manipulative."

"I know Anne quite well," Dixon said. "She's a fierce advocate for children. Haley couldn't be in better hands."

"She would be in good hands here," Bordain argued, "and be with people she knows."

"Mrs. Bordain," Mendez jumped in. "How did you meet Ms. Fordham?"

She huffed a sigh, not happy to let go of the subject of Haley.

"I met Marissa at the art fair in '82," she said at last. "I was one of the judges. I thought her work was extraordinary. So luminous, so full of joy."

"And you decided to sponsor her? Just like that?"

"I have an eye for talent," she said. "I introduced Marissa to the people from the Acorn Gallery. They agreed to represent her art here and at their gallery in Montecito. I persuaded Marissa to put down roots here. Haley was just a baby. They needed a home."

"You own the property she lived on," Dixon said.

"Yes. I lived in that house while this one was being built. My husband couldn't understand why I didn't just stay at the house in Montecito and drive back and forth. He, of all people, should know you can't leave these contractors for a minute. Nothing would be right if I hadn't been here to watch them like a hawk."

"How long ago was that?" Mendez asked.

"I lived in that house most of 1981 and half of '82. Of course this one wasn't finished when they said it would be."

Mendez let her prattle on about how she had fired the carpenters halfway through the project because they had paneled the study in pine with knots when she had specifically told them over and over that she wanted clear pine. The carpenters had probably wanted to put her in a pine box by that point, Mendez thought.

His mother would have told him to be kind. Despite Milo Bordain's snobby character, she was nervous and upset. It made her feel a sense of control to divert the conversation off the main track to more mundane territory—and clearly, control was Milo Bordain's thing. She was a woman used to being in charge and telling other people what to do.

Eventually he brought her back on topic. "Did she ever talk to you about Haley's father?"

"No. I suspected he was abusive, and that was why she came to California, and why she didn't talk about him."

"But she never told you that," Hicks said.

"No."

"Had she seemed nervous lately?" Dixon asked. "Distracted? Upset?"

"No. Marissa was very self-possessed."

"She didn't mention having a problem with anyone?"

"Nothing she couldn't handle."

"What does that mean?" Mendez asked.

"It's nothing, I'm sure," she said. "She had complained to me about that strange neighbor of hers. He's a professor at the college. I don't know why they keep him. The man has something wrong with him. People pay a lot of money to send their children to that school. My husband sits on the board. I've told him several times he should get this taken care of."

"What did Ms. Fordham say about him?" Mendez said.

"Well," she said, avoiding his eyes, "that he was strange and made her uncomfortable. You should be questioning him."

Undoubtedly, Zahn made Mrs. Bordain uncomfortable, Mendez thought. Everyone they had spoken to had told them Marissa Fordham was perfectly at ease with her strange admirer.

"Yes, ma'am," he said. "We've already spoken with Dr. Zahn."

"And?"

"Do you know if Marissa was dating anyone in particular?"

"You didn't answer my question, Detective."

"I'm not going to."

"What Detective Mendez means to say," Dixon explained, shooting Mendez a hard glance, "is that he isn't at liberty to comment on an active investigation."

Bordain was offended. "I consider Marissa and Haley family. I should be kept informed about the investigation. Especially now that—that—box—"

She went pale again and pressed a hand to her mouth. Tears rose up in her eyes.

"*I* could be a target," she said, agitated. "You said so yourselves. Marissa could have been murdered to get to me."

"Why would you think that?" Mendez asked, almost laughing at the absurdity of her statement. Marissa Fordham had been stabbed dozens of times and nearly decapitated, and Milo Bordain thought that was somehow all about her. Unbelievable.

"I'm a wealthy woman. My husband is an important man. My son has a big political career in front of him. People are jealous. Marissa was important to me—"

"Has anyone threatened you directly?" Dixon asked.

"Well, no, but—"

"It's not about you, ma'am," Mendez said bluntly.

She looked to Dixon again for interpretation.

"Most crime is pretty straightforward," Dixon explained. "Most people are murdered because somebody wants them dead. Conspiracies only happen on television."

"Most people don't get a box like *that* in the mail," she returned.

"Can you think of anyone in your life who might want to kill you, ma'am?" Hicks asked.

"No! I don't have any enemies."

"We'll start with your friends, then," Mendez said.

Bordain turned to Dixon again. "What does he mean?"

"Most people are murdered by people close to them," Mendez explained, irritated that she kept turning to his boss, as if he weren't speaking English and she needed a translator. "We'll start by interviewing your husband. Did he know Ms. Fordham?"

"Is he trying to be amusing?" she asked Dixon.

Dixon shot him another glare. "There's nothing amusing about Detective Mendez."

"Where was your husband over the weekend?" Mendez pressed on.

"He's been in Las Vegas on business since Friday."

"He's still there?" Hicks asked. "Have you told him about Ms. Fordham's murder?"

"Yes, of course. But there wasn't any point in him coming back. He had important meetings to attend. He's flying into Santa Barbara tonight. He'll go to the Montecito house."

Mendez arched an eyebrow and made a few notes. "Even after you tell him about the box? Even if you tell him you think your life might be in danger?"

"If I ask him to come here, he'll come here," she said defensively. "I called my son. He should be here shortly."

"Your son's name?" Mendez asked.

"Darren Bordain."

"What does he do?" he asked just to insult her. He knew who Darren Bordain was. He just wanted Milo Bordain to realize not everybody gave a rat's ass.

She huffed a sigh. "Darren runs our Mercedes dealerships. He stars in all the commercials."

"I don't drive a Mercedes," Mendez said. "Did your son know Ms. Fordham?"

"Of course he did. Darren is also very involved in state politics. He's going to be governor one day."

"Were they friends?" Mendez asked. "More than friends?"

"They were acquaintances." She turned to Dixon. "Is this really necessary? My son had nothing to do with Marissa."

"We'll need to speak with him," Mendez said. "And we'll need to have you come into the sheriff's office so we can take your fingerprints."

"My fingerprints?!" she said, shocked.

"For elimination purposes," Dixon explained. "Your prints will be on the box."

"I was wearing gloves when I handled it."

"There's also Ms. Fordham's house," Hicks said. "You were there frequently. It's safe to assume your prints will be among those found."

"I feel like I'm being treated like a criminal," she complained to Dixon.

"Not at all, Mrs. Bordain," Dixon said. "We'll need to be able to identify your prints—and the prints of anyone else who spent a lot of time in Ms. Fordham's home—so we can take them out of the mix and hopefully eventually end up with only the prints of the killer. You can come directly to my office and we'll take care of it in private."

"Thank you, Cal," she said. "At least *you're* a gentleman."

Dixon turned the laser-blue eyes on Mendez, and he knew he was cooked. One poke too many at Her Majesty. "Detectives, can I have a word with you both outside?"

29

"Do you realize who she is, Detective Mendez?" Dixon asked, herding them to one side of the porch, away from the door.

"Sure. She's a snobby, rude, narcissistic bitch."

"You must be talking about my mother."

Mendez felt the bottom drop out of his stomach.

Darren Bordain stood up from the bent-willow bench on the other side of the door and casually put his cigarette out in a pot of his mother's geraniums.

"Mr. Bordain, I apologize—"

Bordain waved it off. "No need. I'm well aware who my mother is. I've been putting up with her for thirty-two years.

"Did she treat you like a servant?" he asked. "Don't feel special. That's how she treats everyone except celebrities, conservative politicians, and people she wants something from."

"Mr. Bordain. Cal Dixon." The sheriff offered his hand.

Bordain shook it. "Call me Darren. No need to stand on formality. I try not to be my mother's son whenever possible."

Ironically, Darren Bordain was physically the spitting image of his mother—same height, same build, same straight blond hair, same green eyes, same square jaw. Every time he looked in a mirror, he saw his mother's face.

His vintage silver Mercedes 450SL convertible was parked out by the sheriff's car. But he had been in no hurry to come in the house.

"I was just trying to work up the energy to deal with her crisis du jour."

"She's pretty upset," Dixon said. "She told you about the box?"

"Yes. She called my office and got my secretary and screamed at her until the poor girl came and got me off the golf course." He took a pack of Marlboro Lights from the pocket of his leather jacket and shook one out. "I had two holes left to play, so I'm a little late. She told me she had already called you guys, so what was I going to do?"

Comfort her, Mendez thought.

"She's concerned she might be a target," Dixon said.

"I'm sure she is," he said, lighting up. "It's all about her, isn't it?"

"You don't think anyone has it in for her?" Mendez asked.

He laughed. "I'm sure a lot of people have it in for her. She's not Miss Congeniality. But if she managed to push someone so far they would kill, why wouldn't they just kill her? Why kill Marissa?"

"Did you know Ms. Fordham?" Dixon asked.

"Sure, of course. She was the daughter my mother never had," he said sarcastically.

"She was included in your family?"

"Hell, no. A woman with an unknown past and an out-of-wedlock child? Marissa was more like a pet or a Barbie doll. Mother gave her a place to live, made a big show out of being magnanimous and a patron of the arts. But Marissa was never invited to Thanksgiving dinner."

"What was your relationship with Ms. Fordham?" Mendez asked.

"We were friends. We ran into each other at functions, had a few drinks, had a few laughs at my mother's expense."

"Were you ever involved with her romantically?"

"No. Not my type. The bohemian artist thing doesn't work for me. I'm told I have a political career to consider," he said dryly. "I should have thought about it, though. Marissa and I together would have given my mother an aneurysm."

"What about your father?" Hicks asked. "Did he have an opinion about Ms. Fordham? Or about the money your mother spent to support her?"

Bordain shook his head. "The Great Man can't be bothered with most of what goes on in my mother's life. He doesn't care what she does. He lives his own life. They're hardly ever in residence in the same house at the same time."

The front door opened then and Milo Bordain locked on her son.

"Darren, what are you doing out here? I called you nearly two hours ago."

He sighed. "Sorry, Mother. I was tied up in a meeting."

He very purposefully dropped his half-smoked cigarette on the porch floor and ground it out with the toe of a Gucci loafer.

"Duty calls, gentlemen."

30

"Nanette Zahn died of multiple stab wounds," Vince said. "Her death was ruled—get this—a suicide. Her son, Alexander, who was twelve at the time, was taken and raised by a cousin."

"Wow," Trammell said. "Do you think the college will give me my money back?"

"Your kid's on a scholarship. You didn't pay any money," Campbell pointed out.

They had gathered in the war room for their end-of-the-day wrap-up and to regroup and make plans.

"The boy was never charged or convicted of anything," Vince went on, peering down through his reading glasses at his notes. "There was a documented history of child abuse. The mother was severely manic-depressive. She couldn't deal with her son's condition—the investigator used the word 'autism.' She blamed the boy, ridiculed him, punished him, tormented him. She reportedly locked him in a closet for days at a time and just left him. He was put into foster care on three separate occasions, but was always returned to his mother once she went back on her medication and her moods evened out."

"What about the father?" Hamilton asked.

"The father was never in the picture," Vince said. "The mother was known to self-mutilate when she was depressed, so it isn't out of the question that she might use a knife to kill herself. But I would have expected her to cut herself, not stab herself. It's extremely rare for a woman to stab herself. She reportedly had three stab wounds to the abdomen.

"Apparently the boy was covered in blood when officers arrived and had sustained injuries consistent with a beating."

"Now we know why nothing showed up in a routine background check," Mendez said. "He doesn't have a record. But he told us he killed her. Where did you get this information?"

"I found out Zahn grew up in a suburb of Buffalo, New York," Vince said. "As it happened I worked a child abduction up there ten years ago. The lead detective on that case is their chief now. He was in a uniform at the time of Nanette Zahn's death. He actually remembered the case on account of the boy."

"What was his take on it?" Hicks asked.

"If the boy did it, it was self-defense. The kid was in a near-catatonic state when the police arrived, and stayed that way for months afterward. No one ever pressed the issue because they knew the family history, and I think they basically felt like the mother had it coming."

"Where does that leave us considering Zahn as a suspect?" Dixon asked.

"Milo Bordain said the victim complained to her about Zahn," Hicks pointed out.

"Everybody else has said she got along with him, didn't mind him hanging around," Mendez said. "I think Mrs. Bordain doesn't like Zahn. He's not her kind of people."

"Vince?" Dixon asked.

"We have to keep him on the list, but he would have had to have had some kind of psychotic break to do what was done to the victim," he said. "He's not psychotic. He has plenty of issues, but he's not psychotic."

"But he may have killed a woman with a knife before," Dixon said.

"Yes."

"If Marissa Fordham had made him angry somehow, said the wrong thing and triggered a memory . . ."

"It's possible."

"Talk to him again. See how he reacts when he finds out you know about his mother."

Vince nodded and jotted a couple of notes to himself while Mendez briefed the group on their conversation with Gina Kemmer.

"We should sit on her," he suggested. "She knows more than she's telling us."

Dixon nodded. "I agree. Campbell and Trammell take the first watch.

I'll bring a couple of deputies in to take the second. Tony, Vince, bring her in tomorrow and have another conversation with her. Turn up the heat.

"Hamilton, what did you find in Marissa's phone records?"

"Her last call was to Gina Kemmer on the evening of the murder," Hamilton said. "Before that, there was a call to the Bordain residence, one to Mark Foster, one to the woman who runs the Acorn Gallery. Nothing really stands out as unusual. These were all people she knew and had friendships with."

"And the bank records?"

"There was a regular monthly deposit of five thousand dollars from Milo Bordain, her sponsor."

"That's sixty grand a year!" Campbell exclaimed. "Shit! I'm taking up finger painting. Bordain will be looking for a new artist to sponsor."

"There were deposits from the Acorn Gallery. She had a balance of twenty-seven thousand in her savings, three thousand, two hundred fifty-one in checking. The trust account for her daughter has over fifty grand in it."

"That's a lot of dough," Vince said.

"She had very few living expenses," Dixon said. "The Bordains own the property she lived on. She had a generous allowance."

"And if she came from money to begin with—" Hicks began.

"So far, there's nothing from Rhode Island on a Marissa Fordham," Hamilton said. "And I haven't found anything in the state of California for Marissa Fordham predating 1981. So far I'd say she didn't exist in this state before 1981."

"Milo Bordain thought she might be running from an abusive relationship," Hicks said. "She might have changed her name."

Dixon sighed and rubbed a hand across his forehead. "Great. I'll call the pathologist. We need to run her fingerprints."

"Haley was born in May 1982," Mendez said. "If Marissa came to California before September '81 then she wasn't running from the baby's father."

"What's the latest on the girl, Vince?" Dixon asked.

"She's being released from the hospital tomorrow. Brain function is normal. There may be some permanent damage to her larynx, but she can talk."

"What's she saying?"

"She doesn't remember being hurt," Vince said. "But we have to be patient. Her memory could come back over time—or it might never."

"Can we drug her or hypnotize her or something?" Campbell asked.

"You'll lose a limb trying to get to her," Vince said. "My wife will have you for lunch."

"And pick her teeth with your bones," Mendez added.

Vince grinned, ridiculously proud. "That's my girl."

"We need the info if we can get it," Dixon said.

"If Haley has information to give, Anne will get it," Vince said. "But she won't put the girl at any kind of psychological risk to do it. And that's the way it should be. So the rest of you bums better get out there and beat the bushes for a killer."

Dixon checked his watch and frowned. "I've got to talk to the press. They want me to comment on Milo Bordain's reward."

"What's your comment going to be, boss?" Campbell asked as Dixon headed for the door.

"No comment."

31

Gina Kemmer paced around her living room like a caged animal, restless and on edge and desperately wanting out. Darkness had fallen outside. She felt as if it were pressing in against the walls of her cute little house, trying to get in and swallow her whole like a monster. She had turned on all the lights in her living room to ward it off.

She was cold and had wrapped a heavy sweater around herself, holding it tight in a manner that made it seem as if she were wearing a straitjacket. Maybe she should have been wearing a straitjacket, she thought. She felt like she might go crazy. Her life had gone crazy, no thanks to Marissa.

Every time she thought of her friend, her memory flashed to that horrible picture of Marissa butchered and bloody, lying dead on the floor. The thing was still lying on her coffee table among her more pleasant memories of times past. She needed to get rid of it. She couldn't have it there. She could imagine the blood seeping out of the photograph and running off it and spreading over the other snapshots of happier times, ruining them.

Her stomach tried to bolt again, but there was nothing left in it to throw up. She went to the kitchen and got a long-handled barbecue tongs out of a drawer. Back in the living room she inched sideways toward the coffee table, trying not to look at the photograph. Hand shaking badly, she tried to catch the corner of it with the tongs, swearing as she knocked it away.

After a couple of tries, she managed to get hold of it. She took it to the kitchen, holding it as far away from her as possible, as if it were the dead carcass of a rat or a snake. In the kitchen, she threw the picture in the trash and the tongs after it, the utensil now contaminated with the evil that had been done to Marissa.

A fresh wave of tears flooded her eyes and spilled down her cheeks. She had never been so scared in her life.

Gina wasn't the kind of person who went looking for excitement or lived life on the edge. That had been Marissa—always the one with the big plan. That was how they had ended up in Oak Knoll: Marissa's big plan.

Sure, Gina had been glad to come along. And it had worked out fine. She loved it here. She loved the town and her home. The boutique was doing well. She was satisfied. Life could have just gone on that way forever. The only other thing she wanted was to meet a nice guy—not even a rich guy, just a nice guy.

Everything was ruined now. Marissa was dead.

She pressed a hand over her mouth and tried to swallow the crying, hiccupping, and choking on it. The local news was coming on with the story of Marissa's murder leading the broadcast. Gina grabbed the remote control and turned the sound up.

First was an exterior shot of Marissa's house, which had always been one of Gina's favorite places, so pretty with the porch and the flowers, and Marissa's fanciful sculptures in the yard. Now it looked abandoned and sinister.

Then coverage went live to a press conference being given in front of the sheriff's office. The sheriff was telling about the autopsy results. That Marissa had died of multiple stab wounds, and that her daughter was in stable condition in the hospital. He confirmed the earlier reports of a $25,000 reward for information leading to the arrest of the killer. The number for the tip line was put up on the bottom of the screen.

Twenty-five thousand dollars was a lot of money. Marissa would have said it wasn't, but it was to Gina. It was to most people. The boutique was doing well, but cash flow was always an issue with a business that had to maintain inventory. She no longer had Marissa to help her out. Twenty-five thousand dollars would take the financial sting out of her death.

But she would have to live to collect it.

Gina's head swam and she had to sit down. The idea that came to her made her dizzy and sick. It was something Marissa would have thought of—something Marissa would have done without hesitation.

The worst they can do is say no. That's what Marissa would have said.

But that wasn't true. Marissa was dead.

Gina closed her eyes and saw the scene from the photograph she had thrown away.

The smartest thing she could have done would have been to pack some things and get the hell out.

But she loved her home. She loved her life here.

She had taken her phone off the hook hours before. Reporters had found out that she had been friends with Marissa. They wanted to interview her. They wanted to ask stupid questions like how did it feel to have her best friend murdered and did she know who the killer was.

Maybe she could sell her story. Maybe that was her leverage.

She muted the television and stared at the sheriff and the number for the tip line. On the coffee table lay the business card the older detective had left for her.

She didn't know what to do.

She picked up the receiver and punched in the number.

The call went through.

"I need to talk to you . . ."

Ten minutes later she was driving down the street, her mind on her mission. She turned the corner at one end of the block just as a plain burgundy Ford Taurus turned onto her street from the other end of the block. In it were two sheriff's detectives come to watch over her and keep her safe.

32

Mark Foster was younger than Mendez expected him to be. He had imagined the head of the music department in a prestigious school like McAster, and a town like Oak Knoll—known for its summer classical music festival—would be old and stodgy in a rumpled brown suit, wearing little wire-rimmed glasses and with white hair growing out of his ears.

Instead, Foster was probably in his late forties, fit and good-looking with close-cropped thinning brown hair. He was dressed in khaki pants and a blue oxford shirt with a knitted brown necktie. The only part Mendez had gotten right was the wire-rimmed glasses.

At seven thirty in the evening Foster was still working, preparing for a rehearsal of his senior honors brass quintet. Mendez and Hicks stood in the conductor's area of the stark white music room that rose up around them in level after level of chairs and black metal music stands. Foster distributed sheet music to the stands near them where his quintet musicians would sit.

"I'll help any way I can," he said. "I was horrified when I heard the news. What's the world coming to? The murders last year, now this. You don't expect that kind of thing here. We live in such a pretty little bubble most of the time. I remember talking with Marissa last fall after Peter Crane abducted that teacher and tried to kill her. We couldn't believe it."

"You were good friends?" Hicks asked.

"We ran in the same circles. Saw each other socially, occasionally met for drinks, that kind of thing."

"When was the last time you saw Ms. Fordham?" Mendez asked.

"A couple of weeks ago at dinner," he said. "It was so weird. I had gone to Los Olivos to try a new little hole-in-the-wall place I'd heard about. I'm a food fanatic," he explained. "I live to find places nobody else has discovered yet. I was shocked to see anyone I knew. But there was Marissa, smiling and waving. She was always so vibrant, so full of life."

"We were told you dated her," Hicks said.

"We went out from time to time," he admitted. "Plus One was Marissa's specialty."

"What do you mean?"

"She liked charity fund-raisers—the social scene, dressing up, having a good time, rubbing elbows with all the right people," he explained. "But she never had to buy a ticket. She was always somebody's Plus One."

"A party girl," Mendez said.

"I guess you could say so, but she wasn't wild. She just liked to have a good time. She was a free spirit. She liked men, and men liked her."

"Was she ever more than Plus One to you?"

"We were just friends," Foster said, his expression carefully blank.

"Did she know you're gay?" Mendez asked.

If Foster was shocked at the question, he did a good job of hiding it. "I'm not gay."

Mendez looked at Hicks, pretending confusion. "Really? Someone told us you are."

Foster shrugged it off. "That's nothing new. Single artsy teacher, hasn't gotten any co-eds pregnant—must be gay. I'm not."

"Huh," Mendez said. "He seemed pretty sure of it."

Foster shrugged. "Well, whoever he was, he was mistaken."

"When did you last speak to Ms. Fordham?" Hicks asked.

Foster thought about it. "Hmm . . . Sunday. She called me Sunday afternoon."

"For any particular reason?"

He shook his head. "Just to chat."

"How did she seem?

"Fine. Normal."

"She didn't say anything about being worried, or that someone was bothering her?"

"No. We talked about the holiday fair coming up. She's been doing some work with silk. She was excited about having pieces for sale in her booth."

"Can you tell us where you were Sunday evening?" Hicks asked.

"Dinner and a movie at a friend's house. Home in bed by eleven thirty. School night."

A door opened at the top of the room and two of Foster's quintet came in carrying trumpets.

"Is there anything else?" Foster asked. "I can postpone the rehearsal if you need me."

"No, thanks, Mr. Foster," Hicks said. "We're done for now."

Mendez handed Foster a card. "Thank you for your time. If you think of anything, please call."

Foster put the card in his pocket. "I'll do that. Good luck. I hope you find the person that did it."

Halfway to the door, Mendez turned around. "Mr. Foster, was Ms. Fordham with anyone when you saw her at that restaurant?"

"Yeah," he said. "She was having dinner with her attorney."

Steve Morgan.

"I told you!" Mendez gloated as they walked across the parking lot. "I knew it!"

"Could have been an innocent attorney-client dinner," Hicks said.

"You don't sneak out of town to an out-of-the-way restaurant nobody knows for a simple client dinner."

Hicks conceded the point.

"That bastard!" Mendez said. "I want him in the box. Now."

"It's not against the law to have dinner," Hicks said. "Or to cheat on your wife, for that matter."

"He's connected to a murder victim."

"He's a lawyer. He'll never consent."

"He's got a big ego," Mendez said, pulling open his car door. "Maybe he'll want to prove us wrong."

"What do you think about Foster?" Hicks asked as they got in the car.

"Single artsy teacher with no pregnant co-eds?" Mendez said. "Sounds gay to me."

"He was pretty cool about it."

"If he's used to people assuming he's gay, maybe it's no big deal to him."

"There's a big difference between someone saying you're gay and someone being able to prove it," Hicks said. "We didn't ask him who he was with at that out-of-the-way dinner."

"Like you said: There's no law against having dinner. Unless he was making out with another guy between courses, it doesn't matter who he was with," Mendez said.

"I see," Hicks said. "It's okay for Foster to meet a boyfriend for dinner, but Marissa Fordham being seen with Steve Morgan gives Morgan a motive for murder. That's some double standard you've got there, compadre."

"Don't ridicule my theory of the crime," Mendez said. "I mean, do you really think the powers that be at McAster would be shocked to find out their music director is gay? That's like saying they'd be shocked to find out half the girls' softball team are lesbians. Would they really care?"

"They'd care if there were photographs," Hicks pointed out.

"So would Steve Morgan," Mendez countered.

33

The adrenaline for the upcoming confrontation coursed through Mendez all the way to the Morgan home . . . then crashed. Steve Morgan's Trans Am was not in the driveway.

"Maybe it's in the garage," Hicks said.

"It was parked outside last night."

"Last night? What are you doing? Stalking the guy?"

"I was just driving around, thinking. I came by here."

"You're obsessed."

"I'm tenacious. It's only obsession if there's nothing to back it up."

They sat at the curb for a moment, Mendez regrouping his thoughts.

"Let's go in," he said. "We'll talk to Mrs. Morgan. Light a fire."

Sara Morgan was not pleased to see them. It took her several moments to come to the door. She was dressed like a welder in bib overalls and a heavy leather apron with equally heavy leather gloves. Her hair was up in a messy topknot with long curls slipping free all around.

She looked like she hadn't slept or eaten in days.

"Detectives," she said, pulling the gloves off. Her hands were raw with cuts and scratches. She had given up on the Smurf Band-Aids. The sculpture she had told him about was taking a hard toll on her.

"What a surprise," she said with no surprise in her voice at all.

"Mrs. Morgan," Mendez said. "Is your husband at home? We need to speak to him."

"What about?"

"It's of a sensitive nature, ma'am," Hicks said.

"Are you going to accuse him of sleeping with Marissa again?" she asked bluntly.

"Uhhhh . . . well . . ."

"Don't bother," she said. "He'll only deny it. That's the first three things they learn in law school, you know. Deny, deny, deny."

"It sounds like you've already had that conversation with him," Mendez said.

Sara Morgan let his statement hang. "He isn't home," she said. "He called to say he'd be late. Again."

Wendy came down the stairs then, her eyes widening a bit at the sight of two detectives in the foyer. She'd grown since Mendez had last seen her. She was going to be a knockout like her mother in another few years.

"Hey, Wendy," he said, smiling. "How are you doing?"

She shrugged with one shoulder. She didn't smile back. "I'm okay. Why are you here?"

Sara Morgan turned to her daughter. "They have some questions about Marissa, about . . . what happened."

Wendy huffed an impatient sigh. "Why don't you just say it? Her murder. Marissa was murdered. Somebody took a knife and killed her."

"Wendy—"

"I'm not a baby, Mom. I know what goes on in the world. People get murdered. People die. It's nothing new," she said with a bitterness in her tone that made Mendez frown.

Wendy looked up at him with unblinking blue eyes. "Do you know who killed her?"

"No," he said. "We're still gathering information. Your mom and Ms. Fordham were friends. We thought she might be able tell us something about Ms. Fordham we don't already know."

Satisfied with that answer, Wendy moved on. "How's Haley? Is she going to be all right? Where is she?"

"She's going to be fine," Mendez said. "Anne Leone—Miss Navarre—is looking after her in the hospital until we can find some relatives."

Wendy's demeanor lightened considerably at that. She turned to her mother. "Oh, Mom! Can I go see her? Please!"

"Wendy loves Haley," Sara Morgan said, her own expression softening as she looked down at her daughter.

"Can I go see her in the hospital? Please, please, please!"

She turned to Mendez again. "I was going to get to be her babysitter next year. After I turn twelve. I could have handled it this year because it's not like I'm a regular eleven-year-old. I'm very mature for my age."

"I know you are," Mendez said.

"I don't know if they'll allow visitors, sweetie," Sara Morgan said.

"I'll ask," Mendez offered.

"Oh, thank you, thank you!" Wendy said, bouncing on the balls of her feet as if the excitement weren't going to be contained in her body. She turned toward her mother. "I'll take her something special. Can I make her a card? Please? Can I go in your studio and make her a special card?"

Her mother ran a hand lovingly over Wendy's tangled mermaid's mane that matched her own. "Sure, sweetie. Make her something really special."

Wendy bolted back up the staircase and disappeared.

Sara Morgan watched her go. There was a fine sheen of tears in her eyes when she turned back to them.

"I don't get to see her that excited very much anymore," she said.

"That must be hard on you," Mendez murmured. It occurred to him that a lot of things in her life were hard on Sara Morgan. He halfway wanted to put his arms around her and give her a shoulder to cry on.

Maybe more than halfway.

"Ma'am," Hicks said. "Do you know where your husband was Sunday night?"

"He was in Sacramento all weekend for a golf tournament. I couldn't tell you what time he got in Sunday night. I didn't hear him. When I came downstairs Monday morning he was sleeping on the sofa."

"I hate to have to ask this," Hicks said, "but do you think your husband was involved with Ms. Fordham?"

"I don't know," she said sadly. "And frankly, I don't want to know anymore. My marriage is as over as it's going to get. I just don't know how to leave it."

"I'm sorry," Mendez said softly, even though a part of him wasn't. She deserved better than Steve Morgan. She deserved to be happy.

Hicks drew breath to ask another question. Mendez headed him off at the pass.

"Thank you, Mrs. Morgan," he said. "We won't take up any more of your time."

"I was going to ask her where she was Sunday night," Hicks said as they walked back to the car.

"Leave her alone."

"If her friend was sleeping with her husband, she had as much motive to kill Marissa Fordham as anyone. Maybe more. And did you see her hands? They're all cut up."

"She's making a sculpture, working with metal."

"Since when? Monday morning?"

Mendez started the car. "Let's go find the asshole she's married to and ask him."

34

Anne had changed into a pair of gray sweatpants and a soft, loose black sweater for the evening, settling in beside Haley on her hospital bed. She thought it would be a wonder if she didn't fall asleep before the child did. She was exhausted from the battle with Maureen Upchurch and Milo Bordain, and the knowledge that neither woman was going to give up.

Maureen would band together with Bordain now if for no other reason than to be against Anne. Milo Bordain would bring her family's influence to bear wherever she could. Not that Anne blamed her. The woman considered Haley family. Even if she showed no outward signs of being maternal, she clearly felt a strong connection.

Anne had Judge Espinoza on her side. She tried to comfort herself with the knowledge that he would not be swayed. A staunch Democrat, he would delight in thwarting the Bordains at every turn.

Haley was busy coloring in the coloring book Franny had brought for her. She wouldn't last for long, either. Her energy came in short bursts followed by long naps. Her little body had been put through a lot, and while she now had a clean bill of health, she would still be recovering physically for days.

She hadn't asked about her mother again.

Anne thought she probably simply couldn't cope with the idea that her mother wasn't here and had closed a door in her memory—temporarily. Anne suspected that when Haley couldn't hold those memories back anymore, the floodgates would open and the emotion would pour out.

There was very little literature to draw from on the subject of childhood memory, particularly childhood memory of traumatic events. Did children's memories function in the same way as adults'? Or were the memories of children more influenced or distorted by emotional responses? Nobody really knew. There was even less information available on how best to pull those memories out and help the child cope with them.

Anne had called her professor for advice. His suggestions had been to tread very carefully, not to ask leading questions, and to go with her gut.

"I'm sure we'll have a lot more data on the subject after this mess down in Manhattan Beach is over," he said. "But for now you've got good instincts, Anne. Use them."

Everyone in the field of child psychology, as well as those on the front lines protecting children from abuse, were watching the developing McMartin preschool sex-abuse case in Manhattan Beach, south of Los Angeles, where staff of the preschool had been accused of horrific crimes against the children in their charge.

It was a case that immediately struck a nerve with everyone who cared about children. People were outraged at the very suggestion of sexual abuse. The allegations had been made in '83. The pretrial investigation was still ongoing three years later. But rumors about how the children involved were being interviewed were bringing more than a little doubt about the veracity of the testimony being elicited—at least among psychologists.

Improper suggestive interviewing techniques could easily mislead and confuse small children, rendering their testimony unreliable—to say nothing of potentially causing psychological damage to the children.

Maybe she knew more about this than she realized, Anne thought. But she still felt like she was working without a net.

Haley had colored a page of chickens all red. Was that because of all the blood she must have seen the night she and her mother were attacked? Or did she just like the color red? Or had there been red chickens at her home out in the country?

"Why are your chickens red?" she asked.

Haley just shrugged and turned the page to a picture of kittens.

"I have kitties," she said. "At my house."

"You do?"

"When can I go home?"

"You're going to come and stay with Vince and me for a while."

"My mommy will miss me. Can my kitties come and stay too?"

"Hmmm ... I don't know," Anne said. "We'll have to see about that."

"When Mommy says that she means no."

Anne smiled and stroked a hand over the little girl's unruly mop of curls.

"Hey, would you draw a picture for me?" Anne asked, reaching for the tablet of blank paper. "Would you draw me a picture of your house and your kitties?"

"Okay. I like to draw."

She chose a brown crayon and started her rendition of a mamma cat and her babies. In the background she drew her house. Far off to one side of the page she drew a large black figure with red eyes.

"Who is that?" Anne asked, holding her breath for the answer.

Haley shrugged and colored the grass yellow.

"Is this a person?" Anne asked, tapping a finger below the imposing character looming off to the side.

Haley nodded.

"Does this person have a name?"

"Bad Monster," she said, and then looked up at Anne. "Are there kids at your house?"

"No. Do you have other kids for friends?"

"Sometimes Wendy comes. She's eleven. That's more than four. That's more than seven. When I'm seven I'm gonna ride a bike."

"Good for you."

"Big kids ride bikes."

"Does your friend Wendy ride a bike?"

"Uh-huh. Her mommy is Sara."

"Sara Morgan?" Anne asked.

"Uh-huh."

"I know Wendy," Anne said. "Does Bad Monster have a name?"

"*Bad Monster*," Haley repeated impatiently. "Can Wendy come and play with me?"

"Maybe," Anne said. "We'll see."

"Uh-oh."

Anne chuckled.

Haley paused in her coloring to take a drink from the crazy purple bendable straw Franny had brought.

"It feels funny," she complained, frowning, tears welling up seemingly out of nowhere.

Anne rubbed her back. "It's okay, sweetheart."

"No! No!" she cried, curling her fingers against her throat as if she were trying to pull something away.

Anne could see the hysteria building. She knew exactly how it felt—like an avalanche coming down, like a tsunami wave crashing.

"You're okay, Haley. I'm right here. I'm not going to let anything bad happen to you," she said as the little girl fell against her, sobbing. "It's okay. You're okay, sweetheart. You're safe."

Anne didn't tell her not to cry. She knew that sometimes crying was like opening the valve on a pressure cooker, and once the steam was released the worst of the panic passed with it. She did what she would have wanted someone to do for her: She was a rock, an anchor, a sponge to absorb the tears and wring them out until they were spent.

After a few minutes she felt Haley's body relax against her. Asleep.

Without moving the sleeping girl, Anne looked at the drawing she had left on the bedside tray and studied Bad Monster. Was Bad Monster black or had Bad Monster worn black clothing? Or was the color associated with fear? Maybe Bad Monster *was* the fear she felt metastasized into an entity, something she could isolate and push away from her sense of self.

The answers were only easy after you had them, Anne thought. Until then there were only puzzle pieces.

35

Dennis was angry. Miss Navarre hadn't shown up all day. He had waited for her, looked for her, asked the stupid nurses where she was and when she was coming. And she never showed up or called or anything.

He had even done his stupid reading assignment and everything. How could she just not show up?

Maybe she was dead. Maybe she was in a car accident and ran her car into the back of a tractor-trailer and cut her stupid head off. That would be funny. He could picture her decapitated head still lecturing him as it lay on the pavement.

That made him laugh.

She would have asked him why he thought that was funny.

He imagined running up and kicking her head like a soccer ball, and her head flying through the air. He wouldn't have to listen to her then.

He laughed harder, but held his pillow up to cover his face so no one would hear him.

The hospital was quiet now. All the crazies were drugged and in bed asleep instead of babbling to themselves in the halls and in the common rooms. The lights in the rooms were off. The lights in the halls were low.

Dennis liked this time of night. He knew what time the nurse would come by. Sometimes he would pretend to be asleep, then a few minutes later he would sneak out of his room and roam around in the dark. He liked the idea that just about everyone else was asleep and he could pretend he had the place to himself and could do anything he wanted.

Sometimes he would sneak into other people's rooms and just stand there watching them sleep, imagining the things he could do to them if he still had his knife.

Sometimes he would hide in the lounge near the nurses' station, waiting. Arlene, the skinny head nurse on the night shift, smoked, and she would go outside to do it because smoking wasn't allowed in the building. The short, fat nurse, Betty, would go with her, and then no one was at the desk.

They were never gone for more than ten minutes, but in ten minutes Dennis could sneak behind the desk and steal stuff. He never took big things. He would steal a pen or some paperclips or candy the nurses kept stashed. Or he would go into the trash and steal a newspaper someone had already thrown away.

He had never been a very good reader, but now it was the only way he could find out what was going on in the world outside the hospital—other than his preferred method of eavesdropping. He always looked for articles about Peter Crane or the Dodgers.

Nowadays the stories with Crane in them were about the trial that would happen sometime soon. There had been all kinds of delays already, and pretrial motions—which Dennis really didn't understand. But there would always be a paragraph about Dr. Crane and what he had *all-ed-ged-ly* done to Miss Navarre, and how he was suspected in those murders where the women had their eyes and mouths glued shut. That was the part Dennis liked to read about.

He imagined now what it would be like to glue Miss Navarre's eyes and mouth shut so she couldn't look at him or tell him what he shouldn't do. That would be cool.

Nurse Betty walked past his door without looking in.

Dennis slipped out of his bed. He counted under his breath to a hundred, then cracked the door open and stuck his head out to see if the coast was clear. The hall was empty.

He went out into the hall in his stocking feet because that way he didn't make any noise at all, and he could run and slide on the slippery floor. He scurried from shadowed doorway to shadowed doorway to the intersection of hallways where the nurses' station was.

The two nurses were at the desk yakking away while Arlene dug in her purse for her cigarettes. Then they were on the way down the hall away from Dennis, going for the front door.

Dennis slipped behind the counter, eyes scanning the lower counter for good stuff. He grabbed some Jolly Ranchers from a candy dish and stuck them in a pocket of his pajama bottoms. He pulled the front page of the newspaper out of the trash and scanned it, his heart jumping at the big black headline: GRUESOME MURDER ROCKS RURAL OAK KNOLL.

Dennis got so excited he thought he might pee his pants. A murder! A *gruesome* murder! Maybe someone had murdered Miss Navarre.

He folded up the paper and tucked it under his arm. He was about to beat it out of there with his treasures when he spotted Arlene's purse sitting open on the desk.

The bag was huge and full of all kinds of junk that looked like it had just been thrown into it like it was a garbage bag. Her wallet was on top. Dennis glanced down the hall. No sign of the nurses coming back.

Very carefully, he opened the wallet. There was a lot of cash. Maybe a hundred dollars. He wanted to take it all, but then she would know she'd been robbed. Better to take what she wouldn't miss right away. He pulled out a twenty from a bunch of twenties, and one ten out of four, and a couple of ones, and stuffed the money in his other pocket.

He was about to put the wallet back when his eye caught on something deeper in the bag. A yellow Bic lighter. It must have been her spare. Now *that* was a prize.

Dennis lifted the lighter and hurried out of the nurses' station. He made his way back to his room the same way he had come, ducking from recessed doorway to doorway. He was halfway to his room when he heard the nurses coming back. The soles of their shoes squeaked against the floor every few steps.

Dennis held still where he was for what seemed like forever, waiting for one of them to come down the hall and catch him. But they stopped at the nurses' station and Nurse Betty said, "Jeez, Arlene, you left your purse sitting open. You should stick it in a drawer. One of the crazies will make off with it."

Dennis snickered to himself and shot down to the next doorway and the next doorway to his room.

He flicked the lighter a couple of times, just to watch the flame burn, excited at the prospects of what he might do with it. Burn this fucking place to the ground.

But not tonight.

Tonight he stashed all his new treasures in his special hiding place under the mattress, and climbed in bed to sleep over the top of them and dream dreams of bright orange flames . . . and freedom.

36

Gina had considered three different choices. She had made the wrong one.

How stupid.

Now she was going to die. Not in the same way Marissa had died, thank God. There was a gun to her back. At least it would be fast.

She should have let bad enough alone. She should have packed her things and left or at least kept her mouth shut or called the sheriff's tip line. Twenty-five thousand was a lot of money.

She was crying. She didn't want to die. Her feet felt like lead weights. She could hardly move them forward.

She begged. She promised. She pleaded.

She was told to shut up and cracked across the back of the head with the gun. Instantly dizzy, she stumbled and went down on her knees in the dirt.

She was told to get up. Hard to do with her hands taped behind her back. Why not just die here, on this spot? What was the difference? Dead was dead.

But her killer had other ideas.

She was yanked upward by one arm from behind. She got her feet under her and moved forward.

There was no light but moonlight and the headlights behind them. There was no road but the fire road. There would be no other traffic.

No one would save her, and no one would find her. Coyotes would eat her body.

She was turned roughly and marched off the path a few feet. The skeletons of a couple of long-abandoned buildings were like modern sculptures in the near distance. On the ground in front of her were what looked like old storm cellar doors.

She hadn't thought of it in years, but now she had the clearest memory of the storm cellar doors at her grandmother's house back East. She had been nine years old. She remembered her brother opening the doors and daring her to go down into the dark, dank cellar. She hadn't wanted to, but he dared her, and she walked down the stone steps only to have him close the doors behind her.

Her killer stepped in front of her, still holding the gun on her, and reached down to open one side of the door, revealing a large hole in the ground.

There was no such thing as a storm cellar in California.

Her killer turned to open the other door.

Gina bolted, spinning and running back toward the fire road. She tripped and fell. Unable to break her fall with her hands, she hit face-first, crying out as small rocks tore the flesh of her cheek as she skidded.

A hand tangled in her hair and yanked hard, pulling her half up off the ground. She never regained her feet. She refused to. She wouldn't make it easy. She had to be dragged and kicked and shoved back to the hole as she cried, "No, no, no, no!"

She tried to dodge sideways at the same time the gun went off and the bullet penetrated her body.

She was falling before she realized she'd been pushed.

She was gone before she hit the bottom of the well.

37

"What do you mean she's gone?" Mendez asked stupidly. He sat at his desk writing up his notes from the day, eating a burrito from the vending machine and drinking a Mountain Dew.

"She's gone, man," Trammell said. "She was gone when we got there. We hung around in case she was just out to dinner or shopping or something, but she never came back. I walked around the house. Nothing looked out of place. No forced entry or anything like that. Looks like she left of her own accord. There's a team of deputies sitting out in front of her house now in an unmarked vehicle. They haven't seen her, either."

"Shit," Mendez said, checking his watch.

It was just 11:37. Gina Kemmer could have gone out with friends. She could have gone to stay with a friend. That made sense. She had been so distraught when he and Vince had left, she might have wanted support and a sympathetic ear.

Or she might have bolted. If she had been caught up in something with Marissa Fordham and Marissa Fordham was now dead, she might have decided the smartest thing she could do would be to get out of Dodge.

"Let's get a BOLO out on her car," he said. "Say she's wanted for questioning in relation to a murder."

He dug his notebook out of his coat pocket and pulled out the sheet where he had written down Gina Kemmer's license plate number and the make, model, and color of her car. He handed it to Trammell, who went to make the call to dispatch.

"Damn," Mendez said. "We didn't leave her alone for that long."

"She's probably with a friend," Hicks said.

Their gray metal desks sat front to front. Both were awash in paperwork.

"She just lost her best friend," Hicks said. "You said she was a mess. She probably wanted a shoulder to cry on."

Mendez thought about it. "I don't know. I've got a bad feeling. If she knows what got Marissa Fordham killed, then she's a target."

"There's not much else we can do about it now."

"I want to get into her house."

"You'll never get a warrant."

"She's a material witness in a murder investigation. She's gone missing—"

"That's a liberal idea of a material witness: She knew the deceased woman. She hasn't admitted to witnessing anything," Hicks said, playing devil's advocate. "It's a free country. She's an adult woman. She's free to go and do whatever she wants. We don't know that she's missing. We've got no one to report her missing. Who's going to write you a search warrant?"

"No one," Mendez said, scowling. He hated being wrong. "If we were on television, I would get a warrant."

Hicks laughed. "If we were on television, we could just go bust into her house without one."

"And we could wear T-shirts and jeans to work, and we'd all drive Porsches," Mendez said.

"And we'd have hot babes all over us," Campbell said.

Mendez looked at him with a straight face. "You don't have hot babes all over you? Man, that's sad."

Campbell fired a wad of paper at him, laughing. "Screw you!"

Mendez sighed. "Damn, I want in that house."

"Hey, man," Hicks said. "I'm just trying to save you from a certain death. If you go knocking on ADA Worth's door at this time of night with what you've got, she'll have your ass."

True enough, Mendez thought. "I'd have to have my fingers crossed while I typed my affidavit."

Every unit on the streets of town and the roads out in the county would be looking for Gina Kemmer's car. If she was parked at the home of a friend in town, it shouldn't take that long to find her.

Mendez tossed the last of his bad burrito into the trash and stood up.

"Where are you going?" Hicks asked.

"I'm going to drive around and look for her."

This was one of the benefits of not having a life: He could feel free to drive around town in the dead of night, looking for a needle in a haystack.

Hicks had opted to go home to his wife, who was pregnant with their third child.

No pregnant wife for Mendez, much to his mother's dismay. *Why you don't marry, Anthony? Why you don't give me any grandchildren?* she would ask practically every time he talked to her, and certainly every time he went to see her. His sisters were no better.

The rest of them had reproduced prodigiously enough he didn't really feel like he had to be in a hurry. He had been too focused on his career to devote much time to looking for a wife.

He had goals. He was still thinking seriously about making the move to a career with the FBI. He wanted to see Peter Crane put away for his crimes first, then he would go after it. It didn't make sense to put roots down deep only to have to pull them up again and relocate to the other coast.

In the meantime, he didn't have any trouble getting a date when he wanted one. But he never let a relationship get too serious.

His thoughts turned to Sara Morgan as he turned down another street, scanning for Gina Kemmer's blue Honda Accord. He had been surprised to hear her say her marriage to Steve Morgan was over. Not because he thought she should have stayed with the bastard, but because it seemed out of character for her to be so candid about something so private.

She looked so wrung out, so fragile, like she was hanging on by a thread.

Her husband was nowhere to be found. Mendez and Hicks had cruised past Morgan's office where he was allegedly working late. No sign of him. They knew him to frequent O'Brien's Pub, but he wasn't there either. Nor had there been any sighting of his black Trans Am in any hotel parking lot. Just like there was no sign of Gina Kemmer's car anywhere.

He would bag it for the night, but not before swinging past the Morgan house to see if Steve Morgan had ever gone home.

There was still no Trans Am in the driveway, but a light burned bright in the garage. It was 1:41 A.M. The house was dark.

He didn't like that. Sara Morgan was depressed, her marriage was failing, she'd just lost a friend to a violent death. . . . It wasn't beyond reason that she could be in that garage with the minivan running, putting an end to her pain.

He parked at the curb, got out and drew his weapon. This was a nice neighborhood—all the more reason for a thief to come calling. Quietly he made his way around the side of the garage where the windows were full-size. Without revealing himself, he peeked inside.

Sara Morgan sat on a tall stool in front of what was apparently the sculpture she had been working on—a tall contraption made of iron and wire and steel mesh. But Mendez didn't think she was even seeing it. She sat with her arms wrapped around herself, and a thousand-yard stare haunting her eyes.

He could have just left. It was none of his business why Sara Morgan was sitting in her garage at one forty-five in the morning. But if she was sitting there contemplating turning that minivan on and sucking down some carbon monoxide . . .

Instead of walking away, he went around to the front of the garage and knocked on the service door.

"Mrs. Morgan? It's Detective Mendez. Are you all right in there?"

It took a moment, but she opened the door and stood back.

"Still looking for my husband?" she asked wearily.

"I was driving by and saw the light," he said. "I just wanted to make sure you were all right."

She smiled to herself, a small, slightly bitter smile.

"Thank you," she said. "I would say I'm fine, but I think you probably won't buy that."

"No, ma'am," Mendez admitted, following her back into the garage.

Her Dodge Caravan was parked on the side of the garage nearest the entrance to the house. The far stall was taken up by an artist's nest of tools and materials and hand torches, with the sculpture at the center of it.

"I wanted to say I'm sorry," he admitted.

"For what?"

"I'm sorry you have to be stuck in the middle of another investigation. It's not your fault, but you have to deal with it. I'm sorry for that," he said. "I don't really know you, but I think you probably don't deserve to have to go through all of this."

She put her head down and her wild mane fell around her face. She swept it back with both hands and looked up at him.

"I don't know anymore what I deserve," she said. "But thank you. I know it's not part of your job to feel bad for me."

"Is there anything I can do to help?" he asked, not sure what he could possibly do to make her life easier, but he wanted to offer—needed to offer—just to let her know she could have some support. "Is there someone I can call to come stay with you? A friend?"

But instead of helping, his offer of kindness seemed to be her undoing. She pressed her hands over her nose and mouth, and squeezed her eyes shut hard. The tears came, nevertheless. A dam had broken somewhere inside her and the pain came rushing out.

Mendez went to her just to put a hand on her shoulder and steady her—or steer her toward the stool she had been sitting on earlier. But at his touch Sara Morgan turned to him, and then she was in his arms, crying her heart out on his shoulder.

He wasn't quite sure what to do with that—what was proper, what was not; what was procedure and what was human. He went with his gut and held her, and let her release the pain and the sadness. He couldn't help but feel compassion for her. And when she looked up at him through those impossibly blue eyes magnified by tears, he couldn't help but feel something more.

He wanted to lean down and kiss her. The invitation was on her softly parted swollen lips. Instead, he pulled a clean handkerchief from his hip pocket and pressed it into her hand.

"You should try to get some rest," he murmured.

She nodded as the moment slipped away.

"I'm sorry," she whispered, embarrassed, dabbing the handkerchief against her cheeks.

"No, don't be. Don't be," he said softly, resting a hand between her shoulder blades. "Come on. You're going to bed."

"And what are you doing?" she asked as they walked toward the door.

"I'm spending the night on your sofa."

38

"Would you like a cup of tea or coffee or something?" she asked him as she led the way through the house to the kitchen.

"No, thank you, ma'am," Mendez said, taking in the surroundings: cream-painted cupboards and a hand-painted border of grapes dripping from vines around the ceiling. Her handiwork, he imagined. Down along a right-angled crease where a cabinet met a wall, she had painted a bright-eyed mouse peeking out of a hole in the baseboard—so realistic he almost startled when he first saw it.

"Please, call me Sara," she said as she filled a mug with water and stuck it in the microwave oven that seemed to take up half the counter. "I'll feel less embarrassed about having a nervous breakdown in front of you."

"Sara, then," he said, thinking it maybe wasn't such a good idea to blur that line. "Do you have any family nearby?"

"I'm from the Seattle area. My parents are there. And my sister."

"Are you close?"

"We used to be," she said. She hit the Cancel button on the microwave before the timer could go off. "She's got a family and a career. She's busy. I'm busy."

"You know, it's none of my business—what's going on in your marriage—but it just seems to me you shouldn't try to go through it alone," he said, then felt like an ass. "I should have stopped at 'It's none of my business.'"

She shook her head and dunked her teabag—something herbal by the scent of it—into the mug of water as she took a seat at the breakfast bar. "It's okay. I'm sure I would say the same thing if I was watching from the outside. From the inside . . . it's not so simple."

"I'm sure it's not."

"I come from a perfect family," she said. "I'm supposed to have a perfect family. I thought I did. What did I do wrong?"

Mendez felt a rush of anger. "You didn't—"

"You don't know that." She smiled at him as if he were a sweet but dimwitted boy. "Nothing happens in a vacuum."

He wanted to say at least ten derogatory things about her husband, but he bit his tongue.

"Maybe I'm too insecure," she said. "Maybe I wasn't paying attention. Maybe—"

"Maybe your husband is a son of a bitch."

So much for his self-control.

"That too," she said, and took a careful sip of her tea. "It's hard on Wendy. I feel guilty for that. I'm the mom. I'm supposed to make her life ideal and shelter her from life's unpleasant side. Instead, her father and I are wallowing there."

"Then you need to change that."

"I know," she admitted. "It's scary."

"Do you think he'll make it hard for you?" he asked.

"I don't know. I hope not."

The bastard was a lawyer. He would know every way possible to screw her over in a divorce. He had probably been stashing assets for the past year. Keeping secrets seemed to be his specialty.

"Are you married, Detective?" she asked.

"No, ma'am—uh, no," he said. He didn't invite her to call him Tony. "No, I'm not."

She seemed to think about that for a minute, as if she might have had a different idea about him.

"We used to be happy," she said. "Not that long ago. And then something changed and neither one of us seemed to know what to do about it. It's hard to explain. It was like one minute we were standing toe to toe, and then all of a sudden there was a chasm between us."

She sipped her tea and shrugged to herself. "Maybe I wasn't needy enough. And now that I am, it's too late."

"When did he become so involved with the Thomas Center?" Mendez asked, steering away from the too-personal details. He didn't need more reasons to want to put his arms around her and protect her. That wasn't his job. It was his White Knight Syndrome, as his sister Mercedes called it.

"Steve has always been involved in women's rights causes. He had a single mother. It was a tough situation for him growing up. She passed away when he was in law school, and he dedicated himself to helping disadvantaged women in her honor."

She smiled an ironic little smile. "That dedication was one of the first things that attracted me to him."

Dedication was one thing, Mendez thought. Lobbying in Sacramento for women's rights was terrific. Donating services to the Thomas Center was admirable. But that dedication also put Steve Morgan in a target-rich environment of women to take advantage of.

Sara sighed and slid down off her stool. "And now that you know more about my life than you ever wanted to know, I'm going to take your advice and go to bed. I have car pool in the morning."

Mendez watched her dump her tea in the sink and rinse out the mug.

She glanced at him over her shoulder. "You don't have to stay. Really. I'll be fine."

He didn't believe her—or he didn't want to believe her.

"You should take your own advice," she said. "Go home and get some rest."

The hell he would, he thought. Her husband had as good a reason to kill Marissa Fordham as anybody. And he had even more motive to kill the wife who was about to divorce him and take half of everything he had—plus alimony, plus child support.

But he said none of that to Sara.

"You'll lock your door behind me," he said as they went down the hall to the front of the house.

"Yes, sir."

She gave him a little salute as he turned to say good night.

"And thank you," she said sincerely. "For stopping to check on me, and for listening to me rattle on."

"That's okay," he said with half a smile. "That's a nice switch for me. In my line of work, most people don't want to talk to me."

"Too bad. You're a good listener."

An awkward little tension sprang up between them. It was like the end of a first date. Who should say what? Should he kiss her? No. Absolutely no.

"Thanks. Well, good night," he said abruptly, and he turned and walked away.

He should have taken her up on the coffee, he thought two hours later. His eyelids felt like they were lined in sandpaper, and his mouth tasted like a dirty sock. He ran his tongue over his teeth and grimaced.

Finally a set of headlights turned onto the street. Steve Morgan's black Trans Am. Mr. Midlife Crisis: driving a teenager's sports car and cheating on his wife.

Mendez remembered interviewing Peter Crane during the investigation into the murder of Lisa Warwick—before Crane himself had taken the spotlight as See-No-Evil. Crane had tried to make excuses for his friend's behavior.

Steve is a complicated guy . . . Steve comes from a tough background—single mom, not much money, desperate times . . .

Sara had given him the same out for being an asshole.

Boo-fucking-hoo, Mendez thought. He came from a tough background himself, but he didn't use it as an excuse for bad behavior. And his mother raised him to treat women with respect, not lie to them and cheat on them.

He didn't wait for Morgan to pull into the driveway. He got out of the car and walked across the street with purpose, coming up alongside the Trans Am as Morgan turned the key off.

Mendez smacked his badge up against the driver's side window then shoved it back in his coat pocket. He stepped back just enough that Morgan could get the car door partially open to get out, only to find himself trapped between the door and the car.

"Is there a curfew law I'm unaware of?" Morgan asked calmly. He smelled just vaguely of alcohol.

"Where've you been all night?" Mendez asked without any preamble of false niceties.

"Working."

"I've been past your office ten times tonight. You weren't there."

Morgan raised his eyebrows. "Ten times? That sounds like harassment to me."

"Where were you?"

"I had a dinner meeting with a client."

"Oh? Did you take her to that nice out-of-the-way little place in Los Olivos?"

Morgan looked annoyed. He worked his jaw a little back and forth like he was grinding his teeth.

"You spoke to Mark Foster," he said and nodded. "Yes, I sometimes meet clients out of town. People here can get the wrong idea if I take a woman out to dinner."

"Yeah?" Mendez said. "And I bet they really raise their eyebrows when you take that woman home and bang her."

"I took Marissa to dinner," Morgan said, maddeningly in control of himself.

Mendez would have been happy to have Steve Morgan take a swing at him. It would have given him a chance to knock the jerk on his ass, and then drag him off to jail for assaulting an officer.

"We met in Los Olivos to try the restaurant—the same as Mark did," Morgan said. "I didn't want to do dinner here in town because people like to jump to conclusions. I don't need anyone calling Sara and upsetting her for no reason."

"Or giving her one more reason to dump your sorry ass," Mendez said. "Is that what Marissa Fordham threatened to do? Tell Sara the two of you were sleeping together? Did she give you the big ultimatum, Steve? Dump the wife or else?"

Morgan actually had the gall to laugh. "Clearly, you never knew Marissa," he said. "She didn't want a husband. She never let any relationship get that serious. She was very happy being single."

Frustrated, Mendez said, "So you met a client for dinner tonight. Who?"

"That's confidential."

"Where?"

"In Malibu. At a private home."

"Convenient. That explains how you can be just getting home at four in the morning. No closing time. Long drive."

"You know, Detective, I don't have to answer your questions at all," he pointed out.

"No," Mendez said. "Is that the tack you take with Sara too? You don't need to answer her questions?"

"She stopped asking."

Heat burned through Mendez like a flash fire. He stepped closer, leaning his hands on the top of the car door on either side of Steve Morgan. "You're a bastard."

"Yeah," Morgan said without humor. "I am."

Mendez leaned in closer. "Is this where you try to make me feel sorry for you because your mother was a junkie whore and you had it so bad you just can't help being the way you are?"

He got his wish. Steve Morgan came with a right that connected hard into his mouth, busting his lip from the outside with knuckles and from the inside with his own teeth. He staggered sideways.

"Fuck you, Mendez!" Morgan said, coming away from the car, pulling his arm back for a second shot.

Mendez came up into his boxing stance, blocked the second punch and hit Morgan with two hard jabs in the face. Blood gushed from Morgan's nose.

He stumbled back into the side of his car and bounced forward again, swinging too hard, too soon. Mendez grabbed the man's fist, stepped to the side, and twisted his arm up behind his back. Using Morgan's own momentum, Mendez swung him around and slammed him across the hood of the Trans Am.

Dogs all around the neighborhood started barking. A light came on across the street.

Mendez cuffed one wrist then the other behind Steve Morgan's back, then turned and spat a mouthful of blood across the hood of the car.

"Thanks, man. You just gave me an early Christmas present," he said.

He pulled Morgan up off the car hood and marched him toward the Taurus at the curb.

"Steve Morgan, you're under arrest. You have the right to remain silent . . ."

39

"Did you have it coming?" Vince asked, pouring himself a cup of coffee.

"Hell, yeah."

Mendez tried to grin with only partial success. He had come up to the ICU straight from the ER. A little centipede line of fresh stitches knitted his swollen upper lip on the left side. Lidocaine still had a firm hold on that side of his face.

Vince had to laugh. "You look like a freaking half-wit, Detective Frankenstein. What the hell happened to you?"

They sat down at a corner table in the otherwise-empty ICU family lounge.

"I had a little run-in with Steve Morgan," Mendez said, talking out the right side of his mouth. "Turns out he has a temper."

Vince raised his eyebrows. "What triggered that?"

"I guess it was something I said."

"Like what? Your mother was a junkie whore?"

"How'd you know?"

"You *said* that to him?" Vince laughed.

"Yeah. I said a whole lot of other shit before that, but he didn't turn a hair. That one—he went off like the fucking Raging Bull."

Vince felt a surge of pride. "That's my boy! You wanted to find his hot button and you did. I hope you gave a good accounting of yourself in that fight, young man."

"He came after me. I had to protect myself. I might have broken his nose, and the one eye was swollen shut. He's still downstairs getting patched up. I left a deputy with him."

"Has Cal heard about this yet?" The sheepish look told Vince the answer was no. "He'll have your ass."

"I was defending myself!"

"You—an ex-marine, Golden Gloves boxing champion—versus a lawyer."

"Hey, he had a hell of a swing!" Mendez protested. "He golfs and plays tennis."

"He's gonna sue your ass."

"He assaulted a law enforcement officer."

"You called his mother a whore."

"Did I? I don't remember. Too bad he doesn't have any witnesses to testify to that."

"Let's back this up, Rocky," Vince said as the red flags started popping up in his head. "What were you doing in his face in the first place at O-dark-thirty in the morning?"

Mendez glanced down for just a second before he started his story. And he glanced down several times more as he told about going to the Morgan house and talking with Sara Morgan.

He wasn't lying. Mendez was as straight an arrow as arrows could be. But he was trying to be evasive about something. Sara Morgan.

"Did you ask her how long she'd been friends with Marissa Fordham?" Vince asked.

The glance down.

"No. She was on the verge of a nervous breakdown. I wasn't going to push her over the edge."

"Uh-huh. Very chivalrous of you."

"What? I was supposed to browbeat her?"

Anger.

"There was no point in it," Mendez said. "She doesn't have it in her to kill someone. Besides, she's going to divorce the husband. That ends her suffering regarding his infidelities."

Denial. Rationalization.

Vince nodded.

Half a scowl. "Don't give me that look."

"What look is that?" he asked.

"You smug bastard," Mendez complained. "Don't you sit there and psychoanalyze me."

"Well, I wouldn't," Vince said, amused. "But it's just so easy."

"Say it, then."

"Say what?"

"You're enjoying this."

"Oh, yeah," Vince said, chuckling.

"So I'm attracted to her," Mendez admitted. "So what? What guy wouldn't be? She's gorgeous and talented—"

"And needs a champion—"

"I kept everything very professional. Nothing inappropriate happened."

"Of course not."

"I mean it!"

"I know you do, Tony," Vince said, serious now. "You're an honorable man. And there's certainly nothing wrong with wanting to stand up for a woman—even if she doesn't belong to you. I mean, really, that's how it ought to be. I just don't want to see you blur a line here."

"Oh, you mean like you didn't?" Mendez said sarcastically.

"Anne wasn't a person of interest—"

"Sara couldn't—"

Vince held up a finger to stop him. "Listen to me. Anne wasn't a witness. She wasn't a suspect. Her involvement in the case—while crucial—was peripheral when we first got together. Then she became a victim. Now Crane's attorneys are trying to get evidence thrown out, claiming I planted it because Anne and I were involved."

"The hell!" Mendez said.

"It's true. They want that tube of superglue excluded. Thank God it's not that important to Anne's case. But if they can get it excluded now, chances are our side doesn't get it back in later. If Crane goes to trial on any of the See-No-Evil cases, and the prosecution wants to establish a pattern of behavior . . ."

"Shit."

"Now back to you, Junior," Vince said. "Don't get me wrong, I like Sara, Anne likes Sara. But if Steve Morgan was having an affair with Marissa Fordham, then Sara had a motive and she has to be considered a person of interest. Even if she wasn't, Steve Morgan is certainly someone we have to take a look at. You can't get involved with Sara."

"I wouldn't," Mendez said, frowning with the working side of his mouth. "She's a married woman."

"Barely," Vince said. "It sounds to me like psychologically she's practically divorced. She's wounded and frightened and needy. You gave her a shoulder to cry on. Tell me you didn't come this close to kissing her last night."

The glance down.

"It's a slippery slope, kid. Stay off it until there's an all-clear. Then—when she leaves that asshole—go for it. Fall in love. Get married. Anne and my kids are going to need playmates."

"Very funny," Mendez said. "What's going on with Anne and the little girl?"

"I'm taking them home this morning before the reporters crawl out of their rat holes," he said.

He didn't have a good feeling about it. He was still worried not only about Haley—and therefore Anne—being a target, but for Anne's level of attachment to the child. What happened when they found a relative and Haley had to be handed over? Nothing good in terms of Anne's emotional health. As good as it might be for her to help the little girl through this ordeal, there would be an end to it, and that was going to be hard.

"You had to let her do it, Vince," Mendez said.

Vince frowned. "Now who's reading whose mind?"

"You've taught me well, Old Man. Has the girl said anything?"

"No, but it's in there. Last night she drew a picture for Anne with a scary-looking figure in it. 'Bad Monster,' she called it."

"That's not much to go on," Mendez said. "We can't put out an APB for Bad Monster."

"Your witness is four."

"This case stinks, so far. My witness is four, I've got to deal with an autistic hoarder who murdered his mother. It looks like the victim's best friend took it on the lam—"

"What?" Vince said, coming to attention.

"Gina Kemmer is missing. In the couple of hours we weren't watching her, she took off."

"I don't like that. There's no sign of her?"

Mendez shook his head. "We've got a BOLO out on her and her car."

"Get in her house."

"I wanted to do that last night, but it was too soon. I wasn't going to get a warrant based on nothing but the fact that she wasn't home."

"That was last night when maybe she was just out to dinner," Vince said. "She's still gone this morning. Now it's a possible kidnapping. Go to ADA Worth and fight for it. We know you're good in a fight."

"She scares me more than Steve Morgan does," Mendez joked, getting up.

"Page me when you get the warrant. I want to be there."

Mendez gave him a mock salute and headed out the door.

Vince dumped the last of his coffee in the trash and headed back to Haley's room. It was time to take his temporary family home.

40

"Where are we going?" Haley asked in her scratchy little sleepy voice.

Anne had awakened her before they left the hospital room, not wanting her to wake up in a panic in a strange place. They had forgotten about needing a child safety seat. Anne held the little girl on her lap and buckled them both in together for the short drive home.

Haley rubbed her eyes now and looked around as they drove out of the parking garage.

"We're going to the house where Vince and I live," Anne said. "Remember? You're going to stay with us for a while."

"How will my mommy find me?"

The question made Anne flinch inwardly. It wasn't in her to lie, but neither was it time to tell Haley the full terrible truth.

"Your mommy got hurt really badly at the same time you did, sweetheart," Anne said carefully. "Do you remember I told you that?"

Haley didn't answer. She looked out the window at the tree-lined street and changed her line of questioning. "Do you have aminals at your house?"

"No, we don't," Anne said.

"I have kitties and chickens at my house." She twisted around on Anne's lap and looked up at Vince. "Can my kitties come and live in your house?"

"Hmmm . . . we'll have to see about that," Vince said.

"Uh-oh."

"We've already had this conversation," Anne said. "Haley told me when her mommy says 'we'll see' that means no."

"What about your daddy?" Vince asked. "What does he say?"

Anne glared at her husband over the top of the little girl's head and mouthed, *Don't push.*

"The daddies say lots of things," Haley answered cryptically.

The daddies, plural. Her quick burst of anger pushed aside, she thought about what she had been told of Marissa Fordham's life: single mother, free spirit, dated casually. Had Haley—fatherless—attached the label of "Daddy" to all of her mother's male friends in the hopes that it might stick to one?

Vince was thinking the same thing.

"How many daddies do you know, Haley?" he asked, one eye on the road, one on the child.

Haley shrugged and made a little face, unhappy with the question.

In the hospital she had asked Vince if he was the daddy. She had asked Franny the same thing.

"Do you have a special daddy?" Anne asked.

No answer, but the somber expression on her face made Anne think she was looking back on a memory she wasn't ready to share.

"Is that your house?" Haley asked as Vince turned in the driveway.

"Yep."

Anne smiled, looking up at the old white stucco Mediterranean she and Vince had chosen to make their home. It was a solid, substantial house that had commanded its spot on that street since the late twenties. A tasteful renovation had brought the house up to modern standards without compromising its character.

She loved her house. It was welcoming and sheltering and safe, with none of the oppressive memories her childhood home had contained from her parents' long unhappy marriage.

Vince led the way to the front door, laden down with duffel bags. Anne carried Haley, who was still a bit weak from her ordeal. Haley looked around with a critical eye, taking in the curved staircase with a glimpse of family room to one side and dining room to the other.

"Does your house have monsters?" she asked.

"No, honey. No monsters," Anne said. "This is a safe house. No monsters will get you here."

The little girl put her head on Anne's shoulder, a thumb inching toward her mouth. "I'm tired."

Anne carried her upstairs to the small guest room nearest the master. The room she had already pegged for a nursery. The walls were painted the softest blue. The double bed was too big for a toddler, but would hopefully give Haley the feeling of being on her own little island of safety with her stuffed animals.

She was asleep before her head hit the pillow.

Anne tucked her in and brushed a hand tenderly over her mop of dark curls. When she turned, Vince was smiling at her tenderly.

"You're a natural at that," he said softly, slipping his arms around her.

Anne hugged him back. "She'll be out for a while. Want some breakfast?"

He nuzzled her neck and growled. "I want you for breakfast."

"You'll have to settle for scrambled eggs," she said, ducking away.

They went downstairs to the kitchen and Anne set about the task of making eggs while Vince made coffee. She loved being domestic with him. They had a nice working rhythm together, as if they had been a team for years instead of months.

"What's going on with the investigation?" she asked.

"They're still digging for background on the victim. I have a feeling there was a lot more to her than met the eye," he said. "She claimed she was from Rhode Island, but there's no trace of her ever having been there. And records of her here in California only go back to 1981."

"Haley was born in 1982," Anne said.

"Yeah. So was Marissa Fordham invented for the sole purpose of being Haley's mother? Who was she before that? And so far no clue to who her father is. And the one person I think can tell us that has gone missing."

"Voluntarily?" she asked cautiously, a low-watt current of unease going through her.

"I don't know. It appears that way," Vince said. "But I admit I don't have a good feeling about it. I think these two gals could have been in something together and it got one of them killed."

"And the other one is missing."

"Ask Haley about her. See if you can get any impressions. Her name is Gina Kemmer. I think she and Marissa go way back."

"All right."

They sat at the table in the breakfast room overlooking the backyard. Anne picked at her food, anxiety chewing at the ends of her nerves. Their yard was boxed in by tall privet hedges, but no fence. A woman was missing. The only witness to a murder was upstairs sleeping . . .

Her heart was beating a little too fast.

"Do you want the deputy in the house?"

"No," she whispered, angry with herself for letting the fear creep in.

"Nervous?" Vince asked.

"Don't say I told you so."

"I won't," he said. "Eat your eggs, Mrs. Leone. I need you strong and healthy to bear my children."

They both smiled at that.

Vince's pager came to life beside his coffee mug. He checked the readout.

"Tony. I've got to go."

41

"We can go in and make sure she's not dead on the floor," Mendez said. "But we can't take anything—unless we've got an obvious crime scene—and then Worth wants me to call her so she can come and make sure I'm not lying."

"That's better than nothing," Vince said. "She's going to dot every *i* and cross every *t* in ink. She's good. She's careful."

The three of them—Hicks, Mendez, and Vince—went into Gina Kemmer's cute little Tudor house with gloves on and paper booties over their shoes. Just in case. Nothing seemed out of place. There were no signs of forced entry or of there having been a struggle in the house.

Someone had cleaned up the broken plant pot and the vomit in the living room. The snapshots that had been lying loose on the coffee table had been put away.

Vince had wanted another look at them. He would have liked to have put them up on a wall and just stare at them, waiting for that one certain something to pop out at him. He had wanted to study the two women—their faces, their body language, how they related to each other. He had wanted to find a date on the back of one of those snapshots that predated 1982.

He opened a drawer in the base of the table. No photos. He looked in a magazine rack, in a small bookcase. Nothing.

Wandering through the house, Vince was struck again by the feeling Gina Kemmer had put roots down here. He didn't think she would pull those roots back up easily and just leave.

The house was neat and clean, but comfortably lived-in. There was an afghan tossed over the arm of the sofa, a couple of jackets hung on the hooks of an antique hall tree near the front door. There was art on the walls—several small paintings from Marissa, and casual groupings of photos, presumably of family and friends.

"It doesn't look like she packed anything," Mendez said, poking his head in the bedroom closet.

The bedroom was tidy. Dust rose and country blue. Very girly. Lace and dried flower bouquets. A couple of well-read romance novels were stacked on the nightstand at the base of a lamp with a frilly shade. Gina Kemmer still believed in fairy tales

. Vince went into the kitchen. The counters were cluttered with canisters and cookbooks. The refrigerator held half a dozen Bartles & Jaymes wine coolers, a rusting head of lettuce, some cheese, and condiments.

On the door of the fridge a multitude of novelty magnets held photographs and notes and a drawing Haley had made.

"Who are these people?" he asked, pointing to a snapshot of Gina and Marissa and two good-looking men at a beach party. The girls were in bikini tops and hula skirts. The men were in baggy shorts, Aloha shirts, and Ray-Bans. All four of them were laughing, having the time of their lives.

Hicks closed a cupboard door and came to look.

"The taller one next to Marissa is Mark Foster, head of the music department at McAster. He and Marissa went out from time to time. The one on the other side of Gina is Darren Bordain."

"You've talked to both of them?"

Mendez nodded. "Don Quinn told us Foster is gay. Foster denies it. I can't imagine anyone would care one way or the other."

"People are funny about their secrets," Vince said. "It doesn't matter if anyone else cares or not. People will guard their secrets like junkyard dogs, and take them to the grave if they can."

"He's the one who saw Steve Morgan having dinner with Marissa Fordham in Los Olivos," Hicks said.

"And Morgan said . . . ?"

" 'So what?' " Mendez answered with a dark look.

"What about Bordain?"

"Fair-haired child of Milo and Bruce Bordain," Hicks said. "He seems to be one of the few guys in town who hasn't gone out with Marissa. They were casual friends."

"What did his mother think about that?" Vince asked.

"He said maybe he should have had a fling with Marissa just to flip the old lady out," Mendez said.

"Marissa was *her* toy, *her* pet," Vince said, thinking about Milo Bordain's attitude regarding Haley. Possessive. Entitled.

"Right," Hicks said. "Good enough to trot out for occasions, but never invited to Thanksgiving dinner, he said."

"Hmmm . . ."

"He also said a bohemian single mother wouldn't be good for his future political career."

"The apple didn't fall far from that tree, did it?" Vince said. "What about Bruce Bordain? Have you spoken with him?"

"He's been out of town," Hicks said. "He was supposed to fly into Santa Barbara last night."

"I'm just curious about the family dynamic," Vince admitted.

"According to the son, Bruce and the missus live separate lives. They hardly ever live in the same house at the same time."

Which could have explained, at least in part, Milo Bordain's need to hang on to the people in her life, Vince thought. She was lonely. It was as simple as that. Being able to keep Haley in her life would fill the void left by losing Marissa, who had filled the void left by an inattentive husband.

"She was a beauty, wasn't she?" Vince said of their victim as he looked at the photo.

"Vibrant" was the word that came to mind. With a wicked smile and dancing dark eyes, there was something about her that just made her seem more alive than anyone else in the picture.

Funny, Vince thought, they were supposed to be looking at Gina Kemmer. She was the one missing. Her situation was urgent. Yet they were all drawn to Marissa. She had definitely been the dominant person in the friendship.

Gina was pretty, but in a quieter way. Blond and fair, she paled in comparison to her friend—physically as well as in terms of her presence. He had never met Marissa in life, but even after death he could feel the strength of her spirit. Gina didn't have that. She had been the shy one hanging on to her friend's coattails.

Mendez had glanced away to look in the trash. He reached into the receptacle and came out with a long-handled tongs at the end of which was the Polaroid of Marissa Fordham, stabbed, her throat slashed, dead eyes half open.

He held it up next to the happy snapshot.

"She was a beauty," he said.

She was no more.

They could only hope her friend had not met the same fate.

42

I'm dead.

But if she were dead, should she have been able to have that thought?

Gina drifted for a time in the blackness with no answer. She couldn't feel her body. It was as if her soul had abandoned it, as if it were no longer of any use to her.

That was the definition of dead, wasn't it? The body died and the soul went on. If a person believed in the soul, then that belief extended to include an afterlife. Heaven and hell.

Was she in hell?

Should she have been?

She wasn't a bad person. She hadn't done a bad thing. But she hadn't stopped a bad thing from happening either.

Maybe that meant she was in purgatory.

Her mother's crazy aunt Celia had always told the kids purgatory was full of dead babies. She hadn't seen any dead babies. She hadn't seen anything but blackness.

She floated then for a while longer. It seemed very peaceful to be dead.

Then—slowly at first—something began to impede on the quiet calm within her. Her mind didn't register what it was. Sound? Feeling?

Pain?

PAIN.

Oh my God, the pain!

Gina came to consciousness with a gasp, like a swimmer breaking the surface from a deep, deep dive. Her eyes opened. Her mouth opened. Her whole body strained as she came free of the blackness that had enveloped her and protected her. She gasped for air once, twice, a third time. Each breath hurt worse than the one before it.

She learned very quickly then to take only shallow breaths, but she took them too quickly and her vision began to dim again. Good, she thought. Dead was better.

But she wasn't dead, and she didn't die. At the edge of consciousness her body was able to regulate its breathing. Gina lay there trying to corral the pain into something she could comprehend. Were her bones broken? Were her organs damaged? What had happened to her? Where was she?

She was no place she had ever been.

Pinpoint beams of sunlight came down from above her, penetrating the dark like lasers. The wall in front of her appeared to be coated with layers of dirt and grime. The thick root of some plant was growing into the space through a jagged crack in the concrete like a long bony finger reaching in to point at her.

Was she in a cell? A basement?

The pain burst out of the flimsy confines of her will and engulfed her, choked her, convulsed through her until there was no room in her being for anything else—not air, not consciousness.

She had no idea how long she was out. It could have been moments. It could have been hours. When she came awake again, nothing seemed to have changed. She hadn't been dreaming—unless she was dreaming still.

No dream. Nightmare.

She felt dizzy and sick to her stomach. The stench of her surroundings went up her nostrils and down the back of her throat. Feces and urine, rodent and decay. Garbage. Sour beer. Her stomach turned itself inside out and she retched and retched.

She wanted to push herself up with her left arm so as not to vomit on herself, but her hands were stuck behind her back. Then she remembered the masking tape around her wrists.

The tape wasn't tight. She twisted her right hand and plucked at it with her fingers, working it off. She went again to support herself with her left arm, but the arm collapsed beneath her, sending a searing pain through her.

Oh my God. Oh my God.

No dream. No nightmare. She was wide awake.

Tears came then, and fear. Where the hell was she?

The memory came back in strobelike flashes. Night. Walking. Choking on her fear. Begging for her life. A gunshot.

A gunshot. She'd been shot. She looked down at herself. Her T-shirt was soaked with blood, a hole burned through the upper left shoulder. She didn't know if the bullet was still in her body or if it had passed through her. Whatever it had done, it hadn't killed her. Hours had to have passed and she hadn't died from loss of blood.

That was one good sign.

Slowly she took stock of her body. She had feeling in her left arm, but it seemed to be useless. Her right arm worked. She moved her left foot, bent her left knee. No damage there. Her right leg was a different story.

The attempt to move her right foot was excruciating. She struggled up onto her right elbow and looked down, panic knifing through her. The foot was turned inward almost perpendicular to the leg bone, as if it had been snapped off at the ankle.

"Help!" Gina called out. "Help! Somebody help me!"

She called out until her throat was raw. She was in the middle of nowhere. There was no one to hear her.

The space she was in was maybe five feet wide. It was a long way to the light. She was a poor judge of distance, but it had to be more than twenty feet. She remembered now the doors, like cellar doors. The doors—cracked and dilapidated—were the ceiling of her prison.

She reached out with her right hand to touch the wall, rough and hard. Concrete. Filthy. Beneath her was garbage—old boards, collapsed cardboard boxes; stinking plastic garbage bags that had been ripped and torn, their contents spilling out: eggshells and coffee grounds and putrid food and milk cartons. And beneath it all was the smell of stagnant water.

She was in an abandoned well, and she wasn't alone.

Slowly she became aware of the feeling of being watched. Her heart pounding, Gina turned her head left inch by inch and came face-to-face with the biggest rat she had ever seen in her life.

43

"No signs of forced entry. No signs of a struggle. No signs that she packed anything in a hurry—or at all," Mendez told Dixon.

They had gathered in the sheriff's office to share the news. Dixon sat back against the edge of his desk with his arms crossed tight across his chest. As always, his uniform was pressed crisp and impeccable. The only wrinkles were the creases Vince could see deepening across the sheriff's forehead and around his mouth.

Dealing with the press was taking its toll. Not only the entire state of California, but the nation was watching this case with a magnifying glass. The national press had moved in. The story of the beautiful artist murdered in the beautiful setting was made even juicier by the back story of Oak Knoll with the sensational See-No-Evil murders and the upcoming trial of Peter Crane.

Throwing gasoline on an already hot fire, the story of the delivery of Marissa Fordham's breasts to Milo Bordain had been leaked by someone to the hungry media pack.

Vince didn't envy Dixon his public relations job on this. Dealing with the press and the public was like trying to satisfy a multitude of two-year-old children who wanted what they wanted NOW. None of them wanted to hear that this case wasn't going to be solved overnight.

"And nobody has spotted her car," Dixon said.

"No, sir."

Dixon stared out the window for a moment. "What do you think, Vince?"

"She was pretty shaken up yesterday," Vince said. He had claimed a seat for himself on the credenza built in along the outer wall of the office.

Mendez and Hicks stood, nobody taking the much lower positioned chairs in front of the desk. Cops.

"She definitely knows more about Marissa and what got her killed than she told us," he went on. "My gut tells me they were in something together. Marissa would have been the leader. Gina probably got dragged along for the ride."

"We're thinking blackmail," Mendez said. The Lidocaine had finally worn out of his face so he didn't have to talk out the side of his mouth. But his lip was still fat beneath his mustache. "There's a reason why nobody seems to know who Haley's father is. And we still haven't located a birth certificate."

"That would explain how she came to have that much money in the trust account for the little girl," Dixon said.

"That would also make sense looking at the crime," Vince said. "The personal quality of the attack, the amount of rage involved, the concentration of stab wounds to the lower abdomen, removal of the breasts—"

"Right down to the knife in the vagina," Mendez added.

"Exactly," Vince said. "The killer's rage was focused on everything that made Marissa a woman—every body part related to reproduction."

"And we have plenty of candidates for the title of Dad, don't we?" Dixon said.

"The list goes on and on," Hicks said. "And those are just the men we know about. It's just as apt to be somebody she *didn't* date openly, right? I mean, the guys she was seeing casually are single men. It might be embarrassing for one of them to have a kid pop up, but it wouldn't ruin anybody."

"Steve Morgan isn't a single man," Mendez pointed out.

Dixon scowled at him. "No. He's a man who's going to sue the department."

Mendez spread his hands. "He assaulted me!"

Vince intervened. "If she was seeing Steve Morgan on the sly, she could have had other married lovers."

"Gina Kemmer probably knows," Hicks said.

"But Marissa Fordham didn't move here until after the baby was born, right?" Dixon asked.

"Right," Hicks said. "At this point, we don't really know where she came here from. She told people Rhode Island, but for all we know she might have come here from Vegas—somebody's drunken weekend indiscretion."

"A threat's not a threat unless it's in your face," Vince said. "Being here in the community is a constant reminder that revelation is just one missed blackmail payment away."

"Has the little girl said anything about her father?"

"No, not specifically. She talks about 'daddies,' plural," Vince said. "She asked me if I was 'the daddy.'"

"Chances are even better that Gina knows who the father is," Mendez said. "If she didn't leave on her own . . ."

"We need to get a helicopter in the air looking for her car," Dixon said.

"You need to be able to go through her house with a fine-tooth comb," Vince said. "If Gina has the birth certificate—or a copy of it—stashed somewhere, it's got the killer's name on it in big black letters."

"The ADA wouldn't give us a search warrant this morning," Mendez complained. "There's no evidence of foul play. There's no evidence Gina Kemmer didn't just leave of her own free will."

"She's got no family in the area to declare her a missing person?" Dixon asked.

"*Nada.* She told us she came up here from LA."

"Then we issue a warrant for her arrest as a material witness," Dixon said. "We'll get our search warrant that way."

"Bill and I talked about the material witness angle last night," Mendez said. "It's a little bit thin. What do we say she witnessed?"

"Get the affidavit started," Dixon said. "I'll call the ADA myself."

"I'll get on it," Hicks volunteered. He hustled out of the room and down the hall to get the paperwork started.

"Do we have anything yet on the box with the breasts?" Dixon asked.

"Latent prints says the box is a mess," Mendez said. "Covered in fingerprints. Prints on top of prints on top of prints. The thing has been handled by who knows how many people."

Dixon blew out a sigh, letting his shoulders slump for just a second. "Nobody at that post office is going to remember one person mailing a plain brown box."

"It'd be great if they had video surveillance in their lobby."

Dixon looked at Mendez like he'd lost his mind. "Video surveillance at the post office? In Lompoc?"

"Someday it'll be everywhere," Mendez said. "Post offices, airports—"

"Right," the sheriff scoffed. "For all those post office crime waves."

Vince chuckled. "First the mini-marts, next the post office."

"I can see it now." Dixon laughed. "Blitz attacks led by rogue stamp collectors."

"I'm telling you," Mendez insisted, taking the ribbing in stride. "And I'll come to the nursing home and rub your noses in it when technology takes over law enforcement."

"You do that, Tony," Dixon said. "Right now, we've got a case to deal with. Vince, why send the breasts to Milo Bordain?"

"The obvious reason would be basically putting an exclamation point on the murder. He destroyed Marissa and expressed his disdain for the woman who paid for her to live in this community."

"You don't think Mrs. Bordain is in any danger?"

"Marissa had to be the primary source of his hatred," Vince said. "The brutality of the crime was intensely personal. Sending the breasts to Mrs. Bordain was something that happened from a distance, suggesting a certain amount of emotional detachment."

"So the answer is no."

"Never say never, but it seems unlikely. I know of a case in Spain where a disturbed man murdered a patron of a particular controversial artist because he believed the artist's works sent satanic messages. He couldn't get to the artist so he eliminated the artist's source of support— a well-known figure in the art community," Vince said. "Marissa Fordham's work couldn't be called controversial in any way."

"Feminist, though," Mendez said. "She did the poster for the Thomas Center for Women, celebrating the strength of women's spirits. That might be considered controversial by some people."

"Jane does say they get a certain amount of mail from strict ultra-conservative religious groups," Dixon said.

"If this is supposed to be some kind of crusade, then you'd be looking at a very different UNSUB," Vince said. "That would be someone more apt to want attention to get their point across. I think we would have heard from the killer either directly or through the press if that was the case."

"So, we're no farther along than we were," Dixon concluded. "Lots of questions, not many answers."

"We need to find Gina Kemmer," Mendez said.

Detective Hamilton knocked on the door and stuck his head into the office. He was bleary-eyed and one ear was red from keeping the phone pressed to it for too many hours.

"What have you got, Doug?" Dixon asked.

"I got Marissa Fordham's social security number from the bank yesterday," the detective said. He came into the open doorway and propped himself sideways against the jamb. They were all exhausted. "It belongs to a woman named Melissa Fabriano. I'm running the name for a record, wants, and warrants in California."

"So you were right," Mendez said. "Marissa Fordham didn't exist before 1981."

"It looks that way. We don't know if Melissa Fabriano exists either, though," Hamilton said. "Could be another alias."

"Only people with things to hide need an alias," Mendez said. "What about Gina Kemmer?"

"What about her?"

"See if she has a record," Dixon said.

"Can I sue the department for cauliflower ear?" Hamilton asked.

"We need computers," Mendez complained.

"I need world peace," Dixon said, pushing to his feet. "And for this case to be solved. If you all can deliver either of those things, get out there and do it."

44

Vince left Mendez to wait for the search warrant for Gina Kemmer's house. He had given instructions to include photographs on the list of evidence to be searched for.

He liked the blackmail angle. It was neat and tidy in its own way. Simple cause and effect. Woman blackmails man. Man reaches breaking point, kills woman.

Why send the breasts to Milo Bordain? The answer that had rolled off his tongue for the sheriff made sense at a glance, but he wasn't so sure it held up to scrutiny.

Sending body parts held an element of gamesmanship. It was usually done to intimidate the family of the victim and/or to taunt the police. A metaphoric nose thumbing. That didn't fit into the neat and tidy blackmail scenario. Why would the perpetrator bother with it? He had a problem—Marissa—and he dealt with it. Why involve Milo Bordain?

He thought about the photograph on Gina Kemmer's refrigerator. Gina, Marissa, Mark Foster, and Darren Bordain.

Mendez and Hicks had said Bordain hadn't dated Marissa but had joked that he should have because it would have driven his mother crazy.

Vince only knew Darren Bordain from the television ads for the Bordain Mercedes dealerships. He must have been in his early thirties. Good-looking in a sort of androgynous way—not unlike his mother. In fact, quite *like* his mother. But where the masculine side of the trait tended to give Milo Bordain a masculine quality, the feminine side of the trait loaned the son a certain elegance to his features.

Mendez and his team needed to delve a little deeper into that relationship. If Darren Bordain had been involved with Marissa, had fathered her child, had been blackmailed by her, the ironic twist would have been his mother's attachment to and support of Marissa. If the son resented the mother enough, sending her a box of body parts wouldn't have been a big stretch.

People would have a hard time imagining a man like Darren Bordain—the elegant, privileged son of a well-respected family; the man who came into their homes every evening during the local news broadcast to promise them a better life if they would drive a Mercedes—being capable of doing the things that had been done to Marissa Fordham. Just as they had had a hard time with the idea of their handsome, friendly, family-man dentist as a serial killer.

Even with Peter Crane awaiting trial for the kidnapping and attempted murder of Anne, there were people in town who simply refused to accept the idea of Crane as a murderer.

Vince knew from long experience that killers hid behind all kinds of masks and came from all walks of life and all socioeconomic groups. Most people didn't want to believe that their next-door neighbor or their insurance man or day care provider could be a killer. They wanted killers to look like Gordon Sells.

Gordon Sells, the uneducated owner of a salvage yard outside of town, had been a person of interest in the See-No-Evil cases. He was a rough-looking, dirty person. He had done time for child molestation. The public would have gladly accepted Sells as the perpetrator.

In fact, human remains had been found on Sells's property, and Sells had since been charged with homicide on a former missing persons case in another jurisdiction where he had been tried and convicted. But the point was, Peter Crane had been just as guilty of crimes just as terrible, if not worse.

The face of evil could be handsome just as easily as it could be frightening.

Vince remembered when Ted Bundy had been sitting in jail in Colorado awaiting trial for the murder of Caryn Campbell, a number of influential political people in his home state of Washington had raised money for his defense.

Despite the fact that Bundy had already been convicted and sentenced to fifteen years in a Utah penitentiary for the kidnapping of Carol DaRonch—one of the lucky few Bundy victims to survive—and had also been conclusively connected to the disappearance of a seventeen-year-old high school girl, Debby Kent, Bundy's supporters couldn't believe the

Ted they knew—smart, charming, handsome, articulate; a volunteer on a suicide hotline; and up-and-comer in local conservative politics—could possibly have committed a vicious sexual homicide.

Now those well-meaning people had to live with the idea that after escaping jail Bundy had probably used the money they had sent him to fund his trip to Florida where he had brutally attacked five female students at Florida State University, killing two, and days later abducted and murdered a twelve-year-old girl.

Evil made its home wherever it could, wherever the conditions were right, wherever that elusive toxic mix of nature and nurture curdled a soul and warped a mind.

What had that cocktail done to Zander Zahn? Vince wondered. A family history of mental illness. A known history of physical and psychological abuse by his mother. A brain that was hard-wired in a way that complicated his attempts to relate to other people. What might all those ingredients produce if the conditions were wrong? A flashback? A rage? A memory of betrayal? A need for revenge?

While Zahn was certainly respected in his field, Vince suspected people would have been happy to peg him as a murderer because he wasn't like other people. There was something wrong with him. A person like that might do anything.

Zahn had murdered his mother. He had killed her by stabbing her repeatedly in the abdomen.

There was no denying that possible connection, Vince conceded. He thought of the photograph Mendez had pulled out of Gina Kemmer's trash. Marissa Fordham, stabbed in the abdomen so many times the area had been shredded into bloody hash.

Zahn had idolized Marissa. Perhaps deep in his psyche she had represented the gentle, loving mother he never had. If he had felt she had betrayed him in some way, could that have caused the psychotic break necessary to kill in the manner Marissa had been killed?

Yes, he thought so.

A call to Arthur Buckman had confirmed Vince's suspicion that Zahn would not be teaching. He had taken the rest of the week off due to his extreme grief over the death of his friend. Rudy Nasser had taken over Zahn's classes.

Vince drove the scenic route to Zahn's home by himself. He hadn't called ahead. He was pretty certain Zahn would have told him not to come, then he would have spent the fifteen minutes it took Vince to get there anyway winding his strange little psyche into knots of anxiety.

He parked outside the gate and pushed the intercom button on the keypad, hoping Zahn would answer. Nothing happened. He tried again. Again nothing.

He looked at the stucco privacy wall that must have been about six feet high. Maybe in his heyday he could have gotten over it without a ladder.

He tried the intercom again. No luck.

He looked from the wall to his car and back. In his heyday he would have scaled the wall somehow. Now he was older and wiser. He maneuvered the car into place beside the wall, climbed onto the hood, then onto the wall, and lowered himself to the other side.

"Not bad for an old man, Vince," he said, dusting off his palms and his clothes.

He had dressed casually for the day in tan slacks and a black polo shirt. The beauty of working for himself: no dress code but his own. He found people didn't always want to talk to the suit and tie he had been required to wear in the Bureau. There were times he wanted people as relaxed as possible when he sat down with them so he could more easily steer them where he wanted them to go psychologically.

He took a moment to just stand there and look around the yard at Zahn's odd collection of things. Coming from a childhood in poor circumstances, both financially and psychologically, Zahn probably derived security from the ownership of things and more security from the orderly placement of those things. And the way Zahn's mind worked, he could probably list every single item and would know exactly where each item was.

What must it be like to live inside a mind like that? Vince wondered. He couldn't find his car keys half the time.

He went to Zahn's front door and pressed the buzzer, pretty sure the professor was watching him from one window or another. The speaker on the intercom clicked, but no one spoke.

"Zander? It's Vince. Are you okay in there? I'm worried about you. I came to see how you're doing."

Silence. Then the sound of a deadbolt turning. The door opened a crack and Zahn peered out.

"Vince. I wasn't expecting you, Vince. I'm not prepared, Vince."

"Hey, Zander, it's just me," Vince said with his most disarming grin. "I'm not the queen of England. You don't need to do anything special for me. I just wanted to make sure you're all right, see how you're doing today. I know this is a rough time for you, Zander, and you're all alone out here."

Zahn inched the door open to the width of his narrow face. His green eyes were huge, the pupils dilated almost to the last edge of the irises. He wore black slacks and a black turtleneck that blended into the dark background and made it look as if his head with its cloud of gray hair were floating free of his body.

"Oh. That's very kind of you, Vince," he said in his hushed, breathy voice. "This is a very bad time. I'm terribly upset. Terribly."

"I know. You've lost your dear friend."

"Yes. And Haley. Where is Haley? How is Haley?"

"Haley is going to be fine," Vince assured him. "Would you like to visit her?"

Zahn's mouth rounded in surprise. "Oh, my. Could that be possible, Vince? Could I see Haley? Could I speak to her?"

"I can arrange that," Vince said, trying to see deeper into the house, curious as to what collections were contained within. "Would you like that? I can do that for you."

"That would be wonderful," Zahn said. "Haley is so sweet, so pure, such a perfect child. Small children don't judge, you know. They haven't yet been taught to judge or to hate. They simply accept what is. Isn't that wonderful? Small children are like Zen masters. They accept what is."

"I never thought of it that way, Zander. You're right. Small children are pure of heart. Life hasn't broken them yet. That comes later, doesn't it?"

Zahn frowned as he considered the question. Looking inward, Vince thought.

"You know, Zander, I'm dying of thirst here. Would it be all right if I came in and got a drink of water?"

"Come in? Come inside? Come inside my home?"

"Yeah. I mean, I know you're a very particular sort of man, and you don't want people touching your stuff. I get that. But I'm thirsty and I'm not feeling too great to tell you the truth," Vince said. "You know I had something terrible happen to me. Did you know that?"

"No. I'm sorry, Vince. I don't know."

"Yeah, well, I got shot about a year and a half ago. Someone tried to kill me."

"Oh my goodness! That's terrible. How terrible."

"Anyhow, I survived, but sometimes I still don't feel so good. I need to sit down and have a glass of water. Would that be okay? I mean, I think of us as friends now, Zander, going through this whole murder thing together."

Zahn looked caught. He didn't want anyone coming into his sanctuary, but neither was he a man with many—if any—friends.

Slowly, and with no small amount of anxiety in his expression, he took a step back from the door, then another.

"Thanks," Vince said, slipping inside. "Thanks a million."

The entry hall was crowded with unopened boxes of Christmas ornaments and decorations of all descriptions—artificial trees and wreaths, balls and tinsel, Santa Claus figures, angel tree toppers. Immediately, Vince took a seat on a bench along a wall to minimize his size and not physically intimidate Zahn in his own home.

Zahn seemed to hold his breath for a moment, as if he were waiting for something catastrophic to happen now that he had let someone breech his boundary.

"I'll get you a drink," he said at last. "Please wait here, Vince. I'll bring it here."

"No problem."

He kept his seat, figuring Zahn might duck back around the corner to make sure. From his vantage point he could see an office crowded with bookshelves that were absolutely packed tight with books. There was a desk, spotless, devoid of clutter.

One wall was entirely covered in whiteboard where Zahn had scribbled math equations that might as well have been Sanskrit as far as Vince was concerned. He could figure his odds at the racetrack. That was as much math as he cared to keep in his head.

In the other room he could see from the bench were file cabinets of all descriptions—metal, wood, new, antique—lined up against the walls and in rows across the floor, stacked as high as five feet with no more than two feet between them. Zahn would know exactly what was in each and every one of them.

"That's quite a collection you have there, Zander," he said about the filing cabinets as Zahn returned to the hall with a glass of water. Vince accepted it and took a long drink. "You keep a lot of paper documentation?"

"Yes. Yes, I do. I keep every paper filed accordingly."

"You know, Tony tells me computers are the way of the future. You remember Tony, don't you? He's all about the high-tech. He says pretty soon we won't need paper. Everything will be on computers.

"It's starting already. Even in law enforcement. Old records are getting converted into computer files. Fingerprints are going into databases," he went on. "Now me, I'm an old-fashioned kind of a guy. I'm a people person. I like to talk to people. Face-to-face if I can. But if I can't—say if the person I want to talk to is in Buffalo, for example—I don't hesitate to pick up the phone and call."

At the mention of Buffalo, Zahn blinked as if he'd been hit in the face with a drop of water.

"Why don't you have a seat, Zander?" Vince suggested, moving down to one end of the bench.

Zahn sat down on the opposite end and began rubbing his palms on his thighs, fretting.

"It's okay, Zander," Vince said softly. "I don't judge, either. I understand sometimes people have to do what they have to do in order to save themselves. It's okay. It isn't always easy to be kid."

Zahn said nothing. He had gone inward. He started rocking a little and kept rubbing his hands against his thighs—still trying to wipe the blood off all these years later.

Vince sat quietly, not wanting to push, letting Zahn absorb and process what he was saying. Nor did he want to wait so long the silence became uncomfortable.

"I know your story, Zander," he said, in that same soft, nonthreatening voice. "I know about your mother. That was a tough time for you. She was hard on you. You were just a boy, trying to be good. I bet you tried really hard, didn't you? You weren't a bad kid. You're just not like everybody else. You couldn't help that."

Zahn rocked a little harder and made a tiny sound in his throat, like a small, trapped animal.

"Nobody blamed you, Zander. It wasn't your fault."

Shaking his head, staring at the floor, Zahn said, "I don't want to tell this story, Vince."

"You don't have to. I know what happened. She tried to hurt you. You protected yourself. Right?"

"I don't want to tell this story, Vince. Stop telling this story. Stop it."

"Being the one to find Marissa," Vince said. "That had to be a pretty terrible shock. It probably brought back some bad old memories, huh?"

Zahn rocked harder, muttering to himself. "No more. No more."

"All that blood," Vince said, watching Zahn rub his hands harder against his thighs.

"You could imagine what happened to her, couldn't you? The knife going into her body again and again. But Marissa was a friend. She didn't have that coming to her, did she? She couldn't have made someone so angry they would do that to her, could she?"

Zahn was perspiring now. His skin had taken on a waxy translucence, and his respiration had become quick and shallow.

Suddenly he stood up. "You have to go now, Vince," he said quickly. "I'm terribly sorry. So sorry. You have to go now."

Vince got up slowly. "Are you upset, Zander? I didn't mean to upset you."

He tried in vain to make eye contact with the man. Zahn shook his head, looking away, looking at the floor.

"No more. No more," he said, his breathing picking up one beat and then another. "You have to stop. Stop now, Vince."

"I'm sorry if I upset you, Zander," he said. "I just want you to know that I know your story now. I understand why you had to kill her. I don't judge you."

That was it. In that instant Zahn went over the tipping point.

Vince watched as his eyes changed, his face changed. He seemed to suddenly get bigger, stronger, and dangerous. The rage erupted from him in a huge, hot explosion of emotion so big it seemed impossible that it had been contained within him.

Screaming, he lunged at Vince like a wild animal.

45

"NO MORE!! NO MORE!! NO MORE!!"

The first blow caught Vince hard on the cheekbone. The second one hit his collarbone. He had to shove Zahn backward to ward off another. He kept his arms pushed out in front of him, hands spread wide, establishing space between them.

"No problem, Zander," he said. "No problem. I'll go, but you have to calm down first. I'm not leaving until you calm down."

Stuck in his rage, Zahn wasn't listening to him, and just kept shouting, his face red, the cords in his neck standing out. He now held his arms stiff and straight down at his sides, his hands balled into white-knuckled fists. It was as if his whole body were in a state of spasm, jerking and trembling.

"Zander! Zander!" Vince shouted, trying to break through the grasp of Zahn's inner demon.

He grabbed Zahn by the upper arms and tried to hold him still, surprised at the strength in the man's slight frame.

"NO MORE!! NO MORE!! NO MORE!!"

"Zander! Stop it! Listen to me! Listen to me!"

Vince gave him a hard shake. Zahn looked at him then with shock, as if seeing him for the first time.

"Calm down," Vince said quietly, his own heart beating like a trip hammer. "Calm down. You're all right. It's all right. Just take a deep breath."

He felt the tension drain out of Zahn from the top down until he all but went limp.

"You're all right, Zander. Let's just have a seat. You're fine."

He steered Zahn to the bench and continued holding on to him until he was seated. He looked stunned, like he had just awakened from a nightmare.

"I'm very tired now," Zahn said in a small, weak voice. "I have to rest now. I'm very tired. I don't know why. Why am I so tired, Vince?"

"It's okay, Zander," Vince said. "You should rest. It's been a rough time for you."

"I'm sorry you have to go now, Vince," he murmured. "I'm very tired." He looked at his watch. "Rudy will be coming soon."

Thank God, Vince thought. He didn't want to leave Zahn alone now. He seemed exhausted and confused almost in the way of someone who had had a violent grand mal seizure.

"I'm just going to sit right outside, Zander, until Rudy gets here."

"Rudy is bringing my groceries," Zahn mumbled. "I can't go shopping. I can't do that. I find that very upsetting to go shopping. Rudy does that for me."

"That's good," Vince said. "You should lie down now, Zander."

"Yes, I'll lie down, thank you. Thank you very much, Vince," Zahn murmured.

He lay down right there on the bench, curling into a ball and going instantly to sleep.

Vince went out onto the front step and sat down. For the first time in ten years he wished he had a cigarette. Zahn's meltdown had been much bigger than he ever would have anticipated. It bothered him to think he had pushed too hard. His instincts were usually better than that.

He cursed the bullet in his brain for knocking his timing off. A little frontal lobe damage. He wasn't as patient as he used to be.

Then again—to cut himself a break—he had never encountered anyone quite like Zander Zahn before. It was difficult to know how far to go with a mind as intricately complex and closed to the understanding of "normal" people as Zahn's. It was one thing to goad a psychopath into an outburst, and something quite different to do the same thing to a fragile individual like Zander Zahn.

At the same time, seeing Zahn lose it was valuable information. Could Marissa Fordham have done something to trigger that kind of mental break in him? Could she have lost her patience with him, made a remark that cut him in the same way his mother might have done years ago?

Now that he had seen Zahn in a full-on rage, it wasn't as difficult to picture. He could have snapped, gone into a dissociative state, gone after Marissa with the knife. He may not have been consciously aware of any of it.

Despite the many times Vince had seen that used as a defense in a murder trial, a true dissociative state was a rare, rare thing to have happen—but it did happen.

He pieced that scenario together, frame by frame in his mind: the horrific murder, Zahn walking home afterward, still in a daze. At some point he would have become aware of this blood-soaked clothing—which would have been a trauma in itself for Zahn. He may or may not have realized how that had happened. He would have disposed of the clothes and scrubbed himself clean.

Zahn's mind may never have allowed him to associate the bloody clothing with what had happened to Marissa and Haley. The human brain has amazing ways of protecting its owner. Zahn's had no doubt compartmentalized many of the traumas of his life, closed the doors on those compartments, and locked them.

"Detective Leone? What are you doing here?"

Vince looked up to see Rudy Nasser at the gate. He had already punched in the gate code, and the gate was rolling back, revealing him standing there with two bags of groceries from Ralph's.

"I came by to check on Dr. Zahn," Vince said as Nasser came up the narrow path that cut through Zahn's mind-boggling array of junk.

"Is he all right?"

"He's resting now. Have you ever seen Dr. Zahn lose his temper?"

Nasser frowned. "Not until the other day when he knocked me down. He's ordinarily very mild-mannered. Meek, really. Why? Did something happen?"

"He's fine," Vince lied. "I was just wondering, that's all. Have you seen him since that happened?"

"Yes, why?" Nasser asked, his dark eyes looking more suspicious by the second.

"Did you talk about what happened?"

"No. I was out of line. I upset him, he reacted. It's water under the bridge."

"He didn't mention it? Didn't say anything? Didn't apologize?"

"No," Nasser said. "Why are you asking me these things? You can't possibly still be thinking Dr. Zahn had something to do with Marissa Fordham's murder."

Vince worked up a placid smile. "I just like to understand how people work, Rudy. I want to know what makes them tick. Details fill the picture in.

"I'm sure you want to get inside," he said, nodding at the grocery bags. "Your ice cream is going to melt."

Still suspicious, Nasser went to the door just the same and let himself in with a key. He turned back before he went inside.

"Should Dr. Zahn have an attorney?"

"Not on my account," Vince said.

When Nasser had gone inside, Vince walked down into the yard and wandered through the maze of collections, just taking it all in. The privacy wall ran around the entire property, but a gate led out the side yard. The path going to it was well worn. This was probably the way Zahn had gone every morning to Marissa's house.

Vince let himself out and followed the trail up a hill where it connected to a fire road. Fire roads were cut all through the California hills as access for firefighting equipment when brush fires ran rampant in the summer and fall. He followed the road up to the crest of a bigger hill.

The country that rolled out below him was gorgeous: the golden hills rising and falling as far as the eye could see, liberally dotted with the dark green canopies of oak trees. He had lived in Virginia for many years, where the fields were lush and green and tough to beat for the title of beautiful, but this landscape had its own appeal.

To the south he could see Marissa Fordham's place, looking like an Andrew Wyeth painting—white and gray against the wheat color of the land surrounding it. A hundred yards to the west he could see what must have been a ranch at some time prior to wreck and ruin. The place looked like it had burned. Only charred matchsticks were standing here and there where buildings had once been. A desolate, lonely place.

After a while he turned and went back down the hill to Zahn's, where he locked the side gate, then manually tripped the entrance gate and let himself out.

Drained to the bone, he got in his car and drove back to town, never knowing that he had been just out of shouting distance of Gina Kemmer.

46

The scream that tore up out of Gina was primal. The rat was unimpressed. It moved toward her, fearless, nose twitching, eyes beady and intent.

"Ohmygod, ohmygod, ohmygod, ohmygod!"

With her right hand, Gina groped for something, anything, grabbing hold of a milk carton. She flung it at the rat, missing it, but getting her point across.

The rat scurried away and disappeared down into the layers of garbage.

Who knew how many years people had been throwing trash down this hole? Who knew what was living in it? Bugs. Worms. Mice. Rats. In Southern California, where there were rats and mice, there were snakes—rattlesnakes.

The idea that snakes might be slithering beneath her body nearly made her vomit again. Her fear was like a fist in her throat. What was she going to do?

With every shallow breath pain burned through her shoulder where she had been shot. Every time she tried to move she could feel her right foot and the lower part of her ankle pull away from the end of her shinbone. The pain was excruciating.

Panic overwhelmed her for a few moments, but quickly wore her out. She lay still on the stinking garbage, trying to think.

She had never been a brave person. She had never had a sense of adventure. She had never had the nerve to live life on the edge of disaster. Marissa had been the owner of those qualities, but Marissa was dead. Marissa couldn't coax her through this, goad her into action, dare her to go beyond her limits. Yet that was what she needed if she wanted to have any hope of living through this.

The first thing she needed to do was sit up so she could better view her surroundings.

On the count of three . . .

With her right hand behind her head, she blew out a breath and tried a sit-up.

It felt like someone was trying to ram a hot iron rod through her left shoulder. Gina cried out, fell back the few inches she had managed to raise her shoulders. This was what she got for ignoring her gym membership.

Do it again. On the count of three . . .

Like a weightlifter straining to push the barbell over his head, she shouted as she fought for it. Her head was pounding with the physical struggle, her blood pressure spiking.

Fight for it! Fight for it!

The voice urging her on was Marissa's.

Gina screamed out. Colors exploded behind her eyelids, squeezed shut against the strain. And then she was sitting up—dizzy, sweating, nauseous, weak, but she was sitting. She pulled up her good left leg, wrapped her good arm around it and pressed her cheek against her knee. She was shaking from the effort.

Damn you, Marissa. This is all your fault.

You went along with it, G.

No one was supposed to get hurt.

It didn't matter now.

Gina took another look around her prison. She had never been in a well before. She was a city girl. She wouldn't have even known what a well was if not for television and the movies.

There were serious cracks in the walls, and places where the concrete had fallen away completely. To her right was a series of iron rungs leading up to the top. It would have been an easy way out if she had two arms and two legs. To climb that high in the state she was in . . . How could she? She had almost passed out just trying to sit up.

For now, all she wanted to do was get her back against the wall behind her so she could rest. This would involve pushing off with her good leg and scooting backward on her butt. An easy mission on the face of it, but the reality was she was on a heap of garbage, not a solid floor. Could she get enough leverage to push? And when she pushed she would then drag the right leg with its hideously broken ankle, and the pain would be blinding.

Stop whining, Gina. Just do it.

Shut up, Marissa.

She couldn't have said how long it took her to work up the strength and the nerve to try. She looked around for something to help her effort, something to use like a crutch or a lever.

Discarded lumber was strewn amid the garbage, odd scrap pieces from someone's home project. Within reach were several short stubs, butt ends of two-by-fours. Not helpful. To her left and away from her was a longer piece—narrower, thinner, but about three feet long.

She couldn't reach it with her right hand. She might have reached it with her left, but her left arm hung limp. Gina flexed the fingers of her left hand, but she couldn't lift the arm.

Slowly she stretched her leg back down and tried to get the toe of her shoe under the piece of wood and move it closer, but managed only to push it farther out of reach.

Exhausted, she brought her knee back up and rested her head.

She had no idea how long she had been in this hole. She hadn't worn a watch. It might have been hours. It might have been days. She hadn't eaten since hearing the news of Marissa's murder. She hadn't been able to keep anything down. She hadn't had anything to drink since just after the detectives had left her house—after the older one had put that photograph in her hand.

The smell of the place kept her stomach turning over and over, but thirst was parching her throat. She looked at the garbage around her. Beer cans. Lots of them—most of them crushed. Soda cans. Empty liquor bottles. She was in the dumping ground of a party spot. Teenagers probably came out on the fire road for a secluded place to drink and smoke dope and do whatever teenagers did now.

Gina remembered a place like that when she and Marissa had been in school—a place out in the hills above Malibu. Her memory drifted back to an illegal campfire, cheap beer, and Boone's Farm wine; "Smoke on the Water" and "Horse With No Name."

They had thrown all their garbage into a cave. It had never occurred to her to imagine there might be somebody trapped in that cave, dying while they partied.

She picked up a half-crushed Pepsi can. The opening was crawling with ants. She shook the can and listened to maybe half an inch of liquid slosh in the bottom. Dreading the idea, she tried to scrape the ants away then closed her eyes and held her nose and raised the can to her lips.

It tasted terrible, but wet. She took one sip, then a second, then spat it out when a cigarette butt slipped between her lips and touched her tongue.

Gina let herself cry for few minutes. She was so tired. She hurt so bad. She knew no one would come here looking for her.

As her gaze settled on what looked like a pile of bloody clothing across from her, she had no way of knowing that above this hellhole and a hundred yards away stood Vince Leone.

47

Anne got out of her car in the parking lot of the mental health facility and took a deep breath—both to enjoy the fresh air and to clear her head before going in to deal with Dennis.

Clouds were gathering, gray and swollen and promising rain. She had always welcomed this time of year when the rains came. After months of baking heat and relentless sun, it was nice to curl up at home with a blanket and a good book and listen to the rain come down.

That sounded like a good plan for the evening. Vince had come home to rest and watch Haley for her while she came to see Dennis. Maybe she would get lucky and have her husband home for the evening, and the three of them could snuggle up on the couch and they could read a book to Haley, or watch a video.

She tried to check herself at the thought. They hadn't had Haley in their home for a day yet, and she was already getting too comfortable with the idea of her being there. *Not smart, Anne.*

She was in Haley Fordham's life for a specific reason. She needed to remember that. At the end of this investigation into Marissa Fordham's death, Haley would go elsewhere, hopefully to a relative who would take her in and love her. Although, from what Anne had gathered, Marissa Fordham had been estranged from her family. So far, no one had even been able to find out where they were.

If no relatives could be located, Milo Bordain would try to get custody. It wasn't that Anne had no sympathy for the woman. If Marissa had been like a daughter to Bordain, then Haley was like a granddaughter. Milo Bordain probably loved the little girl in whatever way she was capable of loving her, but that didn't necessarily make her a good candidate to raise a small child.

Bordain was in her fifties, very staid and proper. Anne didn't have to visit the woman's home to know there would be a long list of rules and things not to be touched by a four-year-old. She could imagine little Haley dressed up in Burberry and Hermès, accessorized like a fashion doll.

Haley had grown up in the home of an artist, an environment full of inspiration and imagination, and probably few boundaries. In going through the clothes Vince had picked up for her, Anne found tie-dyed T-shirts and a pink tutu, a tiny denim jacket hand-painted with baby jungle animals and a fairy costume complete with wings.

Anne set the subject to a back burner as she went into the hospital and signed in at the desk, exchanging pleasantries with the staff. She had to focus now on Dennis Farman.

He was jumping around the room practicing karate moves when Anne walked in. He glanced at her out of the corner of his eye, but pretended not to know she was there, continuing to leap and shout and kick and chop.

Anne took her seat at the table and set her tote bag and purse on the floor.

"That's pretty impressive Dennis," she said. "Did you take lessons?"

"I'm a black belt," he said, crouching and chopping with his arms as he moved around the table.

That was almost certainly a lie, Anne thought, though she had to admit she knew nothing about martial arts. On the other hand, she supposed if Frank Farman had thought to sign his son up for something it would be something macho like karate. The violent aspect would have appealed to him.

"Good for you," she said. "But that's enough for today. Have a seat."

"I don't have to," he said belligerently.

"You do if you want me to stay," Anne said calmly. "If you're just going to goof off and be obnoxious to me, I'll leave."

He jumped up in the air, shouted, and kicked out with one foot. Anne pushed her chair back from the table, gathered her things, and stood up.

"See ya," she said, turning for the door.

Dennis's angry expression fell away. He didn't ask her not to go, but he sat down at the table.

Anne waited for a moment, letting him think she was still considering

SECRETS TO THE GRAVE 219

walking out. He had to realize there were consequences to his behavior—consequences that didn't involve him getting a beating. He needed to learn to take the feelings of others into consideration when he acted out.

He was pouting now as she returned to her seat, staring down with his nose inches from the tabletop.

"I'm sorry I couldn't come yesterday, Dennis," Anne said. "I was tied up in an important meeting."

"More important than me," Dennis said.

She didn't take the bait. "Meetings have to happen when they have to happen. Judges have very busy schedules."

At the mention of a judge, he looked up at her. "Was it about me?"

"No."

"Then why the fuck should I care?"

"No reason," she said, ignoring his language. "What did you do yesterday?"

"Nothing. There's nothing to do here but watch the crazy people. That one weird guy with the dreadlocks pulled his pants down and shit on the floor in the activities room," he said, laughing. "That was pretty funny!"

Oh my God, I have to get him out of here, she thought. She would look into group homes herself. There had to be one somewhere that would be appropriate for him.

"Did you do your reading assignment?" she asked.

"No."

"Why not?"

"You didn't come."

"You should have read it Tuesday. You didn't know I wouldn't come yesterday."

"But you didn't," he argued. "How was I to know if you'd ever come back again? You could have been dead for all I knew. You could have been murdered and stabbed a hundred times and your head cut off."

"I could have flown to the moon," Anne said. "But that wasn't likely. And it wasn't likely that I had been murdered either. That's no excuse not to do your homework, anyway."

"Dr. Crane tried to murder you," he pointed out. "Why wouldn't somebody else?"

"Let's talk about you," Anne said pointedly. "I know you had a session with Dr. Falk yesterday. How did that go?"

"Somebody killed that other lady," Dennis said. His small eyes gleamed with excitement. "They stabbed her a million times and cut her head off."

"How do you know about that?"

"I know stuff," he said evasively.

"Did you see it on television?"

"No." She could see him contemplating whether or not to tell her the truth. Finally he said, "I read it in the newspaper."

"Really?" Anne said, brows lifting in surprise. At least he was reading something. She would have preferred the subject matter wasn't murder, but she wasn't going to be choosy at this point. "I'm impressed. Do you enjoy reading the newspaper?"

"No," he said, frowning, knowing he had gotten himself caught in something now. "Just about murders and rapes and stuff like that."

"Reading is reading," Anne said, determined not to react to his supposed interest in the macabre. He only said those things to rattle her. She hoped. "So you can write me a report about this murder. I want to see two pages tomorrow."

His jaw dropped. "The fuck!"

"Yeah, life's a bitch, isn't it?" she said. "I'm a teacher. I can take anything and turn it into an assignment. I want you to write two pages about the murder. And no copying from the newspaper. I read it too."

"That sucks!"

Anne shrugged. "You've got nothing better to do. You said so yourself."

He hated it when she turned his own words around on him. The rims of his ears turned red and his freckles stood out like polka dots on his cheeks. He made two fists and hit the tabletop in frustration.

"I'll bring you something special tomorrow," she promised.

"Like what?"

"I'm not telling," Anne said, thinking she would make a trip to the bookstore on the Plaza downtown and see if they had something Dennis might channel his reading interest toward. Some comic books, maybe. Superheroes fighting crime instead of committing crime. "But you have to have your pages written. Deal?"

He looked suspicious. "No. What if what you bring me is something stupid like sugar-free gum or some stupid toy or something?"

"What if it isn't something stupid?" Anne challenged. "What if it's something you'll really like?"

"Like what?"

"I'm not telling."

Behind the frustration Anne thought she could see a little glimmer of excitement. Dennis had had a rotten childhood. She was willing to bet neither of his parents had ever surprised him with any kind of gift. Half the time he had come to school in dirty clothes. Not even his basic needs had been taken care of adequately.

Maybe she could show him the world could be a better place for him—not just for the Wendy Morgans or Tommy Cranes of the world. If she could show him that people could take an interest in him and care about what happened to him, maybe he could turn around. It certainly wasn't going to hurt to show him a little kindness.

Or so she hoped . . .

48

Vince smiled as he watched Haley watching Big Bird on *Sesame Street*. The joy and keen interest in her eyes, the unselfconscious quality of her spontaneous dancing along with the character, her singing—decidedly off-key—all spoke of pure innocence and a wonder at the world around her.

He had missed this with his girls. Working long hours and traveling for the Bureau had carved him out a legendary career, but he had missed this. He would be a lucky man to get a second shot at being a father.

Not that he had written himself out of the lives of his daughters. Since his shooting they all had made an effort to stay in touch and to strengthen their relationships.

Anne had accompanied him to Virginia the past winter to meet the girls. Vince had been more than a little nervous about that. Anne was slightly closer to their ages than to his. He worried they would think he had gone off some midlife crisis deep end, taking up with a younger woman, moving to California, leaving the Bureau.

And they had at first. Amy, just sixteen, who had fewer memories of the tensions between her parents when they had been together, harbored more resentment toward him than had Emily, two years older. They still had things to work on, all three of them, but both girls had flown out for the wedding. He felt that was a good start to acceptance of his new life.

He stretched out in his big leather recliner—the Man Chair, Anne called it—in their cozy family room with its warm tan walls and cream-colored carpet. He was exhausted and still disturbed from his encounter with Zander Zahn. All that and he was going to have a nasty bruise on his cheekbone too.

Popped by a professor. The boys in the cop shop would have fun with that. Not that Zahn's meltdown was anything to joke about.

Sighing, he closed his eyes for a few minutes in an attempt to relax his brain.

He had a lot of thoughts and theories turning over up there, and it had physically been a long day. But miraculously the pain in his head receded as he rested and used some of the breathing techniques he had learned from a chronic pain specialist. It rarely completely left him, but rather lurked in there somewhere at its lowest level, keeping him aware it could come out and nail him whenever it wanted to.

Gradually Vince came up out of the restful place his mind had been, and he became aware of the sense of being watched. When he opened his eyes he was looking into Haley's. She stood beside the chair with her rabbit tucked under her arm.

"Hey," Vince said.

"You were sleeping," Haley said in her hoarse little voice.

He wondered if she would ever be rid of that reminder of being choked. At least the bruising on the exterior of her throat would eventually fade away, if not the memory.

"Do you have to take naps?" she asked.

"I like to take naps."

"I don't."

"No? Why not?"

Her expression was very sober as she shook her head. "Babies take naps."

"I'm not a baby," Vince pointed out.

"No." Her little mouth twisted up on one side in a funny smile. "You're the daddy. Why don't you have any kids?"

"Well, because Anne and I just got married. We haven't had time to have kids yet."

She thought about that, deciding it must be a reasonable explanation. "Where's Anne?"

"She had to go have a meeting with someone. She'll be back in a little while."

"I like Anne. She plays with me," she said, as if she and Anne were longtime friends.

She seemed to have no reticence with strangers. But then her mother had been a very social person with a lot of friends who had come into Haley's life on a regular basis. She had probably never had a reason to fear adults—until now. Vince wondered if that would change for her once the memories of what had happened came back to her. Probably.

"Will you play with me?" she asked.

"Sure," Vince said. "What are we playing?"

"We're playing you're the daddy and I'm the little girl."

"Okay. What do I have to do?"

"Read me and Honey-Bunny a story."

"All right. You go pick out a book."

She went to a basket full of toys and books Franny had brought over on loan and pulled one out, then came back and scrambled up in the chair with him, settling herself comfortably into the crook of his arm.

"Do you like to read stories?" Vince asked.

"I can't read," she told him. "I'm just little."

"Does your real daddy read you stories?" He winced a little at the mental image of Anne kicking him in the shins for that.

Haley paid no attention to him as she opened the cover of the storybook.

"What about Zander?" he asked. "Does Zander ever read you stories?"

"Zander is weird," she said without looking up.

"Weird how?"

She shrugged. "Just weird. He doesn't like to touch anything. Isn't that funny? Mommy says he's fraggle."

"What does fraggle mean?"

"I don't know. Why does your shirt have a horse on it?" she asked, scratching at the purple Ralph Lauren logo on the black polo shirt.

"That's a symbol for the company that made it," he said. *Fraggle?* What the heck was fraggle?

"I like horses," Haley said. "I'm gonna get a pony when I'm five." She held up her small hand, fingers splayed wide to show him she knew how much five was.

Fraggle? Fragile?

"Did your mommy say fragile?"

Haley nodded. "Fraggle. What does that mean?"

"When someone is fragile it's easy to upset them or hurt their feelings."

Haley had already lost interest in the subject and was turning the pages of the book.

"Does Zander ever scare you, honey?" Vince asked.

She frowned but didn't answer. "Do you know Zander?"

"Yes, I do."

"Isn't he weird?"

"Yeah, I'd have to say so," Vince admitted.

"Read the story!" Haley said impatiently.

"Does your mommy read you stories?"

"Sometimes. Sometimes she makes up stories. She makes me books sometimes and paints the pictures in them."

"That's very special," Vince said. "Are you missing your mommy?"

A faraway look came into her eyes and she said nothing for a moment. Finally, she said quietly, "My mommy fell down and got hurt."

"I know," Vince said softly. Anne was going to kill him. "Were you there when your mommy got hurt, sweetheart?"

Tears welled up. Vince held his breath.

"You're not playing right!" Haley insisted, lower lip quivering. "You're the daddy! You have to read the story!"

"Okay. All right, honey. Don't cry."

He could only imagine the consequences if Anne came home and Haley told her he had made her cry.

She settled in against him as Vince turned to the first page of the book, her body tense at first, as if she were still trying to ward off the bad feelings he had stirred up with his questions. But as he began to read the story about a princess who wanted to be a fairy, he felt her let go. Before he had read three pages she was asleep, dreaming of a place where bad things couldn't happen, he hoped.

49

"There's no sign of Gina Kemmer, no sign of her car," Hicks said. "One neighbor said she saw her leave her house sometime between five and six o'clock last night. She was alone. She didn't have a suitcase. Everything looked normal."

Back in the war room for the end of the day, someone had ordered pizza and sodas. Chicago-style pizza. That meant Vince had put the call in. Mendez was glad. He was starving. He couldn't remember the last meal he'd had—or decent night's sleep for that matter.

They sat on all sides of the long table eating like they would never see food again. The room was filled with the aroma of herbs and tomato sauce—almost, but not quite drowning out the smell of frustration.

"If she left town of her own accord, she did it without taking so much as a change of clothes or a makeup bag," he said. "What woman does that?"

"None," Dixon said. "If she was snatched from the supermarket parking lot, her car would still be there. If she went to stay with a friend, her car would be parked on the street or in a driveway."

"She could have gone off the road into a canyon," Hamilton suggested. "Or just plain got out of town. Maybe she has a friend in Santa Barbara or someplace else."

"Or somebody has her," Trammell said.

"Or she's dead," Mendez said. "To me this strengthens the blackmail angle."

"Even if there was no blackmail," Hicks said, "Gina probably knows something someone doesn't want her to."

"What do her bank records look like?" Dixon asked, swiping a napkin across his chin to catch a dribble of tomato sauce.

"She has her accounts at Wells Fargo, same as Marissa Fordham," Hamilton said. "The only odd thing is every month she deposits a check for a grand from Marissa Fordham."

"Payoff?" Dixon said. "Or was Marissa just a generous friend sharing her good fortune?"

"A payoff could give Kemmer a motive," Campbell said. "If the generous friend tried to cut her off."

Mendez shook his head. "You had to see this girl yesterday. She was a nervous wreck. She'd never have the *cojones* to stab anyone, let alone do what was done to her best friend. And then put those breasts in a box and send them to Milo Bordain? She couldn't even look at a crime-scene photo without puking."

"Do we have her phone records?" Dixon asked.

Hamilton shook his head. "Not yet."

"What have we found out about Marissa Fordham's alias?" Mendez asked.

"Melissa Fabriano?" Hamilton shook his head as he consulted his notes. "Nothing. No criminal record in the state of California. I went back to the authorities in Rhode Island—on the off chance she really was from there. They didn't have anything on that name."

"So the vic had no criminal record on either of her names," Trammell said.

"Not that I've found so far."

"Why would a person with no criminal record need an alias?"

"She had to be hiding from somebody," Mendez said. "If not the baby's father, who?"

Nobody had an answer for that.

"Damn, this job's a lot harder than it looks," Campbell complained, breaking the tension with a laugh.

"What about Gina Kemmer?" Trammell asked. "Is that her real name? Does she have a record somewhere? If the two of them go back some years, maybe that's how we find out about our vic."

"I'll see what I can find out," Hamilton said. He looked to Dixon. "When are we going to get computers?"

"When they become necessary and free," Dixon said. "There's nothing wrong with your ear and your finger. Use the damn phone."

"Speaking of phones," Vince said. "Any hot tips on the reward line?"

"Oh, yeah," Campbell said. "There are at least five women in the county who believe the killer was their ex-husband, ex-boyfriend, ex-married lover."

"A psychic called to say she would find Marissa's killer for us if we would only pay her the reward up front," Trammell said.

"If she was really psychic, she would have known better than to call," Dixon said.

"It's a big waste of time, but Mrs. Bordain got one of her civic groups to man the phones," Hamilton said. "It's not costing us anything in man hours—unless we get a lead that's worth chasing down."

"Anything from any of Ms. Fordham's gentlemen friends?" Dixon asked.

"Most of them had alibis for the night of the murder," Campbell said.

"Who doesn't?"

"Mark Foster was home alone. Bob Copetti was out of town—we haven't corroborated that yet."

"Steve Morgan was allegedly out of town," Mendez said. "Has anyone followed up on that?"

No one had.

"What about Darren Bordain?" Vince asked. "He knew the victim and Gina Kemmer."

"What's his motive supposed to be?" Dixon asked.

Vince shrugged. "Maybe he's Haley's father. Or maybe he resented Marissa for her relationship with his mother."

Dixon tried to dismiss the idea. "Darren Bordain is the golden child of that family. He's had everything he ever wanted handed to him—an education, a career. He's being groomed for the political arena."

"I doubt any of that comes without strings attached," Vince said. He looked to Hicks and Mendez. "You said he made some wisecrack about he should have had a fling with Marissa."

"Yeah," Mendez said. "He was on the sarcastic side when he talked about his mother, but . . ."

"But what?" Vince asked. "He's too smooth? Too good-looking? Too privileged?"

Mendez thought about it carefully. He did know better than to be fooled by appearances. "No. That's just a big leap from resenting your mother to cutting a woman's breasts off and sending them to Mom in the mail. I just didn't get that vibe from him."

"There's a reason vibes aren't admissible in court," Vince said. "He should get a good look like every other guy who knew the victim. Don't you think so, Cal?"

Dixon raked a hand back through his silver hair and sighed, no doubt weighing the cons of having Milo Bordain coming down on his head.

"Bring him in for a conversation," he said. "But don't make a big deal about it. Very low-key. Tell him we're trying to build a more extensive picture of Marissa's life and a timeline leading up to her death. We want to know who saw her when, who spoke to her, who has a solid alibi so we can eliminate those people from the suspect list."

"That's not a bad idea anyway," Mendez said. "Let's follow all the way through on that. We've got Steve Morgan in jail already. Let's bring him over."

Dixon gave him the eagle eye. "We do *not* have Steve Morgan in jail."

"He assaulted me!" Mendez said, pointing to his fat stitched lip.

"You broke his nose and damn near fractured his eye socket. He wanted to file harassment and assault charges. I talked him out of it."

"You talked a lawyer out of filing charges?" Trammell said. "You're the man, boss."

"He admitted to hitting you first," Dixon said to Mendez.

"So he's a cheat but not always a liar," Mendez said. "Good to know he has something going for him. We should still bring him in to talk."

Dixon stuck a finger at him. "You will have absolutely nothing to do with it. Do you understand me?"

"Yes, sir."

"I mean it."

"Yes, sir. I know, sir."

"Stay away from his house. Stay away from his family."

"Yes, sir."

"I paid a visit to Zander Zahn this afternoon," Vince said, taking the spotlight off Mendez.

Mendez thanked him mentally. He had been waiting to hear Dixon say "stay away from his wife," sure he would have looked guilty, despite the fact that he had not crossed a line with Sara Morgan. A part of him had certainly wanted to.

"He wasn't happy that I knew about his mother's death," Vince went on. "I pressed him a little. He flipped out on me. Total meltdown."

He proceeded to tell the story, complete with an explanation of a dissociative state, and how Zahn could have killed Marissa Fordham and have no conscious memory of it.

"That sounds like something a defense attorney would come up with," Trammell said.

"They'll certainly latch on to it if they can," Vince said. "But true dissociation is rare. It's a mind's way of reacting to overwhelming psychological trauma."

"Like having stabbed your own mother to death," Hamilton said.

"More like a reaction to whatever his mother did to him to precipitate the murder. Say she burned the soles of his feet with a cigarette. His mind goes into a dissociative state to escape the abuse. While he's in the dissociative state, he kills her. When he comes out of it, he may not remember a thing."

"The mind is trying to protect itself by repressing the memories," Mendez said.

"Right."

"So he could have been capable of killing Marissa Fordham," Dixon said.

"Based on what we know now and what I saw this afternoon, yes."

"It looked like a crazy person did it because a crazy person did do it," Campbell said.

"I asked Haley if she was ever afraid of Zahn," Vince said.

"She's talking?" Dixon asked.

"When she feels like it. But she ignores questions that might take her back to what happened. Either consciously or subconsciously she doesn't want to get near those feelings."

"What did she say about Zahn?" Mendez asked.

One corner of Vince's mouth quirked upward. "That he's weird."

"Sharp kid," Mendez said, laughing. "But why would Zahn ransack the house? He can't be Haley's father. You have to actually touch a woman to get her pregnant."

"How would you know?" Campbell asked.

"Shut up."

"And why would he send the breasts to Milo Bordain?" Hicks asked. "That box was postmarked Monday. The murder took place Sunday night. He would have been out of that dissociative state by Monday, wouldn't he?"

"Not necessarily," Vince said. "I admit the breasts in the box don't seem to fit, but they don't seem to fit any scenario we've had so far other than Darren Bordain."

"Maybe that's exactly *why* they were sent," Dixon suggested. "Because it doesn't make any sense. While we're running around in little circles trying to connect that dot, someone is getting away with murder."

50

Two bad things came at once: darkness and rain.

Gina had finally managed to get her back up against the wall, passing out from the pain and the effort at the end of the process. The rain hitting her face brought her back to reality.

There is no soft autumn rain in Southern California. The rain comes with a vengeance, an angry payback from Mother Nature for months of cloudless skies. The rickety doors far above Gina's head were meager protection from the storm.

She needed something to cover herself to keep from getting soaked. The temperature had dropped. She was cold and, she supposed, in shock—although she didn't exactly know what that meant. Biology had never been her strong suit.

What she did know was that she was sitting in the midst of a garbage heap with garbage bags all around her. Most of them had been torn by the rats that were now beginning to emerge from below and from holes in the walls. Too dark to see now, Gina could hear the rustling, the intermittent squeaks. Her skin was crawling and fear was like a writhing thing in her throat and stomach.

Fighting tears, she felt around on her right side and got hold of a plastic bag with her good hand. It was only partially full of garbage, but stinking enough to make her gag, and it seemed to take forever to work one of the tears open enough to empty it.

She screamed as mice fell from it with the trash. It seemed like dozens of them raining down, screeching, and running, scrambling over her body, her arms, her legs, her chest.

Hysterical, she dropped the bag and swatted at them with her good hand, sure they were going inside her clothes and tangling in her hair. Her body jerked and twisted, setting off explosions of pain. The sounds of rodents squealing and scurrying seemed amplified in the confined space of the well, echoing up the shaft and filling her ears, filling her head.

Oh my God. What did I ever do to deserve this?

Shut up, Gina. Stop feeling sorry for yourself. You're not dead.

Marissa's voice.

I'm going crazy, she thought, whimpering.

No, you aren't. Get the bag and cover yourself or you'll die from hypothermia.

I'll cry if I want to.

Crying will only make you look bad.

Gina felt around and grabbed the empty bag. Holding her breath against the stench, she put the thing over her head and did her best to arrange it around her shoulders.

She tipped her head back and opened her mouth, catching the rain-drops, the first clean drink she had had in more than twenty-four hours.

Had anybody missed her yet? Had the girls at the boutique tried to call her? When they only got her machine again and again, had they gone to her house in search of her? They wouldn't have found anything wrong. No one had broken into her home. Her car was gone. She had left of her own accord.

How had her life come to this? She wasn't a bad person. She and Marissa had only set out to do a good thing. Maybe Marissa's method had been questionable, but she had her reasons. And her only motive had been Haley. That they had both benefitted had been incidental to that goal—to provide for Haley.

How could such a noble motive come to such a bad end?

How did she know if any of this was real at all? Gina wondered. Maybe she really was losing her mind. Could she be hallucinating? How would she know the difference?

I don't know what to do, M.

You're going to get yourself out of here, G.

Don't leave me.

I won't.

I'm not as brave as you.

You'll be as brave as you need to be.

51

She had been watching television the night it happened. Not for entertainment, but for the live news coverage of a hostage standoff at the sheriff's office. Dennis Farman's father had a gun to the head of Cal Dixon. Vince was trying to talk him down. The situation that had begun with violence had ended in violence.

At the time that news had come, Anne had no way of knowing if Vince had survived. She had busied herself opening a small gift Tommy Crane had given to her earlier that night—a necklace. A necklace that could only have come from a murder victim.

And then Peter Crane was there, at her home, seeming fine, polite, apologetic. So sorry. A misunderstanding. He needed that necklace back. There had been a mistake. It belonged to his wife.

Anne had told him that was no problem. She understood completely. She just had to go into the kitchen to get it—a lie—thinking she would go straight out the back door and run for her life.

She never made it to the door. Peter Crane had her by the hair—

Gasping for air, her heart pounding out of her chest, Anne sat bolt upright in bed. For a moment she didn't know where she was and panic grabbed her by the throat. She was soaking wet with sweat.

There was a light on in the far corner of the room. Just a soft amber glow to chase away the dark and the bogeymen that came with it.

She was in her own home. She was safe. This was the guest room she had chosen for Haley. She was safe. Haley was safe, sound asleep.

You're safe. We're safe. Everything is fine. She repeated those words again and again and again in her mind.

What she wanted was to have her husband's arms around her, so strong, so warm, and to have his voice whispering those words to her as he held her and rocked her. But Vince had gone back to the sheriff's office for a meeting with the detectives. She hadn't even gotten to feed him. He had ordered pizza for the guys.

She looked at the clock on the nightstand. It wasn't quite ten thirty. Not late. Vince would be home soon—if he wasn't already. He never disturbed her if she was already sleeping when he came home—specifically so as not to frighten her.

Even though Vince hadn't been there, Anne and Haley had the cozy evening she had thought of earlier in the day. After bath time, with Haley in her Rainbow Brite pajamas, they had snuggled together under the covers of Haley's bed and listened to the rain while Anne read to her.

After Haley was asleep, Anne had done some reading of her own, searching her psychology books for anything she could find on children as witnesses to violent crime—she found nothing—and children and traumatic memories—she found practically nothing. She had finally turned out her reading light and fallen asleep with the books spread around her on her side of the double bed.

She got up now, plucking at her sweat-damp T-shirt. The rush of adrenaline had ebbed, leaving her with the familiar and hated feeling of weakness. Leaving the bedroom door open, she went across the hall to change.

Vince was on their bed in gray sweatpants and a black T-shirt, propped up reading. He looked up from his book, his glasses perched on his nose. The television was mumbling to itself in the armoire that housed it.

Anne went into her closet and put on a fresh FBI T-shirt, then went to the bed and crawled up beside him, tucking her head into his shoulder and wrapping an arm across his broad chest.

"Hey, precious," he whispered, kissing the top of her head.

He set his book aside and wrapped his arms around her. Anne knew he could feel the residual tremors going through her as the adrenaline ebbed out of her system.

"Did you have a bad dream?" he asked quietly.

Anne nodded. "I'm okay. I'm okay now."

"I'm sorry, sweetheart."

Tears stung her eyes. "I hate it."

"I know, baby."

"It never goes away."

He didn't tell her that it would eventually, because he knew it wouldn't, and she knew it wouldn't. The best she could hope for was that the incidents would lessen over time. She wanted to wish her nightmares on Peter Crane, locked in a cell in the county jail. The irony was that her nightmares would be his wet dreams.

Vince stroked her back and kissed her forehead.

"What are you reading about?" Anne asked.

"Dissociation disorder. What were you reading about?" he asked. "I stuck my head in and saw you were asleep. Must not have been a thriller."

"Children as victims and witnesses."

"We're some exciting couple," he joked.

Anne found a smile. "Earlier I was reading about a princess who wanted to become a fairy."

"Oh, I've read that one. A real page-turner," he said. "How was your evening?"

"Good. We missed you."

"Mmmmm . . . good . . . How's Haley?"

"She asked when is her mommy coming."

"What did you tell her?"

"The same thing I told her before—that her mommy was hurt very badly and can't come for her," Anne said. "I want to spare her that awful truth, but at the same time I hate that I'm lying to her. She's going to continue to have this building expectation and excitement that Mommy is coming back. I feel almost cruel."

"That's a tough call," Vince said. "You're the expert on kids, not me, but I don't think kids appreciate being lied to any more than we do."

Anne looked up at him. "What about Santa Claus and the Easter Bunny?"

"That's different. By the time they're old enough to figure that out, they get it. You can't wait until the age of reason to tell Haley her mother is dead."

"I know. And I know that at Haley's age, death is a pretty abstract concept. She isn't liable to understand that death is final. It usually takes time for it to sink in and become real for the little ones. I suppose you could say the news is less traumatic for them in an immediate way. That's a blessing. But she's been through so much trauma already . . ."

"Has she talked at all about what happened?"

"Has she named the killer?" Anne said. "No. Maybe she'll get really lucky and never remember any of it."

No sooner had she said it, a piercing scream came from the room across the hall.

Anne bolted.

Haley was sitting up in bed, screaming like she had been the first time Anne had seen her in the hospital. Caught in the grip of a private terror, unable to break free of it or even see past it.

"Haley!" Anne said, sitting on the bed, gently taking hold of the little girl by her fragile shoulders. "Haley, it's me, Anne. You're okay, sweetheart. You're safe."

"Mommy! Mommy! Mommy!" Haley called, then again came the blood-curdling screams.

So much for my wish, Anne thought.

"Haley, you're safe, honey," Anne said and called herself a liar. She knew there was no such thing as being safe from the nightmares. Those would come again and again.

She drew the child to her and held her close. She felt the bed dip beneath Vince's weight as he sat down behind her. He wrapped them both in his arms and held them, his head bent, his cheek pressed to Anne's.

Gradually, Haley's screams gave way to sobs, and gradually the sobs gave way to sniffles and hiccups. Vince went into the bathroom and returned with a damp washcloth to wipe away tears—both Haley's and Anne's.

"I was scared!" Haley cried.

"I know!" Anne said. "You're safe, though, honey. No one can hurt you here."

"That was a bad dream," Vince said. "Do you want to tell us about it, sweetheart?"

Anne stiffened and shot him a look, but Haley nodded her head. She wanted the memory of it out where grownups could look at it and reassure her that she would be safe.

"Was someone trying to hurt you?" Vince asked.

Haley nodded. "The bad monster was chasing my mommy!"

"That's a scary dream," Anne whispered, stroking the girl's hair.

"Does the bad monster have a name?" Vince asked.

"Bad Daddy!" Haley said.

"Does Bad Daddy have a regular name?"

"*Bad Daddy!!*" she said emphatically, angry that the adults were too dense to get it.

"Bad Daddy can't get you here, honey," Anne said.

"I don't like bad dreams!"

"Me neither. I hate bad dreams. I had a bad dream tonight too."

Haley looked up at her, surprised. "You have bad dreams too?"

Anne nodded.

"Why?"

"Because a bad man tried to hurt me," Anne said, "and I was so afraid."

"Were you little like me?"

"No. It happened just last year."

"And you were still afraid?"

"Very. And I still get afraid when I have a bad dream. But when I wake up I remember that I'm in a safe place, and that the bad man can't hurt me again, and then I don't feel afraid anymore."

"What if the bad daddy came here to get me?" Haley asked.

"We won't let that happen, Haley," Vince said. "Anne and I will look out for you. Bad Daddy can't come to our house."

She seemed to mull that over for a moment, not quite sure she should believe such a claim.

"When is my mommy coming?"

Anne's heart was as heavy as a stone in her chest. She looked at Vince. Was this the time? Was there ever a right time? Did she do it now when Haley was already feeling vulnerable and frightened? Or did she tell the white lie and wait another day?

"Mommy isn't coming, sweetheart," she said, a mix of dread and relief churning inside her. She wasn't keeping a terrible secret anymore. She was telling a terrible truth.

Haley's eyes grew rounder. "Why?"

"Your mommy was hurt very badly, Haley. Do you remember when that happened? You were hurt and so was your mommy."

"The bad daddy came," she said, soberly. "Bad Daddy hurt my mommy."

"Yes. Your mommy was hurt too badly, and the doctors couldn't fix her, and she died."

"But when will she come back?"

"She can't, sweetheart. She can't come back."

Anne watched the little girl try to process the information. How could Mommy not come for her? Mommy had been there for her every day of her life.

"I'm so sorry, honey," Anne said, her own tears brimming over the barrier of her eyelashes.

She had been an adult when she had to accept the truth of her mother's death. And even though logically she had known that death meant an end to the terrible suffering cancer had brought her mother, Anne's own pain and grief had still been overwhelming. It still was overwhelming at times.

"But I want my mommy," Haley said, two big tears rolling down her cheeks.

"You don't have to be afraid, Haley," Vince said softly. "You're here with us, and you're safe, and we won't let anything bad happen to you."

"Bad Daddy hurt my mommy," she said, and she started to cry softly, going into Anne's arms for comfort.

Anne held her close and rocked her. She had always been protective of the children in her care when she was a teacher. Mendez had called her a tigress with cubs. But that paled in comparison to what she was feeling now for Haley.

Maybe it was because she had so much in common with the little girl—having been a victim, having lost her mother. Or maybe it was just the time of her life or the fact that she had been thinking so much about becoming a mother. But as she held Haley Fordham and promised to keep her safe, Anne felt a bond forming inside her like nothing she had ever felt before.

She wasn't going to let anyone harm a hair on this child's head. If the bad daddy or anyone else wanted to get to Haley, he was going to have to come through Anne first.

And no tigress would have anything on her.

52

"You're a lucky bastard," Campbell commented.

With the exceptions of Vince and Hicks, the guys had gone back to their desks after the brainstorming session to try to put a dent in their paperwork and check messages that had come in during the day regarding other cases they were working.

"How so?" Mendez asked.

"You don't have to hear it from a wife how you're never home, you work too much, or you pretend to work too much but you've probably got a girlfriend on the side."

"I don't know how anybody has time for a girlfriend on the side," Mendez said. "I don't have time for a girlfriend right in front of me."

"Tony wouldn't have a girlfriend on the side," Trammell said. "That arrow is way too straight."

"Right," Campbell said. "Tell the truth. Did you really pop Steve Morgan because he screws around on his wife?"

"I hit him because he hit me," he said, staring down at his pink message slips.

His mother was cooking dinner on Sunday. His victim in a domestic assault case wanted to talk to him. ADA Worth wanted to prep him for trial for a case he had worked six months prior.

Sara Morgan had called.

A little rush of something went through him. Excitement? Nerves? What was he—fourteen years old?

The call had come in at 7:20 P.M. No message.

He wasn't supposed to go near Sara Morgan or any other Morgan. The boss hadn't said anything about phone calls. But he didn't want to make the call from his desk with the peanut gallery sitting all around.

Stupid. It wasn't like he was involved with her. He wouldn't have any trouble being completely professional. Yet he still had the feeling he would hang up the phone and the chorus "Tony's got a girlfriend" would fill the air.

He wouldn't get the chance to suffer, as it turned out. Dixon walked into the room and pointed right at him.

"Tony, come with me," he said. "Someone just tried to run Milo Bordain off the road."

The rain was coming down in sheets. On the country road to Bordain's ranch, there was little in the way of light. Sizzling road flares put out by the deputy who had answered the call, and the red and blue lights atop his cruiser, gave warning to slow down.

The headlights flashed on Milo Bordain's massive white Mercedes sedan. The car sat almost perpendicular to the road, the back end dropped down in the ditch, the headlights pointing slightly upward into the night.

"She picked a hell of night to have this happen," Dixon said as he pulled the hood of his storm jacket up over the top of his cap.

Mendez followed suit, wishing he had left the office with Vince and Hicks. Maybe if he had a wife and kid waiting at home for him, he wouldn't have been hanging around his desk to get buttonholed for this call on this shitty night.

It was a cold, nasty rain, pelting down like tiny daggers from the sky. Gusts of wind redirected it inside the hood of the jacket and down the neck. The legs of his pants and his socks were wet in a matter of minutes.

"She said she was on her way home!" The deputy had to shout to be heard. He pointed in the direction they had been coming from. "She became aware of a car coming up behind her, too close on her tail. She touched her brakes to back him off. He came alongside her about there and swerved toward her. She panicked, hit the brakes, the car went into a skid, and that's where it stopped."

"Where is she now?" Dixon yelled.

"Emergency room."

"What?"

"Emergency room!"

"How bad?" Mendez asked.

The deputy shook his head. "Didn't look too bad. She banged her head," he said, pantomiming banging his head against his hand. "And a bloody nose."

Mendez jogged over to the Mercedes and shined his Maglite in on the driver's side. The airbag had deployed and there was blood on it. The cause of the nosebleed, he guessed. There didn't appear to be any other damage done inside the car. He shined the light at an oblique angle down the side of the car. There seemed not to have been any contact between the two vehicles.

"Gotta hope she got a tag number!" he shouted at Dixon. "Are there skid marks?"

"Who can see in this?" Dixon turned to the deputy again. "Did she give you a description of the other car?"

The deputy shook his head.

"Could just have been an asshole," Mendez said as they got back in the Taurus. He started the car and turned the heat on full blast. "She pissed him off when she hit her brakes."

"That would just be too easy," Dixon said. He pulled his hood back and pulled the wet cap off his head. "She's convinced herself she's a target."

"It doesn't make sense," Mendez said. "Like her son said, if somebody had it in for her, why not just kill her? Why kill Marissa Fordham with forty-some stab wounds and the mutilation and leaving the knife protruding from the vagina? All this perp did to Bordain is send her a gruesome surprise in the mail."

"Until tonight."

For Mendez, it didn't sit right. The amount of rage in the killing of Marissa Fordham . . . she had to have been the primary target. Little Haley was collateral damage. This business with Milo Bordain was like a game. That was a different kind of killer altogether. One he'd hoped they wouldn't see again in Oak Knoll.

He drove them to Mercy General Hospital and parked under the ambulance canopy at the ER entrance. The triage nurse led them back to the exam rooms.

"How is she?" Dixon asked.

The nurse, a short woman with smoker's skin and dyed-black hair, waved a hand in dismissal. "She's insisting on a CT scan, but she'll be fine. She's shaken up. More scared than hurt. She'll have a good goose egg on her forehead tomorrow, but there's no sign of a concussion."

She motioned to a door and left them. Dixon knocked twice and opened it.

Milo Bordain sat on the exam table, an unimpressed nurse tending to a small cut and abrasion on the left side of Bordain's forehead.

"Cal! Thank God you're here! Someone tried to kill me!"

She did look worse for wear, Mendez thought. Her blond hair was escaping the usually perfect tight bun she wore, and her makeup was mostly gone, showing her age in the harsh fluorescent lighting. In a hospital gown and wearing a paper blanket for a stole, she seemed much less formidable than in her usual layers of designer wear.

"We'll do our best to get to the bottom of it, Mrs. Bordain," Dixon said.

"Ouch!" she cried out and snapped at the nurse who was dabbing something at the cut on her forehead. "That stings!"

"Yeah," the nurse said, unapologetic. "Good thing you don't need stitches."

"If I need stitches, I'm calling my plastic surgeon. I'm not letting anyone here touch my face."

"Can you tell us what happened, Mrs. Bordain?" Mendez asked, pen in hand.

"I came in to town this afternoon to see how things were going with the tip line. Then I came to the hospital to try to see Haley, and she'd been released.

"Nobody told me she was being released today," she complained, irritated. "I wanted to have a chance to see her and tell her I'm thinking about her. And I brought her a little present—"

"About the accident . . . ," Mendez prompted.

Bordain turned to Dixon and spoke as if Mendez weren't there. "He is so rude. I don't understand why you would bring him here with you, Cal. You know he upsets me."

"I can step outside if you'd like to talk about me," Mendez said.

"I need him to take notes," Dixon said smoothly. "So you were on your way home?"

"Yes. And I was already upset about Haley, and still thinking about what happened yesterday, and about Marissa. I want to have a memorial service for her, but I don't know when her body will be released. Then someone told me only a relative could claim the body, but Marissa has no relatives here other than Haley—"

"And the car . . . ," Mendez said pointedly.

She huffed another sigh.

"Suddenly I see these bright headlights coming up behind me," she said. "I knew the car was going too fast for that road in the rain. People drive like maniacs out there—especially the Mexicans."

Mendez exchanged a glance with the nurse, who was also Hispanic

"The car came right up behind me," Bordain went on. "I thought it was going to hit me! You hear all the time about those insurance scams where some uninsured illegal gets you to rear-end them and then bilks the insurance company and sues the law-abiding citizen—"

"But there was only one car," Dixon said.

"Yes. I was angry that he was right on my tail, so I tapped my brakes to tell him to back off. Then he pulled up alongside me and swerved toward me. My heart was in my throat!"

"Do you know what kind of car it was?" Mendez asked.

"No. I'm sorry but I don't know anything about cars."

"What about the driver?"

She closed her eyes, pained and in pain. "I don't know."

She would know if it was a Mexican, Mendez thought.

"Was it a car or a truck?" Dixon asked.

"A car."

"Dark- or light-colored?"

"Dark. Everything was dark. And it was raining so hard I could barely see the road."

"Did you get a look at the driver at all?"

"Just a glance. I was terrified. I was trying to stay on the road."

"But it was a man," Dixon said.

"Yes, I think so. He might have been wearing a watch cap pulled down low, or maybe his hair was black. I didn't get a good look," she said. "He swerved at me. I swerved to miss him. The next thing I knew my car was out of control. I thought I was going to be killed!"

"We saw your airbag deployed," Dixon said.

"I thought it broke my nose! Those things are dangerous!"

"Try putting your face through a windshield," the nurse muttered—more as a suggestion than a comment, Mendez thought. He cleared his throat and rubbed a hand down over his mustache to hide his smile.

"The car didn't stop," Dixon said.

"No. I didn't see it stop."

"You didn't see the license plate?" Mendez asked.

"No. For God's sake, I was trying to stay alive!"

"Were there any other cars on the road at the time?" Mendez asked. "Anyone who might have seen what happened?"

"You don't believe me?" Bordain said, incredulous. Tears filled her eyes. "Oh my God. You think I'm making this up?"

"It's not that, Mrs. Bordain," Dixon said. "Another driver might have a better description of the other vehicle or of the driver, or may have even gotten a plate number."

"No," she said, calming down marginally. "One of my neighbors came along a few minutes later. He's the one who called nine-one-one."

"Have you been drinking at all this evening, Mrs. Bordain?" Mendez asked.

"What? Of course not! I had a glass of wine with dinner. That was hours ago!"

"It's just a routine question, ma'am," Mendez said. "We have to ask."

The nurse elbowed Mendez from behind and whispered in Spanish, "If she was a Mexican, she would be drunk."

Mendez coughed into his hand.

"What's going to happen next?" Bordain asked Dixon.

Dixon sighed and tipped his head like he was about to ram it into a wall. "There isn't much we can do, Mrs. Bordain. With no license plate and no witnesses, there isn't anything to go on."

"Someone tried to kill me!" she said, tears spilling over her lashes.

"I understand that you're upset."

She turned toward the door. "Darren! Thank God you're here!"

Darren Bordain came into the room with rain beading up on his blond hair and on his expensive trench coat. He looked at Dixon and Mendez.

"Gentlemen, we have to stop meeting this way. People will talk," he said. "Are you finished grilling my mother? I'm sure she'd like to go home."

"I have to have a CT scan," his mother said. "I hit my head on the side window, and the airbag almost broke my nose. Someone tried to kill me, but no one is taking it seriously!"

While Dixon reassured her that wasn't the case, Mendez nodded Darren Bordain into the hall.

"Why wouldn't you take that seriously?" Bordain asked. "Someone sent her human body parts in the mail yesterday."

"It's not that we aren't taking it seriously, Mr. Bordain," Mendez said. "There just isn't much for us to go on. She didn't get a good look at the other driver or the license plate of the other vehicle. No one else saw the accident."

Bordain's perfect brow knit. "Do you think she's lying?"

"I didn't say that."

"She's usually a good driver."

"She's had a lot of bad things happen this week," Mendez said. "She's been upset. I'm sure she's distracted, and she's probably exhausted. Things happen. People get embarrassed. They don't want to admit they just went off the road on their own or that they might have had a drink or two. The deputy should have done a Breathalyzer test on her at the scene, but he didn't."

"She had a couple of glasses of wine with dinner," Bordain conceded, "but she was by no means impaired."

"All right. We have to check every angle," Mendez said. "There's no offense intended."

"I understand."

"You had dinner together?"

"Yes, at Barron's Steak House. My parents and I."

"What time did your mother leave the restaurant?"

"Around ten thirty. We all left at the same time."

"You came in separate vehicles?"

"Yes. I went home—to my house. My father had to go back to Montecito. Mother headed back to the ranch."

"She's staying out there alone?"

"No. Hernando and his wife—the caretakers—live on the property. And of course my father will come back now."

Mendez jotted his notes. Despite the fact that Milo Bordain was a racist snob, he couldn't help but feel a little sorry for her. Her husband didn't seem to be giving her much in the way of support after all she'd been through this week.

"Is everything all right with your parents' marriage?" he asked.

"Their marriage is no different than it's ever been. You don't think my father had something to do with this?"

"Like I said: We have to look at all possibilities."

Darren Bordain shook his head. "They have their arrangement. Neither of them complains about it."

"What arrangement is that?"

"They lead their own lives. My father has his businesses, he plays golf, he probably has a girlfriend here and there—although he is completely discreet. My mother makes a career of being Mrs. Bruce Bordain. She has her social circle and her causes. They still enjoy each other's company when they're together. It works for them."

He looked across the hall as an orderly arrived with a gurney to take his mother for her CT scan.

"You know Gina Kemmer, don't you?" Mendez asked.

"Yes, why?"

"When was the last time you spoke to her?"

"She left a message for me yesterday afternoon to ask if I know anything about a funeral date for Marissa. She's a mess," Bordain said. "Marissa was like a sister to her."

"Did she say anything about going out of town?"

"No, why?"

"We've been trying to get hold of her, that's all," Mendez said. "We want everyone who had contact with Marissa in the last week or so to come in and give us an interview so we can build a fuller, more accurate picture of the last week of Marissa's life. I'd like to schedule a time with you, as well."

"Sure," Bordain said. "Call me tomorrow. I'd better go be a good son now and do some hand-holding."

When he was halfway across the hall he turned back. "Is there anything new in Marissa's case?"

"No, sir. Not at this time."

"You'll keep my mother apprised, though, won't you? She may be a pompous snob, but she really is beside herself over Marissa's death."

"Sheriff Dixon will personally see to it," Mendez said as Dixon came out of the room and Bordain went back in.

"I will personally see to what?"

"Mrs. Bordain," Mendez said as they started down the hall.

Dixon gave him a look. "Jesus, Tony. What did I ever do to you?"

53

Sara had spent much of the evening curled into one corner of the sofa, wrapped in an afghan her grandmother had made for her hope chest twenty years ago. Twenty years ago—when she had still believed in white knights and happily-ever-after.

She sat there staring . . . thinking . . . trembling . . . crying . . . Funny how the cycle had become weirdly comforting after a while.

Steve hadn't come home the night before. Sara had gone to bed after Detective Mendez had left. She had taken a sleeping pill and hadn't stirred until the alarm had gone off at seven. When she opened her eyes, her husband was not in bed beside her—not that that was unusual.

Groggy from the pill, she dragged herself downstairs to put out breakfast for Wendy. There was no sign Steve had spent the night on the sofa, which he did more often than not lately—when he came home at all.

She had no idea where he went on the nights he didn't come home. He usually claimed he had slept at the office, but Mendez had told her there had been no sign of Steve at his office that night.

Mendez had come by to check on her. He had been concerned to see the garage light on in the middle of the night. He had offered her sympathy and protection. Mendez, a relative stranger, had acted like a husband, while her husband had become nothing short of a stranger to her over this past year.

Wendy came downstairs for breakfast.

"Where's Daddy?" she asked, pouring cereal in a bowl.

"I don't know," Sara said. "He didn't come home last night."

"Yes, he did. His car is in the driveway."

But he wasn't home. Wendy went through the house calling for him.

Sara went into the garage to find no sign of him. When she went out to his car and saw blood on the driveway, she started to panic.

He wasn't anywhere in the yard. He hadn't fallen in the pool. He wasn't dead in the street.

Sara called the sheriff's office, then called another mother to take over car pool for the day. Distraught, Wendy had refused to go to school. She became convinced her father had been murdered.

A deputy had come to the house, looked at the car and the blood, and followed the same route through the yard and the garage and the house.

"Daddy's dead, isn't he?" Wendy said, crying, her arms wrapped tight around Sara's waist. "He's been kidnapped and killed! And now he's dead!"

"No, sweetie," Sara said. She wanted to say those things only happened on television, but she couldn't. Wendy had seen a murder victim herself. Her best friend's father was sitting in jail awaiting trial. One of her classmates had attacked her and stabbed another child.

"I'm sure there's a reasonable explanation," Sara said. "I'll call the office. Maybe Don knows where Daddy is."

While the deputy was in his car on the radio, Sara called Don Quinn to ask if he had heard from Steve.

Yes, he had. He had been Steve's one phone call from jail. Steve had been arrested for assaulting a sheriff's detective.

"And it didn't occur to you to call me and let me know what was going on?" Sara said.

"Steve asked me not to."

"And you thought that was okay?" The tone and volume of her voice went up with her blood pressure. "To let me go out of my mind with worry. To upset Wendy to the point that she's sick to her stomach. You didn't see anything wrong with that?"

"I don't know what to say, Sara. I thought Steve would call you himself."

"You didn't think that," she said bitterly. "You didn't think about Wendy or me. Just like he didn't think about Wendy or me. The two of you can rot in hell together for all I care!"

She slammed the receiver down and burst into tears, beyond the end of her rope. Wendy bolted from the room and upstairs.

That was it, Sara realized as the tears subsided, the last straw. She was done.

She dried her eyes and went outside as the deputy came up the sidewalk looking uncomfortable.

Sara held a hand up. "I know. I just spoke to my husband's partner."

"I'm sorry, ma'am," the deputy said.

"You don't have anything to be sorry for. Thank you for your time."

The adrenaline drained down through her, taking her energy with it as she went back to the house. She felt like she was eighty years old as she climbed the stairs to go to her daughter's room.

Wendy was busy putting her dolls into a garbage bag while tears streamed down her cheeks.

"Sweetheart, what are you doing?"

Wendy didn't look up. "I'm giving them away."

"Why?"

"Because they're stupid," she said angrily. "I'm too old to play with stupid toys for little kids."

Sara's heart broke all over again. Wendy was throwing away her childhood. She felt hurt and angry. No one seemed to be taking her feelings—the feelings of a child—into consideration. Maybe if she stopped being a child . . .

"Don't," Sara said softly.

She knelt down by her daughter and took a baby doll gently from her hand. She remembered the Christmas she and Steve had given that doll to Wendy. She had been five and covered in chicken pox. Sara had put red dots all over the doll so Wendy wouldn't feel so alone, sequestered away from her cousins for the holiday, missing out on all the fun. She and her new baby had chicken pox together, and Steve had played doctor and Sara had played nurse, the two of them devoted to their child, the three of them a wonderful family.

She looked down at Wendy and touched her face, and said, "Do you know how much I love you?"

They held each other and cried for a long time, letting go the emotions both of them had been trying to bottle up for too long. When the emotions had run themselves out, Sara took her daughter by the hand and led her over to the window seat.

"We need to talk," she said.

"You and Daddy are getting divorced," Wendy said flatly.

"I'm so sorry, honey," Sara said. "This isn't what I ever wanted for us."

Wendy leaned against her as they sat on the window seat, pressing her head against Sara's shoulder. "I wish things could be like they used to be."

"Me too," Sara whispered, stroking her daughter's hair. "I wish that too. I would give anything for that. But that isn't going to happen, and we can't go on the way we are. This isn't good for any of us."

"This is so not fair!" Wendy cried. "You and Daddy are supposed to love each other forever!"

"I know," Sara said, guilt and sadness weighing on her. "That's how it should be."

"I don't understand why Daddy can't just be happy with us. You're beautiful and smart, and, and I—I t-try to be g-good—"

Sara held her daughter tight. "It's not your fault, honey. You haven't done anything wrong. I don't know why Daddy can't be happy. I don't know."

She had asked herself that question so many times, never really finding an answer. She had blamed herself. Steve had blamed her. According to him, she was too jealous and she didn't trust him. But he had proven she couldn't trust him. And how could she not be jealous when her husband spent most of his time with other women—either working for the women's center or sleeping with a lover.

How many nights had she stared at the ceiling instead of sleeping, wondering what about her was so lacking? She had even asked him outright. He hadn't had an answer.

"You haven't done anything wrong," she said, not sure if she was talking to herself or to Wendy. "Daddy loves you, baby. You know he does. No matter what happens between Daddy and me, you need to know that we both love you so much."

"Then why isn't he here?" Wendy asked bluntly.

She was a smart girl—too smart at times. Too observant, too spot-on in her assessment of the situation. She was so much more aware and sophisticated than Sara had been at her age.

She was asleep now—or at least Sara hoped so as she sat there in the corner of the couch, waiting for Steve to come home. She figured he would at some point because his Trans Am was still parked in the driveway with his golf clubs in the trunk.

He hadn't bothered to call. No one had bothered to call. There had been no call from the sheriff's office. There had been no call from

Detective Mendez. Sara had finally tried to call him but was only able to leave a message. She wanted an explanation from somebody. What had happened? What had triggered her husband to become so violent that he would actually punch someone? Did he have a reason? Had he just gone off? Should she be afraid?

She didn't know who Steve was anymore. He had become so withdrawn, so angry, over the last year and a half, and she didn't understand why. He had a good life, a successful career. Had he just so grown to resent her and their marriage that he had become this sullen, bitter—now violent—man?

Had he loved Lisa Warwick? Had he loved her so much that her murder—now more than a year ago—had set him on this downward spiral?

Or was there a darker trigger in his mind?

He had never acknowledged his involvement with Lisa, but Sara had no doubt that he had moved on to another affair. Probably more than one. Possibly with Marissa.

The notion had eaten away at Sara's mind, at her soul, at her self-esteem.

Lisa Warwick was dead. Marissa was dead. Her husband had attacked a sheriff's detective.

Her heart started tripping. She could hear the voices of Mendez, of the local news anchor.

"Ms. Fordham is deceased."

"Multiple stab wounds . . . Reports of near-decapitation . . . Sexual mutilation . . ."

She felt sick and weak and out of control.

Lights flashed by on the street and turned in at their driveway. She could hear car doors open and close, men's voices. The car backed out of the driveway and drove away.

Sara turned the lamp on beside her as the front door opened and Steve came in. He looked into the living room at her, then back at the suitcase sitting at the foot of the stairs.

"Is this yours or mine?" he asked, coming into the room.

He looked like he'd been hit by a truck. His purple swollen nose appeared to be held on to his face with adhesive tape. Both eyes were black, but the left one was swollen nearly shut. He had gone to jail for punching a detective, but it was clear the detective had punched back.

Sara thought of Mendez and his thinly veiled anger toward her husband.

"You never sleep here anyway," she said. "You might as well have a change of clothes with you, wherever you go."

" 'Oh my God, Steve,' " he said sarcastically, feigning shock. " 'What happened to your face?' "

"Oh, please," Sara said, getting up from the couch. She crossed her arms in front of her. "Don't expect sympathy from me at this hour. You couldn't even be bothered to call and tell me why there's blood on the driveway, and I'm supposed to feel sorry for you? Wendy thought you'd been killed. She was sick with panic."

"But you weren't."

"Come out of the hallway," she said. "Your voice will carry upstairs. Your daughter is asleep."

He stepped into the living room and she could see him gather himself in the same way he would in court.

"Did you think I was dead?" he asked. "Were you worried sick?"

"Yes, I was worried," she admitted. "I didn't know what to think. I don't even know who you are anymore. You're not my husband. You're not the man I married. You're not the man I fell in love with. Who are you? I don't understand what's happened to you, Steve. I don't get it."

"You never did," he said with a touch of tragic bitterness in his voice that only made Sara angrier. He would bring out his flair for the dramatic to try to make her feel guilty, to try to pretend he was the wounded one.

"What does that even mean?" she asked. "Are we going back again to your tragic, terrible childhood? I've been telling you for fourteen years what a remarkable person I think you are for making it through and making yourself into the human being you are—or were, at least.

"Enough with that, Steve. You're a grown man. Stop playing the sympathy card already. Stop trading on your mother's misfortunes. The statute of limitations has run out."

"That's easy for you to say," he muttered. "Miss Perfect Family."

"I'm not apologizing because my mother wasn't an IV drug user," Sara said. "It's not my fault you had a rotten childhood. You wanted my perfect family, remember? You married my perfect family. We had our own perfect family. Now you're the one destroying it."

"You've always been jealous of the time I spend on the Thomas Center—"

"Don't start with that," she warned him. "Don't put this on me. I'm not taking it. I'm not the bad guy. You want to volunteer? That's great. You're a humanitarian. But you don't do it at the expense of your family. You don't do it at the expense of your daughter or me. Marriage is supposed to be a partnership. You're more devoted to Don."

"That's not true—"

"Really?" she said, pretending shock. "Who did you call this morning?"

"He's my attorney."

"And did you ask him to call your wife and explain to her why your blood is on the driveway and why you're missing?"

"Maybe I was embarrassed."

"Maybe you didn't give a shit," she said. "I don't know who you think of anymore, Steve, but it certainly isn't me and it certainly isn't Wendy."

"I love my daughter," he said vehemently, taking an aggressive step toward her.

The omission of her name from that sentiment cut Sara like a knife. She wouldn't have believed she had any illusions left about their relationship, but it still hurt.

"Then why do you do these things, Steve?" she asked. "Wendy isn't stupid. She knows when you don't come home at night. She knows what that means. An eleven-year-old girl shouldn't feel compelled to come to her mother and tell her she knows all about affairs, and why does her father have to do that?"

"And I'm sure you haven't tried to tell her otherwise," he snapped.

"Why would I? I'm supposed to lie for you? I'm supposed to lie for you and look like a fool to my daughter? I'm not stupid, either. You think I don't know that you weren't in Sacramento last weekend? Did you think I wouldn't check up on you when you've done this to me time and time again over the last year and a half?"

"Where do you think I was?" he asked, challenging her.

Sara refused the bait, careful with her answer. "I don't know where you were."

"Really, where do you think I was?" It was a taunt more than a question. He moved back and forth in front of her like a shark in a tank. "Do you think I was with Marissa?"

Sara said nothing, but caught herself taking a step back from him.

"You think I was having an affair with her, don't you?" he said. "That's why you were suddenly so interested in her, wanting to be friends with her, hanging out with her. Did you think she would just tell you? Did you think she would just turn to you one day and say, 'Oh, by the way, Sara, I'm fucking your husband'?"

"Stop it," she said quietly, her voice trembling with anger and something she didn't want to call fear. He continued his pacing, back and forth, back and forth, inching in on her with each turn. She took another step back toward the bookcase built into the wall behind her. With his battered face he looked monstrous and aggressive.

"That's what you believe," he said. "Just like you believed I was having an affair with Lisa Warwick. Why don't you want to hear it?"

She didn't say anything. She wanted this conversation to be over and for him to just leave.

"Really, Sara," he pushed, coming toward her, in her face. She tried to take another step back and couldn't. Something like satisfaction flashed in his eyes.

"Do you think I was with Marissa?" he asked quietly. "Do you think I was stabbing her forty-seven times and cutting her throat?"

"Stop it!" she said again, staring into his face and not recognizing him. This man was a stranger to her. She didn't know what he might do.

"Why?" he asked, enjoying her fear. "Am I scaring you? Do you really think I could do that?"

Sara tried to step sideways to get away from him. He grabbed her arm hard and shouted in her face.

"Answer me! Answer me! Do you think I'm a murderer? Do you?"

"STOP IT!! STOP IT!!" Wendy screamed.

Startled, Steve stepped back as Wendy flung herself at him, hitting him with both fists.

"STOP IT! STOP IT! I HATE YOU! I HATE YOU!"

"Wendy!" Steve grabbed hold of her and she kicked him and struggled and squirmed.

"Let go of me! I hate you!"

"Don't say that!"

He dropped down on one knee and tried to gather her close. She swung sideways to evade him, hitting him with her elbow in the bridge of his already broken nose.

Steve fell to the side then came up on his knees, his hands to his face, blood pouring out of his nose, between his fingers and dripping onto the carpet.

Sara caught her daughter as Wendy flung herself against her, sobbing.

"Look what you've done," Sara said as the man who used to be her husband looked up at her with tears in his eyes. "Look what you've done to us. Get out. Get out before I call the sheriff's office."

And that was end of the fairy tale.

54

The inky black of night paled to charcoal gray. The rain kept coming down.

Even beneath her trash bag garment Gina felt wet and cold to the bone. She had spent the night shaking, drifting in and out of consciousness. Every time she wanted to let go and sink into a deep sleep, Marissa's voice shouted her awake.

Stay awake, stay alive!

Gina kept one long stick of the discarded lumber in hand to swat at the rats and mice that crept near, smelling her blood, smelling her fear. Though in the dead of night she was no better off than a blind woman with a white cane, feeling around for danger while danger kept just out of reach.

Over and over during the night she had caught herself thinking this couldn't possibly really be happening. Marissa couldn't be dead. And she couldn't have been attacked by someone she had considered a friend. Yes, she had made a threatening remark, but she never would have followed through on it. She had been out of her head with panic. A true friend would have known that. A true friend wouldn't have shot her and left her for dead because she had said something stupid.

She was so tired. She knew she was in danger of dying from hypothermia. Her body wasn't making enough energy to try to keep itself warm. With the cold rain coming down, that would only intensify. Dehydration was only making the situation worse.

Her body needed fuel. She hadn't eaten in—what?—three days now? As enough light filtered down the shaft of the well, she tried to make out some of the garbage that had fallen from the bag she was wearing. She looked for anything that might be edible, something that wouldn't be moldy or rotten.

Using the stick for a reaching tool, she inched a crumpled potato chip bag toward her, and found a few chips and a mouthful of crumbs. They were stale and soggy, but they were calories, and the salt tasted good. She mentally thanked the unknown teenagers who partied at this desolate spot.

Over the next hour, Gina became more skilled with the stick, snagging a wrapper with three bites of a Snickers bar inside, and a McDonald's bag with a couple of stray French fries, a packet of ketchup, and a dried crescent of bun from a not-quite-finished hamburger. She ate all of it and prayed it stayed in her stomach.

If I can find enough strength—

You have to, G. You will.

If I can get up—

Get up! Don't think about it. Get up!

I'm trying!

No, you're not!

Shut up!

"Shut up!"

The sound of her own voice startled her, making her realize she had drifted off again. She had stopped worrying that she was hallucinating. Whatever dire condition hallucinations indicated, it was better to have company—even if the voice existed only in her mind.

The saltiness of the junk food had made her thirsty. She found a discarded water bottle with half an inch of dirty water in the bottom. Using her T-shirt over the mouth of the bottle, she filtered the water into her own mouth and drank it, grimacing at the taste, and fighting not to gag.

A rat scurried over her feet and disappeared into the empty McDonald's bag, only its long naked tail sticking out. Gina shrieked and jumped, the pain exploding in her broken ankle and racing up her leg like a wildfire. She swung her stick at the McDonald's bag and the rat shrieked and jumped and ran backward out of the bag, then leapt onto the thick vine hanging down the wall and disappeared into the crevice where the concrete had broken away.

Gina cursed and screamed—at the rat, at her predicament. But she quickly realized the favor the rat had done her. Adrenaline was pumping through her veins now, bringing energy, dulling pain.

She looked to her right, to the iron rungs cemented into the wall. Her only way out of this hole. She looked up at the doors above her. It had to be twenty-five feet. That didn't sound like much if the distance was horizontal, but the distance was vertical and more than three times the height of the average household ladder.

Gina had the use of one arm and one leg. Her left arm hung useless at her side. Her right ankle was so badly broken the foot was turned perpendicular to the shinbone.

You have to do it, Gina.

I know.

You have to do it now.

I know. I know! I KNOW!!

Get mad!

I AM!!!

To prove her point, Gina lunged to the right with her upper body, caught hold of one rung, and pulled as hard as she could, a roar of fury and pain and frustration tearing her throat raw.

Her body moved a matter of inches. Her consciousness dimmed. She pulled in a deep breath that burned in her left shoulder and ribs, and pulled again at the rung as hard as she could. She swung her left leg to the side and with the toe of her foot pushed off the wall, shoving herself another few inches closer to the ladder.

She had moved herself a total of two feet. Exhausted, she let go of the rusty iron rung and fell against the filthy wall, banging the side of her head on the next rung down.

She was sweating and weak. All over her body tiny erratic electrical impulses were causing individual muscles to twitch and tick.

And she had twenty-five feet to go . . . straight up.

55

Mendez stood in the middle of the road, hands on his hips as he stared at the skid marks. It was still raining enough to be miserable, though the storm system had blown out its worst effort during the night.

"Looks like just one car," Vince said. "That's a pretty good skid."

"She definitely had an accident," Mendez said. "Nobody doubts that. The question is why."

"Where's the vehicle?"

Milo Bordain's car had been removed from the scene, but the marks where it had sunk into the shoulder of the road remained.

Mendez gave him a sly look. "I'm sure Mrs. Bordain had it moved so some Mexican wouldn't come along and steal it."

"Present company excluded," Vince joked, "who would want to do her harm?"

"That's the thing. She may be irritating, but that's not a motive for murder—or for sending mutilated body parts to her in the mail.

"She had dinner with her husband and her son at Barron's last night. She had a couple of glasses of wine with the meal—"

"How'd she do on the Breathalyzer?"

"She didn't. She refused the deputy that was first on the scene."

"Did they take blood at the hospital?"

"We don't have it yet that I know of," Mendez said. "She only wants to deal directly with Cal. He can have her. He didn't say anything last night about a blood-alcohol level."

"Anyways, we know she had some alcohol in her system," Vince said.

"Some. She appeared sober—for what that's worth. Her speech wasn't slurred. Her eyes weren't glassy. She was pretty upset, and very adamant about what happened."

"And the son?" Vince asked.

"Showed up at the ER like a good son. He didn't act like he'd just tried to run his mother off the road," Mendez said. "He's coming in today for an interview regarding Marissa and Gina."

"I'll want to watch that."

Vince looked up and down the tree-lined stretch of road. No homes were visible. On one side of the road was a grove of lemon trees. On the other side of the road shaggy-haired red cattle with big horns grazed along the bank of a large man-made pond.

"That's Bordain property," Mendez said. "She told us she raises exotic cattle."

"This property has to be worth a fortune," Vince commented. "The way Oak Knoll is growing, there'll be developments out here within the next ten years."

"Bruce Bordain made his money in parking lots and strip malls, but the guy is a real estate mogul," Mendez said. "If there's money to be made out here, he'll be first in line."

"And if the missus doesn't want to give up the Barbie Dream Ranch . . . ?"

"Nobody brutally murders a woman just to be able to cut her breasts off and send them to someone as a scare tactic," Mendez said.

"No," Vince agreed. "There would be a lot more to the story. Whoever killed Marissa had it in for Marissa. Period. That murder was all about her. This other business . . . I don't know."

He checked his watch. "Let's go. I want to make sure Zahn is okay."

He hunched his shoulders inside his trench coat as they walked back to the car. Rain ran off the brim of his hat. Who ever said it never rains in Southern California lied. It rained, it poured, and it was damn cold when these storms came in off the Pacific.

"I spent half the night reading up on dissociative disorders," he said as they got back in the car. "Not surprisingly, there's overlap with post-traumatic stress disorder. I want to make sure that in bringing back the memories of his mother's murder I didn't push Zahn into any kind of long-lasting break with reality."

"You couldn't have known that would happen, Vince," Mendez said. "You said yourself: True dissociation is rare."

"I know, but still, I feel responsible," he admitted. "I certainly knew going in he's a fragile individual."

"Nasser was with him when you left yesterday."

"Yeah, I know."

I know, but . . . , Vince thought. He hadn't been able to shake the lingering sense of guilt. He had broken the lock on that small dark box in Zander Zahn's mind that contained the memories of what had happened to his mother—what he had done to his mother. What if Zahn couldn't get that box to close again?

On the other hand, perhaps it had been Marissa who had unwittingly opened that box and had paid a terrible price for doing it.

"Besides, Zahn brought up the subject of his mother's murder in the first place," Mendez said as he started the car. "He can't be that sensitive about it."

"It's one thing to use the words 'I killed my mother' and something else to pull up those memories in Technicolor," Vince said.

Rudy Nasser met them at Zahn's gate. He was dressed for a hurricane in a black storm jacket with the hood pulled up over his head.

"How was he after I left yesterday?" Vince asked as they walked up the narrow gravel path toward the house.

"He seemed fine."

"He wasn't agitated?"

"No, why?" Nasser asked with a suspicious look. "What did you do to him?"

"I talked to him about his mother."

"He didn't really kill her, did he?"

"He doesn't have a record for it," Vince hedged. It wasn't his place to tell Zander Zahn's story. If Zahn wanted Nasser to know, he would tell the story himself.

"The conversation stirred up some bad memories for him," he said. "I feel bad that he was upset."

Nasser pressed the buzzer at Zahn's door. "You're not used to dealing with him. It's difficult for most people to have any kind of a conversation with him. His mind plays by a different set of rules."

He rang the buzzer again, frowned and pushed back the sleeve of his raincoat to check his watch.

"Maybe he's sleeping in," Vince suggested.

Nasser shook his head. "He's an extreme creature of habit. He gets up at three A.M. every day to meditate."

And then he would take his hike over the hills to Marissa Fordham's house, Vince remembered. Every day.

"He meditates, then he takes his walk," Nasser said. "He should have been back by now."

"He walks around in the rain?" Mendez asked.

"The walk is ritual," Nasser explained. "Rain, shine, whatever."

"You have a key," Vince said, his nerves itching. "Use it."

Nasser let them in and called out for Zander Zahn. The house was silent.

Nasser called again.

The silence seemed to press in on Vince's eardrums.

"Where's his bedroom?" he asked.

"Upstairs on the left."

They went up the staircase, made narrow by foot-high stacks of *National Geographic* magazines. Nasser knocked on Zahn's closed bedroom door.

"Zander? It's Rudy."

Not even the air stirred.

Vince turned the knob and opened the door.

In contrast to the rest of the house, Zahn's bedroom was nearly empty. He seemed to have chosen the smallest bedroom for himself. The only furniture was the bed—neatly made—a dresser with nothing sitting on it, a nightstand with a lamp, and a chair. Three of the walls were bare. On the fourth was a huge collage of photographs of Marissa and Haley Fordham.

The photos dated back to when Haley was just an infant with impossibly huge brown eyes and a mouth like a tiny rosebud. Casual snapshots of Marissa and Haley were mixed with faded pictures cut from newspapers and magazines featuring Marissa and her art. Marissa and Gina at a picnic. Haley on the beach. Toddler Haley offering Zahn a flower. Zahn looking uncertain how to respond to such a spontaneous gesture.

Vince had seen a few shrines in his day—shrines built by sexually obsessed stalkers. Zahn's collection of photos was not that. Marissa and Haley had been his adopted family. There was nothing sexual or sinister about it.

He went into the small spotless bathroom but did not find Zander Zahn hanging from the shower curtain rod.

The three men split up then, each going through a different part of the house searching for its owner.

"He's not here," Mendez said as they met up in the foyer. "But you need to see something."

He led the way down a hall crowded with coatracks to a room at the back of the house. The room was lined with shelves and crowded with tables, and every available inch of space on those shelves and tables, and every bit of wall space, was occupied by prosthetic human body parts.

There were arms with hooks for hands, arms with plastic hands; whole legs, lower legs; hands, feet, and women's breasts.

One entire bookcase was filled with prosthetic female breasts of every size and description.

"Try to tell me this isn't creepy," Mendez said.

Vince looked around the room at all the spare body parts, wondering where Zahn had come by them and why he had felt compelled to bring them home.

"Look on the bright side, kid," he said. "At least they're not real."

56

"He owns a car, which Nasser says he rarely drives," Mendez said. "The car is sitting in the garage. There was no sign of Zahn in the house."

They sat in the break room where a television monitor was showing Detective Trammell interviewing Bob Copetti, a local architect who had gone out with Marissa Fordham from time to time. The sound was turned down to a mumble. Copetti's alibi for the night of Marissa's murder had checked out.

"Anything to suggest foul play?" Dixon asked.

"No."

"He couldn't have gone somewhere with a friend?"

"He doesn't have friends."

"He goes for a walk in the hills every morning," Vince said, pouring himself a cup of coffee. "Something could have happened to him on a trail."

"It's pouring rain," Dixon pointed out.

"Every day, no exceptions. He's an obsessive-compulsive creature of habit," Vince said, stirring a mega-dose of cream into his drink. "The fact that he isn't where he's supposed to be is a major red flag."

"Do you think he could have Gina Kemmer stashed somewhere?" Dixon asked.

"That seems unlikely to me," he said, taking a seat across the table from the sheriff. "He had a close connection to Marissa. There's a possibility he could have snapped and killed her while in a dissociative state. If Gina had been there at the scene, he might have gone after her in a continuation of the same episode, but he wouldn't have gone after her later. I would make book on that.

"If Zander Zahn is a killer, the murder was spontaneous and situational," he said, "and there'd be a better than even chance he doesn't remember the crime at all. He wouldn't consciously go looking to commit another murder."

"I'm not sure then what it is we're supposed to do, Vince."

"I'm concerned for Zahn's mental state. He went over the edge yesterday. Now he's missing. I don't know that he wouldn't hurt himself."

"And you feel responsible for that."

"Yeah, I do," he confessed.

Dixon nodded. "If there's a chance he's lost in the hills out there, then we send out the Search and Rescue team."

"Do you still have the chopper up looking for Gina Kemmer's car?" Mendez asked.

"They'll go back up when the weather subsides. The radar shows there should be a break around noon."

"Is that thing equipped with a thermographic camera?" Vince asked.

Mendez had read about thermographic technology. The military already had it. Thermal-imaging cameras could read the infrared radiation emitted by all objects, making warmer objects—such as humans—stand out against cooler backgrounds—like the ground. For law enforcement it would mean being able to locate a human on the ground in circumstances where the person may not be visible to the naked eye—at night for instance.

Dixon barked a laugh. "Are you high? You spent too many years working for the federal government."

"I'll take that as a no."

"That would eat a big chunk out of my budget for a year!" Dixon said. "I'm excited we're getting a fax machine. I've got a Search and Rescue team with a German shepherd. That's the best I can do."

Vince held up his hands in surrender. "I get it."

The sheriff took a swig of his coffee. "What's going on with our littlest witness?"

"The memories are there," Vince said. "She's having nightmares. But she hasn't named a name. She talks about the bad monster and Bad Daddy. Bad Daddy was chasing Mommy. Bad Daddy hurt Mommy. The trouble is she asks every man she sees if he's the daddy. Because she doesn't have a father in her life, she's preoccupied with the idea."

"What if we put together a photo array of the men her mother dated?" Mendez suggested. "Maybe she'll react to one of them."

Dixon nodded. "It's definitely worth a try."

"I agree," Vince said.

"We'll start taking Polaroids of these guys," Mendez said, tossing his coffee cup in the trash.

Hamilton stuck his head in the door, looking to Dixon. "Bruce Bordain is here."

"I'll see him in my office." Dixon stood up. "Tony, you come with me."

"I get to be there when he tells you to fire me?"

"Why should I have all the fun alone?"

"Tony," Vince said, going for a refill on the coffee. "Did you find photographs at Gina Kemmer's house?"

"Yeah. They're in a box in the war room."

"Great. Thanks."

"Do you know Bordain?" Mendez asked Dixon as they went down the hall.

"I've met him. He's a good guy, a bit of a hustler. Don't play golf with him, you'll lose your shirt."

They went into Dixon's office and the sheriff stuck his hand out to a very tan, very handsome, smallish man with thinning dark hair slicked straight back a la Pat Riley, the LA Lakers coach. Bruce Bordain, the parking lot king of California.

"Bruce, thanks for coming in."

Mendez had expected Bruce Bordain to be a man as big as his fortune. But what he lacked in physical size, he made up for in magnetism. It beamed from him like an aura.

"Cal," he said, flashing a big white smile. "How's that slice?"

"Bad as ever. I'm taking up miniature golf. I don't lose so many balls," Dixon said, sitting back against the edge of his desk. "Bruce, this is my lead detective, Tony Mendez."

"Tony." Bordain gave his hand a firm shake. "How about you? Does the boss here drag you out on the course?"

"Not me," Mendez said, shaking his head.

"He can't play badly enough to lose to me," Dixon joked. "Tony's on our softball team. Hell of a shortstop. Have a seat."

Bordain took one of the chairs in front of the desk. Mendez took the other. They settled in like they were just three guys talking sports and shooting the shit. It was hard to imagine a man as loose and affable as Bruce Bordain being married to a woman as buttoned up and stuffy as Milo Bordain.

"How is Mrs. Bordain this morning?" Dixon asked.

"Stiff, sore, out of sorts," Bordain said. "She's pretty shaken up about what happened last night."

"Rightly so," Dixon said. "Good thing she was driving that German tank."

"She thinks you don't believe her about someone trying to run her off the road."

"It's not that," Dixon said. "I explained to her last night that without more information about the other car, there really isn't anything we can do."

"If the other car had made contact with her car, we'd at least have paint transfer, and we could be looking for a car with matching damage," Mendez said. "I went back out to the accident site this morning. We don't even have skid marks from a second car."

"Could be she just pissed off the other driver when she hit her brakes," Dixon said, "and he swerved at her to scare her."

"Well, it worked," Bordain said. "It takes a lot to rattle my wife, but she hardly slept last night. First that business with the box—and, Jesus, why would anyone do something like that?—now this accident."

"You don't have any reason to think someone would try to kill her, do you, Mr. Bordain?" Mendez asked.

"I can't imagine why anyone would want to do that. I mean, Milo can rub people the wrong way, but she's got a good heart and she's certainly not involved in anything dangerous. She's passionate about her causes, but none of her causes are controversial."

"What about you?" Dixon asked. "Has anybody threatened you for any reason? Do you have any development projects going on that someone might be against?"

"I've got a big project going in Vegas," Bordain said. "But believe me, I've greased all the right palms. Besides, it's a parking structure. Nobody is against more parking spaces. It's not like I put up nuclear power plants."

"And how are things between you and Milo?" Dixon asked.

Bordain raised his eyebrows. "Fine. You don't think I would try to have her killed, do you?"

"No. I was thinking more along the lines of her trying to get attention from you."

"Oh. No." He shook his head. "Are you married, Cal?"

"Divorced."

"Tony?"

"No, sir."

"Milo and I have been married thirty-seven years," Bordain said. "After that many years a good marriage is like a business partnership. We each have our strong suits, we each bring something to the partnership, and we don't get in each other's way. We're way past romance. We're old friends. We've got our system down and it runs like a well-oiled machine."

"And your wife feels the same way?" Mendez asked.

"Milo has everything she wants. She's very good at being Mrs. Bruce Bordain. She makes it a full-time job. She doesn't want me underfoot every day."

"I'm going to have to be a little indelicate here, Bruce," Dixon said. "Is there another woman in your life who might want to see Milo go away?"

Bordain didn't even blink at the suggestion that he cheated on his wife. "No. I've learned to make sure that doesn't happen. Pay now, not later. There are no angry women in my life."

"Your wife supported Marissa Fordham in a very substantial way," Mendez said. "Do you know of anyone who might have objected to that?"

"I imagine there are artists Milo doesn't support who weren't happy about that, but I don't know any."

"Did you have any objection?" Dixon asked. "Sixty grand a year and a place to live. That's a lot."

"Cal, I have more money than I could ever spend," Bordain said with the big grin. "What do I care if Milo wants to buy herself an artist? Believe me, she spends more money than that on clothes every year."

"What about your son?" Mendez asked, thinking of Vince's theory that Darren Bordain may have resented his mother's relationship with Marissa Fordham. "How did he feel about that relationship? Your wife made mention Marissa was the daughter she never had."

"Why would Darren care about that? He had to be glad for the distraction on Milo's part. The more time she spent with Marissa, the less time she spent smothering him."

"How well did you know Marissa?" Mendez asked.

Bordain shrugged. "Well enough to have a conversation with her. It's god-awful what happened. Do you have any idea who did it? Do we have another Peter Crane running around?"

"We don't think so," Dixon said.

"And the little girl? Has she said anything? Milo said you think she may have seen the killer. Has she named anyone?"

"Not yet," Mendez said. "The woman taking care of her has training in child psychology. She'll try to draw the memories out."

"She's what? Four years old?" Bordain said. "How reliable can she be? She could say anything. She could name someone just to make an adult happy that she answered the question."

"Anne knows what she's doing," Dixon said. "She'll be very careful in how she goes about it. And of course no one would be convicted on the testimony of a child alone. There has to be evidence to back it up."

"And then what will happen to her?"

"We're trying to find relatives," Mendez said.

"Milo has it in her head she should have the kid. She's fretting about it constantly."

"It's best that the girl is where she is right now," Dixon said.

"Do you think you could arrange a visit, Cal?" Bordain asked. "Milo is beside herself with everything that's happened. It would cheer her up to see the girl. She's the closest thing to a grandchild Milo is going to have any time soon. Darren is still happily playing the field."

"I'll see what I can do," Dixon said, noncommittal.

"It would mean a lot," Bordain said, getting up. "It could be worth, say, some new piece of equipment the sheriff's office needs."

He smiled again like the Cheshire Cat.

"I'll give that some thought," Dixon said.

"Let me know."

He reached out and shook Dixon's hand again, then turned to Mendez.

"Detective Mendez. Think about that golf game. I have a standing tee time at the Oaks country club. You should come."

"At the Oaks," Mendez said as Bordain disappeared down the hall. "I should come as what? His caddy?"

"I'm sure he pays well," Dixon said.

"He just offered you a bribe."

"Yes, he did."

Mendez thought about it for a moment. "Do you think he'd spring for a thermographic camera?"

Dixon chuckled and waved him toward the door. "Don't you have a murder to solve?"

57

You can't pass out, G.

I know.

If you pass out, you'll fall. If you fall back down, you'll die in here.

I know. I'm not stupid.

I'm not so sure about that.

Very funny. I'll remind you, you're dead. I'm only half dead.

Shut up and climb. We can't both be dead. You have to live. You're the only one who knows the truth, G. You have to live to tell the truth. For Haley.

I'm so sorry I didn't tell it already. I'm so sorry, M. I was so afraid. I'm still so afraid!

You have to be brave now, G. For me. For Haley.

Gina licked her cracked lips and looked up. She didn't even like getting on a step stool to reach the highest shelf in her kitchen cupboards.

She put her stick in her left hand, reached up with her right and grabbed hold of the rusty iron rung. It was nothing more than a piece of bent rebar cemented into the wall. Who knew how long this well had been here or how long it had been abandoned and therefore not maintained in any way. Gina didn't know if the rungs would even hold her.

She took a deep breath and pulled, got her good leg under her, and pushed herself upright. Colors burst before her eyes while black lace crept in on her vision. There were no words to describe the pain. Trying not to focus on it, she held on to the rung, hanging her full weight from her good arm as she lifted her good foot and placed it on the bottom rung of the ladder.

She had raised herself six inches off the bed of garbage. Her muscles twitched violently. Her stomach rolled with the bad food and bad water she had consumed. She had to fight hard to remain conscious.

Marissa shouted at her.

Way to go, G! Do it again!

I'm going to fall!

No, you're not. You can do it! Do it again!

Gina looked up at the next rung. She would have to let go of the one she was holding in order to reach the next one. She would have to bring her foot up one, then spring upward to catch the next one with her hand.

She thought about what a miserable failure she had been in gym class. Marissa had been athletic enough to climb up the dreaded rope that hung from the gym ceiling. Gina could barely climb the stairs without tripping.

Holding tight she struggled to get her leg up where it needed to be. She panted a few breaths, then sucked one in, held it, and pushed herself upward, reaching for and grabbing the next rung up.

Ohmygod, ohmygod, ohmygod.

Gina hooked her arm through the rung and clung tight, her consciousness dimming again with the pain. If she got out of this alive, the first thing she would do would be to hire a personal trainer.

Of course, she would be destitute and homeless, but if she lived in her car, maybe she would be able to afford it.

Marissa's laughter filled her head.

You are such a dork, Kemmer!

At least I keep you amused.

You'll make it, G. You'll make it, and you'll train with that guy Lance at Ultimate Fitness.

Hot Lance with the washboard abs and round butt?

And the piercing blue eyes and tight workout shorts.

Will he fall in love with me and sweep me off my feet?

No, but he'll screw your brains out!

Gina's own laughter startled her.

What the hell did she have to laugh about?

She had twenty-three feet left to go.

58

There were years of friendship contained in the box Mendez had pulled out of Gina Kemmer's house. Years and years.

Vince spread the contents of the box out on a table that ran along one wall of the war room. He had removed the boxes of files pertaining to the See-No-Evil cases and put them under the table. One crime at a time.

Gina's box contained framed photos, photo albums, and packages of photographs that had never made it out of the envelope from the drugstore that had developed them. All of Gina Kemmer's life condensed into three-by-five and five-by-seven rectangles.

Vince went through them, separating them into groups—as to his best guess, at least. Family, school, friends, vacations.

Gina came from a nice, normal-looking family. Dad wore a crew cut. Mom wore cat-eye glasses. There were three kids: two boys and a girl—the youngest. They lived in a brown ranch-style house in Reseda, according to the loopy handwriting on the back. Reseda September 1969.

They vacationed at Big Bear and Yellowstone. There was Gina with Minnie Mouse at Disneyland. Robbie, Dougie, and Daddy at a Dodgers game in June 1972.

Funny the things that built a life. All these little moments knitted together. Another Christmas, another Easter, another Halloween.

He thought of his own family, and how many of these photos his girls had packed away in boxes. Photos without him in them. A familiar hollow ache filled the center of his chest. He made a mental note to call them on the weekend. They were always home Sunday night.

He would be in the next set of family photos. Him and Anne and the children they would have together. He thought of last night, sitting with his arms wrapped around Anne and Haley both.

He thought of Zander Zahn, who probably had no photos from his childhood—nor would he want any reminders of that painful, horrible time. He wouldn't want even the memories—which was why he kept them locked away in his strange compartmentalized brain.

He surrounded himself with things instead of memories. Tangible things he could touch and hold. Things that would never leave him. How telling that room of human prosthetics—no whole person in his life, just parts and pieces made of plastic. They couldn't hurt him.

Vince took a deep breath, sighed, and rubbed his hands over his face, turning his attention back to Gina Kemmer's photographs.

He found the first one of Marissa dated 1971. Even as a young teenager she had been striking with her shining dark eyes and her dark hair falling around her shoulders in waves. She was dressed like a hippy in bell-bottom pants with a peace sign hanging around her neck and a leather headband across her forehead. Gina was in a similar getup. The back of the photo read—in schoolgirl handwriting—Missy and Me, Sept. 1971.

They had grown up together. Best friends. Like sisters. School. Boyfriends. Holidays. Trips.

So why the big lie? Why say they only met here in Oak Knoll in 1982? Who would have cared where they had come from? Who would have cared how long they had known each other?

And why had Melissa Fabriano changed her name? Had she just wanted to reinvent herself? Had she been running from someone in LA? Maybe her family hadn't been as idyllic as the middle-class Kemmers of Reseda.

Maybe Haley's father had been abusive. Maybe there was no blackmail scheme. Maybe the abusive father of her child had finally found her and put an end to her perfect secret life in perfect Oak Knoll.

Then why wouldn't Gina have given up his name? She would have been in danger from him too. Why wouldn't she just give him up?

The door opened and Mendez came into the room with a bag from Carnegie West Deli.

"If there's a hot pastrami on rye in that bag, I'll kiss you full on the mouth."

"No tongue," Mendez said. "I'm not that kind of girl."

He set the bag on another table and started dragging sandwiches out of it.

"Finding anything?" he asked, nodding at the photographs.

"More questions than answers, so far. Gina and Marissa go way back. Gina and Melissa, I should say. They go back to seventh or eighth grade."

"So why pretend they didn't?"

"That's my question. If Marissa was running from someone in Los Angeles, came up here and changed her name, who would care if she and Gina knew each other?"

"Maybe Marissa wanted the whole new identity—needed it for whatever reason—but Gina didn't want to be bothered with living a lie."

"Maybe . . ."

Vince got up and stretched, picked up his sandwich and breathed in the aroma through the wrapper.

"I gave up pastrami ten years ago," he said. "At the same time I quit smoking. The big midlife health kick."

"And then?"

"I got shot in the head and lived. A little pastrami isn't going to kill me."

"You gonna take up cigarettes too?" Mendez asked, eyeing his meatball sub for a spot to attack it.

"I'm indulgent, not stupid," Vince said. "So did Bordain want you fired?"

"No. He invited me to go golfing. He's nothing like his wife."

"You liked him?"

"He's hard not to like. Charming, charismatic, accessible. He's the guy guys want to hang out with and ladies want to hang on his arm. But he talks about his marriage like it's a business arrangement."

"It probably is. It looks like it works out for both of them."

"That's not the kind of marriage I want."

"Mr. Romance."

"And you're not?"

"I am, absolutely. Guilty as charged, and happy as a half-wit at the county fair," Vince confessed. "But not a lot of people get that lucky. Not everybody wants to. The highs are really high, but the lows suck. Middle of the road is safer."

"Dixon asked him if he had a girlfriend who might want his wife dead. He said he's learned to make sure that doesn't happen. Pay now, not later. What do you think that means?"

"Hookers. Cash on the dresser. Cheaper than a mistress."

"I guess." Mendez shook his head and sighed wistfully. "The world's an ugly place, Vince."

"Not always," Vince said, picking up a photograph of Gina Kemmer and Marissa Fordham in bikinis on a beach. He looked at the back. "Life's a knockout in Cabo San Lucas, circa . . ."

He stared at the back of the snapshot, turned it over, and stared at the front.

Mendez stopped chewing and talked with his mouth full of meatball sub. "What?"

"March 1982."

"What about it?"

"Haley was born in May 1982." He put the photo down and tapped a finger on the very flat belly of Marissa Fordham/Melissa Fabriano. "Does that woman look seven months pregnant to you?"

"Maybe the date is wrong."

"Why would the date be wrong? Gina learned from her mother to always put the date on the back of the picture. Every photograph on this table has a date written on the back of it. Why would any of them be wrong?"

"But she's obviously not pregnant."

"Obviously not."

"Wow." Mendez shook his head as if he'd been dazed. "We're busting our asses trying to find out who Haley's father is. We don't even know who her mother is."

"Who's the daddy?" Vince said, feeling a whiplash coming on. "Who's the baby?"

59

"When is my mommy going to stop being dead?"

Anne brought a bowl of tomato soup to the kitchen table and sat down next to Haley on the banquette. Haley had tossed the question out like she was asking the time of day. Matter-of-fact in the way of small children whose lives drift in and out of fantasy. Death was unreal, but a unicorn might live in the bushes outside the house.

"People don't stop being dead, sweetheart," Anne said quietly.

Engrossed in her coloring, Haley didn't even look up. "Yes, they do. They turn into angels."

"Oh. Well, yes," Anne said, once again feeling out of her depth. She had no way of knowing what belief system Marissa Fordham had subscribed to or what she had instilled in her daughter. "Then what happens?"

"They go to heaven and fly around, and they come for Christmas, and whenever we need them." She looked up at Anne then. Some of the blood had left the whites of her eyes, but the effect was still startling. "How come you don't know that?"

"I do," Anne said. "I was just testing you. Have some of your soup, sweetie. It'll feel good on your throat."

Haley knelt on the cushion of the banquette and leaned over her bowl, blowing on the soup to cool it.

Anne glanced at the paper she had been drawing on. Oddly shaped cats and kittens of all colors ran along the bottom third of the page. She wondered how Vince would feel about having a kitten in the house. Or two.

She reached over and brushed Haley's hair back to keep the ends from dipping in the soup, and revealed the dark bruises that ringed her throat. They had faded to a mix of blue and yellow. She could almost feel Peter Crane's hands close around her throat and had to swallow hard a couple of times to push the feeling away. She hadn't been able to wear anything tight around her neck since, no turtlenecks, no scarves, no short necklaces.

"Where's your mommy?" Haley asked. She scooped up a spoonful of soup and sipped at it, giving herself an instant tomato-soup mustache.

"She's an angel in heaven," Anne said.

"That's good. Does she know my mommy?"

"Maybe."

"Where's your daddy?"

"He lives in a house in another part of town."

"Why?"

"Because that's his house."

"How come you don't live in his house?"

"Because this is my house. Vince and I are married and this is our house."

Haley thought about that and ate some more soup. "I would live in my daddy's house."

"Would you?" Anne asked. "Where is your daddy's house?"

"I don't know."

"What does your daddy look like?"

"I don't know."

"Is he a big guy like Vince?"

"No."

"Does he have a mustache?"

"No."

"Does he have orange hair?"

Haley laughed. "No! That's silly!"

"Does he have blue hair like a Smurf?"

"No!"

"Does he have no hair at all?"

The little girl fell into a fit of giggles, flopping down onto the cushion. Anne scooped her back up.

"Come on, silly, eat your lunch before it gets cold."

Haley took a few more spoons of soup. Anne knew her well enough by now to see the little wheels of her mind turning as she thought hard about something.

"Anne?" she said at last.

"What?"

"Would you be my mommy until my mommy stops being an angel?"

Tears stung her eyes as Anne hugged Haley tight and kissed the top of head. "I'll be your mommy for as long as I can be," she whispered. "How about that?"

Haley nodded and squirmed around onto Anne's lap, and stuck her thumb in her mouth, suddenly tired.

"Are you ready for a nap, sweetie?" Anne asked softly.

"No."

"No? You look pretty sleepy."

"No!" she whined.

"Why not?"

"Bad Daddy will come!"

"What if I stay right with you so Bad Daddy can't get you?"

The tears started with two big drops. "No! Bad Daddy will get you too!"

"No, baby, that won't happen. We're safe here. Remember?"

Haley was unconvinced, sniffling and crying a little, all around her thumb.

"You know what?" Anne said. "We're not going to think about Bad Daddy now. We're going to play a game. Do you want to play a game?"

"W-w-w-hat game?"

"We're going to play Imagine That. Do you know that game?"

Haley shook her head.

"You know what Bad Daddy looks like," Anne said. "What color are his clothes?"

"B-b-b-black."

"Not anymore," Anne said. "We're going to make them white. White with big pink polka dots. Can you imagine that?"

Haley hiccupped and nodded.

"And he has big huge floppy clown shoes on. Can you imagine that?"

She nodded a little quicker this time.

"And does he have a big round red nose?"

Another nod.

"And it honks like a horn when you pinch it. Can you imagine that?"

"Uh-huh."

"It's not Bad Daddy anymore. He's just a silly clown. Can you imagine that?"

No answer this time. Anne peeked down. Sound asleep.

She scooted back on the banquette to a more comfortable position with Haley sleeping against her. It was almost one o'clock. Sara Morgan had called and asked if she could bring Wendy over, a visit that would be good for both Haley and Wendy.

Anne knew Wendy was struggling, and Sara sounded stressed down to her last nerve. She and Steve probably weren't going to make it. That was going to be especially tough on Wendy. Anne wanted her to feel like she had a safe haven if she needed it in the future.

Damn. She wasn't going to have time to get to Dennis today. She would have to call and let the nurse supervisor know. And she would call Dr. Falk as well.

Guilt swept over her in a cold wave. She hated missing a session with him, especially when she had made a promise. She had stopped at the bookstore and picked out a couple of comic books for him for his reward. Of course, the odds that he had done the assignment she had given him were long. Still, she hated not being able to keep a promise to him. He had had too many people let him down in his short life.

You can't save everybody every day, Anne, she told herself.

60

"What do you mean Marissa Fordham isn't the little girl's mother?" Dixon asked.

Most of the detectives had come into the war room for lunch, to have a little ham and cheese with their homicide. Eight-by-tens of the Marissa Fordham crime-scene photos were plastered all over one wall.

Vince showed Dixon the photograph of Gina and Marissa in Cabo San Lucas in March 1982, and explained about the significance of the dates.

At the end of the story, Dixon just stared at him, dumbfounded.

"I'm confused," he said at last. "If Haley isn't Marissa's child, then whose child is she?"

"I don't know," Vince said. "I don't know what to say."

"You think Marissa was blackmailing the supposed father, but the kid's a ringer?" Dixon said. "Jesus, Mary, and Joseph. I thought I'd heard everything."

"Haley was an infant when Marissa moved here," Mendez pointed out. "No one here ever saw her pregnant."

"And yet everyone would assume the child was her child," Dixon said. "Huh. So . . . where did she get the baby?"

"That's the sixty-four-thousand-dollar question," Vince said. "You can't just walk into a store and buy a baby."

"But you can always steal one," Mendez suggested. "Or she could have adopted."

"The murder might not have anything to do with blackmail at all," Hamilton said, flicking pickles off his tuna salad. "We haven't really come up with any solid evidence to support the theory. There's nothing fishy in her bank records. She could have been stashing money elsewhere, but everything looks legit so far."

"Besides," Trammell said, "in this day and age, who would pay blackmail without proof the kid was really his kid? A paternity test is a lot cheaper than paying someone to keep their mouth shut."

"Blackmail is a poker game," Vince said. "If you really didn't want a big scandal attached to your name, would you call the woman's bluff? Maybe she's got pictures of you and her together in a compromising position or two. She can for sure prove to God and everybody you were having sex with her. If you don't pay, the majority of the shit hits the fan whether the kid is yours or not."

"Then everyone assumes the kid is yours anyway," Mendez said.

"By the time the paternity test is done, who gives a shit?" Vince said. "All the damage to your reputation, your marriage, your career, whatever, has been done."

"Maybe Bruce Bordain has a point," Dixon said. "If you're the kind of guy who's so inclined, pay up front."

He heaved a sigh and let his shoulders sag for a moment while he thought.

Vince sat back in his chair wondering how this was going to impact Haley's life. She'd just lost the only mother she'd ever known. Did she have a birth mother out there somewhere looking for her, wondering where she went and what became of her; wondering if she was even alive?

"Okay," Dixon said. "Where Haley Fordham really came from is irrelevant with regards to the theory of the crime that Marissa was blackmailing a man who believed he was Haley's father. It doesn't matter if he really was or not. It matters what he believes.

"We proceed as planned," he said. "If this crime was about blackmailing a man for having an illegitimate kid, we need that man to go on thinking that's the case—and that we're zeroing in on him. And if that's not what the crime was about, it doesn't matter at the moment."

"It matters to whoever that baby really belongs to," Hicks pointed out.

"The murder is our first priority," Dixon said. "We wrap that up, then we'll start looking back at infant abductions in the summer of 1982. We know now that Gina and Marissa both came up here from LA. We'll start with abductions in LA County, Orange County, Riverside, and Ventura. But we need to catch a killer first."

"Or," Mendez said, "find Gina Kemmer alive."

Dixon grabbed up the receiver as the phone on the table rang. His eyes went immediately to Mendez.

"He'll be right there," he said, and hung up. "Sara Morgan is here to see you."

Mendez went out into the hall with Dixon on his heels.

"I don't want you speaking to her alone," the sheriff said. He held his hands up to forestall the objection rising in Mendez's throat. "It's not that I don't trust you, Tony, it's that Steve Morgan is an attorney and you're already skating on thin ice with him."

He nodded, impatient to get to her. Something had to be wrong for Sara Morgan to bring herself to the sheriff's office.

"Fine," he said. "Vince knows Sara. Just let me ask her if she's comfortable with that."

He had already started down the hall before Dixon could answer.

The receptionist had brought Sara into the small waiting area outside of the detectives' offices, where a sign on the wall instructed all detectives to turn their guns in at the desk. She looked like hell. His first impression was that she had two black eyes, and his temper had already begun to spike before he realized the dark around her eyes was from stress and lack of sleep. She looked thin and fragile, as if a man might be able to snap her in two.

If one had already tried, Mendez was going to kill Steve Morgan with his bare hands.

"Sara? Is something wrong?"

He could see she was trembling as she stood up.

"Can I speak to you privately?" she asked, her voice so small, he could hardly hear her.

"Is this about Steve?" he asked, putting a hand on her shoulder to steady her.

"Yes."

"Okay. Because of what happened between Steve and me, I'm going to have to have someone else sit in with us. You know Vince Leone. Is it all right if he sits in with us?"

Head down, she nodded.

"All right. We'll go back here," he said, letting his hand fall to the small of her back to guide her gently through the office with its small sea of desks, and down the hall to the interview rooms.

"Are you all right?" he asked quietly.

"No," she said.

"Is there something I can get you before we sit down? Would you like a glass of water or some really bad coffee?"

She tried to smile and shook her head.

"Where's Wendy? Is she okay?"

"She's with Anne."

"Okay. Good. That's good."

He looked in the glass inset of the door to interview room one. Vince was already waiting. He stood up as Mendez opened the door and held it for Sara.

"Sara," Vince said easily. "I understand from Anne that Wendy is visiting Haley this afternoon."

"Yes."

"Have a seat, honey," he said, pulling out a chair for her at the small table. "You look a little shaken up."

Mendez took the chair on the far side of the table and planted his forearms on the tabletop to keep from reaching over to touch her. That didn't stop Vince, who reached over and patted her hand.

"It's okay, Sara," he said in his quiet, almost fatherly voice. "You're okay. You're among friends here, right?"

She nodded, squeezing her eyes shut against gathering tears.

"Between me and Tony here, we've heard about every kind of wild story there is," Vince went on, trying to put her at ease. "So nothing you come up with is going to shock us."

Sara drew a shallow, shuddering breath. "I think my husband might have killed Marissa."

Vince's brows sketched upward ever so slightly. "What makes you say that, Sara?"

"I suspected he was having an affair with her," she said. She was shaking so hard, she wrapped her arms around herself as if she were freezing.

Mendez stood up, took his sport coat off and draped it around her, giving her shoulders a comforting squeeze.

"When did you first start thinking that?" he asked, sliding back into his seat.

"Last winter when the project for the poster for the Thomas Center started. Then I found out she was a client—that she'd been a client for a while. Do we have to go over all of this now?"

Vince reached over and took one of her hands in his. "I'm sorry, honey. I know it's hard. This is a tough time for you. You know you're not alone, right? We're here for you."

Sara nodded and glanced at Mendez. "I told him to leave. I told him to get out."

"You told Steve to get out?" Mendez said. "When did you do that?"

"Last night. He never called in the morning to tell us what had happened. Wendy saw his car in the driveway, but he wasn't home, and there was blood . . . We didn't know what to think. Wendy thought he'd been killed."

Mendez wanted to bang his head against the wall, feeling stupid and guilty. "Oh, Sara, I'm so sorry. I can't believe he didn't call you. I would have called you if I had known."

"It's not your fault my husband is a bastard," she said. "Just like it's not my fault his mother was a prostitute.

"Everything is somebody else's fault where Steve is concerned. He didn't used to be that way," she said. "He's changed so much in the last year and a half, I don't even know who he is anymore."

"His behavior has changed?" Vince asked. "How?"

"He used to be happy. He loved us being a family. We were his dream come true. And then he started working more hours and getting more wrapped up in his work for the women's center, and he just started to change.

"I know you thought he was having an affair with Lisa Warwick when she was killed. And then, of course, Peter Crane was arrested. Peter and Steve were friends. That was hard on him. He just seemed to withdraw more and communicate less."

"You and Marissa were friends, right?" Vince asked.

Sara shook her head. "I knew who she was. I didn't try to get to know her until last April or May."

"After you already believed Steve was involved with her?" Mendez asked.

"Yes. I wanted to know . . . If he was in love with her, I wanted to know why. Why her? Why not me?" she asked, the pain in her voice so raw, Mendez wanted to take her in his arms and hold her.

Vince shifted his chair a little and leaned forward, still holding Sara's hand, his knees now almost touching hers. She gave him her other hand, wanting the contact, needing to feel Vince's strength.

"It's okay, Sara," he whispered. "You hang on to me as tight as you need to, honey, all right?"

She was almost doubled over from the emotional pain. Mendez left his chair and squatted down beside her so he could hear her. He braced a hand against the back of her chair. He wanted to reach up and wipe the tears from her cheek.

"Steve wasn't in Sacramento last Sunday," she said. "I don't know where he was. I told him last night that I knew he wasn't where he said he was. And he got really angry, and he said to me, 'Do you think I was with Marissa? Do you think I was stabbing her forty-seven times and cutting her throat?'"

The hair went up on the back of Mendez's neck. He and Vince locked eyes.

"Is that exactly what he said to you, Sara?" Mendez asked.

"Yes. He was trying to scare me. I didn't even know who he was when he said those things."

"Why didn't you call me?"

"I just wanted him gone," she admitted. "I just wanted him to leave. And Wendy was so upset—"

"Did Wendy hear him say that?" Vince asked.

"I don't know. I don't know what she heard. I thought she was upstairs in bed. Steve was shouting at me, and suddenly she came in the room and hit him and screamed at him that she hated him. It was awful. I just wanted him away from us."

"And he left?" Vince said.

"Yes."

"Do you know where he is now?" Mendez asked.

"I don't know. He could be at work. He probably is. It's raining. He can't golf."

Mendez got up and left the interview room, going across the hall to the break room where Dixon and Hicks stood watching the closed-circuit television showing the interview.

"Has that information been leaked to the press?" he asked. "The number of stab wounds?"

"Not officially," Dixon said. "Multiple stab wounds is all we've released. If the press has a number, they might have gotten it from the morgue."

"I can't believe whoever did that to Marissa Fordham would have counted the number of times he stabbed her," Hicks said. "He was in a rage, a frenzy."

"I know," Mendez said. "But forty-seven? That's pretty damn close to right. We can't discount that out of hand just because it seems unlikely. What do we know? Maybe that's a significant number to him for whatever reason. We need to talk to him."

"He's not going to come in voluntarily," Dixon said. "We've got no evidence of anything, Tony. Remember evidence? It's what we use to prove guilt in a court of law. If we try to bring him in for an official questioning now and he lawyers up—which he'll do because, hello, he's a lawyer—we're fucked."

"He could be a killer."

"You're not going near him," Dixon said calmly.

"No, because I would fucking kill him for what he's putting her through," he said honestly, pointing at Sara on the monitor.

"We need to get him to talk to Vince," Dixon said. "And you need to calm down."

61

"Bill," Dixon said, "would you give us a minute?"

"Sure, Boss." Hicks raised his brows at Mendez as he exited the room, leaving the two of them alone.

Dixon looked at him hard with the laser blue eyes. "Are you sleeping with Sara Morgan?"

"No!" Mendez said, sure he probably looked more guilty than offended.

"Because I'm watching your body language with her, and I'm seeing ownership there."

"Vince is holding her hands!"

"I'm not worried about Vince. I'm worried about you," Dixon said. "He's giving her the Uncle Vince treatment. You busted her husband's face yesterday—and don't give me that 'he hit me first' bullshit. He may have hit you first, but you hit him to hurt him. I don't like that, Tony."

There wasn't much he could say to that. He looked down at the floor. Dixon waited with the patience of a man who had interviewed a few hundred criminals in his time.

"I feel bad for her," Mendez confessed. "She's a beautiful, talented, intelligent woman. She doesn't deserve to be treated the way he's treated her."

"And you're the white knight riding to her rescue."

Mendez said nothing.

"That's admirable, Tony," Dixon said. "I mean that. You're a good guy. Any mother would be proud to have you for a son. But you're walking a fine line here. If it pans out that we like Steve Morgan for this murder, I can't have one single solitary drop of impropriety muddy the waters."

"Yes, sir."

Dixon studied him for long enough that he wanted to move away from his boss's scrutiny, but he held his ground like a good marine.

"I'm not trying to be a hard-ass here, Tony," Dixon said. "But I want you to remember two things. First, you're a detective and you've got a murder to close. Second, Sara Morgan is vulnerable right now. She's going to go for the first safe port in the storm. Don't jeopardize your case or your career just to get your heart broken."

Mendez worked the muscles in his wide jaw, embarrassed at the whole conversation. Jesus. He felt like a high school kid getting dressed down by some girl's father for trying to unhook her bra in the movie theater.

"No, sir," he said.

Dixon, sitting on the break room table with his arms crossed over his chest, looked completely unconvinced.

"You're not to be alone with her," he said.

"Yes, sir."

The sheriff heaved a sigh. "Darren Bordain is waiting for you in two. I want you to take a few minutes and get your head where it needs to be, then you and Bill go have a talk with him."

"Yes, sir."

Dixon gave him a fatherly pat on the shoulder as he left the room. Hicks came back in with a Snickers bar from the vending machine down the hall and the same raised-brow expression he had left the room with.

They both sat down on the table and stared at the television monitor. Vince was still talking with Sara, asking her questions about Marissa Fordham.

"Did Marissa ever hint or let on to you that she and Steve might be involved?"

"No. She was never anything but friendly and kind. It's hard to describe Marissa. There was always this feeling of openness about her, and yet, you knew there was something more going on deeper down. I'm sure that doesn't make sense."

"No, I think I know what you mean," Vince said. "Some people have a lot of layers. Only the top one looks uncomplicated."

She nodded.

"So, even though Marissa wasn't giving off that vibe, you still had that feeling something was going on."

"From Steve. He avoided talking about her. He was secretive about meeting with her." She paused, weighing what she was about to say next. "Steve and Wendy and I ran into Marissa and Haley during the music festival, and Haley looked at Steve and called him Daddy."

The admission clearly hurt her. Vince patted her shoulder.

"Don't take that too much to heart, Sara," he said. "Haley has some confusion about the daddy issue."

Turning from the monitor, Hicks gave Mendez a sideways look. "You going back in there?"

"No."

"You need a cup of coffee?"

"I need a drink."

"Later."

"Damn straight."

"Bordain is in two waiting for us."

"I know," Mendez said, still staring at the monitor screen. It irritated him that Vince was touching her. Just as it irritated Vince when Mendez came within two feet of Anne. Hmmm . . .

"Come on," Hicks said, sliding off the table. "Let's go see what the Golden Child has to say for himself."

Darren Bordain sat in the interview room impeccably dressed in a pinstriped suit that looked like it might cost more than Mendez's car. He smiled easily as Mendez approached the table and stretched out his hand.

"How is your mother doing today?"

"She's been busy telling everyone about her harrowing brush with death last night," Bordain said. He sat back in his chair, relaxed, with his legs crossed. A pack of cigarettes and a lighter lay on the table in front of him. "I'm sure you'll see it on the news at eleven."

"Do you not believe her?" Hicks asked.

"My mother isn't given to lying."

"But you don't seem very concerned about it if someone really did try to kill her."

"They didn't succeed," Bordain pointed out.

"You all left the restaurant last night around ten thirty, right?" Mendez asked.

"Yes."

"And you went straight home?"

"Yes."

"Were you alone?"

"Yes," Bordain said, getting annoyed. "I thought I was here to help you build some kind of timeline to do with Marissa."

"We need to do the same thing with your mother's case," Mendez said. "Might as well kill all the birds with one stone, right?"

"I suppose, but I don't like the implication," Bordain said. "Am I a suspect in what happened to my mother?"

"We just need to have a clear picture of everything that took place last night, Mr. Bordain," Hicks said.

"Well I didn't run my mother off the road," he said. "I don't know how much clearer I can make that picture."

"We're paid to be suspicious of everyone, Mr. Bordain," Mendez explained. "Most interpersonal crime is committed by people who know their victims. Family is always one prong of an investigation like this. It's not personal on our part."

"It's difficult not to see it as personal from where I'm sitting," Bordain said.

He shook a cigarette out of the pack on the table before him and lit up, blowing smoke at the acoustic tile ceiling.

"I know I make a lot of sly remarks about my mother," he said. "But I wouldn't kill her, for God's sake."

"We aren't accusing you, Mr. Bordain," Hicks said.

"Think of it this way," Mendez said. "Our questions might be an irritation to you, and you might feel like we're being insulting or insensitive, but the person we're working for is usually injured or dead and she won't ever have the luxury of feeling irritated again."

Bordain conceded the point with a nod of the head. "Well put. I'll stop my whining now."

"When was the last time you saw Ms. Fordham?" Hicks asked.

"I saw Marissa Sunday, a week ago—the Sunday before she was killed. There was a fall festival at the Licosto Winery between here and Santa Barbara. Food by local chefs, wine tasting, rides in a horse-drawn wagon and games for the kids. There was sort of a loose group of us from Oak Knoll. Marissa brought Haley. How is she, by the way?"

"She's doing well, considering," Mendez said. "Her memory is getting clearer every day."

Bordain frowned and tapped the ash off his cigarette into the small ashtray that had been provided for him. "I hope that's a good thing."

"If she can name her mother's killer, why wouldn't it be?"

"You're kidding, right? Didn't she see the whole thing? Would you want a memory like that in your head for the rest of your life? Better for her if she never remembered any of it."

"Better for the killer too."

"I suppose."

"Did Marissa ever tell you someone was bothering her, that someone in her life scared her, anything like that?" Hicks asked.

Bordain raised an elegant eyebrow. "Marissa? Scared? No. What's that beer commercial about grabbing all the gusto?"

"Did she ever say anything to you about Haley's father?"

"No. I got the impression that was a sore subject. As open and free a spirit as she was, there was always a little reserve in Marissa. It was like you got ninety-eight percent of her, which was a lot—until you started thinking about that missing two percent that she never gave to anybody. I think she'd gotten hurt somewhere along the line. I assumed by Haley's father."

"Do you know who he is?"

"No. She had Haley when she moved here. I assumed he was wherever she came from."

"The East Coast."

"I guess so."

"Would it surprise you if I told you Marissa came up here from Los Angeles?" Mendez asked.

"Nothing about Marissa would surprise me."

"Would it surprise you to know her real name wasn't Marissa Fordham?"

Bordain shrugged. "I don't know. Why would I care? She was who she was. Are you going to tell me she was a secret agent or something? In witness protection?"

"How did you feel about your mother's relationship with Marissa?" Mendez asked. "The daughter she never had."

"Well, since I can't be the daughter my mother never had, it was okay by me."

"Your mother spent a lot of money on Marissa."

"My mother spends a lot of money. Period. Luckily, my father is filthy stinking rich. My mother's hobbies have no impact on my life."

"It didn't bother you even a little bit?" Mendez asked.

Bordain gave him a hard look. "No. I liked Marissa. She had a great joie de vivre. If she could get my mother to foot the bill, more power to her."

Mendez pushed a little harder. "Why do you think someone would murder Marissa, cut off her breasts, and send them to your mother?"

"I don't know. Isn't that your department?"

"That's a very personal offense," Mendez said. "First, the murder. Stabbing is a very personal crime. Sending the breasts to your mother, also a highly personal gesture. It's a big Fuck You, if you'll pardon my language."

"I don't know what you want me to say."

"Have you been in Lompoc recently?" Hicks asked.

"No. Why would I go there?"

"You've got a car dealership up there."

"Yes, but we've got a good manager. There's no reason for me to go there when I can pick up the phone. I divide my time between here and Santa Barbara."

"Where were you last Sunday night?" Mendez asked.

"The night Marissa was killed?" Bordain tried to laugh. "You want my alibi?"

No one laughed with him.

"We need to know where you were."

He stalled, lighting another cigarette. His hands shook a little. "I was at Gina's house."

Mendez exchanged a long look with Hicks.

"You were with Gina Kemmer?"

"Not in the Biblical sense. She had a couple of friends over. Marissa called and said she was busy. We ate a pizza and watched a couple of movies. I was home by eleven thirty."

"Have you heard from Gina lately?" Mendez asked.

"A couple of days ago." He looked increasingly uncomfortable with the pace and nature of the questions. "You asked me that last night. Why?"

"Where were you this past Wednesday from, say, five o'clock on?" Hicks asked.

Bordain sighed impatiently, tapped off his cigarette, took another drag, and blew the smoke out his nostrils. "I worked until about six, had a couple of drinks at Capriano's, ate some dinner . . ." His memory seemed to start failing then. "I don't know. I went home. I don't account for every hour of every day of my life, do you?"

"I'm pretty much here," Mendez said. "You didn't see Gina Kemmer that day?"

"No. She called me that afternoon about a funeral for Marissa. I didn't see her. Why?"

"Gina Kemmer has been missing since late Wednesday afternoon," Hicks said.

"Missing?" Bordain said stupidly, as if he didn't understand the meaning of the word.

"Right," Mendez said. "She won't be able to corroborate your alibi for the night Marissa died because no one has seen or heard from her in two days."

Bordain looked from one detective to the other.

"I think I should go now," he said, standing up abruptly. "I don't like the turn this is taking."

Mendez sat back in his chair and spread his hands. "If you haven't done anything wrong, there's nothing for you to be uncomfortable about."

"Look," Bordain said, snatching up his cigarettes and lighter. "I had nothing to do with Marissa's murder. I did not send severed breasts to my mother in the mail. I did not try to run her off the road. Wherever Gina is, I didn't put her there."

"Would you be willing to take a polygraph?" Hicks asked.

"No, I would not," he said. "And you have no reason to keep me here, so—"

"You're free to go at any time," Mendez said. "We just need to get a quick photo of you before you leave."

"For what?"

"For Haley. We'll be showing her photographs of all the men in her mother's life to see if she has a reaction—"

"Absolutely not," Bordain said, angry. "You're going to put me in a lineup for a four-year-old child who's been traumatized and is probably brain damaged? Go to hell."

They watched him go to the door and stand there. Mendez got up and made his way over to let him out.

"Some people who come in here aren't as free to go as others," he said.

Bordain said nothing, but walked out and wasted no time getting to the end of the hall. Vince came out of the break room to watch him go.

"He didn't take that well," Mendez said.

Vince shrugged. "Go figure."

62

Halfway up the ladder the world went silent. Gina had no idea how much time it had taken her to get this far. It seemed like days must have passed. Each step up was more difficult than the last, her body was more exhausted, her mind drifting in and out of reality. With each step she had to rest longer, and with each rest she felt more inclined to just go to sleep and fall into the next dimension.

She thought she might be crying, but it was as if all aspects of her—body, mind, spirit—were drifting apart and losing the connection to one another. Marissa had stopped talking to her. Silence rang in her ears.

She was close to giving up. The little bit of rotten food she had eaten had come back up from the pain and the effort of moving. What adrenaline she had used to start the climb was spent.

Starving and dehydrated, she had no energy reserves to draw on. Unknown to her, the concentrated acid in her empty stomach had begun to eat through the stomach lining. She was aware of that pain because it was new and sharp. The pain in her broken ankle was so enormous and had been so continuous that in a weird way it had become like deafening white noise in her head. The pain in her shoulder where she had been shot throbbed now like a bass drum. Infection had begun to set in.

I just want to lie down.

No one told her not to.

She couldn't remember how long she had been standing on this rung. She had hooked her good arm through the iron loop and put her head against the dirty concrete wall to rest. Just for a minute . . . and then another . . . and another . . .

In one tiny corner of her mind she was very afraid, but that little voice wasn't strong enough to wake her. It tried to shout, but seemed so far away.

I don't want to die!

Her pulse was shallow and quick. She wondered dimly if that meant not enough blood was getting to her brain.

If she could just lie down and rest. If the pain would stop for just a while . . .

If she could just let go . . .

Then she did let go, and her body felt weightless, and it seemed to take forever just falling and falling.

NO!!!

"No!"

And BANG! Like that, all the disparate parts of her being slammed back together, and her body jerked as if she had been given an electrical shock. She grabbed tight to the iron rung as her good foot started to slip.

Climb! Marissa's voice shouted. *Damn it, G., climb!*

Dry wracking sobs shaking her, Gina forced herself to reach up for the next rung.

Even as she did it, she was thinking, *I can't do it. I can't make it. I'm so tired. I feel so weak.*

You can do it, Gina! You have to. Do it for me. Do it for Haley. One more. Come on. Come on!

One more.

And then one more.

Her head hit the rotten door. She pushed it open.

And then she was lying on the ground, in the mud, the steady cold rain drenching her to the bone.

63

"I love a school holiday," Franny said, pouring the coffee. He made himself at home wherever he was, particularly in Anne's kitchen. "Thanksgiving, Christmas, Sixth Graders Putting Cherry Bombs Down the Toilets Day."

The resulting plumbing catastrophe had given the children and teachers of Oak Knoll Elementary an unexpected long weekend.

"I'm glad for the company of another adult," Anne said. "The mind of a four-year-old can be exhausting to keep up with."

"They haven't been dumbed down by society yet at that age," Franny said, doctoring the coffee with cream and cinnamon. "Everything is possible."

They went into the family room with its big bank of windows looking out on the backyard. The rain was still coming down. Haley and Wendy were busy with dolls at one end of the room. Franny and Anne each took a big stuffed leather chair near the windows.

"Haley asked me if I would be her mommy until her mommy is done being an angel," Anne said.

"Oh!" Franny's eyes filled with tears. "That should be in a children's book!"

"A children's book about death?"

"They take it better than we do. What did you tell her?"

"Yes, of course. I'd keep her forever," Anne admitted wistfully.

"Maybe you will."

"I can't think that way. I'm sure she has relatives somewhere. Everyone does, right?"

"That doesn't mean she should go and live with them," Franny said. "What if her relatives are toothless rednecks living in travel trailers in one of those fried food states in the middle of the country? Oh! What if they're carnie people?" he asked, getting carried away with himself, as usual. "Next thing you know Haley's in a sideshow as the Bearded Baby."

Anne chuckled, appreciating the distraction that was her friend.

"This is a nice way to spend a rainy afternoon," she said. "Good company, a hot drink, watching kids play."

Franny smiled at her until his eyes disappeared.

"What?"

"You're going to be such a good mom!" he said.

"If Vince and I ever get to sleep together again," Anne said dryly.

"You've been staying with Haley?"

Anne nodded. "She's having some pretty scary nightmares."

"You know all about that. Has she named the k-i-l-l-e-r yet?"

"No. She calls him Bad Daddy. She says he was dressed all in black. Vince is going to bring home some kind of photo lineup of men who knew her mother. Maybe she'll pick one out. But there's always a chance the killer wore a mask."

"Don't you think he tried to k-i-l-l Haley because she could identify him? Why else?"

"Maybe he's just plain evil," Anne said. "How about that?"

"Mommy Anne!" Haley called as she came running from the other end of the room. "Look at my dolly Wendy gave me!"

"That's a really special doll, isn't it?"

"I'm gonna call her Kitty," Haley announced, "because I want a kitty."

"Okay! That's a good name!"

Anne rolled her eyes at Franny as Haley scampered away. "We're lobbying heavily for a kitty."

"She couldn't be cuter if she was my child," Franny said.

The front doorbell rang and Anne jumped like she'd been given an electric shock. She could almost feel the blood drain from her face. This was part of her post-crime sentence, to panic at the sound of the door-bell when she wasn't expecting anyone.

Franny frowned. "I'll see who it is."

Anne followed him at a distance to the front of the house, trying to calm herself, to tell herself there was no reason to panic. Peter Crane was sitting in jail. He wouldn't be on the other side of her door ready to attack her.

No. It wasn't Peter Crane at the door, but a whole other kind of threat Anne realized as she heard Franny say, "Maureen Upchurch. How's your nephew? Has he been incarcerated yet?"

"What are *you* doing here?"

"Unlike some people, I have friends," Franny said.

Anne moved around him to see Maureen Upchurch and Milo Bordain on her front step.

Because of her aversion to surprise guests and because of Vince's background with the FBI, she and Vince had taken great pains to keep their address private. But of course Maureen would have access to her address because of Haley. And here she was, looking as put out as always.

"This is a surprise," Anne said. "What can I do for you ladies?"

"And she uses the term loosely," Franny whispered behind her. Anne stepped back on his foot.

"It's just a formality," Maureen said, "but I insisted to Judge Espinoza that I make the obligatory home visit so my office can retain some kind of record of this situation."

"A phone call would have been nice," Anne said.

"The visits are drop-ins for a reason," Upchurch countered.

"Oh my God!" Franny exclaimed, slapping his cheeks. "I'll go hide the sex toys!"

Milo Bordain, impeccably turned out in a Burberry plaid raincoat, turned to Maureen Upchurch. "Who is that person?"

Franny stepped around Anne and offered his hand. She didn't take it. "Francis Goodsell, three-time California Teacher of the Year in the kindergarten division. Love the scarf. Hermès?"

Milo Bordain touched a gloved hand to the scarf wound around the throat of her camel cashmere turtleneck as if she were afraid he might try to strip it from her.

Anne focused on the Child Protective Services supervisor. "And did you tell Judge Espinoza you'd be dropping by unannounced with a third party in tow? Because if you're such a stickler for the rules, Maureen, I'm pretty sure tagalongs aren't in the book."

"That's my fault," Bordain said. "Maureen knows how badly I want to see Haley. She was kind enough to invite me along. I hope you don't mind, Anne."

"I do mind," Anne said bluntly.

"But Haley is like a granddaughter to me," Bordain went on, tearing up. "I've lost her mother—"

"Yes, I know," Anne said, "and I'm terribly sorry for your loss, Mrs. Bordain. Really, I'm not trying to be difficult. But as Haley's guardian I'm trying to maintain a certain amount of structure for her. Having people just show up can be overstimulating to a small child, especially to a child who's already had a sudden traumatic upheaval in her life."

"But Haley knows me," Bordain argued, the tears threatening to spill over. "I've been worried sick about her! Thinking about how frightened she must have been, wondering what kind of terrible memories must be plaguing her. I would have tried to arrange something with you myself, but I didn't have any way of contacting you. And I brought her a little gift," she said, holding up a shoebox-size package wrapped in rainbow paper with a big pink bow.

Anne held fast for a moment, weighing the pros and cons. She saw Milo Bordain as a threat to her custody of Haley, but it was probably smarter to have the woman for a friend than an enemy. And she did know what loss was. Anne knew what a hole her mother's death had left inside her. Milo Bordain was suffering the loss of a surrogate daughter. That loss was clearly taking a toll on her. Even the most expensive makeup couldn't conceal the dark circles under her eyes or the deepening lines on her forehead and around her mouth.

Finally she sighed. "Let me go tell Haley you're here so she isn't taken by surprise."

She walked toward the back of the house with Franny right beside her.

"I'm going to the kitchen," he whispered. "To make a crucifix out of garlic to ward them off."

Anne went into the family room.

"Haley, sweetheart," she said, sitting on the ottoman next to the couch where Haley was busy tucking her new doll in bed. "Someone is here to see you."

Haley's eyes got big. "Is it my mommy?"

"No, sweetie. It's Mrs. Bordain. Do you remember her?"

Haley scowled and shook her head.

"Maybe you called her something else. Wendy, did you ever meet Mrs. Bordain at Marissa's house?"

Wendy, now engrossed in a *Brady Bunch* rerun on television, shook her head.

"Haley! It's Auntie Milo!"

Bordain and Maureen Upchurch had invited themselves inside. They came into the family room, a formidable duo—Bordain as tall as a man, Upchurch as big as a house in a black tent for a raincoat.

Haley, already overtired from playing with Wendy, immediately started to cry. Bad Daddy was big and came in black clothes.

Anne picked her up and turned so Haley couldn't see them.

"Maureen, please take your coat off. The black coat is scaring her."

"My coat? Why would that scare her?"

Anne glared at her. "Take off the coat."

Understanding dawned on Milo Bordain's face.

"The attacker must have worn a black coat," she said, then snapped at Upchurch. "Take your coat off, Maureen."

Anne ignored them both, trying to quiet Haley.

"It's okay, sweetheart. Your auntie Milo missed you so much she had to come see you, and she brought you a present."

The flow of tears stopped, one big one dangling on the edge of her eyelashes. She took a shuddering breath and looked at Milo Bordain.

"Hi, Haley!" Bordain made her voice higher and softer. "How are you?"

"My mommy is an angel now," Haley said.

"I know, darling. We miss her, don't we?"

Haley nodded, thumb zeroing in on mouth. She rested her head on Anne's shoulder.

"She tires easily," Anne explained. "Have a seat."

She settled herself on the sofa with Haley on her lap as Milo Bordain chose the ottoman. Anne gave her a point for that—sitting as close as possible instead of choosing a chair six feet away. Upchurch was busy checking the tables for dust and looking with envy at the quality of the furniture.

"Haley," Bordain said, leaning forward with the gift. "I brought you something special for you to have here at Anne's house."

Haley took the present and tugged on the bow.

"We'll keep that for you to wear in your hair," Anne said, setting the ribbon aside.

Her bout of tears forgotten, Haley had moved on to the box, dispensing with the rainbow paper in short order.

"It's a kitty!" she exclaimed, pulling the stuffed toy out of the tissue paper.

"I thought you were probably missing your kitties at your house," Bordain said. "This is a kitty you can take anywhere."

Anne felt her heart soften a little more toward Milo Bordain. She had actually put some thought into the gift and had clearly paid attention to Haley's obsession with cats and kittens.

"What do you say, Haley?" Anne prompted.

"Thank you, Daddy Milo!"

"Auntie Milo," Anne corrected her.

"It's all right," Bordain said. "Haley tells me I should be a boy because I have a boy's name."

Haley was through with the adults, off the couch and taking her new treasure to show her friend. "Wendy, look at my kitty! I got a kitty, but it's not a real one. It just looks like one."

"That's cool, Haley!" Wendy said. "Let's put her with your dolls. What are you going to name her?"

"Scaredy Cat."

"Scaredy Cat?"

"She's obsessed with the idea of the daddy," Anne said.

"That's Marissa's fault," Milo Bordain said with a hint of bitterness. "I told her time and again she should get married and give Haley a father, but she wouldn't listen to me."

"Did she bring boyfriends home?" Anne asked.

"Not in any way that was improper. Marissa was a very conscientious mother. But she had a lot of male friends. I always thought it was confusing for Haley. She calls every man in her life Daddy."

"She has friends with conventional families, a mommy and a daddy," Anne said. "It's normal for her to want that too."

"How is she coping?" Bordain asked. "I've been so worried about her."

"It's a roller coaster. Children Haley's age think death is temporary, and they haven't developed psychologically to a place where they have the tools to think through a grieving process like adults do—and it's difficult for us. We can only imagine how confusing those feelings are to a child.

"So one minute Haley might be upset that her mother is gone, and the next minute she's engrossed in a cartoon or talking about becoming a fairy princess. As she grows up and begins to comprehend more, she'll likely go through different stages of grief at different ages. It's a long process."

"And has she said anything about what happened or who attacked them?" Maureen Upchurch asked, planting herself in Vince's Man Chair.

"She's having nightmares about a figure all in black," Anne said. "Bad Daddy. No name. She may never say a name. Her subconscious mind may never let her."

"Poor little thing," Bordain said, distressed. "Her whole life has been turned upside down!"

Haley came back with her new toy tucked under her arm. "Where are my real kitties?"

"I had Hernando bring the mother cat and kittens to my house so we can feed them and take care of them," Bordain said. "They're living in the barn with the horses and the chickens. You should come visit them sometime soon."

Haley lit up and turned to Anne. "Can we, Mommy Anne? Can we, please?"

Anne felt sucker punched, and there was nothing she could do but sit here and take it on the chin. Consciously or unconsciously, Milo Bordain had set her up.

"Mommy Anne?" Bordain arched a brow.

"That's what Haley likes to call me," Anne explained. "It gives her a little sense of security."

"That seems completely inappropriate," Maureen Upchurch said.

"She's four," Anne returned. "Let her have that if she wants it."

Haley, impatient with the grown-ups, hopped up and down. "Can we, please, please, please?"

"I would love it if you would bring Haley out to see them!" Milo Bordain said, recovering from her instant reaction of disapproval. "Haley would so enjoy that. She loves all the animals. Don't you, sweetheart? We have cattle and horses and sheep and goats and chickens.

"You should bring her," she said to Anne. "I'll have Hernando and Maria set up a picnic for us by the reservoir."

Before Anne could draw breath for an excuse, Haley was right there with the big eyes and hopeful little cherub face.

"Mommy Anne! Can we go? Can we go, *pleeeeeeeeze?*"

"We'll see," Anne said.

"Uh-oh," Haley said, looking at her auntie Milo. "That means no."

"It means we'll wait and see," Anne said.

"I don't see why you wouldn't bring her," Bordain said, getting irritated.

Franny saved her from the awkward moment, emerging from the kitchen with a tray laden with drinks and cookies, calling, "Tea time for all the kitties! I mean kiddies!"

Anne took the two women on a tour of the house to satisfy Maureen Upchurch's jealous curiosity, then herded them out the front door with an excuse about nap time and a promise to call Milo Bordain about the possible trip to the ranch.

When she came back into the family room, the girls were tucked side by side on the couch watching a purple dinosaur on television, Haley with her thumb in her mouth and her eyelids at half-mast. Anne dropped down in her leather chair by the window and looked at Franny.

"I didn't see that coming," she said. "I should have, but I didn't."

"You're a parent now. You're officially sleep deprived."

"How can I compete with a ranch?"

"You can't, but you've got it all over that one in the warm fuzzy love department. The only thing fuzzy about that old tranny cow is her whisker stubble."

Anne laughed wearily at the terrible remark. "She's a what?"

Franny rolled his eyes. "Oh, please, Anne Marie. You ruin all my best lines by being tragically un-hip. T-r-a-n-n-y as in t-r-a-n-s-v-e-s-t-i-t-e! If she doesn't have a set of balls under that skirt, she's hiding them somewhere."

"You are just awful."

"Honestly!" He laughed. "How she hatched that gorgeous son of hers is beyond me."

"Who's her son?"

"Darren 'You deserve a Mercedes' Bordain! Don't you watch television? He does all the ads. He's gorgeous! And so well-dressed."

"He sounds like the man for you."

"Of course he's totally in the closet. He's so deep in the closet even last year's fashion can't see him in there."

"That could mean he's straight," Anne argued.

"You want to spoil all my fantasies."

"You think every good-looking man is secretly gay."

"I don't think Vince is gay."

"Thank God," Anne said. She breathed a big sigh. "Oh, Franny . . . Please tell me it's five o'clock somewhere."

"Darling, it's always five o'clock somewhere," he said, producing a glass of red wine from behind the lamp on the end table.

Anne took a sip, savored it, swallowed, and sighed. "I love you, Franny."

"I know, sweetheart," he said. "Everyone does."

64

Vince sat in his car for a while just looking at the offices of Quinn, Morgan and Associates: Attorneys at Law. Theirs was a well-respected practice, specializing in family and civil law.

Steve Morgan hadn't made partner by being reckless or an idiot. On the contrary. Vince knew him to be very intelligent, very closed, and very careful.

He had sat down across from Steve Morgan a couple of times during the See-No-Evil cases. The cops had all but had a photo of him having sex with victim Lisa Warwick, but he had never cracked. Not even the threat of DNA technology—which they didn't exactly have yet, but made for a good bluff—not even that had rattled him. He never admitted the affair.

What he knew about Steve Morgan was this: He had come from a difficult background. Prostitute mother, no father figure in his life.

He professed a great love for his mother, which Vince had sometimes found in men with such backgrounds to be a veil to cover a deep hatred. Boys growing up in that situation with no positive male role model in their lives often felt vulnerable and unprotected by their only parent, their mother. They grew up watching their mother degrade herself, and watching other men degrade and objectify her. This generally led to the boys having a disdain and lack of respect for women and to harboring a seething anger, which could erupt into violence with the right trigger.

Steve Morgan was intelligent, had done well in school, had graduated at the top of his class from the University of California at Berkeley, where he had met Sara. Then came law school at the University of Southern California. Top honors. Next: a couple of good jobs in the greater Los Angeles area. Marriage, a baby, a move to Oak Knoll for a

SECRETS TO THE GRAVE   309

better quality of life and a job with Don Quinn, whom he had met on his first job out of law school.

And during all of this, he had been an active advocate for the rights of underprivileged women. Admirable.

But the wheels had started coming off the tracks for Steve Morgan, and the question was, why?

Inasmuch as he had shot down Tony's theory of Steve Morgan being involved with Peter Crane in the See-No-Evil murders, it wasn't a stretch to take a man with Morgan's psychopathology and put him in the role of killer.

And that type of killer's victimology? Prostitutes, disadvantaged women . . . free-spirit single moms with lots of boyfriends.

What were the odds of having two highly intelligent, organized, sexually sadistic serial killers in a town the size of Oak Knoll—at the same time, no less? Astronomical. And that the two would have been friends? Vince would have to have the mathematical mind of Zander Zahn to calculate those numbers.

That was something that would only happen in Hollywood on a movie screen, like Jack the Ripper and the Marquis de Sade teaming up to take on one town.

Not that Vince didn't know of teams of killers. He had interviewed both Larry Bittaker and Roy Norris, notorious for the incredibly brutal torture killings of five young women in Los Angeles in 1979. And Kenneth Bianchi and his cousin Angelo Buono, who had also gone down in LA in 1979 for killing ten young women in the infamous Hillside Strangler cases.

But a team took the exact right two people with the exact right mix of bad chemistry. One partner was always dominant, the other a follower. And when the chips were down in a police interview room, invariably one would turn on the other one in a heartbeat in order to secure a more lenient prison sentence. Because psychopaths care only about themselves and their own well-being, they possess no loyalty to a partner.

Vince was confident Morgan had not worked in concert with Peter Crane in the See-No-Evil murders. Crane's killings had been the highly methodical and ritualistic work of a man with a very specific sexually sadistic fantasy.

Marissa Fordham's murder had been a rage killing, pure and simple.

She had been stabbed and stabbed and stabbed and stabbed until her killer's rage was spent. The removal of her breasts and the placement of the knife protruding from her vagina had been postmortem statements.

Now Vince had to find out if Steve Morgan possessed that kind of rage.

He got out of his car and flipped up the collar of his coat against the continuing drizzle, and walked across the street to the office of Quinn, Morgan, et al. He greeted the receptionist with his most charming smile.

"Vince Leone to see Mr. Morgan," he said.

The young woman frowned and whispered, "I'm sorry, Mr. Morgan isn't seeing clients today."

"Please just let him know I'm here," Vince whispered back. "I think he'll see me."

He helped himself to a butterscotch from the candy dish on the counter while the woman called Morgan.

The outer office was very tastefully done in shades of gray with touches of teal and burgundy. It said MONEY, but quietly, and established a feeling of calm and trustworthiness one would want from a family attorney.

"You can go right in, Mr. Leone," the receptionist murmured.

"Thank you."

Steve Morgan sat behind his big desk looking like the losing side of a prizefight. Mendez had popped him good. Both eyes were black—one more so than the other—and his nose was a mushy purple lump taped to his face. That the guy wasn't going to sue the department suggested to Vince a big whopping dose of self-loathing. On some level Morgan must have thought he had it coming.

"I must really be a suspect now," Morgan said. "They've brought out the Big Gun."

Vince held his hands up. "No tricks up my sleeves. I'm not a cop anymore. I'm retired from the Bureau."

"I will argue that you're acting as an agent of the sheriff's office."

"Nothing you say here can or will be used against you in a court of law."

"So you're just here for the hell of it?"

"I saw Sara today."

"Oh."

Vince helped himself to a seat. They looked at each other for a moment. Each trying to read the other's mind before the chess match began.

"Is she having me arrested?"

"For what? Have you broken the law?"

"She was pretty upset when she threw me out of my own house last night."

"Sounds like you had a pretty big helping of upset yourself."

"I don't like being accused of things I didn't do," Morgan said. "Especially by my wife. You know, I took those vows pretty seriously."

"Until when?" Vince asked. "You and I both know you cheat on her, Steve. Don't bother with the big show on my account."

Morgan sighed. "I suppose it won't matter if I tell you my marriage is none of your business."

"No, because it is now—seeing how Sara came and talked to me about it."

Morgan narrowed his good eye. "Why would Sara talk to you?"

"Sara and Anne have gotten to be friends over the last year. You might not know that—you being so busy and all with other women and whatnot."

"Then why wouldn't she talk to Anne instead of you?"

Vince smiled. "Because Anne can't get your ass thrown in jail if need be."

Morgan was unfazed. "Which brings me back to my original question: Is Sara having me arrested for something?"

"No."

Vince scanned the desktop. Morgan had made no attempt to hide the fact that he was drinking. A heavy crystal tumbler sat to the left side of his blotter with three fingers of something in it. Jameson Irish whiskey from the bottle sitting on top of a book containing California divorce law.

"I like Sara," Vince said. "She's a nice gal. She's smart, she's talented. Beautiful—that goes without saying, right? And she loves you."

"Hard to believe, huh?"

Vince shook his head. "Nah. I can see it. You're a good-looking guy—usually. You're a go-getter. You're compassionate to the less fortunate in your community. You do good works. She tells me you've overcome a lot in your life. That's admirable. Why shouldn't she fall in love with you?"

Morgan gave a barely perceptible shrug.

"She had your baby," Vince went on, "gave you a beautiful daughter. The two of you had it all."

Steve Morgan took a stiff swig of the whiskey and sat back in his chair.

"And then I fucked it all up, right?"

Vince shrugged. "You tell me. The wheels started coming off the tracks somewhere along the line. Did you start to think she couldn't really understand you? Her being from a nice family, how could she really get it?

"Or did you start to think you just really don't deserve it? She's out of your league. You might as well fuck it up and show her instead of waiting for her to figure it out on her own.

"Most women marry down, you know. It's a known fact," Vince said. "This is the voice of experience talking here. I'm one lucky son of a bitch, and I know it. I have to look over my shoulder every day, looking for the other shoe to drop. But I cut myself some slack and figure not to look a gift horse in the mouth, you know? Horses bite."

It was a good sign, he thought, that he hadn't been asked to leave. That meant something. Morgan was listening. Was he processing or was he just sitting there thinking how full of shit this jackass from Chicago was?

"Do you ask yourself these questions, Steve?" he asked quietly. "You're a smart guy. Jesus, look at the diplomas," he said, pointing to the wall at one end of the room. "How can such a smart guy be so fucking stupid? Do you ask yourself that?"

"Every day," Morgan murmured, and took another sip of the whiskey.

A little jolt of excitement went through Vince. Score. He wasn't just talking. He had given something up. He felt unworthy. Maybe he didn't get it himself how he could have something so perfect and throw it away with both hands.

"Can I have a couple fingers of that?" Vince asked, gesturing to the bottle of Jameson.

Morgan shrugged. "Why not?"

He reached around to the bookcases behind him and came back with another tumbler, which he handed across the desk. Vince poured himself a drink and took a sip, savoring the smooth smoky quality of the liquor.

"That's nice," he said. "The Italians can stomp a grape, but you can't beat the Irish for whiskey."

Morgan lifted his glass in a toast to the sentiment.

"So," Vince said. "What do you think? Have you broken it? Is it over?"

"You tell me. She talked to you."

Vince gave him a pained expression. "It doesn't look good."

The barest hint of a sad smile creased Steve Morgan's mouth. "I make a living persuading people to see things my way."

On the face of it, that sounded as if he meant to try to win Sara back. But Vince had a feeling it meant he had already succeeded in convincing Sara she should leave him.

"You scared her pretty bad last night," Vince said. "What was that? The coup de grace? Really drive it home what an asshole you are? Or do you really want her to think you might have killed that woman?"

"She already thinks it."

"Might as well be true?" Vince asked.

Morgan said nothing, but poured himself a little more to drink.

"You were supposedly in Sacramento when it happened," Vince said. "But you weren't, were you? And don't bother lying about it because Cal Dixon has a guy who can track that shit down like a freaking bloodhound."

"I wasn't where I said I would be."

"You were with a woman."

"I plead the fifth."

"You'd rather get charged with a murder than admit you're an adulterer when everybody who matters already knows you fuck around? That doesn't make any sense."

"It might to the person I was with."

"It does if that person was Marissa Fordham."

"It wasn't."

" 'Do you think I was stabbing her forty-seven times and cutting her throat?' That's what you said. How did you pick that number, Steve?"

"Why? Was I right?"

"Damn close. Close enough to raise an eyebrow," Vince said. "Not that most killers keep count when they're going at it with a knife like that. But I can tell you, stranger things have happened."

"If I did, I'd be crazy to say so," Morgan said.

"Yeah," Vince said. "Like a fox."

Morgan slowly drank the last of his whiskey and set the glass down without making a sound. He looked Vince right in eye and said, "You have no evidence linking me to Marissa's death because there is no evidence linking me to Marissa's death because I didn't kill her. I'd like you to go now, Vince. Thanks for stopping by."

65

Crawl, G. Don't just lie there. Crawl!

Marissa was on her hands and knees in the mud, bending down in her face.

Crawl! Damn it, Gina! You can't give up now!

But I'm so tired, and it's so nice right here.

No, it isn't. Are you stupid? It's raining. You're facedown in the mud!

I'm so warm. I'm hot. Why do I have all these clothes on?

Oh my God. You're not hot. You're cold. Do you hear me? Do you hear me?

Shut up, Marissa. I hear something.

A very distant whup, whup, whup, whup.

It's a helicopter, stupid.

Don't call me stupid. This was all your idea.

I was trying to do good. We did something good!

You're dead.

Then how can you see me? How can you hear me? Gina? Gina!

All she wanted to do was go to sleep, but Marissa grabbed her good arm and pulled it straight out in front of her, and tried to drag her.

Crawl! You have to do this for Haley! You have to get to the fire road. If you get to the fire road they'll find you!

The fire road. She remembered being driven onto the fire road and marched up it with a gun in her back in the dead of night.

Who?

Who what?

Who will find me?

I don't know! Firemen. Big, hunky firemen.

I love firemen. My dad was a fireman.

No, he wasn't. Your dad sold insurance.

It's my hallucination.

Oh, for God's sake! Crawl, Gina! You're going to die if you don't start crawling! You don't want to die. You can't die! You're the only one who knows the truth. You have to do this for Haley! Crawl, Gina!

For Haley. Gina gathered her strength to try. She tried to dig into the rocky ground with her good hand, feeling fingernails break. She had to gain some kind of purchase. She pulled her good leg into position and pushed off, shoving herself forward.

She expected to feel pain, terrible, blinding pain. She felt nothing. It was as if her brain had become unplugged from her body. She was so weak, so very weak, but she was free of the pain.

Marissa grabbed her arm again and pulled. Gina moved her good leg and pushed. She gained maybe a foot.

How far is the fire road?

Not far. Keep going. Keep pushing.

The process was repeated again and again with rest breaks in between. With each effort she felt weaker and weaker until she couldn't pull her good leg up more than a few inches, and she couldn't move herself any farther than that.

I can't, Marissa. It's too far. It's too late.

What else have you got to do with your time? You might as well go until you die.

I don't want to die. I don't want to die. I don't want to die.

She didn't want to die. She couldn't die. She was the only one who knew the story.

66

"I don't know what more I can tell you guys," Mark Foster said, following Mendez and Hicks back to the interview rooms. "I don't feel like I can be that much of a help."

"It's like I told you over the phone, Mr. Foster," Hicks said. "We're trying to establish a really detailed outline of Ms. Fordham's life in the week or so leading up to her murder."

"Things that might seem insignificant to you could fill in the puzzle for us," Mendez said. He opened the door to room two and motioned Foster in.

Everyone took a seat at the small table. Foster looked around, seeming a little uneasy.

"I've never been in this situation," he admitted. "All I know is what I've seen on television."

"We're not going to shine a light in your face or bring in a big dude with brass knuckles," Mendez assured him. "Unless we don't like your answers."

They all laughed politely.

Foster was in his uniform of khaki pants and blue oxford shirt, but had added a sweater vest to the ensemble, and a blue blazer to ward off the chill of the day. He looked too warm now.

"Would you like a cup of coffee?" Mendez asked. "It's a rotten day out there."

"No, I'm fine, thanks," Foster said, drying the raindrops off his wire-rimmed glasses with a handkerchief. "I saw on the news you're looking for Gina Kemmer. Have you found her yet?"

"No. Nothing yet. You were friends with her, right?"

"Yes."

"You spoke with her the day she went missing," Hicks said.

Foster's eyes opened and widened. "What? When?"

"Wednesday. Late afternoon."

"Uh . . ." Foster's wheels were spinning as he searched his memory—a little frantically, Mendez thought. "Wednesday . . . Oh, yeah. I was really busy that day. Gina called. She wanted to talk about a memorial for Marissa. I didn't have time to get into it."

"When did you last see her?"

"Sunday night. She had some friends over. You don't think anything has happened to her, do you?"

"We don't know," Mendez said. "I spoke with her the afternoon she went missing. She seemed extremely upset."

"Well, losing Marissa that way . . . ," Foster said. "They were like sisters. She was hysterical when I first spoke to her after the news broke."

"Did she mention anything—any reason she thought someone would have wanted to harm Ms. Fordham?" Hicks asked.

"No. My God, we were both in a state of shock. You don't think the killer would have gone after her too, do you?"

Mendez lifted a shoulder. "It's possible."

Foster shook his head. "I can't imagine the kind of mind that does something like that. People are saying she was stabbed seventy-two times and her body was mutilated. That's insane. That person has to be insane, right?"

"That's not our call to make," Mendez said. "We just catch them and lock them up."

"I hope you're close to catching this one."

"You said the last time you saw Marissa was in Los Olivos—"

"Actually, that's not right. I saw her a week before she died at the Licosto Winery. They were having their fall festival. Great wine. Chefs from all around the area. Marissa was there with Haley. How is Haley?"

"She's doing well," Hicks said. "We're hoping she'll be able to identify the killer for us."

"That's a lot to put on a four-year-old child."

"She's our only living witness."

Foster shook his head, troubled by the thought.

"Did anything seem to be bothering Marissa that day?" Mendez asked.

"Marissa let things roll off her back," Foster said. "She'd had a little set-to with Mrs. Bordain that morning, but she just shrugged it off."

"What was that about?"

"Something ridiculous," he said. "I know Milo pretty well from working on the summer music festival committee. She's a force to be reckoned with but she always believes she's got the best of intentions. I always say whenever two or more are gathered Milo will form a committee and organize something."

"She's manipulative," Mendez said.

"It never occurs to her that other people have opinions different from her own," Foster said. "She's got all her people in her circle and she wants them to do what she wants them to do. Marissa was the exact opposite. She would go along with the program most of the time, but she'd put her foot down and say no every once in a while just to let Milo know she could."

"Can you give us a 'for instance'?" Hicks asked.

"Sure. For instance, Milo is very politically inclined. She and Bruce are big contributors to their party. She wanted Marissa to appear and participate in a fund-raiser for a candidate. She had Marissa's dress chosen, the appointments made for the hairdresser, the whole thing. But Marissa didn't share the same political views as the Bordains, and she refused to do it. Milo didn't speak to her for two weeks."

"Was that a difficult spot for Marissa to be in? Having to please her sponsor?" Mendez asked.

"Not within the bounds of reason. But Milo isn't always reasonable. She's spoiled. She wants things her way or she'll pick up her Barbie dolls and go home."

"What about Darren Bordain?" Hicks asked.

"What about him?"

"You're friends."

"Yes."

"How did he feel toward Marissa?"

"They were pals. They liked to trade Milo war stories."

"Did they ever seem like more than friends?" Mendez asked.

"No."

"Did they ever seem like less than friends?"

Foster's brow furrowed in confusion. "They were friends. I'm not sure what you're fishing for."

"Mrs. Bordain's attachment to Marissa and Haley seemed almost familial," Mendez said. "Maybe that made for an odd family dynamic. Maybe there was some jealousy."

"Oh God, no." Foster shook his head. "If anything, that made Marissa and Darren allies."

"Is there any chance Darren could be Haley's father?" Mendez asked bluntly.

Foster's brows popped upward. "I don't think so. I mean, you'd have to ask him, but I don't think so."

"Is there any chance you could be Haley's father?" Hicks asked.

"No," without emotion. "I don't know who Haley's father is. Marissa never brought it up. No one else saw a need to. It wasn't important."

"It might have been important to someone," Mendez said. "It might have been important enough to kill for."

The door opened and Dixon stuck his head in and crooked a finger at Mendez.

"What's up?" Mendez asked, stepping into the hall and pulling the door closed behind him.

"I want you and Hicks at Mercy General. Search and Rescue found a woman out in the hills. It could be Gina Kemmer. It doesn't look good."

"Where did you find her?" Mendez asked.

They stood inside the doors to the ambulance bay in the Mercy General ER with the leader of the Search and Rescue team, Tom Scott, forty-something and built like an NFL linebacker—a mountain of muscle with the chiseled face of a cartoon superhero.

Hicks came back from the trauma unit with a grim face and a nod. "It's her."

"She was about fifty yards off a fire road up in the Dyer Canyon area. The dog found her. We were up in that general area looking for a guy. My young dog took off. He's just in training. I was gonna give him hell for that. So I went after him and when I came over the rise, here he was trying to drag this woman by the arm. He'd pull on her and bark at her and pull on her some more.

"Thank God for him. There's a lot of chaparral and scrub up there. We wouldn't have seen this lady. The chopper had gone over that area earlier and didn't see anything."

"What kind of shape is she in?" Mendez asked.

Scott rolled his eyes and shook his head. "Bad. GSW to the left shoulder. Looks like a through-and-through, but red and hot and full of pus. Broke her right ankle like nothing I've ever seen. Snapped both bones clean. You could turn her foot clear around."

"Oh my God," Mendez said.

Hicks went a little pale at the vivid description.

"Severely dehydrated. Severely hypothermic," Scott went on. "She was absolutely delirious when we got to her. Hallucinating, the whole nine yards."

"Is she conscious now?"

"No. I'll be really surprised if she makes it. I don't know what all she went through out there, but it was terrible. She had what looked like rat bites on her hands, on her legs, on her face. And stink! Like we pulled her out of a Calcutta sewer."

"Did she say anything when you found her?" Mendez asked. "Did she identify a perp? Anything?"

"No. She was babbling. Incoherent. By the time we got her in the chopper, she was out. I've never seen a BP that low and still have a pulse."

He nodded out the glass doors at the Search and Rescue vehicle where his partner was waiting. "I'm gonna go get my paperwork in, but I'll meet you guys out at the scene and show you everything."

"Shit," Mendez said as he watched the big man walk away. "We can't catch a fucking break."

"Us?" Hicks said, looking back toward the trauma unit. "You should see her. If you've got any favors to call in with the big guy upstairs, it's time to use them."

Mendez crossed himself. "God help her. God help us. The sooner the better."

67

The place where Gina Kemmer had been found, dragged from the brink of death by a German shepherd dog, was situated in a scrubby, rocky no-man's-land between several properties, among them Zander Zahn's home, Marissa Fordham's home, and the Bordain ranch. The spot was back off the fire road Zander Zahn had taken nearly every day over the hills to begin his morning with his free-spirited friend, Marissa, and her daughter.

There was nothing quiet or secluded about the area now as daylight was fading. The fire road was clogged with vehicles from the sheriff's office. Portable lights had been set up to focus on the spot where Gina had been found by Search and Rescue, and ran farther back off the road to what had at one time been a group of ranch buildings, now long abandoned and reduced to little more than sticks.

"We followed the drag marks back here," Tom Scott said loudly to be heard above the three helicopters circling the area—one from the SO, and two up from a television stations in Los Angeles. "It looks to me like she crawled out of this old well. Whoever shot her dumped her down there and left her for dead. That's some hell of a will she's got, getting herself out of there."

Mendez and Hicks both added the beams of their Maglites to the hole in the ground. The well was no more than five or six feet across and probably twenty feet or so down to the most horrific, stinking pile of garbage Mendez had caught a whiff of in a while.

"Jesus," he said. "If the fall doesn't kill you, the smell will."

"People have been throwing their garbage down this hole for years," Scott said. "Probably half the people in this valley do it. There's nothing to stop anyone coming up here. Kids from town party out here too.

There's a lot of beer cans around. Shit, I used to come up here when I was in high school."

He shined his light into the well and specifically on the rusty bent lengths of rebar cemented into the wall one above the other as a crude ladder. "I'll bet she caught her foot on one of these rungs on her way down. That's how she snapped that ankle like a toothpick."

"There's things moving down there," Mendez said.

"It's a friggin' rat smorgasbord down there," Scott said. "The rats get down in there through burrows or tunnels in the earth and come into the well where the old concrete has fallen away. God knows what all's down there. Rats, mice, snakes, scorpions."

"God knows, but we're going to have to find out," Hicks said. "Are you *sure* she was down in there?"

"I can't swear to it, but that's what it looked like to me. And by the way that girl smelled—she was down in there for a while."

"She's been missing since Wednesday afternoon," Mendez said.

The big man was impressed. "Wow. If this gal pulls through after all that, I've got to meet her. She must be something."

Funny, Mendez thought, he wouldn't have said so, having met Gina Kemmer. He would have pegged her for the more timid of the two friends. You never knew how people would handle adversity until push came to shove.

Hicks went over to snag one of the crime-scene team to send him down the hole.

"You couldn't pay me to go down there," Scott said.

Mendez laughed. "With those shoulders, you wouldn't fit, man."

"Good! I got no truck with mice. Mice come at me, seriously, man, I'll scream like a little girl."

"It takes a big man to admit that, Tom."

The CSI came with Hicks, protesting. "Are you fucking kidding me, man? You want me to go down there?"

"You're a crime-scene investigator," Hicks said. "There's a crime scene."

"I don't get paid enough for this."

"You've got to take that up with the county commissioners," Mendez told him. "In the meantime, I want to know if there's any evidence down there."

"Watch out for the mice!" Tom Scott called down after him as the investigator made his descent.

"Fuck you!"

The Search and Rescue leader laughed, then stood back and looked around, sobering.

"Seriously, man, this would be a lonely place to die."

Zahn's place was maybe a quarter mile or more over one hill. Marissa Fordham's house probably half a mile to the south. The Bordain ranch was even farther away to the north and west. Nobody would hear you scream up here. No one would hear your cries for help coming up out of the well. There was nothing up here but rabbits, coyotes, and rattlesnakes.

It wasn't hard to figure why someone had brought Gina Kemmer up here to kill her.

He turned again to Tom Scott. "You didn't find any sign of our missing math genius?"

Scott shook his head. "Nope. *Nada.*"

It was hard to picture Zander Zahn shooting someone. But it was even harder to picture him stabbing someone, and he had certainly done that. Where the hell had he gone?

But anybody living out in this area could have known about this spot. Anybody who hiked these hills. Anybody who might have taken a long walk with Marissa Fordham.

"You guys owe me big time," the evidence tech said, making his way back up the ladder with a big brown paper evidence bag hooked over one arm.

"Whatcha got there, Petey?" Hicks asked.

"Black clothes with what looks to me like dried blood. Looks like they were drenched in it."

Scott pulled him up the rest of the way out of the hole like he was a toy and set him on firm ground. He opened the bag and Hicks reached in and pulled out a large black sweatshirt that was rumpled and stiff. They all shined their lights on it.

"Drenched in it," Mendez said. "Somebody took a fucking blood bath."

And odds were good the blood that someone had bathed in was Marissa Fordham's.

"Gentlemen," he said. "We've finally got ourselves some evidence."

68

"We've finally got something," Dixon said. "Hallelujah."

"I've got deputies canvassing the area residents to find out if anybody saw anything Wednesday night," Mendez said, shrugging out of his coat. "It's the freaking wilderness out there, but maybe we'll get lucky.

"Has there been any word on Gina Kemmer?" Hicks asked.

"She's critical," Dixon said. "It's anybody's guess if she makes it through the night."

"She made it this far," Mendez said. "She should have been dead out there three times over."

"Let's hope she's still got some fight in her," Dixon said.

"Do we have someone on her room?" Mendez asked. "The killer is the only one in the state who isn't going to be impressed with her story of survival."

"The state?" Dixon said. "Try the country. I've got the networks on my ass for interviews. I'm told there's hardly a hotel room to be had in town. Between Marissa's murder, Haley, Zander Zahn, and Gina's story, the eyes of America are on us. Again."

"Our killer is going to start getting twitchy now," Vince said. "If he wasn't already. It was one thing to leave a four-year-old behind with the potential to ID him. It's something else to have a grown woman able to do it. He's going to start feeling cornered now. He's made too many mistakes."

"Darren Bordain was pretty twitchy today," Mendez said. "He refused a photograph, refused a polygraph. And his alibi for the night of the murder is Gina Kemmer, who has been conveniently missing."

"He certainly didn't like being in the spotlight today," Vince said. "From his body language, I'd say he's hiding something."

"He could have been involved with Marissa," Hicks said. "He could have believed he was Haley's father. Maybe he found out he wasn't. Maybe he found out Marissa never had a baby."

"And she never would have a baby," Dixon said. "I spoke to the pathologist today. She couldn't say when, but Marissa Fordham had had a hysterectomy at some point in her life."

"That would certainly piss me off," Campbell said. "Finding out after four years of paying blackmail that not only is the child not mine, it's not even hers?"

Mendez nodded, trying the scenario out. "Bordain finds out. He's furious. He snaps. He kills her. His mother made a big deal out of Marissa—the daughter she never had. He sends her the breasts to say 'Here's the fucking daughter you never had. She was a fraud and I killed her.'"

"That fits well," Dixon said. "Too well. Darren Bordain is a smart guy. Would he do something so obvious as send those breasts to his mother in the mail? I'm still leaning toward misdirection with the breasts. Someone's playing with us."

"Vince, what about Steve Morgan?" Mendez asked. "Did he talk to you?"

"Yeah, he did. He's a cagey bastard," Vince said. "I've known some tough nuts in my day, but this guy doesn't crack. He gave me a couple little glimpses inside, then shut the door."

"But could he be a killer?" Dixon asked.

"I'm not sure," Vince admitted, still turning the interview over in his head. He was exhausted from the mental game. His brain hurt from the effort. He could feel himself flagging.

"There's something in him that makes him want you to believe he could be that rotten," he said. "A lot of self-hatred."

"What did he say about knowing the number of stab wounds the vic had?" Hicks asked.

"Lucky guess."

"My ass!" Mendez barked.

Vince shrugged and spread his hands, wishing he had something more definitive to say. "I don't know. If he did it, if he knew that number—which would be unlikely—why would he say it?"

"To poke us in the eye," Mendez said. "He knows we don't have anything on him."

"He admits he wasn't where he said he was on the night of the murder," Vince said. "But he wouldn't tell me where he was, either. He was with another woman, but he isn't going to give her name up unless he absolutely has to. And at this point, he doesn't."

"Let's say he was with Marissa," Mendez said.

"But why would he kill her?"

"She threatened to tell Sara."

"So what?" Vince said. "Sara has been pretty well convinced for a year or more that he's cheating on her. She got closer to Marissa to try to prove it. He knew that. What would be the point of him killing her?"

"He has a volatile temper," Mendez said, his frustration beginning to show. "Maybe he just snapped. Maybe she called his mother a junkie whore."

"That'll get you punched in the kisser. We know that for a fact," Vince said. "Morgan is a complicated guy. And he's undergone a dramatic change in his personality in the last year. That's a red flag. He's become self-destructive in his relationships for a reason."

"He was sleeping with two women who were both murdered," Mendez said. "That tells me either he killed one or both of them, or he didn't stop somebody else from killing them. If that was me, I would feel responsible either way."

Mendez and his White Knight Syndrome. But was Steve Morgan really so different? Vince wondered. If his motives for helping disadvantaged women had been altruistic all along, then he was no different in that respect. He came to the rescue. His wife had gotten left out of the process because he didn't see her as needing saving—or being sympathetic to his cause, for that matter. Sara was jealous of the time he donated to others.

"Peter Crane was his friend," Vince said. "Lisa Warwick was his lover. He probably thinks he should have been able to prevent what happened, but he didn't.

"Now—if he was seeing Marissa—Marissa is dead too. Let's say he didn't kill her. He sinks deeper into self-destruction. He picks a fight with a cop. He picks a fight with his wife, he tries to scare her off, letting her think he might be a murderer. Ultimately, to punish himself."

"I still don't think we can rule him out," Dixon said.

"No," Vince agreed. "You can't rule him out. Not until we know where he was the night she was killed. Or where he was when Gina went missing."

"I'll tell you where he was when Gina went missing," Mendez said. "He was AWOL. Bill and I were trying to track him down. He told his wife he was working late, but he wasn't at his office. He told me later that he was having dinner with a client in Malibu. I'd say he pulled that out of his ass. He didn't show up at home until the middle of the night. I was there waiting for him."

"What about Bordain?" Dixon asked.

"He doesn't account for every minute of every day," Hicks said.

"Meaning he doesn't have an alibi."

"I would say so."

"Mark Foster?"

"We were talking to him early that evening," Hicks said. "Then he had a rehearsal. After that, nothing."

"We know approximately when Gina left her house that afternoon," Mendez said. "But we have no way of knowing when she met up with our bad guy. It could have been early, it could have been late."

"Maybe this, maybe that," Dixon complained. "This is giving me a headache. I want something we can take to the bank. Have we got that photo lineup put together for the little girl yet?"

"Bordain refused to have his photo taken, we don't know where Zahn is, a big no on Steve Morgan," Hamilton said. "But I was able to put something together with photos from other sources—the college, the local papers, *Oak Knoll* magazine. It's not ideal. It won't stand up in court. But it's better than nothing."

"Our witness is four. She won't hold up in court either, but we need something to go on. It's worth a shot." Dixon looked at Vince. "Is Anne okay with this?"

"Yeah. I gave her the heads-up already. But if you want it tonight we'd better get on it, pronto." He lifted his arm and tapped the face of his watch. "Four-year-olds have bedtime."

69

"I wish we didn't have to do this so late," Anne said. "Nighttime is difficult. She already doesn't want to go to sleep because of the nightmares."

"We don't have a choice, sweetheart," Vince said. "We've got a killer running around loose who's going to be on the ragged edge when he finds out Gina Kemmer isn't dead. Time is of the essence here."

Anne sighed. "I know."

She stood at the door to Haley's room and looked at Haley, sitting on her bed in her pink pajamas playing quietly with Honey-Bunny and the new stuffed toy cat Milo Bordain had given her.

Sara had picked Wendy up and gone home right after dinner. Anne and Haley had gone through what Anne wanted to make a nightly ritual of a bath, quiet time, then story time, then bed. Routine would help give Haley a sense of stability, and the downward progression of activities would help teach her to relax and quiet her mind.

Anne knew from her own experience over the last year the value of that kind of routine. Now she could put what had been a difficult experience for her to a positive use for Haley. But tonight she would interrupt that routine to potentially draw out the most terrible memory a child could possibly have: the memory of a monster.

Vince rested a hand on her shoulder, reading her emotions perfectly. "We'll show them to her together," he said. "You and me. Okay?"

"Okay," Anne said. "Let's get it over with."

Vince turned to Mendez. "Keep your fingers crossed."

Mendez took a seat on a bench in the hall to wait.

Vince pressed Anne into the room with a hand on the small of her back. Her heart was thudding in her chest.

"Haley? We're going to play a little game, sweetie," she said, feeling like a wolf in sheep's clothing.

Haley looked up at her, wide-eyed and innocent. "What kind of game?"

"We're going to look at some pictures," Vince said, sitting down on the edge of the bed. "I'm going to put them down on the bed, then you're going to look at them and tell us if you know any of the people in the pictures."

Haley got on her knees and leaned sideways into Anne, chewing on the tip of her index finger as Vince laid the pictures out.

Anne watched her face carefully, looking for any nuance of expression that might indicate recognition.

Haley reached out a finger. Anne held her breath.

"That's Zander," Haley said, pointing at the wide-eyed math genius with his wild cloud of gray hair. She looked up at Vince and crinkled her nose. "Isn't he weird?"

"He looks kind of funny in this picture, doesn't he?" Vince said. "Do you know anybody else here?"

Haley studied the pictures one by one. With the exception of Steve Morgan, Anne only knew who they were because Vince had told her. The head of the music department at McAster. An architect. Steve Morgan's law partner.

Darren Bordain in a photo from a magazine—a shot of him and his mother dressed to the nines at a charity function. He was almost a carbon copy of Milo.

Steve Morgan, handsome, dressed for golf, a wide white grin splitting his features. It was hard for Anne to look at him so happy when she knew he was making Sara and Wendy miserable with his bad behavior. Here he was in a lineup as, at best, a man who cheated on his wife, and at worst a murder suspect.

Haley looked at all of them very carefully. Anne held her breath. Vince was holding his breath and watching the little girl's reactions as carefully as Anne was.

Finally, Haley looked up and smiled like a pixie. "These are all my daddies!"

She proceeded to point to each face and name them.

"Daddy Mark and Daddy Don and Daddy Bob and Daddy Steve and Daddy Milo and Daddy Darren and Zander."

"Daddy Zander?" Vince asked.

Haley shook her head. "Just Zander."

Anne felt limp with relief. As much as the detectives needed a positive ID, she couldn't help but be glad Haley hadn't looked at these men and seen the face of the person who had choked and smothered her.

"Do you see Bad Daddy?" Vince asked.

Haley ignored him and turned instead to Anne. "Mommy Anne, will you read me a story?"

"Sure, sweetheart. In a few minutes. You get under the covers and I'll be back before you know it."

"You won't turn the lights off?"

"Nope. I won't turn the lights off."

"Bad Daddy comes when the lights are off."

"Bad Daddy can't come here," Anne said, gathering the pictures back up off the bed.

She followed Vince into the hall, pulling Haley's door only partially closed.

Mendez got to his feet with a look of tense expectation.

Vince shook his head. "No go. It may have been too dark for her to recognize the killer that night. Or she might only relate that person to Bad Daddy if he was dressed all in black."

"You know, people don't look the same when they turn on you," Anne said quietly. "I remember how Peter Crane looked when he was above me, choking me. His eyes went flat and cold, like some kind of beast's. The angles of his face stood out as if the skin were being pulled tight against the bone. He didn't look like Tommy's dad, or everybody's favorite dentist, or the man who had come to my door just minutes earlier. It was like he was wearing a mask and then he took it off and I saw what he really was."

Vince slipped his arm around her and drew her closer to him, just to let her feel that he was there and strong and protecting her.

"Haley may not have recognized the man who hurt her," she said. "Because it wasn't a man who hurt her, it was a monster."

Mendez sighed, defeated. "I'd better call my mother and ask her to light a candle for Gina Kemmer then, because she's the only one left who can ID this guy."

Good, Anne thought, as she slipped away and went back into Haley's room. Just relating her own experience in a few brief sentences had brought the terrible image of Peter Crane's face that night back to her mind with such sharp clarity it was painful. Her heart was beating quick and shallow, and she felt weak both physically and mentally.

If Haley could be spared that . . .

"Let's make up a story tonight," she said, settling in beside her little charge.

Haley snuggled into her, thumb at the ready. Anne brushed her hair back and kissed her forehead and began.

"Once upon a time there was a land where there were no monsters and no mean people and no bad daddies . . ."

When Haley had drifted off, Anne slipped from the bed and padded downstairs in her stocking feet. The house was quiet except for soft smoky saxophone music drifting out of Vince's office. He was sitting at his desk with only the desk lamp on, concentrating, peering down through his reading glasses at notes he had made.

He glanced up at her and smiled, took off his glasses and set them aside. He looked tired. Anne tunneled her fingers into his thick hair and smiled back.

"Come to bed, Daddy Vince," she said.

"Mmmm . . ." He pressed his cheek to her breast and sighed. "I am so exhausted, so wiped out, so out of gas . . . and I still want you, Mrs. Leone."

He pulled her face down to his and kissed her, a deep, slow, sexy kiss.

"But . . . ," Anne said as they emerged back into the real world.

"But . . . I want to go over these notes one more time. I can't shake the feeling that there's an answer in here somewhere and I'm just not seeing it."

"Maybe you've been looking at it too long."

"Can't see the forest for the trees? Maybe so. It's probably hiding right in front of me. I'm just beating myself up over Zahn," he admitted. "I pushed too hard. I'm afraid I might have triggered something in him he can't get back from."

Anne brushed a thumb over the bruise on his cheek where he told her Zander Zahn had struck him. "We can't know somebody else's tipping point. Most of the time, we don't even know our own until it's too late.

"I looked at those pictures tonight . . . ," she said. "I'm sure not one of those men ever believed they could do what was done to that woman. And yet, one of them probably did."

Vince nodded, then broke the darkness of the thought.

"How'd you get so smart?" he teased.

"I married well," Anne said, smiling. "Come upstairs. You can tell me a bedtime story."

They walked up the stairs hand in hand.

Vince spoke softly. "Once upon a time there was husband who loved his wife . . ."

70

Thunder rumbled. In the distance Dennis could see flashes of lightning far away. He loved it when it stormed at night. But the rain had stopped for now, which suited him fine. The fire would burn better without rain.

Dennis felt like he had a thunderstorm inside his brain. Anger rumbled and grumbled then *BANG!* Flashed like lightning. He was so mad he wanted to just run shouting, spinning around, flinging his arms, crashing into things. Then he wanted his hands to turn into knives and he would slash his way through crowds of people and blood would be spurting everywhere. He would spin and turn and cut people in half and cut their heads off.

And at the end of his rampage would be Miss Navarre. And he would stab her and stab her a million times like the guy that killed that lady in the newspaper. He would stick his knives inside of her and down her throat and in her eyes and through her brain. And she would be alive the whole time until he cut her head off.

She didn't care about him. She didn't show up again. And nobody told him she wasn't coming. He had worked so hard to write his report about the murder like she wanted him to. Two whole pages.

Dennis didn't like to write. It was hard for him. He didn't always get the letters to go the right way, and he didn't understand punctuation. He wrote what came in his head, but it didn't always come out like it did for other people like stupid brainiac Tommy Crane or Wendy Morgan. They did everything right. Dennis did everything wrong.

But he had done his writing assignment for Miss Navarre because she said she would bring him something cool if he finished it. Nobody had ever given Dennis anything special because of something he had accomplished. Mostly because he never accomplished anything. Besides, his dad had always said he was stupid and would never amount to anything, so why should he try?

Miss Navarre probably thought the same thing, and that was why she hadn't shown up. Why bother? Why should she take time out of her life for him when she could be teaching kids like Tommy and Wendy? Or because she could be fucking the FBI guy, which she probably did all the time because she was a whore.

Dennis was going to show her. He would accomplish BIG things starting tonight.

He dug way under his mattress and started pulling out his stash. He put his money and candy and stuff he wanted to take with him into a plastic bag with a drawstring that someone had thrown in the trash.

He hid the bag under his dirty laundry in the closet, then got out the stuff he needed to start the fire. Fires. He had it all planned out. He knew exactly where to start.

The nurse had gone by half an hour ago. He would have plenty of time now.

Dennis slipped out of his room and looked up and down the dimly lit hall, then darted away from the nurses' station, going to the empty room at the far end of the hall. The lights from the parking lot glowed in through the window, allowing him to see well enough.

Dennis had snuck into this room and hid several times over the past year. This was the room where the staff dumped extra pieces of equipment—extra wheelchairs, extra poles for IV bags, bed trays, chairs. A couple of green oxygen tanks were shoved way in the corner of the room most difficult to see from the door—and farthest away from the sprinkler in the ceiling.

There was all kinds of stuff to burn in the room—paper towels, old newspapers. Dennis wadded up paper and made a pile on the floor. He tipped one of the oxygen tanks onto it. He had seen this done on a TV show. Oxygen tanks could explode. The idea that he could make something explode just about gave Dennis a hard-on.

This was something he was good at—starting fires. Ever since he was a little kid he had been fascinated with fire. Practically every time he could get his hands on some matches or a lighter he would set something on fire. Maybe just a piece of paper or a pile of leaves. He liked to steal cigarettes and light them and burn bugs and spiders alive with the hot tip.

Maybe Miss Navarre would give him something really special for burning the hospital to the ground, he thought, and had to try really hard not to laugh out loud.

Dennis flicked the lighter and stared at the flame as it licked the air. He took the wadded-up pages of his writing homework and set them ablaze, then tossed them onto the pile of crumpled paper and quickly exited the room.

He made his way back to his own room with two stops to start fires in the wastebaskets in the rooms of other patients who were sleeping. When he got back to his room, he grabbed his plastic bag of stuff and waited by the door.

It seemed to take a long time before the fire alarm went off. Dennis had begun to think all his fires had burned out, and he was going to be really disappointed. But then several things happened at once. The fire alarm went off. Someone started screaming. And the oxygen tanks in the room at the end of the hall exploded.

All of a sudden people came running down the hall past his room. Dennis opened the door and stepped out. Orange flames were coming out of the door at the end of the hall. Nurses were pulling patients out of the rooms nearby. Other patients were wandering into the hall on their own, drooling and confused.

Nasty black smoke came rolling down the hall, stinking with the smell of plastic burning. Right across the hall from Dennis, a man came through the door screaming, his flaming arms raised straight up in the air.

Dennis stared at him, transfixed, then bolted.

In the chaos of people running and screaming, alarms blaring and sprinklers going off, no one noticed a twelve-year-old boy go right out the front door and disappear into the night.

71

Hiding.

The thought came to him in the hazy gray of predawn.

Hiding in plain sight.

Vince slipped out of bed, pulled on some sweatpants and a T-shirt, and went across the hall. Anne had gone to Haley in the middle of the night when Bad Daddy had paid a visit to the little girl's dreams.

He looked in on them now and felt a tug at his heart. They were curled up together, sound asleep. They could have easily been mother and daughter with their dark hair and turned-up noses.

As trying as the circumstances were, Haley had seamlessly fitted into their lives as if she belonged there. When he thought about it, Vince had a hard time believing it had been only a few days.

He went downstairs to the kitchen and made a pot of coffee, which he drank too hot, but he needed the jolt of caffeine.

Hiding.

The word came to him again as he went into his office and turned on the desk light. Settling in his chair, he put his glasses on and started digging through the notes he had made regarding Zander Zahn.

According to the cop in Buffalo, Zahn's mother had abused the boy in various ways, including *locking him in a closet for days at a time and just leaving.*

He picked up the phone and dialed Mendez, who answered with a mumble.

"Wake up, Junior," Vince said. "You need to get a search warrant."

* * *

"We searched the house yesterday," Mendez said. "He wasn't in it. What makes you think he's here now?"

They stood outside the gate of Zander Zahn's property. Fog had rolled in over the mountains from the coast, giving the valley an eerie, otherworldly feeling. It seemed fitting.

A small flock of reporters had followed them out of town but were being kept at bay by deputies. One of the most brilliant mathematical minds in the country was missing and possibly attached to a brutal crime. America was salivating for the story.

"He feels safe hiding," Vince said.

"Didn't his mother lock him in a closet?" Hicks asked. "Wouldn't that do the opposite? Make him claustrophobic?"

"For some people it would," Vince agreed. "For others, the cage is safer than the world outside the cage. Zahn needs everything to be controlled and orderly. If he's panicking because he feels out of control, I think he'll hide, and the smaller the space the better."

"Oh my God," Rudy Nasser said. "I've found him a couple of times in his office at school under his desk. I never understood why."

"That's why," Vince said. "He was probably feeling overwhelmed. Under the desk was the handiest safe place.

"We've got to look anywhere physically possible for him to hide," Vince said. "And I mean anywhere. Closets, cupboards, inside these refrigerators in the yard. Everywhere."

Nasser punched in the code for the gate, and the search began. Mendez, Hicks, and two deputies took the house. Vince walked the yard with Rudy Nasser, looking in Zahn's collection of refrigerators and freezers.

"I always thought Zander's obsession with that woman would end badly," Nasser admitted. "But I never saw any of this coming."

"Why were you so against him being friends with Marissa?"

"When he was around her or talked about her, it was like he went to another dimension. Dreamy and strange—not that Zander isn't strange anyway. It just seemed unhealthy to me. I try very hard to keep him focused on his work as much as possible. With her, his head turned into a helium balloon and he floated away."

"You think he was in love with her?"

"Yes, and she should have discouraged him."

"Have you ever seen a photograph of Zander's mother?" Vince asked.

"No, why?"

"I'm betting she resembled Marissa, or Marissa resembled her."

"You think he had a mother thing for her?" Nasser asked, clearly creeped out by the idea.

"Not as in Oedipus," Vince clarified. "I think in Zander's mind she might have represented the mother he didn't have."

He pulled open the top of a long chest freezer and peered inside. Clean as a whistle.

"I didn't know Marissa," he went on, "but by most accounts she was a great mother and a lovely, vivacious person who was open to the world around her. Zander's mother was a manic-depressive who tormented him for being different and locked him in a closet when she didn't want to deal with him."

"I didn't know about his mother," Nasser said.

"No. And you, being a healthy young man with an eye for the ladies, looked at Marissa Fordham and saw a sexual being. Zander doesn't look at the world like that. I think he looked at Marissa and saw the essence of her—the mother, the free spirit, a woman who embraced life and feared nothing."

"Life terrifies Zander," Nasser said. "He fears everything—except numbers."

"Numbers won't burn you with a cigarette for being odd."

Mendez called from the front door. "Vince, you need to come see something."

"Can you top the room of artificial limbs?" Vince asked as they went inside.

"No, but I may be able to explain the room of artificial limbs."

They went into Zahn's kitchen and Mendez pointed to a broom closet filled with white trash bags, stuffed with who knew what. He plucked up one of the bags and held it open for Vince to look inside.

Prescription bottles filled the bag. Prescription bottles full of pills. Vince reached in and grabbed up several, holding them at arm's length and squinting to read the labels.

Antidepressants, medications for panic disorders, a new drug Vince had come across in his recent reading on obsessive-compulsive disorder.

"The crazy bastard's been hoarding his own medication," Mendez said. "You might have given him a nudge the other day, but I'd say he already had one foot in the deep end."

"Oh, man . . ." Vince sighed and shook his head.

"This stuff is meant to help him," Mendez said. "The guy's a freaking genius. Why wouldn't he take it?"

"Maybe he didn't like the side effects. Maybe he didn't trust his doctor not to poison him. Maybe the OCD just wouldn't let him."

Whatever the reason, the result wasn't good.

With no sign of Zahn on the property, the search disbanded. Vince got back in the car with Mendez, who waited his turn as the others maneuvered their vehicles around and negotiated their way through the gridlock of news trucks and reporters.

"Let's go back to Marissa's place," Vince suggested.

"Why?"

"The continuation of my hunch," Vince said. "We needed extra bodies to get through Zahn's place. If he's over there, better it's just you and me."

The crime scene having been fully processed, and the press having moved on to more immediate matters like Gina Kemmer and the missing Zander Zahn, attention had fallen away from Marissa Fordham's home. A deputy was still stationed at the end of the driveway to chase away the morbidly curious, but Dixon had pulled the sentry that had been stationed under the pepper tree in Fordham's front yard.

In the setting of fog and dead grass, Marissa Fordham's house looked like it had been abandoned for a long time. Funny how that happened when people left a place. Suddenly the paint looked dull and chipped, and the windows that had been filled with light looked like gaping black holes. The flowers Marissa had tended dutifully when she was alive were weedy and in need of care.

They went inside the house and stood in the living room silently for a moment, looking around. Very slowly, Mendez turned the knob on the coat closet in the entry, and opened it. No Zahn.

They moved through the house methodically and quietly, checking closets and cupboards, finally coming to Marissa's bedroom, where the initial attack had taken place and the walls and ceiling had been spattered with cast-off blood from the killer's knife.

Vince put a finger to his lips and motioned for Mendez to stay back.

"Zander," he said, moving toward the closet. "Are you in here? It's me, Vince."

No reply.

Vince closed his fingers around the old white porcelain doorknob and slowly, slowly turned it.

"I'm going to open the door, Zander," he said. "Don't be afraid. I just want to see you and make sure you're okay."

He eased the door open inch by inch.

Naked and wild-eyed, Zander Zahn was crouched, coiled like a spring on the floor of the closet, clutching the handle of a very large knife.

Later, Vince would remember thinking *I should have seen it coming*, but in the next instant, as Zander Zahn leapt at him, there was no time to think at all.

72

"He did what?"

Anne felt all her blood drain to her feet. Willa Norwood, her CASA supervisor, stood in her hallway just inside the front door looking ridiculously festive in her colorful African dashiki and kufi hat.

"They think he set fire to the mental health center."

"Oh my God," Anne said. "I have to sit down."

"It happened last night around midnight," Willa said as they walked through the house, through the family room where Haley was curled up on the couch watching cartoons, and on to the kitchen.

"He set fire to his own wastebasket six months ago," Anne said. "How could they let him get hold of matches again?"

"I don't know. Apparently, the fire started in a room they use for storage," Willa said. "Why it wasn't locked, I don't know. But Dennis has been caught messing around in there before."

"Did someone see him?" Anne motioned to her supervisor to take a seat at the breakfast table, and dropped onto a chair herself.

"Another patient says Dennis came into his room and set fire to his wastebasket. This is really bad, Anne."

"I know. I've been trying to think of somewhere to move him—"

"No," Willa said.

The expression in the woman's eyes made Anne's heart thump in her chest.

"I mean it's *really* bad. One of the other patients suffered third-degree burns when he tried to move the wastebasket." She took a deep breath to deliver the worst of the news. "And an oxygen tank went through a wall and killed the woman in the next room."

"Oh."

The word came out on a breath that seemed to empty Anne's lungs entirely, and she sat there, unable to move or speak or think, until her head swam.

"Oh my God," she whispered. Dennis had killed someone. Intentional or not, he was now the thing he claimed to admire most—a killer. "Where is he? I'll have to— Maybe Franny can watch Haley—"

"We don't know where he is, Anne," Willa said. "He's gone."

"Gone? Gone where? He's a twelve-year-old boy with no money and no home."

"In all the confusion with the fire and the explosion and dealing with the wounded, nobody saw him leave. He's missing."

The hospital had an open campus. Anybody could come or go anytime they wanted. Even patients—unless they were on a locked ward— could walk out of the building and off the property, and occasionally did. Staff usually kept everything under control, but the scene would have been chaotic. Everyone would have been concerned with the fire and the casualties.

Dennis had killed a woman. He would be able to read about himself in the newspaper.

"This is my fault," Anne said.

Willa reached across the table and put a hand on Anne's arm. "No, it isn't. You've done more for that child than anyone in his life."

"I couldn't get there to see him yesterday. I promised him I would be there and I would bring him something special if he did his writing assignment."

"That doesn't give him an excuse to set the hospital on fire."

"Everybody in his life has let him down. I was trying to be the one person who wouldn't do that to him."

She shook her head and swore under breath. Her thoughts tumbled like kaleidoscope pieces. "What do we do now?"

"The sheriff's office has been notified. They're looking for him. I don't think you should do anything."

"Yeah." Anne sighed. "I've done enough already, haven't I? The court wanted to send him to a juvenile facility after the first incident. I begged for that not to happen."

"You were trying to do what you thought was best for the child, Anne. That's all you can do."

"He'll be going there now."

"There's no getting around that."

"No."

"You did the best you could, girl," Willa said, patting her hand.

"I know," Anne said. "I just wish it could have been good enough."

Dennis had walked what seemed like most of the night before getting to his old house, careful not to let anybody see him. He was good at that. He used to roam all over town in the night, looking in people's windows and watching them have sex and stuff. Once he had seen a man fucking a blow-up doll. That had been crazy.

He didn't know what had happened to his family's house or any of their stuff. With his mother dead and his father dead and himself stuck wherever the court put him, his stupid half-sisters had gone away to live with some relative who didn't want anything to do with him.

Ha! They'd be surprised when they saw his picture in the paper.

To his shock, when Dennis had finally gotten to the house, practically everything had been ripped out of it—walls and floors and carpets. A big, huge trash bin was parked in the driveway, and it was full of junk like old drywall and linoleum and a broken toilet.

Dennis decided it didn't really matter to him that all the Farman stuff was gone. They hadn't had anything very nice anyway. And most of Dennis's prized possessions had been in his backpack that the detectives had taken away from him. They had probably divvied up the good stuff, like the pocketknife he had stolen from his father's dresser, and the cigarette lighter he had taken from his mother's purse. Probably nobody had wanted the dried-up rattlesnake head.

He had spent a cold night in the house with no blankets and no bed, but he was an outlaw now, so he had to just get over it. Today he would steal some stuff and find a place to hide it. He had always heard that bums lived in Oakwoods Park. Maybe he would live there too.

When it got light out he walked to the convenience store hoping, hoping, hoping with his fingers crossed that the old raghead guy that owned the place wasn't working. He had chased Dennis out of the store a million times for shoplifting stuff and trying to look at the dirty magazines.

That Paki bastard—that was what Dennis's father had called the old man, so Dennis called him that too.

Luckily the person behind the counter was a big, fat, pimple-faced

girl, and the store was really busy with people getting coffee and doughnuts and burritos and stuff, so she didn't notice Dennis.

He cruised the aisles, lifting a little thing here and there and slipping
them into the big pouch pocket on the front of his hooded sweatshirt.
A Slim Jim, some Lifesavers, a tire gauge—just because he'd always
wanted one.

He could have whatever he wanted now. He was calling all the shots.
Nobody could tell him what to do—especially not that stupid twat Miss
Navarre.

The television bolted to the wall behind the counter was showing the
morning news. Dennis watched with one eye, waiting to see a picture of
himself on the screen.

Some woman had been rescued after falling down a well. There were
no new leads in the murder investigation of local artist Marissa Fordham. Some crazy-looking white-haired guy had gone missing. Finally
the screen filled with a shot of the county mental health center with
flames shooting out a window on the second floor.

Dennis inched closer to the counter and strained to hear. According to the reporter, the fire had been contained to the second floor and
damages to the building were minimal. But—and here was the exciting
part. Dennis almost shit his pants when he heard it—one person had
gone to the hospital with third-degree burns, and one had been killed—
KILLED!—when an oxygen tank had blown through a wall.

He had killed somebody! The excitement was almost too much for
him. Holy shit! He had killed somebody! He was a killer!

To celebrate, he bought himself a breakfast burrito and a Mountain Dew with some of the money he had stolen from the nurse. Then,
because he was feeling like such a hotshot killer and all, he decided he
would buy himself some cigarettes.

"And a pack of Marlboros," he said.

The pimple-faced girl looked down at him. "Get real and get lost."

"They're for my mom."

"No, they're not."

"Yes, they are, and she's a real bitch. You want me to go and get her?
She's in the car."

The girl looked out the window like she was looking for his mother,
then rolled her eyes and gave him the cigarettes and his change. Stupid cow.

Dennis took his stuff and left, not sitting down to eat his burrito until he was out of sight of the store.

He felt different now than he had twenty minutes ago. Twenty minutes ago he had been just a kid. Now he was a killer. He felt bigger and stronger and meaner. He was going to show everybody just how bad he was. And he was going to start with that bitch Miss Navarre.

73

He hadn't counted on the knife.

Zahn came at him like a wild animal, and Vince flashed on what Anne had said: *You know, people don't look the same when they turn on you.*

"Vince!" Mendez shouted, drawing his weapon.

Zahn's arm came down in an arc, the light catching on the blade of the knife. By reflex, Vince caught hold of the man's wrist and stepped to the side to get out of the path of the weapon.

"Zahn! Drop the knife!" Mendez shouted. "Drop the fucking knife!"

But Zahn didn't hear him. What was reasonable and civilized in him was gone, overridden by fear and demons. He struggled to pull free of Vince's grasp, the two of them crashing into the bed frame, falling against a nightstand.

Madness fueled and intensified Zahn's strength. Vince had half a foot and a good fifty pounds on him, and all he could do was stumble backward on his heels as Zahn continued his attack.

"DROP THE FUCKING KNIFE!" Mendez shouted again.

From the corner of his eye Vince could see him trying to maneuver around them to get a clean shot.

Zahn twisted and yanked free of the hold Vince had on his wrist, stumbling backward and banging hard into the wall. Vince took the chance to dive across the box spring to the other side of the bed.

"DROP THE DAMN KNIFE!!"

"TONY! DON'T SHOOT!" Vince shouted.

Zahn stood there, looking stunned, looking like he didn't know where he was or who he was or who they were. He looked at the knife in his hand, his arm still cocked at the elbow, ready.

"Zander!" Vince said. "Zander! It's me, Vince. Put the knife down."

Zahn stared at the knife in his hand, fascinated. He stared at the knife and at his arm as if it weren't attached to his body.

Mendez had taken the stance to fire, his arms straight out in front of him, his finger on the trigger of the weapon. Everything about him was pulled as taut as a string on a bow. His dark eyes were as bright and hard looking as polished onyx.

"Zander, put the knife down," Vince said, lowering the tone and volume of his voice. "You need to put the knife down. Isn't your arm getting tired?"

Zahn looked uncertain. His fingers flexed on the handle of the knife.

"Aren't you tired, Zander?" Vince asked. "You've had a rough day."

He let the quiet hang, imagining his words trying to find a way into Zahn's brain and, once there, struggling to be routed and processed.

"I'm very tired, Vince," he said in his small, soft voice. The look in his wide eyes was still glassy and far away. He seemed to be staring into another dimension. "I'm very tired. Terribly tired."

"So let's put the knife down," Vince said, moving slowly down to the foot of the bed. "You don't need that thing. Put it down and we'll sit down and you can rest."

"I'm so very sorry," Zahn said.

"It's okay. Everything's okay. No harm, no foul, right?"

He took a slow step toward Zahn, keeping one arm stretched out in front of him, just in case.

"No," Zander murmured.

"Did you come here to see Marissa?" Vince asked quietly.

"Marissa. Marissa is gone."

"You miss her, don't you," Vince said. "She was a very special person, wasn't she? She accepted you for exactly who you are, didn't she?"

"Marissa," Zahn murmured. "Marissa is gone."

"I'm sorry for that, Zander. She was special to you and now she's gone. That's a scary place to be, isn't it? She left you alone, and you don't feel safe. But you're safe with us. So why don't you put the knife down?"

"I'm sorry," Zahn said, his hand flexing on the handle of the knife. "I'm so sorry."

"What are you sorry for, Zander?"

"I'm so sorry. Very sorry. Terribly sorry."

"Why are you sorry, Zander?" Vince asked. "Did you do something wrong? Did you do a bad thing, Zander?"

He began to rock slightly with his upper body, a sign of agitation.

"Very bad," he said. "I'm very bad. Terribly bad. Bad, bad."

"I don't think so, Zander," Vince said. "Why don't you put the knife down and we'll talk about it. Your arm must be very tired by now."

Zahn rocked a little harder.

"So tired," he said. "Very tired. I'm sorry."

"Did you hurt Marissa, Zander? Is that why you're sorry? Did you hurt Marissa?"

"Marissa, Marissa. Mommy, mommy. I'm so sorry."

"Did you hurt Marissa, Zander?"

"Very tired. Terribly tired. Have to go now."

With that Zander Zahn brought the knife down and plunged it into his own stomach.

74

Oakwoods Park held special memories for Dennis. He had grown up playing in the woods away from the playground and picnic area where everything was neat and tidy. The wooded, wild part of the park was way more fun. He had spent hours in there playing war, and Indians, and pirates, and pretending he was a kidnapper. That was his favorite. He would kidnap some other kid and tie them up and scare the crap out of them. That was fun.

Out in these woods was where they had found the dead lady last year. Him and Cody had been chasing Tommy Crane and Wendy Morgan, and they had gone tumbling down a bank. Tommy had practically landed right on her. She was mostly buried, but her head was sticking out of the ground, and one hand with a finger almost chewed off by a dog.

When nobody was looking Dennis had snapped the finger off and stuck it in his pocket.

He walked through the woods now, looking for, and finding, a good spot to stash his stuff. He would camp there tonight, but he was going to have to steal a blanket because it was fucking cold and the ground and all the dead leaves on it were wet. He wouldn't complain, though. He was a man now. He would suck it up.

The next thing he needed was a disguise. His picture was going to be all over the news, and the cops were going to be looking for him. With his red hair, he was going to be easy to spot.

He picked his way through the woods to the edge of the playground where a couple of kids were kicking a soccer ball back and forth. They looked like they were maybe fifth graders. Both of them were smaller than he was. The one was wearing a black baseball cap with the Raiders logo on the front.

"Hey!" he said, walking up to the boys. "Can I play?"

The kid with the cap looked up at him. "Who are you?"

"I'm the guy that's gonna kick your ass. Gimme the ball."

The other kid snatched the ball up off the ground and held it, ready to run.

"You better gimme the ball," Dennis said. "I killed someone last night. I can kill you too, you little dick."

The kid's eyes got big and he took off running.

Dennis grabbed the other one by the arm with one hand and smacked him upside the head with the other.

The kid screamed like a girl. Dennis took his ball cap and knocked him to the ground, then turned and ran for the woods before somebody's parents showed up.

That had been easy. But of course it was. He was a badass stone-cold killer now. Taking a hat off a kid was nothing.

With his new prize shoved down on his head, he went walking. He needed a weapon. He wished he could get a gun, but nobody was going to sell a gun to a twelve-year-old boy, even if he had killed somebody.

Knives were better anyway. He had really liked the way it felt when he had stuck his pocketknife into Cody's guts. He had relived that moment over and over in the year since. It made him get excited thinking about it, and thinking about how it would feel when he stuck it in Miss Navarre.

It was kind of like fucking, he thought. If he was fucking her, he would stick his thing in her over and over and make her scream. When he stabbed her, he would stick his knife in her over and over, and she would scream.

Cool.

He cut through the alleys in the neighborhood near his old school. The houses here were old and most of them had garages that weren't attached, which was good because no one inside the house would hear him looking around. And a garage would be a good place to find a weapon. People left all kinds of shit in their garages.

He picked a garage that had a small side door that wasn't locked, and let himself in. There was all kinds of cool stuff hanging on the walls and piled on a workbench. Power tools, garden tools, regular tools.

A screwdriver might be good, he thought. He picked one up and felt the weight of it in his hand, and practiced stabbing with it. Not bad.

Among the garden tools was a machete, which was the coolest thing, but it was too big. He couldn't go around town carrying a machete and not have people notice.

Then he found it. Hanging on a pegboard at the back of the workbench were some woodworking tools—chisels and gouges and stuff. Most of them were four to six inches of blade with a curvy wooden handle that would feel really good in the hand.

Dennis stood on a cooler to reach them and selected two—one for each hand. One was thin and sharp and had a groove running down the center of the blade. The other one was straight and pointed.

They fit perfectly in the pouch of his sweatshirt.

Happy, he let himself out the side door and continued on his way. Miss Navarre's house was only a couple of blocks away.

Dennis had been to her house before. Not because she had ever invited him, but because he had come in the night to try to look in her windows. It was a really nice house with a big porch on the front and roses in the yard.

Dennis's heart was pounding as he went up the sidewalk with his hands stuffed in the pouch of his sweatshirt. He didn't really have a big plan. He figured she would maybe invite him inside depending on whether or not she had seen the news about him being a killer. She would be surprised to see him. That was for sure.

He almost got the giggles as he thought about the things she might say to him.

You shouldn't kill people, Dennis. That's not nice.

How can I give you your surprise if you started the fire with your homework?

She was going to be sorry she hadn't come to see him.

Dennis rang the doorbell and stuck his hand back in his pouch, his fingers touching the handle of his weapon. His heart was beating fast. His palms were sweaty.

The door opened and a skinny old man scowled down at him. He had to be a hundred, and he was dressed like a golfer.

"Who are you?" the old man demanded.

Dennis swallowed hard.

"I'm Dennis. Is Miss Navarre home?" he asked, trying to crane his neck so he could see inside the house.

"My daughter doesn't live here anymore," the old man said. "She finally got married."

"She was my fifth-grade teacher," Dennis said. "I just wanted to see her 'cause . . . she was the best teacher I ever had. And . . . I mow lawns now and she told me that maybe I could mow her lawn."

"Well, she doesn't live here. She lives over by the college. This neighborhood wasn't good enough for her," he said bitterly. "I'm well rid of her, though. She wasn't much of a housekeeper."

Dennis didn't know what to say about that.

A short, plump lady with black hair piled high on her head came up then from somewhere inside the house.

"What you doing standing there with the door open? You let in all the cold. You catch your death," she said with a funny accent. She looked like maybe she was Chinese or from an island someplace or something. Dennis wasn't sure.

"You should be so lucky," the old man snapped at her.

"You catch your death, I don't get paid," the woman said. "Why you think I keep you alive, old man?"

"For the witty repartee."

The woman zeroed in on Dennis. "What you want, little boy?"

"He wants to visit Anne," the old man said, waving a hand at Dennis as if to dismiss him. "Write down her address for him."

75

"He's in surgery," Mendez reported, handing him a cup of coffee.

Vince sat in a chair in the ER waiting area, drained and stunned. He had already replayed the entire scenario over in his head half a dozen times, trying to make sense of the things Zander Zahn had said.

What had he been apologizing for? Killing Marissa? Killing his mother? Killing himself? When had he been bad? Thirty years ago? A week ago?

Marissa, Marissa. Mommy, mommy.

Had he confused the two and killed Marissa? Or was he saying she had been the mother he never had?

"Wow," Mendez said. "Brilliant guy like that . . . I guess it's true what they say about it being a thin line between genius and madness."

"I guess," Vince murmured.

"So he was in a dissociative state when he came out of that closet at you?"

"Something like that."

"He sure as hell looked crazy. Do you think he snapped like that when he went after Marissa?" He snapped his fingers as a thought popped into his head. "I've got to get his blood type so we can match it to the blood on the sweatshirt—in case he cut himself during the attack."

Vince said nothing.

Mendez looked at him, brows furrowed. "Are you okay?"

"Sure."

"We just closed our case, man. It's all over but the paperwork."

"The crazy guy did it," Vince said with none of the enthusiasm Mendez was looking for.

"Well, he did," Mendez said. "He all but confessed."

Vince tipped his head. "All but."

Getting irritated, Mendez got up and began to pace. "What the hell do you want? A fucking Perry Mason moment?"

"Yeah, that'd be nice." Vince got up and threw his coffee in the trash.

"You're not still thinking you pushed him over the edge?" Mendez asked. "He'd already killed two people before you ever met him, Vince. The guy is a wack job."

"Forgive me if I'm not happy about that," Vince said.

The doors whooshed open, and Cal Dixon came in, trailed by a dozen reporters all shouting questions at the same time. Dixon ignored them and motioned to Mendez and Vince. The three of them went into an exam room while deputies and hospital security chased the riffraff back outside.

Mendez told the story. Dixon stood with his arms crossed over his chest, intent on every detail. Vince sat on the exam table with his forearms on his thighs, and said nothing.

"So that's it?" Dixon said. "Zahn went crazy and killed her."

"And then he went crazy again and tried to kill Gina Kemmer," Vince said. "And then he went nuts again and sent a box of breasts to Milo Bordain. And one more time when he tried to run her off the road for no real reason."

Mendez sighed his frustration. "He lost it and killed Marissa, and tried to kill Haley. Then he had to try to cover it up, so he shot Gina and dumped her down that well. He walked that fire road every day."

"You can't pick and choose," Vince argued. "He's either crazy or he's not. And if he went into a dissociative state and killed Marissa, it's unlikely he would have had any memory of it after. He wouldn't try to cover up something he didn't know he did."

"He had to know it when he found his bloody clothes the next day," Mendez argued. "He knew he killed his mother. He told us about it."

"And who told him? The cops, the psychiatrists, the social workers."

"Maybe he's not crazy at all," Dixon ventured. "Maybe crazy is an act. It got him off before. Why not use it again?"

"You never met him. You never talked to him," Vince snapped. "He isn't an act."

"Why are we chewing each other's tails about this?" Dixon asked.

"Because it doesn't fucking make sense, that's why," Vince said, irritated. "Why all the bullshit with Milo Bordain?"

"Maybe he doesn't like her," Mendez said. "Maybe to make it look like her son did it."

"We're talking about a guy who finds it too overwhelming to go to Ralph's to buy groceries, but he would pack human breasts in a box and drive all the way to Lompoc to perpetrate a conspiracy on the Bordain family?" Vince said, incredulous. "What is in your fucking head?"

"He practically said he did it!" Mendez said.

"But he *didn't* say it, did he?"

"He stabbed himself with an eight-inch chef's knife!"

"And what happened to 'Steve Morgan did it'?"

A stout red-haired nurse in scrubs pulled the door open and stuck her head in. "Shut the fuck up! People in Milwaukee can hear you!"

Mendez held a hand up. "I know. If Zahn mailed the breasts to Milo Bordain, somebody in that post office is going to remember him. You don't meet that guy and then forget about him. Bill and I will go up to Lompoc and show them the photo of Zahn."

"Good," Dixon said. "It would be nice to have something besides conjecture to give the district attorney—if Zahn lives."

"We'll probably have his blood on that sweatshirt," Mendez said.

"If he cut himself," Vince came back, "then where are the wounds? He didn't have any wounds on his hands."

"If Gina Kemmer makes it, we'll have an ID."

"What's the latest on her?" Dixon asked.

Mendez frowned. "Not very good. She's fighting infections. They can't seem to keep her blood pressure stable, and they don't know why."

Still agitated, Vince slid off the table and moved with purpose toward the door.

"Where are you going?" Mendez asked.

"To call Rudy Nasser. He should know what happened."

76

"Anne? Why does life suck so much?"

Needing to escape the pall of misery at her own home, Wendy had begged for another visit with Anne and Haley. Sara Morgan, no doubt as at a loss for explanation as her daughter, had dropped her off.

They sat on the couch side by side not watching the movie blabbering to itself on the television. Haley had curled up on one end of the couch pretending to be a cat and had fallen sound asleep.

"I know it seems like it does sometimes," Anne said.

"Sometimes? *All* the time," Wendy said dramatically. "Look at all the bad stuff that's happened! Tommy's dad and Dennis Farman and the space shuttle and Chernobyl. And Haley's mom, and now my mom and dad are getting divorced, and Dennis killed somebody!"

It was hard to make an argument against all of that, but Anne tried to find something positive.

"I've had a lot of bad stuff to deal with in the last year," she said. "But I also met Vince, and we fell in love and got married."

"I'm never getting married," Wendy declared. "I don't know why people bother when they only get divorced in the end anyway. Marissa wasn't married, and she was way cool. And she had Haley."

"It's not easy to be a single parent," Anne said. "It's a big job for two people to do it well. What does Haley talk about all the time?"

"Kittens."

"Besides kittens."

"Daddies."

"She's never had a dad, but she wants one so badly she calls every man Daddy," Anne said.

"She'll learn they're not all they're cracked up to be," Wendy said.

"I used to think my dad was so cool, but he's just a jerk. He's so mean to my mom."

"Mean in what way?"

"He's always mad and says mean things and makes her cry."

"I'm not going to try to make excuses for your dad," Anne said. "I don't know what his problem is, but I think it's safe to say he has one."

Wendy rolled her eyes. "Yeah. Duh. Like his affairs with other women. I hear them argue. I'm not deaf and I'm not a little kid. I watch *Dynasty*. Mom thinks he had an affair with Marissa. I hope that's not true."

"I hope so too."

"Marissa was so cool!" Wendy said. "She just loved life and did what she wanted to—but in a good way. She was so nice. She used to ask me about my dreams and what I want to be and all that. And when I told her, she was just like 'Wow, Wendy! That's so great! You go for it!' "

"I wish I had met her," Anne said.

"And she did all this really beautiful art and helped my mom with her art," Wendy went on. "I don't want to know if she did bad things. My mom liked her. How could my mom like her if she thought Marissa was having an affair with my dad?"

"I don't know," Anne said. "It doesn't seem like they could have been friends if that was the case."

It seemed so strange and wrong to be talking about affairs with an eleven-year-old, but Wendy clearly knew what she was talking about—at least to a point. Anne wanted her to feel like she could bring up any subject at all when they talked. If they talked about affairs when she was eleven, what would twelve bring?

"People make life so complicated," Wendy said on a wistful sigh.

They sat quietly for a moment, Wendy toying with the half-dozen cheap silver bracelets she wore on one arm.

She looked up at Anne again. "Can I sleep over? Please? I don't want to go home. You and Vince are cool. I could sleep with Haley."

"What about your mom?" Anne asked. "She's feeling pretty down right now. Don't you think you should stay home with her and keep her company? She's hurting too, and I'm sure she's feeling very alone."

Wendy frowned and pulled at a loose thread on her purple leg warmers. "I know."

Anne put an arm around her shoulders and gave her a hug. She remembered all too well being the one who comforted her own mother when her father was so rotten to her. It had been Anne her mother leaned on in the face of Dick Navarre's incessant infidelities. Anne remembered thinking how unfair it was that she had to be the adult when she was really just a kid. She had blamed her father mightily. She still did.

She made a mental note to call and check on him just the same—because that was what her mother would have wanted her to do. Dick was never happy whether she called or didn't call. Finding fault was his specialty. Thank God he had Ling, his nurse, to spar with now.

"Maybe we can try to talk your mom into coming and staying here for a few days," Anne said.

Wendy brightened at the idea. Thank God there were moments when she still seemed like the child she deserved to be instead of the small adult her world was forcing her to be.

"That would be awesome!" she said. "It would be like we were having a big slumber party—except for Vince."

"Vince would deal with it."

Haley stirred on her end of the couch. Anne reached over and pulled her blanket up around her shoulders.

"Are you going to get to keep Haley?" Wendy asked.

"I don't know."

"Where else would she go? She wouldn't get sent to an orphanage or something, would she?"

"No, that won't happen. First the authorities have to find out if she has any relatives."

Wendy made a face. "That awful Mrs. Bordain. I pretended not to know her yesterday. She is *such* a word I'm not supposed to say."

"You know her from Marissa?"

Wendy nodded. "But she doesn't know me 'cause I'm just a kid and I might as well be a rock for all she could care."

"She cares about Haley, though," Anne said. "Haley is practically a granddaughter to her."

"What-ever," Wendy said. "She was always in Marissa's face. 'Do this, do that. Don't do this. Don't do that.'"

"Really?" Anne said, trying to reconcile what Wendy was saying with Milo Bordain's portrayal of the grieving near-mother.

"I heard her yelling at Marissa once. She's all, like, '*I could take this all away from you!*'" she said, doing a wicked impersonation of Milo Bordain. "And then Marissa was, like, '*So could I, and you know it!*'"

"I wonder what that meant," Anne said.

Wendy shrugged. "I don't know. Mrs. Bordain saw me then and yelled at me for eavesdropping."

So could I, and you know it.

What could Marissa have taken away from her sponsor? Herself? Haley?

"How about some warm apple cider?" Anne suggested. "With cinnamon sticks. It's such a nasty day."

Anne got up and pulled her sweater around her as she went to the kitchen. The rest of the house was not enjoying the warmth of the fireplace in the family room.

She turned on just the light above the stove and moved around the room gathering what she needed. Even though it was still afternoon, the gloom outside was almost nightlike. The fog had never lifted all day, and the sky seemed only to get heavier and closer to the ground.

She wondered where Dennis was, if he had found a place out of the elements. The sheriff's office was supposed to call her if they picked him up. How the hell was she supposed to help him now? Twelve or not, he would almost certainly be sent to a juvenile facility now until he was eighteen. She would try to get him sent to one with a good psychiatrist on staff . . .

She turned and looked out the bank of windows, a chill going through her. She hated having the shades up when it was getting dark out. More often than not she felt like someone was out there looking in at her.

It didn't occur to her as she lowered the blinds that someone actually was.

77

"Did you know he wasn't taking his medication?" Vince asked.

Nasser shook his head. "He's very secretive about personal things. I picked up the prescriptions for him, but what happened after that was not my business."

They stood in the ambulance bay, in the damp cold. Nasser had needed a cigarette. He wore the collar of his pea coat turned up against the chill. It made him look a little sinister with his dark features and razor-trimmed goatee.

"Did he ever mention a woman named Bordain to you?"

"I don't recall. Why would he?"

"She was Marissa's patron. She owns the property where Marissa lived."

"Oh . . . ," he said. "I know who she is. Zander was afraid of her."

"Afraid?"

"She intimidated him, made him feel small."

"Do you think Zander is the kind of guy who would try to get back at somebody for something like that?"

"Zander? What would he do?" Nasser asked. "Cast an evil mathematical equation on them? He won't even go in a convenience store to buy gum."

"That's what I thought."

They were quiet for a moment. Nasser finished his smoke and stubbed out the butt in the giant sandpit atop an equally giant trash receptacle by the door.

He nodded toward the building. "It's taking a long time."

"It was a long knife," Vince said.

"Do you think he'll make it?"

"I don't know."

"He's such a fragile soul," Nasser said. "It's like he was never meant for this world, you know?"

"He's had a tough row to hoe."

"Do you think he killed Marissa?"

"No. I don't," Vince said. "Let's take a ride. Maybe we can prove it."

They sailed out the dark country road in Nasser's old 3 Series BMW. The muffler needed some help, and the ragtop quaked like it might fly off at any moment.

Zahn's place was creepy in the gathering gloom, the fog slithering around the old refrigerators and rows of strange garden statuary. The house was black and unwelcoming. Coyotes yipped and howled in the distance.

Nasser let them in and turned on the hall lights.

Vince went into the room with the collection of filing cabinets that were stacked so close together he could barely fit between the rows.

I keep every paper, Zahn had told him.

It hadn't occurred to him when they were searching the place in the morning because they were searching for a man, not a document. Not even Zander Zahn would have attempted to hide himself in a filing cabinet.

When it came to him, it seemed so simple he wanted to kick himself. If Marissa had wanted to put Haley's birth certificate someplace nobody would look, what better place than in the home of a hoarder? And who better to trust it to than her strange friend Zander? Zander, so devoted to her, so enamored of her. Of course he would hide it and never tell a soul. His loyalty to Marissa was absolute.

The cabinets were jam-packed with files on every subject imaginable. One entire row that had to be fourteen feet long and five feet high held nothing but math papers. It looked like every math paper Zahn had ever completed in his life.

Cabinet after cabinet after cabinet was crammed with the paper detritus of Zahn's life, and everything he had ever found odd or interesting or pertinent or relevant. All of it alphabetized or otherwise organized, of course. There was just so much of it. Cabinets of financial records, copies of medical records, articles on the nature of genius and the mysteries of autism and its cousins.

"Can I help?" Nasser asked.

"I'm looking for any kind of a file pertaining to Marissa or Haley Fordham."

"Okay. I'll start over here."

They worked quietly for what seemed like hours. Finally, just when Vince thought his eyes were going to give out in the poor light, he found it. The file was simply marked M. He pulled the folder out of the drawer and studied the document.

"What is it?" Nasser asked, trying to get a look.

Vince closed the folder. "Motive."

He carried the folder into the hospital with him and went in search of Mendez, finding him in the ICU, staring through the glass wall into Gina Kemmer's room with Darren Bordain standing beside him.

"How is she?" Vince asked.

"No change. No better. No worse," Mendez said. "We tracked down her family in Reseda. Her parents are on their way."

"Good. That might make a difference if she can hear their voices."

"I wanted to go in and talk to her," Bordain said.

"Family only," Mendez said.

"My friends are my family. Gina and Marissa were part of the group."

"Rules are rules," Vince said. He locked eyes with Mendez and tipped his head away from Bordain.

They took three steps to the side before Mendez spoke quietly. "Zahn didn't make it."

Vince sighed.

"The surgeon said they would get one leak plugged and another would spring. That was a hell of a big knife. Between the damage to the organs, the blood loss and sepsis, he just wasn't strong enough to pull through."

"Maybe he'll find some peace now."

Vince thought of what Nasser had said: *He's such a fragile soul. It's like he was never meant for this world, you know.*

Maybe he would find more compassion in the next one.

Mendez's eye finally caught on the manila file folder tucked under Vince's arm. "What's that?"

"This?" Vince asked, as if he had forgotten about it. He handed the folder to Mendez. "A little light reading."

Mendez flipped it open and looked the document over from top to bottom twice, his eyes going wide.

"Ho-ly shit."

"Yeah." Vince nodded. "I thought you might say that."

78

Vince had called to say he would be late again and to go ahead with dinner. Anne brought the girls into the kitchen to "help" and to keep her company.

"What are we having?" Wendy asked.

"Macaroni and cheese—and not the kind that comes out of a box," Anne said, gathering ingredients from the refrigerator and putting them on the island. "The real deal, like my mother used to make. Haley, do you like macaroni and cheese?"

Haley was on all fours on the banquette, playing with her stuffed cat. "Meow. Yes. Meow. Meow."

Wendy laughed. "Haley, are you a kitty?"

"Meow. Meow. Meow."

Anne filled the pasta pot with water and put it on the stove to heat, then cut up an onion and diced it in the food processor.

"Mommy Anne? When can we go and see my kitties?"

"I don't know yet, sweetie. We'll wait for a nice sunny day."

"Will that be tomorrow?"

"I don't know."

"I hope it's tomorrow."

"Haley, what are the names of your kitties?" Wendy asked.

"Scat and Mittens and Kittywampus."

"Kittywampus?" Anne said. "That's a funny name."

How nice is this? she thought as Haley told a story about Kittywampus. She had grown up in a home that was often filled with tension and sadness and her mother's desperation to be the best possible wife to a man who deserved nothing of the kind. Anne had tiptoed through that minefield her entire childhood, and unlike Wendy, by the time she was eleven she had wished every day that her parents would get divorced.

This was how a family should be. Enjoying each other. Being together. The picture was only incomplete in that Vince wasn't there. It didn't matter to Anne that these girls weren't her children. She loved having them, getting to know them, figuring out their burgeoning personalities and how their little minds worked.

Life was good.

Until the doorbell rang.

Wiping her hands on a dish towel, Anne went to the front of the house, muttering her too-familiar ritual that she was all right, she was in a safe place, Peter Crane would not be standing on her doorstep.

But Dennis Farman was.

79

"Do you spend much time in Los Angeles, Mr. Bordain?" Mendez asked.

Darren Bordain was nervous and suspicious, and had been from the second Mendez had asked him to come back to the sheriff's office with him. His first instinct had been to say no, but he had thought better of that when Mendez asked him why not.

Refusing made it look like he had something to hide. He had already refused to let them take his photograph. He had refused to take a polygraph. If he refused to come in to look at a new piece of evidence he might be able to shed some light on, the cops were surely going to think he had something to hide.

"I go down there maybe once a month."

"Business? Pleasure?"

"Usually some of each. I went to school at UCLA. I have friends there."

"Did you know Gina or Marissa from LA?"

"No. I told you before: I met them both after they had moved here in—what?—'81, '82," Bordain said. "Why are you asking me this? I thought you wanted to show me something."

"We'll get to that," Mendez said.

The closed file folder lay on the table between them. Bordain eyed it like it might open and a rattlesnake would pop out of it and strike him.

"You also told us you never dated Marissa," Mendez said.

"That's right. We were just friends. We hung out with the same people."

"You didn't find her attractive?"

"Of course I found her attractive. She was a beautiful woman."

"A beautiful, single, free-spirited woman," Mendez said. "It's probably not a stretch to think she wasn't all that hard to get in bed."

"That's insulting."

"To you?"

"To Marissa. She wasn't like that."

"She was a single woman with a child."

"That doesn't mean she was easy."

"And you were never tempted to find out?" Mendez asked.

"No."

"Even though you admit it would have yanked your mother's chain if the two of you had gone out."

Bordain rolled his eyes and shifted positions on his chair for the tenth time. "Just because I can yank my mother's chain doesn't mean I always take the opportunity to do it."

"And last night, when you went home after dinner, did anyone see you?"

"I don't know. Ask my neighbors," he said, clearly annoyed. "I thought we went over all of this. I did not run my mother off the road."

"Hmmm . . ."

Mendez pulled the file folder to him, opened it and looked at the document, sighed and closed it again, returning it to its resting place.

"You're telling me you didn't know Marissa before Haley was born," he said.

"That's right. I'm telling you that, but you don't seem to be comprehending it."

"It's not that, Mr. Bordain. It's just that I have some documentation here that contradicts what you're saying in a pretty big way."

Bordain looked at the file folder but didn't touch it. Sweat was beginning to bead on his upper lip. He wiped it away, shook a cigarette out of the pack on the table, and lit it.

People always thought they looked cooler and more relaxed when they smoked. The thing they never accounted for before they lit up was that if their hands were trembling even a little bit, with the cigarette perched between their fingers it would then look like they had Parkinson's disease.

Darren Bordain's hands were shaking.

"And I have some problems with your explanation of your whereabouts both the night Marissa was killed and last night when your mother was run off the road," Mendez admitted. " 'Home alone' is one of those alibis that really isn't."

"I wasn't aware at the time I would need an alibi."

"It seems like you're home alone a lot for a guy who gets around town," Mendez said. "Dinners with friends, all those civic and charity functions you go to. You go home alone. That doesn't make sense to me. You're rich, charming, good-looking. I wouldn't think you'd ever have to sleep alone."

"Maybe I'm not as promiscuous as you would apparently like to be," Bordain said, flicking ash into the ashtray. Flicking too hard because he was nervous, a good bit of it missed the ashtray and landed on the table. He swore under his breath, stuck the cigarette back in his mouth, and quickly brushed the ashes onto the floor.

"And then there's this," Mendez said, slowly tapping his finger on the file folder. He did it over and over and over and over, the sound seeming to fill the otherwise silent room like water dripping from a faucet.

He could almost see Darren Bordain's nerves fraying.

"Why don't you just show it to me and get it over with?" Bordain snapped. "Whatever it is, there's probably a logical explanation for it."

Mendez pretended to think about it, then shrugged. "Okay."

He opened the folder and slid it across the table.

"You should pay particular attention to the box marked 'Father.' "

As he looked at the birth certificate the color drained from Darren Bordain's face, then rose back up again, bright red.

"That's a lie."

"That is an official document from the county of Los Angeles."

Bordain shook his head. "It can't be. It's not. I am not Haley's father."

"No? We showed her a photograph of you. She called you Daddy."

"She calls every man Daddy."

"Yeah, but apparently with you it's official," Mendez said, tapping his finger on the birth certificate. "Do you happen to know your blood type, Mr. Bordain?"

"A-negative."

Mendez raised his brows. "Really? Because we've got the sweatshirt you wore the night you killed Marissa. Man, it was soaked in blood."

"Marissa's blood, not mine."

"Marissa's blood—AB-positive. Lots of it. But also a little A-negative," he lied. "She must have scratched you, or you cut yourself. Knives get slippery when they're covered in blood."

"This is ludicrous!" Bordain shouted up at the ceiling, throwing his arms up. "I didn't kill Marissa!"

"What's that cut on your wrist?"

Bordain looked at his left wrist and quickly pulled the cuff of his shirt over it. "I—I—must have done that on the golf course."

"They golf with knives now?" Mendez asked. "That might make it interesting enough to try."

Bordain pushed his chair back and got up. "I'm done now. That's it. I don't have to talk to you. I'm free to go."

He went to the door and turned the knob, but it didn't open.

"It's like I told you yesterday, Darren," Mendez said. "Some of our guests are not as free to go as others."

80

"Dennis. What are you doing here?" Anne asked.

How the hell had he gotten her address? Their phone number was unlisted. She had a P.O. box for an address on her business cards.

"How did you find me?" she asked.

"I asked your dad."

"You went to my father's house."

Dennis nodded. "Uh-huh. He's really old."

"And he gave you my address?"

"Uh-huh."

Oh my God. That man will be the death of me yet.

Anne's gaze skated past Dennis to the sheriff's radio car sitting parked at the sidewalk. The deputy was eating a sandwich, paying no attention. Why would he pay attention to a little boy in a baseball cap? His assignment here was to keep Anne and Haley safe from a murderer.

"I set the hospital on fire," Dennis announced.

"I know. I heard about that," Anne said calmly.

"It was really cool," he said, his eyes lighting up in that glassy, unnatural way they did when he talked about killers and crimes. "This one guy came running out of his room and his arms were on fire! And he was screaming and shit. It was so cool! And then this oxygen tank exploded and *BAM*!! It went right through a wall and killed a lady!"

Anne's blood ran cold at his obvious delight—not just in his attempt to shock her but in the actual details of what he had done. The burned man and the dead woman meant absolutely nothing to him except in terms of his own amusement.

"Why did you do that, Dennis?"

He shrugged, his hands tucked into the big pouch on the front of his too-big hooded sweatshirt. "'Cause I wanted to. 'Cause I was mad. You said you were gonna come yesterday, and you didn't. You said you would bring me something cool, and you didn't."

"I called to say I couldn't make it, Dennis."

"No, you didn't," he said, getting angry. "You never called. You don't care about me. You're such a liar!"

"Dennis—"

"Shut up!" he shouted, his temper about to erupt. "You're just a lying, fucking cunt and I hate you!"

Before Anne could react Dennis had pulled his hands out of his pockets and came at her swinging and screaming. She wasn't aware of what he had clenched in his fists until she felt something sharp and pointed stick her in the breast. By the time it registered he had struck her twice more.

There was nothing she could grab to hit him with. She didn't want to run backward into the house. If Dennis saw Wendy or Haley she knew he wouldn't hesitate to hurt either one of them.

She tried to grab at his arms as he swung at her, and his weapons cut her hands and forearms. She shouted at him, "Dennis! Stop it! Stop it!"

Wendy had heard the commotion and came running from the kitchen. As soon as she saw Dennis, she started screaming at the top of her lungs. And right on her heels came Haley.

"Wendy, run!" Anne shouted as Dennis struck her again. "Take Haley and run!"

Haley stood at the end of the hall, shrieking.

Oh my God, Anne thought as she tried to fend off her attacker, *she's seeing it happen all over again.*

Dennis was in a frenzy. He was big for his age, and strong, and with strength of purpose he kept coming at her, shouting and swinging and pushing her backward into the house. They were now out of sight of the deputy parked at the curb.

"I fucking hate you!" Dennis yelled, bulldozing into her.

Anne's feet tangled with his and then she was falling backward. The back of her head struck the floor so hard it bounced. Blackness rushed in from the outer edges of her vision.

Dennis Farman came down on top of her, one arm raised high, ready to plunge a blade into her chest.

81

"I did not kill Marissa," Darren Bordain said.

Mendez got out of his chair. "Why don't you have a seat for a little longer? I've got to step out and get a cup of coffee. Would you like one?"

Bordain looked at him like he had lost his mind completely. "Do I want a cup of coffee? No, I don't want a fucking cup of coffee! No, I don't want to sit down!"

Big sweat stains ringed the underarms of his blue oxford shirt with the neat little logo embroidered on the pocket: MEF.

"I'll be right back," Mendez said, unfazed.

He let himself out of the interview room and went across the hall to the break room where Dixon, Hicks, and Vince were watching the monitor.

Vince smacked him on the back. "Good job, Junior."

"You've got him back on his heels," Dixon said. "I can't believe he hasn't asked for a lawyer."

"I think he wants to tell you something," Vince said. "But he can't quite do it."

"If he confesses to killing her, then it's out there," Mendez said. "He can't take it back."

Vince went to the machine and rewound the tape. "Watch him when you ask about the nights in question. Watch what he does."

Mendez stared hard at the monitor as the moments that had just happened unfolded again in front of him.

"Watch him here when you ask him about last night, if anyone saw him at home. Watch how he kind of closes his shoulders like he wants to wrap his arms around himself."

"Protective?" Mendez said.

"And the same thing here when you press him about his alibis," Vince said. "He's hiding something."

"The fact that he's a murderer?" Hicks suggested.

"Press those points again," Vince said. "See what he does."

"Okay."

Mendez poured two cups of coffee and went back across the hall.

"I brought you one anyway," he said, setting the cups on the table. "It's not half bad today. Someone brought Irish Cream beans in."

Bordain had taken his seat and lit another cigarette. He ignored the coffee. His hands were still trembling.

"I did not kill Marissa," he said again. "I had no reason to kill Marissa."

"I'm thinking you got tired of her blackmailing you."

"No one is blackmailing me."

"It's ironic, isn't it?" Mendez said. "You say you toyed with the idea of going out with her because it would wind your mother up like a top—but you get her pregnant and have a child out of wedlock and you keep that information to yourself—and the old lady would really blow a gasket over that."

"It's not ironic. It's not true."

"You can't account for your whereabouts the night she was murdered. Your name is on her daughter's birth certificate. And you're sitting here in front of me sweating like a whore in church."

"I was at Gina's house the night Marissa was killed," Bordain said.

"Gina, who is still conveniently in a coma."

"I didn't try to kill Gina."

"Is that why you wanted to go into her room this afternoon? To say your last good-byes and accidentally pull a plug?"

"That's ridiculous."

"She can't help you, Mr. Bordain. By your own admission, you left her house and were home alone by eleven thirty."

Bordain closed his eyes and swallowed hard. Mendez waited, watching his shoulders draw inward toward his chest, holding whatever it was inside.

"Darren," Mendez said quietly, leaning across the table. "There's nothing worse than murder. That's the big enchilada. It doesn't get worse than that. Whatever it is that you're not telling me could not possibly be worse than that."

Bordain smiled bitterly as tears came to his eyes. "You're not from where I'm from."

"I'm going to read you your rights and put you in jail. Does that go over big where you're from?"

"You don't have any proof that I killed Marissa."

"Not as much as I'd like," Mendez acknowledged. He tapped the edge of the file folder against the table. "But I've got a hell of a motive."

"She's not my child. She couldn't be my child."

Again the protective posture.

"Why?" Mendez asked.

"I didn't kill Marissa."

"Find me someone to corroborate your alibi."

Bordain put his elbows on the table and buried his face in his hands. "I can't," he said in a tortured voice.

That wasn't *I can't* because there was no one to corroborate his story, Mendez thought. That was *I can't* because he wouldn't reveal the name of the person who could.

Mendez found himself staring at the logo on the pocket of Bordain's shirt. He'd seen it before. Not in a store. He didn't pay attention to stuff like that. His sister Mercedes did most of his fashion shopping.

MEF.

He thought back over half a dozen conversations with different people over the week. Where was Darren Bordain the night of Marissa's murder? Gina Kemmer had some friends over, including Darren Bordain and Mark Foster. Where had Darren last seen Marissa? At the Licosto Winery event—the same last place Mark Foster had seen her. Who had Mark Foster been having dinner with the night he saw Marissa having dinner with Steve Morgan in Los Olivos—Darren Bordain? If they asked Steve Morgan, would he say Bordain?

Not a logo. A monogram.

Mark Foster. Mark E. Foster, the "not gay" head of the McAster music department.

Darren Bordain had either accidentally or who knew why gotten up that day and put on the shirt of his lover, Mark Foster.

"You're gay," Mendez said. "You were with Mark Foster when Marissa was being murdered."

Bordain didn't answer. He apparently would have rather gone to prison as a murderer than admit it.

"You're wearing his shirt," Mendez pointed out.

"Am I?" Bordain said. He was rattled, but he wasn't going down without a fight. "The laundry must have made a mistake."

"Did Marissa know?"

"We never had a conversation about laundry services."

"Did she think keeping the secret of your sexual orientation might be worth some cash?"

Darren Bordain was the only heir to Bruce Bordain's fortune, and Milo Bordain's only hope for a grandchild. He was being groomed for a big political career in a party that would never embrace a gay candidate. The scandal would be huge—worth killing over.

But Darren Bordain had kept that secret for a very long time, and he wasn't going to give it up now.

"Do you really want us digging into this?" Mendez asked. "Tell me the truth now and it doesn't have to go any farther than this room."

Bordain laughed at that. "Right."

"You'd rather we start digging around, asking your friends . . . your enemies?"

"I don't need an alibi," Bordain said, pulling his composure completely back in place. "I never slept with Marissa, nor did I kill her. And since I know you can have no evidence of me having committed a crime because I have not committed a crime, I'll be leaving now or calling my attorney. The choice is up to you."

Mendez sighed. They had nothing to hold him on. If he called an attorney there would be no chance at any further conversation with him. Damn. He'd had Bordain on the ropes there for a minute. He wanted more time.

Mendez sighed and tapped the file folder against the table again. He still had Bordain's name on Haley Fordham's birth certificate.

"Am I supposed to believe there's another Darren Bruce Bordain walking around Southern California?" he asked.

"Actually, yes," Bordain said. "Yes, there is. He's my father."

82

Anne got her arm up in time to block him and swung her other arm in from the side to try to hit Dennis in the head. But that wide swing left her right shoulder vulnerable and he was quick enough to stick his weapon into the hollow of her shoulder all the way to the hilt.

This was incredible. She was down. He had the complete advantage over her. He was striking her, stabbing her with two different weapons. She was going to be killed in the hallway of her own home by a twelve-year-old boy she had only ever wanted to help.

And somewhere behind her a four-year-old child was witnessing her second murder in less than a week.

She could hear Haley's hysterical screams.

Where had Wendy gone? Had she run out the back door to go get the deputy who was sitting in his car curbside eating a baloney sandwich, oblivious to what was happening in the house he was supposed to be guarding?

Above her, sitting on her stomach, Dennis was still raging. His eyes bugged out of his head. His face was so red she couldn't see his freckles. His mouth tore open, a gaping maw with a wild animal sound pouring up out of some terrible part of his soul.

The scent of urine was strong. All control gone, he had wet his pants in the frenzy.

As he raised an arm to stab her again, Anne tried to twist her hips beneath him to throw him off.

"STOP IT!! STOP IT!! STOP IT!!" Wendy screamed.

Suddenly Dennis Farman's head snapped to the side and blood spewed from his mouth and cheek all over the wall.

"STOP IT!! STOP IT!!"

Wendy, wielding a poker from the fireplace in the family room, struck at him again, hitting him on the shoulder, and once more, hitting him in the side.

Dennis fell sideways and over, dazed.

The deputy called from out on the lawn. "Mrs. Leone? Is everything all right in there?"

No, Anne thought as she lay there on the floor, cut and bleeding. Everything was not all right.

Nothing was right at all.

83

Darren Bruce Bordain.

The name had been in the family for generations, alternating generations using the first name Darren or the second name Bruce as the name they went by.

Mendez got up and left the room again, going across the hall, where his audience of three were all looking as stunned as Mendez felt.

"What the hell do we do now?" he asked.

"We're supposed to believe Bruce Bordain is Haley's father?" Hicks asked.

"Thinks he is," Vince corrected him.

"And Darren Bordain is so afraid of being outed that he'd rather go to jail as a murder suspect," Mendez said.

"He knows he isn't going to jail. He's too damn smart to fall for that," Dixon complained. "And now we know the whole damn family had a motive to want Marissa Fordham dead. What a freaking nightmare."

"Your cup runneth over, Cal," Vince said. "Daddy Bordain Senior fathered her child and she blackmailed him. Bordain Junior fathered her child and she blackmailed him. Or Junior is light in the loafers and she knew it and she blackmailed him. I don't know which motive I like better."

"No matter which one we go after, the press will smell a story like stink on shit and the Bordains will have my head on a platter," Dixon said.

"Press the gay angle first," Vince suggested. "The Bordains will circle the wagons around their own. Mark Foster is an outsider."

Dixon nodded. "Bill, go pick up Mark Foster and bring him in."

"And Bordain?" Mendez asked.

"Stall him," Vince said. "Let him think Foster is already here in another room."

"Okay."

Round Three, Mendez thought as he walked back to the interview room. A grim-faced deputy came down the hall as Mendez started to open the door.

"Is Vince Leone here?"

"In the break room. What's wrong?"

"Someone just tried to kill his wife."

84

Vince didn't wait for an invitation to go back into the trauma unit at Mercy General. He crashed the double doors like a bull in a china shop, sending staff scurrying like frightened mice.

He barged into the exam room without thinking, scaring the hell out of his wife. Then he pulled her into his arms and hugged her too tight, immediately loosening his hold at her whimper of pain.

"Oh my God. Oh my God," he murmured, carefully stroking her hair back from her face. "Baby. Oh Jesus. Are you okay?"

She nodded. Not satisfied, Vince looked her over. Her hands and forearms were raked with cuts and gouges. She had bled through the paper gown in several places on her chest, most notably in her right shoulder.

"Jesus Christ," he muttered. "Where's the doctor? Have you been seen yet?"

"We just got here."

"So where's the fucking doctor?"

"Don't yell at me!" Anne snapped.

Vince put his hands on her shoulders. He didn't know who was shaking worse, Anne or him. "I'm sorry, baby. I'm not yelling at you."

"Yes, you are!" she accused in a harsh whisper. "And keep your voice down. You'll wake Haley."

For the first time Vince saw the little girl curled up on the exam table, nearly swallowed whole by a big gray blanket.

"She's sedated," Anne said, turning to brush Haley's hair with the fingertips of her bloody hands. "She saw what happened. She wouldn't stop screaming, and I had blood all over me. It was horrible!"

"Hush, hush, hush, sweetheart." He tried to calm himself as much as he tried to calm Anne. He was breathing too fast, and he felt light-headed. "I'm sorry, honey. God, you scared the living shit out of me. When the deputy came and said—"

He stopped himself and pressed his lips against hers and stroked his hand down the back of her head—it came away red and sticky with blood. "Oh my God." He stepped out into the hall and shouted, "Where's the goddamn doctor?"

The big redheaded nurse from earlier planted herself in front of him with a ferocious scowl. "Sir, you have to calm down or you're going to get thrown out of here."

"Yeah? And who's gonna do that, Sunshine? You?" Vince demanded, poking a finger at her. "Ten of you couldn't get me outta here! That's my wife in that room, and I want her seen by a damn doctor!"

"Vince! Stop it!"

Anne had come to the door, battered and torn, wearing her most fierce expression.

"Stop it and get in here right now!"

"I like her," the nurse declared. "She's too good for you. Behave yourself and listen to her. The doctor will be here in a few minutes. He's dealing with a head injury down the hall."

"I'm sorry, honey," he said, following her back into the room. "You should lie down. Please lie down."

"I don't want to lie down," she said, her big brown eyes filling with tears. "I want you to hold me!"

"Oh, sweetheart."

Vince took her into his arms as if she were made of spun glass and held her while she cried. His heart was pounding so hard he thought it might burst.

"Tell me what happened."

The story came out in fits and starts. Vince did his best not to react the way his brain wanted to react. He wanted to fly into a rage. He wanted to find Dennis Farman and beat his brains out against a wall. He swallowed all of that down so as not to upset Anne, who was more upset about Wendy and Haley than about herself.

"All I could think was that I was supposed to protect her and here I was making her relive that attack all over again!" she said.

"It wasn't your fault, Anne."

"Of course it was my fault!" she said angrily. "You warned me not to stay involved with Dennis, but I couldn't listen to you. I had to try to help him, and look what's happened!"

"Baby, you didn't tell him to burn the hospital down. You didn't tell him to kill people. You didn't arm him. You didn't tell him where we live. How did he find out where we live?"

"Don't even ask me that right now. I'm so upset!"

"Shhhh . . ." Vince held her and rocked her some more. "Where's Wendy?"

"Down the hall somewhere with Sara. How am I ever going to face Sara again? Her daughter comes to visit me and ends up having to beat a kid in the head with poker! Why do these things happen to me?"

"I don't know, sweetheart," he said, holding her close again. "I guess they happen because you care too much. If you didn't give a shit about Dennis Farman he would have gone off to juvie a year ago to begin his lifelong career of incarceration. If you didn't care about Haley, she'd be with Milo Bordain, for God's sake."

He pulled back a little and stroked his hands ever so carefully down the sides of her face. "If you didn't care so much . . . I wouldn't be so crazy in love with you that I would go out of my mind like I just did and make a big ass of myself in a public place."

Anne tried to smile a little, but the tears were right there to threaten. "I just feel like I've made such a mess of things. Now what's going to happen with Haley? She was put in danger because she was in our home! Maureen is going to get her taken away from us!"

"Over my dead body," Vince promised. "Or hers."

"Milo Bordain will be petitioning the court tomorrow for custody."

"Don't you worry about the Bordains. They've got problems of their own tonight."

Someone rapped on the door. Vince scowled at the doctor that came in.

"It's about damn time."

"Vince . . ."

He shut his big mouth and stood back, barely resisting the urge to lose his temper every time the doctor touched Anne in a way that caused her pain. He was almost sick at the sight of the wounds Dennis Farman had inflicted on her. Only one was very serious, thank God. But several would need stitches and bandages, and would have to be watched for infection.

Anne excused him from the room for that part, and he didn't argue, knowing he wouldn't be able to take watching the love of his life being poked with needles.

He walked out the doors to the ambulance bay, needing the damp, chilly air to clear his head. He had forgotten his coat at the SO, and was still in the same shirt he'd been wearing when Zander Zahn had lunged at him with a knife. He wanted to wash the day off with a hot shower and crawl between the sheets naked with his wife.

The adrenaline had all drained out of his system, leaving him weak and shaking. He sat down on a bench, leaned his arms on his thighs and hung his head down, working at regulating and becoming more aware of his heartbeat and breathing.

With a clearer head, the realization of what he might have lost tonight was sharp and stark. For the second time in a year, his love, his second chance at life, his precious Anne had almost been taken from him.

Finally able to have one quiet moment to appreciate that, he allowed himself to feel that fear and cry.

Having been poked and washed and stitched and stuck with needles, Anne was finally able to dress in a pair of surgical scrubs borrowed from a nurse. She sat on the exam table waiting for Vince, petting Haley's hair.

The idea of CPS taking her away was unbearable. The idea of her going to live with Milo Bordain was unthinkable. The idea that Anne herself had put the little girl through a second living hell tonight was devastating.

What would this trauma bring to Haley, so close on the heels of losing her mother and almost losing her own life? Anne was terrified at the possible psychological damage this might have done. She was going to have to think hard about her future as an advocate if there was any chance of putting her loved ones in harm's way.

Of course, if she hadn't been an advocate, Haley would probably have never come into her life at all.

The little girl blinked her sleepy eyes open and looked up at Anne.

"Mommy Anne? Are you an angel now?"

"No, sweetie," Anne whispered. "I'm fine."

"You fell down," Haley said, tears coming. "That boy made you fall down!"

"But I'm all right now, sweetheart, and that boy will never ever come to our house again."

"He's mean like Bad Daddy!" she said, the anxiety building in her expression and her voice. She started to cry. Scrambling up onto her knees, she reached for Anne, and Anne pulled her close.

"Is that what Bad Daddy did to your mommy?" Anne asked, hating the need to do it.

Haley nodded against her shoulder, crying harder, edging back toward the hysteria that had gripped her earlier.

"Bad Daddy knocked my mommy down and hit her and hit her!"

"Oh, no. I'm so sorry, honey. I'm so sorry you had to see that. You must have been so afraid."

Anne held her tight as the terror of that night came back over Haley like a terrible black wave. She could see the picture in her mind's eye— the black figure knocking Marissa Fordham to the floor, the arm rising and falling again and again as the killer plunged the knife into her body over and over and over.

"Were you afraid, sweetheart?"

Haley nodded, sobbing. "I-I-I w-w-a-s hi-ding!"

"That was a good thing to do," Anne said.

"B-but then I-I said no!" Haley cried. "I said, 'No, no, don't hurt my mommy!' "

Oh my God, Anne thought. She could easily imagine Haley running from her hiding place, rushing to her mother's side. The killer couldn't leave her there alive to tell the story. Thank God he hadn't turned on her with the knife.

Had she been able to see his face? Had it been too dark? Was he someone she had known and trusted or a stranger she had never seen before?

"Did Bad Daddy say something to you?" she asked.

"Noooo!" Haley wailed. "I want my mommy!"

Now the grief came, howling and tearing out of her like a wild animal. Anne held her tight and rocked her and offered what comfort she could. When a nurse stuck her head into the room to ask if she needed help, she shook her head no. She let Haley release the emotion instead of stopping it short.

It didn't take long to run out. Her energy store depleted itself quickly, and she gave up and settled against Anne. Anne whispered to her and stroked her hair and told her she was safe, feeling like a liar in the wake of what had happened with Dennis.

A sense of security would be a long time coming for Haley . . . and for herself. She felt as if what strides she had made in her own struggle with the aftermath of crime had been taken away from her, and she had been pushed backward down that long tunnel. The sense of despair that came with that was so heavy, all she wanted to do was lie down and escape into sleep, and pray that the nightmares wouldn't follow her there.

85

"How long have you and Darren Bordain known each other?" Mendez asked.

For the first time since he had met Mark Foster, he saw a little crack in the man's stoic good nature.

"Not this again," Foster said, closing his eyes and heaving a sigh. "Darren didn't kill Marissa."

"That's not what I asked you."

"I've known Darren five or six years."

"And how long have you been involved?"

"Involved in what way?"

"How long have you been lovers?"

"Oh my God." He looked at Hicks. "You dragged me down here for this? What's wrong with you people? Why are you so hung up on the idea that I'm gay? I'm not gay—not that it's anyone's business. Darren is not gay. And will you make up your minds? First you think he's Haley's father, but now you think he's gay? And what would it matter? If he was gay, he really wouldn't have any reason to kill Marissa."

"He would if he didn't want her spreading his little secret around," Mendez said. "That information would be very valuable to him, I would think."

"You know his mother," Hicks said. "How would she react to news like that?"

"I have no idea."

"You told us you know her really well," Mendez said. "I barely know the woman at all and I can tell you she's a narcissistic, racist snob. Homophobic wouldn't be much of a stretch."

Foster massaged the back of his neck, literally trying to rub out the pain that this experience was. "Is there a point to this?"

"Oh, yeah," Mendez said.

"Will we get to it anytime soon?"

"What about his father?" Mendez asked. "He seems like that kind of macho man's man who wouldn't be too pleased to hear his son really doesn't have his same interest in strippers and hookers."

"I don't really know Mr. Bordain."

"You don't run in the same circles."

"No," Foster said. "Really. Why are you asking me these questions? Why don't you ask the Bordains? Why don't you ask Darren? He's here, isn't he?"

"What would make you think that?" Hicks asked.

"He called me and told me before you brought him down here."

"Why would he do that?"

"Because a bunch of us were going out to dinner. He called to say he wouldn't make it."

"Thoughtful."

"Yes. Is that a crime now?"

"No," Mendez said. "Did he happen to mention to you that he's wearing one of your shirts?"

"What?"

Mendez ran a forefinger along the breast pocket of his own shirt. "Monogrammed. M-E-F."

"There must have been a mix-up at the laundry."

"Mmmmm . . . I suppose that could have happened. Or maybe you left it at his house the night Marissa was killed."

Foster wasn't quite sure what to do with that. He waited to see where Mendez would go with it.

"Here's the thing, Mark," he said. "We have Haley Fordham's birth certificate with Darren Bordain listed as being her father."

"That's impossible."

"Why would you say that?" Hicks asked. "If Darren is straight, why wouldn't that be possible?"

"Because Haley was already born before Darren ever met Marissa."

"He says," Mendez stipulated. "The problem with Darren's story is that he doesn't really have an alibi for the night Marissa was killed, and he potentially has two very strong motives to want her dead. Now, he says he was home alone, which doesn't help him out. I don't believe him. I think there's someone who could corroborate his alibi. I don't believe he was home alone. I think he was with someone, and he's trying to protect that person."

"If you're that person, Mark," Hicks said, "you can clear this up right now and everyone moves on with their lives."

"Why would you believe me?" Foster asked. "Darren is my friend. I could lie for him. You would have to corroborate my story, and you'll do that by going around asking everyone I know if I'm gay and if Darren is gay. Since you're going to do that anyway, I might as well go home now and leave you to your work."

"You're not going to back him up," Mendez said.

"He hasn't told you he was with me," Foster countered. "There's nothing for me to back up. And there's nothing for either of us to gain by me saying I was there."

Frustrated, Mendez sat back and tapped a pen against the tabletop. This was what he got for getting into a chess match with a smart guy. It was so much easier with the average stupid criminal.

"All right," he said on a sigh. "Then this is going to get ugly, and there's nothing I can do about that except apologize in advance."

"You'll understand if I don't accept your apology, Detective," Foster said, getting up, "if you're going to drag my name through the mud and jeopardize my career by creating a scandal over something that doesn't exist."

"Yeah," Mendez said. "I guess it's easier for you to blame me for that than to accept responsibility for your own choice not to answer my questions or own up to who you are."

Foster gave him a cold look through his steel-rimmed glasses. "You don't have any idea who I am."

"No," Mendez agreed. "And you've been keeping that secret for so many years, I wonder if you know the answer yourself."

"I live with who I am every day," Foster said. He turned to Hicks. "If you don't mind, Detective, I'd like to go home now."

"Strike two," Mendez said, walking into the break room.

"Go home," Dixon said. "Tomorrow is another day."

"Any word about Anne?"

"Dennis Farman somehow found their house. He attacked her with a couple of wood gouges he stole somewhere. She's cut up, but she'll be fine."

"Jesus," Mendez muttered. "She's the only person on the planet who ever tried to do a kind thing for him. Where's the little shit now?"

"In restraints at Mercy General. Apparently, the little Morgan girl was at the scene and clocked him a good one in the head with a fireplace poker."

"Way to go, Wendy."

"He'll be transferred to the juvenile detention center as soon as the doctor clears him to go," Dixon said. "As far as I'm concerned he can rot there until he's eighteen."

Mendez shrugged his sport coat on and headed for the door. "Be sure to tell them to hide all their matches."

86

Dennis lay in his hospital bed, staring up at the ceiling. He couldn't move his hands because he had been tied to the bed. His head felt like a pumpkin that had been bashed with a baseball bat.

Stupid Wendy Morgan. He'd show her one day.

He would show them all.

It wasn't like he'd never been hit in the head before. One time his dad had knocked him in the side of the head with a beer bottle and he had gotten half knocked out and started puking and everything. He'd had a ringing in that ear for two weeks after.

Miss Navarre hadn't come to see him. He hoped that meant he had killed her and she was dead now. That would mean he had killed two people, and he wasn't even a teenager yet. Nobody was ever going to mess with him again. He felt like a pretty tough guy thinking about that.

Then he thought about what would happen next, and he didn't feel so tough, after all. He wouldn't be sent back to the hospital on account of he had tried to burn it down. He would be sent to juvenile detention, and no one would ever come to see him. Ever.

Nobody wanted to help him. Nobody would ever care how he felt or what he thought ever again. He had killed the one person in his life who would have done those things—Miss Navarre.

He had no one. No one at all. And he never would again. He was rotten and bad and good-for-nothing like his dad had always said. And not one person in the whole world cared. He was all alone.

For the first time in a long time, Dennis Farman cried himself to sleep.

87

"So, what's this all about, Cal?" Bruce Bordain asked.

He was irritated and making only a half-hearted effort to conceal it. The blindingly white smile had been downsized. There was certain tension in his body. He hadn't appreciated having a deputy interrupt his breakfast for a command performance at the sheriff's office.

"You couldn't just pick up the phone and talk to me?" he said to the sheriff. "I've got a plane to catch before noon."

"We'll try not to keep you, but this is a conversation we don't want to have over the phone, Bruce," Dixon said, leading the way back from his office, past the detectives' squad room.

"Do I get a heads-up as to what this is about?" Bordain asked. "I don't like surprises unless they're twenty-two with big tits and jump out of a birthday cake naked."

"Well," Dixon said, opening the door to interview room one and motioning Bordain in, "then it's a pretty safe bet that you're not going to like this one."

"And you're bringing me back here to the dungeons for this?" Bordain said. "Should I have brought my attorney with me?"

"I don't want someone walking into my office while we're having this conversation, Bruce. If you decide at some point that you'd be more comfortable with your attorney present, you're free to call him."

The last remnants of the bullshit smile faded away. "I don't like the sound of this."

"Have a seat," Dixon offered.

Bordain took the chair facing the door with his back to the wall. Dixon took the seat at the end of the table. Mendez took the seat with his back to the door, but turned the chair sideways.

"Bruce," Dixon began. "I asked you the other day how well you knew Marissa Fordham—"

"And I told you, well enough to have a conversation."

"How intimate would that conversation be, Mr. Bordain?" Mendez asked.

"What's that supposed to mean? Are you asking me if I was screwing her? You think I was screwing my wife's pet artist right under her nose? Do you think I have a death wish?"

"We're more interested in the year prior to when Milo began sponsoring Ms. Fordham," Dixon said.

"In 1981," Mendez specified. "You would have met her in Los Angeles. Her name was Melissa Fabriano then."

Bordain didn't even blink. "Never heard of her."

"We've come to find out she spent some time working at Morton's downtown," Dixon said, "as a hostess. You're a steak man, aren't you, Bruce?"

"I like a great cut of beef," he said. "And I'll admit it: I like a great piece of ass too. But I never laid eyes on Marissa until Milo introduced me to her."

Mendez tapped the edge of the file folder against the tabletop and exchanged a meaningful look with Dixon.

"Have you spoken to your son recently, Mr. Bordain?" Mendez asked.

"I spoke to Darren yesterday. He came out to the ranch to check on his mother. We had breakfast."

"Do you know if Darren had a relationship with Ms. Fordham prior to her moving here?"

"I wouldn't know. Darren doesn't share the details of his love life with me. What is any of this getting at?"

"We spoke with Darren last night," Dixon said. "He also denies knowing Marissa prior to her moving here in 1982."

"Well I'm glad we've cleared that up," Bordain said, getting up out of his chair. "Neither my son nor I knew Marissa Fordham before she became Marissa Fordham."

"The problem with that," Dixon said, "is that we've come into possession of a document that suggests otherwise."

Bordain's eyes went straight to the file folder. He sat back down.

"Which is what?" he asked.

Mendez opened the file and moved it across the table.

"This is a photocopy," Dixon said. "We have the actual document in safekeeping."

Bordain pulled a pair of reading glasses out of the chest pocket of his pale yellow shirt and perched them on his nose. Mendez watched him for any sign of an emotional reaction as he read the document. There was none. Bruce Bordain hadn't gotten where he was by not being able to play poker.

"It's a lie," he said, and shoved the file back across the table.

"It's a pretty convincing lie," Dixon said, "by all appearances."

"It's still a lie."

"Marissa Fordham moved up here with her infant daughter in 1982," Mendez said. "Your wife began to sponsor her almost immediately—"

"Milo is an art lover."

"—paying her a monthly amount of five thousand plus providing her with a place to live and work. That seems to be the coup of the century according to professionals in the art world."

"Somebody has to win the lottery."

"And this incredibly lucky young woman also just happens to have a birth certificate naming one Darren Bruce Bordain as the father of her child?" Dixon said. "Are we supposed to believe that's a coincidence, Bruce? Because I have to tell you, in case you didn't know it, I didn't fall off the turnip truck yesterday."

Bordain rubbed a hand across his face and scratched behind one ear, looking off to the side and at the floor.

"And we still haven't gotten to the heart of this, have we?" he said.

"Was she blackmailing you?"

"That's not it," Bordain said. "Come on. Go for the big one, Cal."

"Mr. Bordain, where were you on the night Marissa Fordham was murdered?" Mendez asked.

"I was in Las Vegas the entire weekend." He pulled his wallet out and withdrew a business card. "If you'd like to speak to my companions for that night, call this number."

Mendez took the card and looked at it. Pinnacle Escorts. "Pay up front," Mendez said, "not later."

"Apparently, my son needs to learn that lesson."

"You're going to leave your son hanging out to dry on this, Bruce?" Dixon asked. "I didn't peg you for that."

"He has to take responsibility for his own actions."

"Oh, he has," Mendez said.

"Then there you have it."

"Last night he owned up to being gay."

Bordain came halfway out of his chair and jabbed a finger at Mendez. "That's a fucking lie!"

"It would be if it wasn't true," Mendez said.

"My son is not a faggot! He's— He's— He's just trying to get out of this!" he said, pointing to the file folder. "It's his kid. The woman called him and told him she was pregnant. He sent her a check to get an abortion. She didn't do it. Then she showed up here with the baby. I'm not having my son marry some hippy artist with a love child. He's got a future to think about."

"So you paid her off," Dixon said. "Does Milo know why she's writing those checks?"

"Of course she knows."

"And she's fine with that?"

"Milo knows her job. She's protecting her son."

"That'll be the best spin you can put on the story," Dixon said. "Darren got a woman pregnant. Boys will be boys. And that definitely proves he's a boy's boy. Then the family took the woman and child in to support them. Very magnanimous. Definitely the right thing to do.

"The problem is, Bruce, the girl is dead."

"I didn't do it," Bordain said. "I was in Vegas."

"With access to a private jet and a bevy of handsomely paid alibi witnesses," Mendez said. "Is that going to hold up?"

"Like the fucking Hoover Dam," Bordain said. "Because it's true."

"And Darren couldn't have done it," Mendez said. "Because he was busy fucking his gay lover."

A huge vein bulged out on Bordain's forehead, throbbing. "That's a lie! You shut the fuck up!"

"You can't have it both ways—so to speak," Mendez said dryly. "Either Darren fathered this woman's child, got tired of the blackmail and killed her, or he couldn't have killed her because he was in bed with his boyfriend. Which is it, Mr. Bordain? Which of those is the lesser of evils for you?"

"You could both take a paternity test," Dixon said. "Then there's no question who did what to whom."

"Last I knew we had an amendment to the Constitution protecting us against self-incrimination," Bordain said.

He stood up again. This time he really meant it. "We're through here. If you want to speak about this further, Cal, call my attorney. He's in the phone book under 'Fuck You.'"

88

"If Bruce Bordain did it—or had it done," Hicks said, "why would he turn around and send the breasts to his wife? Or try to run her off the road?"

"To make it look like someone has it in for the family," Campbell said.

"But it looks like someone just has it in for the wife," Trammell pointed out.

They helped themselves to doughnuts if for no other reason than to perpetuate the stereotype. The war room smelled like grease and coffee.

"My money here is still on Darren," Mendez said. "Unless Mark Foster steps up, he's got no alibi. And even if Foster comes forward, it's like he said himself last night: 'So what?' That's like uncorroborated accomplice testimony. It's useless. Why wouldn't his lover lie for him? Isn't that part of the job description?"

"And your mother wonders why you're single," Campbell said.

"Well, come on," Mendez said. "Really. Wouldn't you rather have people think maybe you bat from the other side of the plate than have them suspect you of murder? You go to prison for murder."

"A pretty boy like Bordain goes to the can he'll find out all about being a good boyfriend," Trammell said.

"Say he thinks he's Haley's father—or he finds out that's been a hoax all along—either way," Mendez went on. "He kills her and makes it look like some lunatic did it. He sends the breasts to Mom for good measure. Then he tells everybody he couldn't have done it by admitting to something that's so scandalous no one would ever think he was lying about it."

"Right," Dixon said. "And who believes Milo Bordain knows about all of this and is just blithely writing the blackmail checks while treating Marissa Fordham like her long-lost daughter?"

Hamilton issued a low whistle. "These people would make Shakespeare's head spin."

"Tony," Dixon said. "You and Bill go up to Lompoc with that photo array and add a shot of Bruce Bordain. If one of them sent that box, there's our killer."

"That's a great plan, boss," Hicks said. "Except for one thing."

"What's that?"

"It's Sunday."

"Shit. How did that happen?" Dixon scowled.

"What about Gina Kemmer?" Trammell asked.

"No change in her status," Hicks said. "The doctors aren't very hopeful."

"Then we don't have a choice. We need to speak with Milo Bordain."

"The problem with that is going to be that Milo Bordain isn't going to want to speak with us," Mendez said. "There's no way her husband will allow it."

"She'll do it if she thinks she can move everyone around the chessboard the way she wants them," Dixon said. "I'm going to offer her the opportunity to set us straight. I think she won't be able to resist."

"Good luck, Boss," Mendez said. "Just one question: Are you up-to-date on your tetanus shots?"

"I'm fine. What about you?" Dixon asked, heading toward the door. "You're coming with me."

89

Gina, you have to wake up.
    Why?
    You have to wake up so you can tell the story.
    But this is so nice. It's like sleeping, only better.
    You can't just stay this way. All your muscles will atrophy and your body will feed on itself until you look like a petrified cadaver.
    Gross.
    And you know your mouth is hanging open, don't you? You're drooling.
    You're such a bitch, M.
    I love you too.
    Gina's mouth began working first, opening and trying to close. So dry. Parched. She needed a drink. No one noticed. The nurses were busy. One had checked on her not that long ago. They wouldn't look in on her for another fifteen or twenty minutes unless one of her monitors went off.
    That was all right. She was already tired from the effort of moving her mouth. She would rest awhile and try again later.

Open your eyes, G.
    What? I'm trying to rest. Go away.
    You're done resting. You have to open your eyes.
    They're stuck shut.
    You have to open your eyes. There's so much for you to see.
    Like what?
    You'll see.

See what?

You'll see when you open your eyes.

You're so annoying.

Her eyelids weighed a thousand pounds. Gina tried to lift them. They were like stone weights. Maybe they had coins on them. She had seen that in an old Western movie—when someone was dead, the undertaker put coins on the corpse's eyelids to keep them shut.

Maybe she was dead after all.

But if she was dead, how could her heart start beating faster? It wouldn't beat at all.

She must not be dead.

She tried harder to open her eyes. A little wedge of blurred colors appeared. But that was the best she could do for now. She would try again later.

Promise me, G.

I promise, M.

90

The weather system that had settled rain and fog over the area for the last several days had moved out, leaving the air crystal clean and the sky a sparkling, brilliant blue. The drive out to the Bordain ranch was like being in a video for a luxury car—except that they were in the usual ordinary Ford from the SO fleet of unmarked units.

This road, lined with spreading oak trees and white board fences, was where Bordain Motor Cars shot their commercials for the Mercedes dealership: a beautiful silver sedan slinking around the curves of the road, Darren Bordain leaning against the white board fence looking elegant and wealthy, telling all viewers they deserved a Mercedes.

The Bordains' shaggy red imported cattle grazed in the emerald green grass along the edge of the blue reservoir. As Mendez turned in at the gate and they rolled down the driveway, exotic-looking chickens of all colors with fantastic plumes atop their heads clucked and squawked as they pecked at the ground beneath the lush pepper trees.

Milo Bordain, in a huge straw hat and loose gardening clothes, was tending her roses, looking calm and relaxed. Not what Mendez had expected from her, considering the circumstances. She barely looked up at them from her work.

"Of course I knew all about it," she said, snipping the huge wilted head of a salmon-colored rose from its stem. "I'm not a fool, Cal. I know how the world works. I know men."

"And you were fine paying blackmail to Marissa Fordham?"

"I never considered it blackmail. I considered it an investment. It wasn't as if Marissa didn't have something to contribute to the world. She was an amazing artist."

"Who happened to have your son's illegitimate child," Mendez said.

She glanced at him like he was an annoying horsefly buzzing around her.

"I've told you Haley is like a grandchild to me."

"Because she is your grandchild."

"Now that her birth certificate has surfaced, I've already spoken with our attorney about beginning adoption proceedings. The records will remained sealed, of course. It isn't necessary for the entire world to know the circumstances of Haley's birth."

"That news could hurt Darren's political future," Dixon said.

Milo Bordain laughed. "If I told you how many very powerful political figures in this state have a love child or two on the side, you would be embarrassed at your naïveté, Cal."

"But how many have gay lovers?" Mendez asked.

For once, she spoke directly to him. Now the claws came out. "My son is not gay," she snapped, "and if you persist in this line of investigation, my husband and I will sue you personally and the sheriff's office for slander and defamation of character."

"You would rather believe that Darren murdered Marissa than that he prefers male company?"

"Darren didn't murder Marissa. He had no reason to. Marissa had no reason to blackmail anyone. She was very well taken care of."

"I heard she was getting tired of being controlled by you," Mendez said. "That maybe she was over being the daughter you never had."

"That's nonsense. Marissa was an artist. Artists have their fits. She may not have always appreciated my guidance, but she certainly appreciated the results," she said. "I introduced her to all the right people, exposed her work to an audience she would never have had access to on her own."

"And rubbed her face in it every chance you got, I'm sure," Mendez said.

Milo Bordain looked at Dixon, irritated. "Why do you continue to allow him to upset me, Cal?"

"That's his job."

His answer didn't please her. She should have been the queen of something, Mendez thought. Back in the day when monarchs could order people's heads cut off—like Marissa Fordham's.

"Maybe you were the one who got tired of her," he suggested. "She was rebellious. She didn't show proper appreciation for all you did for her. She knew all the Bordain secrets."

SECRETS TO THE GRAVE 403

"That's absurd!" she said, tears springing to her eyes. She turned to Dixon. "I loved Marissa!"

"Not enough to let her marry your son," Mendez pressed.

"Marissa had no interest in getting married! She had her art, she had Haley. She was happy with her life! I'm devastated by what happened to her!" she went on. "I don't know who killed her, but it certainly wasn't me or my husband or my son!

"Are you forgetting that I've been threatened too?" she asked. "Someone sent me that— that— *box* in the mail! Someone tried to run me off the road! What are you doing about that? Anything?"

"We'll pursue it if we get a lead," Dixon said. "There's nothing we can do right now."

"You'll do something when I'm dead on the floor," she snapped. "That's a great comfort to me! And I heard that Kemmer girl was found not far from here. This killer is lurking out here and you're wasting precious time accusing people who had no reason to be involved—"

Mendez's pager interrupted the tirade. He excused himself and went back to the car to radio in. When he got the message, he ran back, dismissing Milo Bordain from his mind.

"We have to go," he said to Dixon. "Gina Kemmer is conscious."

91

"She's drifting in and out," Hicks said as they met at the elevators near the ICU. "She fights for it, she's with it for a few seconds, and then she goes back under."

"Has she said anything?" Dixon asked.

"Not that makes any sense. She mumbles when she's out. Stuff like 'stop it, go away, leave me alone.'"

"I wonder who she's talking to?" Mendez asked. "Her assailant? She hasn't mentioned a name?"

"No."

"Is her family here?" Dixon asked.

"They left to go have lunch."

She looked like hell. The rat bites had scabbed over and the bruises were in full bloom. Somehow Mendez figured she would have thought she looked pretty good compared to the alternative. She should have been dead. The shot that had been meant to kill her had passed through her shoulder doing the least amount of damage possible. She had been plucky enough to survive on garbage and tenacious enough to get herself up a ladder with only two good limbs.

Vince was sitting beside her, waiting. He had done most of the talking the day they had interviewed her. His voice was strong and distinctive. If Gina was going to connect with any of them, it would be with him.

"How's Anne?" Dixon asked.

"Sore, tired, upset," he said.

"That kid's just bad," Mendez said. "My mother would say he's the son of the devil."

"I don't think even the devil would claim him," Vince said. "Twelve years old and he's done. He's broken. What are we supposed to do with him?"

"Lock him up and throw away the key," Dixon said. "How's the little girl? She was there."

"Seeing Dennis trying to stab Anne scared her pretty badly. On the upside for us, it seemed to shake loose some memories. Still no name for the killer, but she's closer to having access to it in her mind—if it's in there."

Gina Kemmer stirred and mumbled, "Knock it off."

Vince leaned closer to her. "Are you talking to us, Gina? It's Vince Leone. Do you remember me? I came to your house a couple of days ago."

Kemmer stirred and whimpered.

"Can you open your eyes and talk to us, Gina?"

"No," she said, her voice small and weak.

"Sure you can," Vince said. "You crawled out of a well with one arm and one leg. If you can do that, you can open your eyes and talk to us. Come on. You can do it. You have to fight for it, Gina."

"No, Ma-ris-sa. Stop."

Vince bobbed his eyebrows. "Is my voice getting higher?"

Mendez laughed. "If she thinks you're Marissa, she must be hallucinating."

"Hey, you've never seen me in a skirt."

"Ay, yi, yi, I could go blind just thinking about that," Mendez said.

"Come on, Gina," Vince said. "You're missing all the fun here. Open your eyes and talk to us."

Mendez thought he could see her struggling to follow Vince's instructions. Her brow knitted. A frown curved her mouth.

"Thatta girl," Vince said. "You're almost with us, Gina. Come on."

She lifted her eyelids as if they weighed a hundred pounds apiece.

"Hey, there she is!" Vince said. "These are a bunch of ugly mugs to wake up to, huh?"

She parted her lips as if they had been stuck together. Mendez took a glass of water from the bed table and slipped the straw between her lips. She drew on it enough to get a little bit of moisture.

"You've had a rough few days," Vince said. "Do you remember?"

She nodded slightly.

"Do you remember that someone shot you, Gina?"

She nodded again. Just that much effort was wearing her out. Her respiration had picked up a beat and seemed a bit labored.

"Do you remember who that was, Gina?" Vince asked.

She nodded again, then visibly worked at gathering her energy to say the name.

"Mark."

92

Sundays in Oak Knoll were days for music. A concert by the McAster Chorale, chamber music on the Plaza downtown, a student playing the Spanish guitar in the bookstore.

Mark Foster had gathered his honors brass quintet at the old Episcopalian church for a special preview of the upcoming winter festival.

The pews were nearly full. Cultural activities were always well attended in Oak Knoll. Between the academic community of McAster and the large population of white-collar retirees, no performance of any kind went lacking for an audience.

The quintet was in the middle of "Lo, How a Rose E'er Blooming" when Hicks and Mendez walked into the back of the church with a pair of uniformed deputies. The deputies made their way up the outside aisles. Mendez and Hicks walked up the center aisle and stood politely, waiting for the song to end.

Foster turned to bow to the crowd's applause. His face dropped at the sight of them. The deputies came in from the sides.

"What's going on here?" Foster asked.

Mendez stepped forward. "Mark Foster, you're under arrest for the kidnapping and attempted murder of Gina Kemmer. You have the right to remain silent—"

Foster went chalk white and looked at the deputy approaching him with handcuffs.

"Don't run," Mendez warned him. "Don't do it."

But like any cornered animal, Foster's strongest instinct was flight.

People in the audience gasped and shrieked as he bolted to the left of Hicks and dashed for a side door. Mendez sprinted after him, catching him by the back of the collar as he got the door open, and running him through the door and face-first into a stone pillar.

Slapping his own cuffs on Foster—now sporting broken glasses, a broken nose, and a split lip—he said, "I told you not to run."

Vince was waiting for them in the interview room. He had made himself at home with a cup of coffee, a couple of file folders, a notepad he was scribbling on when they came in the door.

He glanced up at Foster over the top of his reading glasses.

"Mr. Foster," he said, standing up and offering his hand—reminding Foster he was still in cuffs. "Vince Leone."

"Mr. Foster had it in his head he might outrun me," Mendez said, depositing Foster on a chair.

Vince frowned. "Oooh . . . never run, Mr. Foster. It makes you look guilty."

"I haven't done anything."

"Then why did you run?" Vince asked, taking his seat. "See how that works?"

"I'm being harassed."

"No, I believe you're being arrested. Which will follow with being booked and fingerprinted and deposited in the county jail."

He made a couple of notes, referred back a few pages, took his glasses off and set them aside.

"Gina Kemmer regained consciousness this afternoon."

"That's good news," Foster said.

"Not for you. Gina tells us you shot her and dumped her down an abandoned well and left her for dead."

"That's absurd!" Foster said, trying to laugh. "Gina is a friend! She's confused. She must have a concussion or something."

"No, actually, she doesn't. She broke her leg during the fall, but she didn't hit her head. There's nothing but layers and layers of garbage down at the bottom of that well. A pretty soft landing."

"Why would I do that to her?" Foster asked.

"Here's another tip for you: Never ask a question you aren't going to like the answer to.

"When Marissa was killed, Gina got scared, on account of she knows a lot of secrets," Vince said. "She's a sweet kid, Gina. She doesn't have the stomach for secrets. She just wants to have her little store, and live in her little house, and have her friends. That's all Gina wants.

"But her best friend gets killed, and she's afraid maybe she knows who did it. She figures to get out of Dodge before something bad can happen to her. But she should take a rack of cash with her—just in case. So she calls a friend—you. You'll give her a little 'loan,' she thinks.

"The next thing she knows, she's in the trunk of your car."

Foster shook his head. "That never happened."

"I can tell you haven't done this a lot, Mr. Foster," Vince said. "Tip number three: Don't deny what can be proved absolutely."

"We've impounded your vehicle, Mark," Mendez said. "It's in our garage, and as we sit here, evidence technicians are going through that trunk with a fine-toothed comb—literally. All they need to find is one hair."

"Do you own a handgun, Mr. Foster?" Vince asked.

"No."

"If you do, and it's registered, we'll find out," Mendez said.

"I don't own a gun."

"Does Darren Bordain own a gun?"

"You would have to ask him."

"Oh, we will," Mendez said.

"You don't strike me as the kind of guy who reacts aggressively to situations as a rule, Mark," Vince said. "You must have felt very threatened by Gina. You must have thought she could cause you to lose something or someone very important to you. Your career, for instance."

"She threatened to tell Bruce Bordain about you and Darren, didn't she?" Mendez said. "Bruce sits on the board at McAster. If he wanted you gone, you'd be gone."

"You define yourself by your career, don't you, Mark?" Vince said. "You're proud of what you've achieved. People your age don't reach the status you've reached in your world, do they?"

"Or did you do it for Darren?" Mendez asked. "If Gina let that secret go . . . Bye-bye, political career. I wouldn't be surprised if the old man disowned him, either. Even if Haley Fordham is his kid."

Foster sighed. "You might notice I'm not participating here. I don't have anything to say—other than that I didn't do it."

"We have a victim ID," Mendez said. "You're not going to come out on the right side of this, Mark. You need to think about how you can salvage something out of this mess. If Darren killed Marissa—"

"Darren didn't kill Marissa."

"How can you know that—unless you were with him that night."

"I know because I—"

Dixon rapped on the door and opened it, grim faced. "Mr. Foster's attorney is here. Courtesy of Darren Bordain."

93

"He was going to confess!" Mendez exclaimed. "Ten more seconds and he would have confessed! He was going to say he killed Marissa. Ten more seconds!"

They had adjourned to the war room while the Bordain attorney consulted with his new client.

Vince tuned out Mendez's rant. He went to the whiteboard and made a new entry on the timeline for Wednesday evening.

Apx. 6:00–6:30pm: G. Kemmer abducted by M. Foster.

Gina's explanation had been sketchy and piecemeal. She hadn't been able to give them more than a few words at a time before exhaustion pulled her back under. The doctor had finally intervened and kicked them out of her room.

"Let's think this through," Vince said, turning away from the board. "Go back to Wednesday. Gina is scared. We'll assume because she knows who killed Marissa. She decides she needs to get out of town before something happens to her. She goes to Mark Foster. If she thought Mark Foster killed Marissa, she would never have gone to him."

The excitement drained out of Mendez's expression, leaving just the frustration. "But he was about to say—"

"What you wanted to hear?" Vince asked. "He could have just as easily been about to confess to having been with Darren Bordain."

"Why else would Foster have tried to kill her?" Hicks asked.

"She threatened him," Vince suggested. "She knew about him and Bordain. She and Marissa facilitated the relationship. They were together as a foursome a lot. Foster and Bordain both gave Gina as their alibi for part of Sunday night."

"She was a beard," Hicks said.

"So she's desperate for cash to get out of town. If he hesitates, that's the thing she has to hang over his head. Maybe it's like I said to Foster: She threatened to expose them to Bordain's father. He sits on the board at McAster. Bruce Bordain can ruin Mark Foster's career. Gina can ruin Mark *and* Darren. The next thing Gina knows, she's in the trunk of a car."

"And Foster just happens to dump her in the same abandoned well Marissa's killer dumped the bloody sweatshirt?" Mendez said, skeptical.

"That well is a public dumping ground by the sound of it," Vince said. "It's located equidistant between Marissa's home and the Bordain ranch. Foster could have hiked out there in those hills. Or Darren could have told him. Or Darren could have been the one to take her there for all we know at this point."

"Either way," Mendez said. "I don't think it was a coincidence that sweatshirt was down there. I think we've got to give a hard look at both Bordain *and* Foster now. Even if Gina didn't suspect Foster, that doesn't mean he didn't do it."

"At least we know the girl is going to make it now," Dixon said. "As soon as she's strong enough, we'll get the whole story."

"Do we know if Darren Bordain owns a weapon?"

"We can't find out until tomorrow," Hicks pointed out.

"In the meantime," Dixon said, "we'll get a warrant to search Foster's home and office. And we sit on Darren Bordain. I'll get Trammell and Campbell to take the first watch."

"It's coming together, boys," Vince said, almost satisfied . . . but not quite.

He picked up dinner at Piazza Fontana on the way home, begging off from the glass of wine Gianni Farina wanted to share. All Vince wanted was to get home, back to Anne and Haley.

He had been loath to leave them that afternoon when he had gotten the call that Gina Kemmer had regained consciousness. Haley had been restless and out of sorts, acting out in little bursts of anger.

Anne felt she was probably struggling with the memories and emotions that had shaken loose when she had witnessed Anne being attacked by Dennis Farman. If those memories were starting to bubble up to the surface of Haley's consciousness, an ID of her mother's murderer could be forthcoming.

Meanwhile, Anne was struggling with her own feelings. Between the PTSD and her doubts and depression over how she had handled Dennis Farman, she was in a tough place, and Vince wanted nothing more than to be there for her as a sounding board, or to reassure, or just to hold her.

He knew how she was feeling. He still couldn't help but wonder if he had handled Zander Zahn more carefully, if Zahn would still be alive.

As he turned into their driveway, his car filled with the aromas of lasagna and chicken piccata. He thought how different it was to come home to someone who could share his day, and he could share hers, instead of locking up his professional self at the end of the day and trying to be someone he wasn't with someone who didn't really know who he was.

"You're a lucky man, Vince," he said, and headed into the house to spend the evening with his wife.

94

"I want to see my kitties!" Haley whined.

They sat at the breakfast table trying to start the day in between Haley's outbursts. First she hadn't wanted to get out of bed, then she hadn't wanted to get dressed. Anne had given in on that one for the moment, saving it as a bargaining chip for after breakfast. Next had come the raisin toast rebellion, now this.

Anne knew where the bratty attitude was coming from. The little girl was struggling with the memories and emotions that had been churned up because of Dennis's attack. She was frustrated and afraid of those feelings, and didn't have the tools to deal with them. Consequently, they came out in little fits of temper, and her attempts at taking some control over her environment came out in small acts of defiance.

Of course, understanding didn't make it any easier on the nerves to listen to a whining child.

Vince gave Haley a look that made her sit down on the banquette. "Enough," he said quietly. "Or you won't be going anywhere, young lady."

Big tears welled up in Haley's eyes and she started to wail.

They both ignored the tantrum.

"Are you sure you're feeling up to doing this?" Vince asked.

"No, but I think it will be a good diversion," Anne said. "For both of us."

As much as she didn't want to spend time with Milo Bordain, Anne had decided it would be a good day to take Haley to see her kittens at the Bordain ranch. Let Haley get some fresh air and exercise, and focus on things that were external instead of trying to cope with the tangled ball of feelings inside her head.

The same went for herself. Fresh air and the chance to be around animals and the beauty of nature would do her a world of good.

"Don't let that woman rattle you," Vince warned. "She thinks she's going to a-d-o-p-t. No one has told her yet that she has no standing because the paternity isn't what she thinks it is."

Vince had explained the situation to her as they knew it so far. Everyone was waiting to hear from Gina Kemmer, who was probably the only person involved who knew the true circumstances of Haley's birth.

Anne was trying to put the possibility that Haley had parents out in the world out of her mind. She had to make herself believe that Marissa Fordham—who by most accounts had been a caring, wonderful mother, and a caring, wonderful person—hadn't stolen this precious child. There had to be another explanation.

Haley had given up on her little fit and was nibbling on a piece of blueberry muffin.

"We're going to take a ride in a police car, Haley," Anne said. "That'll be fun."

"Why?"

"Because," Anne said, "if you finish your breakfast and brush your teeth and get dressed, the deputy will take us out to your auntie Milo's ranch to see your kitties."

Haley lit up at that.

That was the end of the bad attitude.

Vince went off to the hospital to see if Gina Kemmer would give them more revelations as she regained her strength.

Anne dressed in jeans and an oversize blue flannel shirt, accommodating both her stiffness and her bandages, and brushed her hair back into a ponytail. She put Haley in bib overalls, a little turtleneck, and pigtails, and off they went to the country.

The day was beautiful, as was the drive through the valley to the Bordains' ranch. Anne and Haley sat together in the backseat of the radio car, behind the cage like a couple of common criminals.

Haley looked out the windows. "This is the way to my house," she said. "Do you think if we went to my house my mommy would be there?"

"No, sweetheart. Your mommy is an angel in heaven, remember? Do you think your kitties will be excited to see you?"

She nodded and played with the stuffed cat Milo Bordain had given her, practicing her meowing.

When they pulled into the Bordain yard and parked, Haley couldn't get out of the car fast enough. Milo stood waiting for them, dressed in riding breeches and a hacking jacket, every hair perfectly in place.

Haley ran toward her. "Where's my kitties? Where's my kitties?"

"How about a hello for your auntie Milo first," Anne said.

"Helloauntiemilo, where's my kitties?"

Milo Bordain smiled one of her very practiced committee-chairwoman smiles. "Anne, I'm so glad you decided to bring Haley. I've missed her so much!" She bent over, trying to get Haley's attention. "I've missed you so much, Miss Haley!"

Haley scowled. "Where's my kitties!!"

"Haley," Anne warned. "No bad attitude or we go home."

"The cats are in the barn," Bordain said, defusing the moment by leading the way.

Tucked back against the hills, the ranch was like something from a magazine. Every inch of it was landscaped for effect with old climbing roses and white potato vines and purple morning glories dripping from fences and arbors. Pepper trees and huge spreading oaks studded the property. Flower beds full of pansies edged the paths and outbuildings. Beautiful gray horses with long flowing manes and tails grazed in green paddocks. Colorful chickens hunted and pecked, scattered around the setting like the perfect farmyard accessories.

"This is absolutely beautiful," Anne said.

"Thank you. It's been a lot of work, but I enjoy it," Bordain said. "We were city people for so many years, but we love it here. Oak Knoll is a wonderful town. We both enjoy being involved with the college and the various civic groups. Bruce enjoys playing the gentleman rancher on the weekends."

"Is Mr. Bordain here very often?" Anne asked, trying to fill in the blanks of Marissa Fordham's life. If Milo was here on her own most of the time, it made sense that she had more or less adopted a second family in Marissa and Haley.

Milo Bordain forced a little laugh. "He's a very busy man. He's expanding his parking lot kingdom to Las Vegas now. He's there today."

She was a lonely woman, Anne thought. And now her son was coming under the scrutiny of detectives in the death of her surrogate daughter. The tension was showing in her manner and in the fine lines across her forehead and around her mouth. She was probably feeling threatened. Marissa had been taken away from her, now her son . . . She would want more than ever to maintain her connection to Haley.

Haley ran ahead of them into the barn.

"She's struggling a little bit with the memories that are coming back to her," Anne said. "That's manifesting in some difficult behavior."

"She's remembering more?"

"Yes. At first she was very vague. Now she's starting to talk in more detail about what happened."

"Really? But she hasn't named the killer."

"No."

"Well, I wish she would so the detectives would stop trying to blame my son. It's ridiculous to think Darren would want to harm Marissa. It's absolutely ludicrous," she insisted, anger rising. "I have to say I'm very disappointed in Cal Dixon."

Haley came racing out of the barn. "Mommy Anne! Hurry up! Come and see my kitties!!"

Thankful for the interruption, Anne picked up her pace, reaching out her hand. Haley grabbed hold and tugged at her, dragging her toward the barn and the promise of kitties.

95

Gina was awake and alert when Vince got to the hospital. Though she still looked worse for wear, there was some color in her face, and her eyes were clearer.

"I hear they're moving you to a regular room today," Vince said. "That's a big improvement. We thought we'd lost you, young lady."

"I guess I'm tougher than I look," she said, but she didn't sound strong. She still sounded weak and fragile, and Vince knew what energy she had would be quickly spent.

"I think you're probably tougher than you ever imagined," he said. "That's good to know, huh?"

"But I wish I hadn't had to find out," she confessed. "Did you arrest Mark?"

Vince nodded. "That had to be a terrible shock for you. I'm sorry."

"It still doesn't even seem real. I would never have done anything to hurt him or Darren. We were friends! I was just *so scared*. All I could think about was running away. I thought Mark would help me. When he told me no . . . I was already in a panic. I said the first stupid thing that came into my head."

"You threatened him," Vince said.

Gina nodded, tears squeezing out of her closed eyes. "I never, never, never would have followed through. He should have known that. I can't believe he reacted the way he did. He was always such a nice guy—I thought."

"We can know people really well, Gina, and never know what they're truly capable of when they're cornered. Mark has held that secret inside him most of his life. He's feared it, feared what it could do to everything he's worked so hard to achieve."

"Why can't people just be who they are?" she asked. "It's not like there aren't gay men in the music world. He wasn't going to be the only one."

"He was going to be the only one named Mark Foster," Vince said, "with his parents and his upbringing—whatever that might have been. He was going to be the only one involved with Darren Bordain, who's supposed to have a big political future ahead of him."

"I guess so," she said quietly, her emotions already taking a toll on her strength. The color was fading from her cheeks. "It was the most horrible moment of my life—when he turned on me like that. It was like—I can't even describe it. It was like he was someone I'd never seen before in my life. That was the worst moment—worse than when he shot me."

Vince could see her energy flagging. She was still fighting an infection, to say nothing of her emotional and psychological exhaustion.

"Gina, I know you're tired, and we've got a lot to talk about, but we won't try to do it all now. I just need to ask you, do you know who killed Marissa?"

She was quiet for a moment as she looked inward, not liking what she saw. "I thought I did. Now . . . I don't know."

"Who did you think it was?"

"Bruce. Bruce Bordain."

96

"Hell of a deal," Hicks said. "Can you imagine either one of those men—Foster or Bordain—doing what was done to Marissa Fordham?"

"No, but one of them did."

"A person has to be out of their head to do something like that and then just walk around like nothing ever happened."

"I don't know," Mendez said. They were creeping around the streets of Lompoc, trying to find the post office. "The other night Anne was talking about when Crane attacked her, how he didn't look like the man she knew. It was like he was a monster inside and the mask came off when he went after her. Maybe there's something to that."

"When I first made detective I worked a rape case," Hicks said. "A guy posing as a gas company employee got this gal to let him into her apartment. Normal-looking guy. Friendly enough. She wasn't suspicious of him at all until he set his toolbox down and turned around.

"She said it was like he had turned into a different person. He turned around and just looked at her and she instantly became terrified. He beat her in the head with a claw hammer and raped her, and she said, during the rape every once in a while, he would pause and lick her like he was a dog or a wolf. And she said she could see in his eyes then that he wasn't human."

"Did you catch him?"

"Yeah. The guy managed a lamp store, had the wife and kids, the whole deal. Looked as normal as could be."

"There it is," Mendez said, pointing to the right.

They parked and went inside. Two people were working the desk: a surfer burnout with a bleached stand-up hairdo, and a large woman with bright blue eye shadow and long claw fingernails.

They waited their turn behind a woman buying stamps and a man picking up his mail after a long vacation. When they got to the male clerk Hicks introduced them and explained what they were there for. Mendez placed the photo array—such as it was: a mishmash of actual photographs and pictures cut from *Oak Knoll* magazine—on the counter.

"He would have been in probably a week ago today," he said.

"Dude, I don't know," the surfer clerk said. "They all look familiar to me. Do you know how many faces come through here every day? I don't remember."

He seemed like remembering his own name might sometimes have been a struggle for him.

"It's very important," Hicks said.

"What was in the box, man?"

"Human body parts," Mendez said.

Surfer clerk stared at them. "No way."

"Way," Mendez said.

"No way! You can't send human body parts through the mail, dude. That's against regulations."

"Yeah, well, imagine what he did to get them," Mendez said. "That's seriously against the law."

Surfer clerk grimaced. "Wooo . . . Dude."

He turned to his coworker. "Monique, come look. You remember people."

Monique finished up with a registered letter, then moved over. "Is this about that woman down in Oak Knoll? She was stabbed ninety-seven times? I seen that on the news. That's some bad shit y'all got going on down there. What's with you people? You had that serial killer too. They putting something in the water down there? It's like y'all got the vortex of evil going on."

"We hope not," Hicks said.

Monique studied the photos one at a time, very methodical, looking carefully at one, then setting it aside, looking at the next one. Surfer clerk waited on the next customer.

"These here are some good-looking men," Monique said. "I don't mind no men like this coming through here—you know what I'm saying? This one here, he look like a movie star," she said, holding up the photo of Steve Morgan. "He's bad, though. I can tell. He got that pout. I don't never trust no good-looking man with a pouty mouth."

She took a good long look at Mark Foster. On the next one she stopped.

"He looks familiar," she said.

Darren Bordain.

"I think he might have been in here," she said. She stared at the picture and chewed her bottom lip. Something wasn't striking her quite right.

"He would have had a brown box about yea big," Hicks said, guesstimating the dimensions of the box with his hands.

Monique thought about that.

"He's very charming . . ."

She frowned and shook her head. "No. I don't remember that. That's not what I'm remembering with that face."

She turned the photo over—not really a photo, but a page cut out of *Oak Knoll* magazine. Mendez had folded the other people in the picture out of the way—the Bordains and another prominent area family at a charity event.

"Oh!" Monique cried out. She tapped a long, curved purple fingernail on the picture. Her eyes were as wide as if she had been frightened. "*That one* I remember!"

97

"Bruce Bordain?" Vince said. "Bruce thought he was Haley's father?"

Gina nodded wearily. "It's a long story."

"You need to tell me the short version of it now, Gina," Vince said.

Bruce Bordain had been in a hurry to catch a plane the day before. If he had left the country, they couldn't lose any more time than they already had getting on his trail.

"I'm so tired," she said.

"I know you're tired," Vince said, glancing out the glass wall to check for anyone watching. He'd gotten tossed out of her room once already for overtaxing her. "But this is so important, Gina. We want to bring Marissa's killer to justice, right?"

"Yes," she said. Her respiration had begun to quicken. "Of course."

"Was Marissa involved with Bruce?"

"Yes. For about a year."

"And at some point she told him she was pregnant."

"She was," Gina said.

"Gina, I saw photographs of you and Marissa just a couple of months before Haley was born. She wasn't pregnant."

Frustration and exhaustion furrowed her brow. Another few tears squeezed out between her lashes. "I'm so tired."

"I know, sweetheart. I'm really sorry," Vince said, "but this is so important, Gina. Is Haley Marissa's daughter? Is she Bruce Bordain's daughter?"

"No."

Marissa had been pregnant, but Haley wasn't her daughter, nor was Bruce Bordain her father. Vince swore under his breath. Now he'd opened an industrial-size can of worms and his witness was running out of gas.

"But Marissa was blackmailing the Bordains?" he said.

"You make it sound so dirty," she said. "It wasn't like that. She was trying to do something good. For Haley."

"Gina, Bruce Bordain has been paying for four years for a child that isn't his. Did he find that out?"

"He might have," she admitted in a small voice. "Marissa was tired of it. She'd had it with Milo trying to manipulate her and treating her like she was a doll to play with. At first, she had wanted him to pay for what he'd done to her. But it wasn't worth it."

"What had he done to her?" Vince asked.

Tears ran from the corners of Gina Kemmer's closed eyes. She was slipping away from him, slipping away from the bad memories.

"Gina?"

"Mr. Leone?" The nurse supervisor came into the room with her hands on her hips. "Don't make me throw you out of here again."

Vince staved her off with one finger raised. "Just one more question."

"Mr. Leone . . ."

"Gina, what had he done to her?"

He had to lean in close to hear her.

"He killed her . . ."

98

"*That one* I remember," Monique the mail clerk said.

The picture was of the Bordain family—Bruce, Milo, and Darren—and another prominent Oak Knoll family in formal dress at a charity fundraiser.

Mendez had expected her to point to Darren Bordain.

She hadn't.

Nor had she pointed to Bruce Bordain.

She pointed to Milo.

"Are you sure?" Hicks asked, sounding as doubtful as Mendez felt.

"I'm sure all right. I'm not forgetting that nasty piece of business any time soon. She was so rude!"

"She came in here with a box to mail?" Mendez asked.

"Yes. And she had it wrapped in brown paper and trussed up with string like a Thanksgiving turkey," Monique said. "And I explained to her very polite that we don't want packages wrapped in paper and tied up with string because it gets caught in the machinery. Well, you would have thought I'd told her to stick it where the sun don't shine. And I wished I had!"

Milo Bordain.

Mendez couldn't even hear Monique the mail clerk going on. He was trying to get his head around this new twist in the Bordain tale.

He nodded to the door. Hicks thanked the clerks and followed him out onto the sidewalk.

"*Milo* Bordain?" Mendez said as they emerged from the Lompoc post office. "Milo Bordain?"

No other words came. They stood on the sidewalk outside the post office, oblivious to the citizens of Lompoc going in and out of the building. Mendez knew his partner's brain was doing the same thing his brain was doing: spinning its wheels crazily.

"I don't get it," Hicks said. "She mailed that box to herself?"

"She *packed* that box herself?" Mendez said, sick at the thought.

He couldn't help but picture the murder scene, the incredible brutality, the blood. He could imagine Marissa Fordham's screams of terror as she tried to escape her killer.

"That can't be right," Hicks said, rejecting the idea entirely. "The postal worker; she's got to be wrong. That can't be what happened."

"She recognized the photograph," Mendez said. "We didn't even ask her to look at that photograph. And the attitude. That's Milo Bordain all over."

Hicks shook his head. "There's no way. No woman could do that to another woman. Women don't kill like that—hands-on, crazy, violent. Cut another woman's breasts off? No."

A woman with a toddler in tow caught the last of that and gave them a wide berth on her way into the building.

"Maybe she mailed the box but didn't know what was in it," Hicks said.

"How could she not know what was in it?"

"The husband or the son gave it to her to mail."

"To mail to herself?" Mendez said. "And she drove way the hell to Lompoc to do it? That doesn't make any sense."

"And Milo Bordain as a homicidal maniac does? No woman could do that to another woman. No way."

Mendez put his hands on top of his head and walked around in a little circle.

"Marissa Fordham was the daughter she never had," Hicks said. "The little girl was like her granddaughter."

"*Was* her granddaughter," Mendez said. "Or so she thought."

"Then why would she try to kill the girl?" Hicks asked. "What grandmother does that?"

Mendez tried to lay out a scenario that worked. "Milo Bordain and Marissa get into it. Maybe Marissa wanted more money or maybe she was done with it. Either way, Milo snaps and goes nuts. She realizes too late that the little girl saw her and can identify her. She has to kill her, too."

"A woman can snap and kill somebody as easily as a man," Hicks conceded. "But the mutilation? Shoving the knife in the vagina like that?"

Two elderly women leaving the post office gasped and stared.

Mendez got the picture out and opened it flat. Bruce Bordain, Darren Bordain, and his mother at a charity function.

"Look at them side by side," he said. "If not for the age gap, they could be brother and sister. Twins, even."

"The son dresses up in drag," Hicks ventured. "Mom is on the masculine side. He's on the feminine side. He pretends to be her and brings that box up here to mail it."

"That would make a hell of a movie," Mendez said, "but it doesn't make any sense."

Hicks threw his hands up. "What part of this lunatic family does?"

"I don't know," Mendez said, digging the car keys out of his pocket. "But we're not going to figure it out standing here. Let's try to find a pay phone and call the boss."

99

After the bright sunshine, the interior of the barn was so dark, it took Anne a moment to adjust her eyes.

The barn was cool and smelled of fresh hay and horses. Haley let go her hand and ran halfway down the center aisle then turned right. Anne followed. A door stood open to a feed room. A wide sliding door opened out onto a patch of shaded grass where two tiger-striped kittens were taking turns pouncing on a string of orange twine.

Haley dropped down on her knees in the grass and snatched at one end of the string. The kittens bounced into the air in surprise, dashed away, then came back in stalking mode.

Haley squealed and giggled in delight at the antics of the kittens. Anne stood in the doorway watching her, so happy to see her happy. She deserved to have some time to think nothing but little girl thoughts about kittens in the grass.

"Mommy Anne! Come and play with my kitties!"

Anne got down on the grass beside her and paid careful attention while Haley showed her what to do with the twine to make the kittens pounce on it.

"This one is Scat," she said. "And the one with the white paws is Mittens."

Scat bounced up on his toes with his back arched and his tail straight up in the air, then turned and dashed back into the barn. Haley ran after him, running smack into Milo Bordain's legs.

She looked up at the tall woman whose face and hair seemed stark white against the black backdrop of the dark barn.

"Oops!" Anne said, laughing.

But Haley didn't laugh, and Milo didn't laugh.

Haley took a step back and then another, her eyes on Milo Bordain. "Haley?" Anne said, puzzled by the expression on her face.

Bordain leaned over. "Haley? What's the matter? You remember me. Auntie Milo."

Haley's lower lip began to tremble and tears welled in her eyes.

"B-b-b-bad," she stammered.

"You didn't mean to run into your auntie Milo," Anne said. "It was an accident."

"B-b-b-b-ad," she said again. "Bad Daddy. Bad Daddy!"

It took a second for Anne to understand, but then the pieces snapped into place. Swallowed by the black background, with just her face standing out, Milo Bordain must have reminded her of the man who had attacked her mother. Darren Bordain was a prime suspect. He was the spitting image of his mother.

"Bad Daddy! Bad Daddy!"

Milo frowned sharply as Haley began to wail and shriek, only succeeding in making herself look more menacing.

"Haley!" she snapped. "Stop that!"

Before Anne could react, she took the girl by the upper arms and gave her a shake.

"Haley! Stop it! Stop it right now!"

Anne bolted forward and scooped Haley into her arms, ignoring the pain of her own injuries as she pulled the little girl tight against her. She wanted to knock Milo Bordain on her ass.

"Don't frighten her more!" Anne snapped.

"She knows me, for heaven's sake!" Bordain snapped back. "She's being ridiculous!"

"She's four!" Anne shot back.

Haley cried harder.

"What have you been putting in her head?"

"Nothing!"

"Cal Dixon and your husband are trying to frame my son—"

"That's absurd! They're trying to get to the truth—whatever it might be."

"Darren did not kill Marissa."

Anne walked away from her and the argument, cradling Haley's head against her shoulder. "It's okay, sweetheart. You're okay."

Haley cried and twisted in her arms. "No!!"

"Maybe we should just go," Anne said. She turned back toward Milo Bordain. "We should just go. This isn't a good day for anyone. We can come back another day."

"No!" Milo said, instantly contrite. "No, please don't go. I'm so sorry I lost my temper. I'm just beside myself with everything that's gone on this week.

"Don't go. I have a picnic lunch all ready," she said. "We'll go down by the reservoir. Haley, don't you want to go for a ride in the golf cart?"

Haley looked up at her. They were out of the shadows of the barn now. The apparition that had frightened her was gone, replaced by a person she had known her whole life.

"Should we go for a ride in the golf cart?" Bordain said, forcing a smile.

Still unhappy and out of sorts, the little girl put her head back down on Anne's shoulder and murmured, "Mommy Anne . . ."

The muscles in Milo Bordain's square jaw tightened against her annoyance at Haley's name for Anne.

"It's okay, sweetie," Anne said. "Do you want to go for a ride and have a picnic?"

"The cart is right over here," Bordain said, leading the way.

The golf cart, like everything else to do with Milo Bordain, was decked out elaborately, made to look like a Mercedes-Benz with the big logo on the front.

Anne got in and tried to set Haley on the middle of the front seat, but Haley crawled back into her lap and started to suck her thumb.

We should have gone, Anne thought. To hell with Milo Bordain's feelings. Haley's feelings were all that mattered. And yet, she couldn't quite bring herself to tell the woman to turn the golf cart around and go back.

They drove through the field bordered by white fences and shaded by big trees. Shaggy red cattle watched them pass with only mild interest.

The reservoir—a grand name for a man-made pond the purpose of which was firefighting—shone like a blue jewel under the clear sky. Milo had sent her minions out earlier to make a picnic spot ready complete with a table and a red-and-white-checked tablecloth. A large wicker picnic basket sat on one end of the table with baguettes sticking up out of it and red and green grapes spilling over the side.

"You went to a lot of trouble," Anne said.

"Oh, no, not at all. Nothing is too much trouble to make a nice event. All it takes is organization."

And cheap hired help, Anne thought. She pointed at the table and leaned down to Haley. "Look, Haley, isn't this special?"

Haley was unimpressed. She nudged a toe against the dash of the fancy golf cart and whined around the thumb in her mouth. "Mommy Anne . . ."

"You really shouldn't let her call you that," Bordain said, irritated.

"If it makes her feel more secure," Anne said, "there's no harm in it."

"You're not her mother."

"I know that. Haley knows that."

"You're not going to be either."

Anne bit her tongue again, remembering what Vince had said at breakfast. Milo Bordain believed her son was Haley's father. No one had told her differently.

"Haley knows her mommy is an angel in heaven. Isn't that right, Haley?"

"I wouldn't be so sure about that," Milo muttered half under her breath.

We should have gone home, Anne thought again. This was a mistake. Why subject Haley—and herself—to this unpleasant woman? Just to be polite? Just to keep the peace? Her tolerance for this kind of social posturing was almost nil, and yet here she was.

Now they were stuck out in a field with Milo Bordain, and Anne realized, well away from the ranch buildings. Well away from the deputy who had brought them out here. A vague sense of unease stirred inside.

We should have gone home . . .

100

Vince went back to the SO to speak to Dixon in his office about what Gina Kemmer had told him.

"She said Marissa was involved with Bruce Bordain for about a year. At some point she says Marissa did get pregnant, but then she turned around and admitted that Haley isn't Marissa's daughter—or Bruce Bordain's for that matter."

"But she was blackmailing him?"

"Yes, but Gina said Marissa was done with it, that she had wanted Bordain to pay for what he'd done to her, but that it wasn't worth the hassle to her anymore. She was tired of having to live under Milo's thumb."

"What had Bruce done to her?" Dixon asked.

Vince shrugged. "I don't know. She said he killed her."

Dixon's brow furrowed. "What the hell does that mean?"

"I don't know. That's when I got asked to leave," Vince admitted. "Gina says there's a lot more to the story. She claims they were trying to do something good."

"For themselves?"

"For Haley. But Gina thinks Marissa was going to tell the Bordains Bruce wasn't the father."

"Four years of child support to a kid that wasn't his," Dixon said. "At the rate they were paying her, that's about a quarter of a million dollars. I have to think that would be enough to piss off anybody—even Bruce."

"Do you know where he is?"

"He flew to Vegas yesterday."

"I'd call Vegas PD and see if they can't sit on him for you," Vince said. "If there's anything to this, he's a definite flight risk."

"And he was willing to throw his own son under the bus for this," Dixon said. "That's cold."

"I don't know," Vince said. "It's like you said to him yesterday—that's probably the best spin he could put on it. If the world thinks Darren got Marissa pregnant, that would dispel any rumors about him being gay."

Dixon's phone rang before he could even think about it. He hit the button marked Speaker.

"Sheriff, Detective Mendez is on line one. He says it's urgent."

Dixon punched line one. "Tony, what have you got for us?"

"Are you sitting down?"

"Yes."

"We showed the photo array to the postal clerks."

"Who did they ID?" Vince asked. "Bruce?"

"Milo."

"I beg your pardon?" Dixon said.

"Milo Bordain. The clerk was adamant about it. I don't know what to say, boss. I'm not sure what it means."

Vince felt the bottom drop out of his stomach. He was halfway to the door before Dixon could speak.

"Where are you going?"

"Anne took Haley to Bordain's ranch."

101

"I didn't know Marissa," Anne said. "What was she like?"

"She was lovely, of course," Milo Bordain said as she brought the food out of the picnic basket. Grapes, cheeses, crackers, bread. Haley was on a mission looking for butterflies. Anne kept one eye on her, making sure she didn't wander too close to the water.

"She was talented," Bordain said. "So talented, but headstrong. She could have been internationally known, but she lacked the discipline necessary. I tried to guide her, but she wouldn't always take the best advice."

"Do you know a lot about the art world?" Anne asked in all innocence.

"I know talent," she said defensively. "And I know people. I'm very good at putting the right people together to make things happen. This is partly why I'm so disappointed in Cal Dixon. He could have gone places. Now, after the way he's botched this investigation . . ."

"It isn't over yet," Anne said, hoping to defuse Bordain's rising level of tension. "Things could turn in another direction."

"They had certainly better," Milo snapped. "Everything I do for this community, and this is the thanks I get? Having my son's name dragged through the mud?"

"Haley!" Anne called. "Come have something to eat."

So we can get the hell out of here.

Haley climbed up on the picnic bench, looked at the spread, and announced, "I don't like this kind of food."

"This is a very nice lunch, young lady," Milo said.

"Have some grapes," Anne suggested.

"No."

"How about a cracker?" Anne said.

"No! I wanna go play with my kitties!"

"No playing until after lunch," Milo declared.

Haley got a mad face. "You can't tell me. You're not my mommy!"

The look on Milo's face frightened Anne. "Don't you talk back to me, young lady! You'll grow up to be an arrogant little bitch, just like your mother!"

Haley started to cry.

Anne wanted to lash out at Bordain, but something, some instinct stopped her—self-preservation, fear? All she knew for certain was that it was past time to go. Milo Bordain's behavior was becoming increasingly erratic.

"I'm sorry," Anne said to their hostess, getting up from the table. She put an arm around Haley, still standing on the bench. "This is just not the day to do this. I think we should leave."

Bordain arched a brow. "After I've gone to all this trouble?"

"I'm really sorry," Anne said, "but this is a difficult time for Haley."

"She's just being a brat," Bordain said. "If you would discipline her—"

"It's not that simple," Anne said.

"I've told you time and again—"

"Mommy Anne . . . ," Haley whined. "Mommy Anne—"

"Stop calling her that!" Milo shouted.

Haley sobbed.

"Okay, that's it," Anne said. "We're done here. We're going home."

"You can't just leave," Milo said. "After I've gone to all this trouble—"

"Nobody asked you to go to any trouble," Anne said.

"Isn't that just like you?" Bordain said. "You've never appreciated anything I've ever done for you. You're nothing but an ungrateful little whore!"

Fear went through Anne like a bolt of lightning. Milo Bordain wasn't speaking to her. Milo Bordain didn't know her, had never done anything for her. She was talking to Marissa.

Automatically Anne's eyes went to the picnic table and the knife that had been left there to slice the bread.

"You think you can just leave me?" Bordain said.

"Mrs. Bordain," Anne said firmly. "Who do you think you're talking to? I'm not Marissa."

Bordain wasn't listening. Her mind had gone to a different place. She took a menacing step toward Haley. Anne drew her back a step on the bench.

"Stop it!" Bordain shouted. "Stop that crying!"

"Bad Daddy!" Haley shouted back. "Bad Daddy! You hurt my mommy!"

Oh my God, Anne thought. She meant it. Haley hadn't mistaken Milo Bordain for her mother's killer. Milo Bordain *was* the killer.

Bordain lunged for Haley with both hands, going for her throat. Haley screamed. Anne swept her off the bench, set her on the ground, and shouted, "Run, Haley! Run for help!"

Terrified, Haley ran a few steps and turned around, sobbing, "Mommy! Mommy, no!!"

Milo Bordain was six feet tall and outweighed Anne by a good fifty pounds. When she grabbed Anne by the hair and slapped her, Anne saw stars. Bordain pulled her arm back to hit her again. Anne dropped to her knees, pulling the bigger woman off balance and loosening her hold.

Bordain fell sideways against the table, sending food and drinks flying. Anne scrambled forward on her hands and knees, grabbed the bench, grabbed the edge of the table as she tried to get her feet under her.

They lunged for the knife at the same time.

One of them struck the end of the handle and the knife spun out of reach.

Anne dashed around the end of the table and lunged for the knife again.

Bordain threw herself halfway across the table and grabbed the knife, blade first, cutting her hand. An animal roar tore up out of her chest, not of pain but of rage.

Haley was screaming and screaming. Anne could see her in her peripheral vision, out of harm's way. But then the little girl came running.

"No!! No!! Don't hurt my mommy!!"

Bordain wheeled toward her, the knife clutched in her bloody hand.

On the wrong side of the table, Anne grabbed the first thing that came to hand—a loaf of French bread—and swung it like a bat, hitting Bordain in the side of the head, diverting her attention from Haley.

"Leave her alone!" Anne shouted, not knowing if Milo Bordain could even hear her. The woman's eyes were like flat pieces of colored glass. Her face was twisted grotesquely as she came at Anne with the knife.

Anne ran around the end of the table and leaned down to scoop Haley off the ground, the only thought in her mind: *Run!*

Already wounded herself, she was going to pick up thirty pounds of wiggling, screaming child and try to run.

It never occurred to her that she wouldn't be able to do it.

She never felt the knife slice her side as she grabbed up the girl and ran.

The buildings of the ranch seemed so far away. It seemed like her feet pounded the ground but gained no ground. In the distance, she could see the deputy running toward them, but not getting any nearer.

She could hear her own breathing, the air rasping in and out of her lungs. She could hear her feet thudding against the ground. And in the far, far distance she thought she could hear a siren.

She didn't dare look back.

Then suddenly something hit her shoulder from behind and she was falling.

Trying to shield Haley, Anne twisted as she fell, hitting the ground with her shoulder. At the same time, the deputy planted himself and shouted for Bordain to drop the knife.

She didn't.

"Drop the knife!" the deputy shouted.

Milo Bordain looked at the knife in her hand, some kind of terrible realization dawning.

"Drop the knife!"

Slowly her fingers peeled away from the handle. The knife fell to the ground. Bordain fell to her knees, emotions tearing through her. She opened her mouth to cry, but no sound came. She curled into a ball, her broad shoulders heaving as she sobbed silently.

Trying to suck in some air, Anne pushed herself up onto her knees. Haley flung herself into Anne's arms, crying and crying.

"Mommy! Mommy!"

"It's okay!" Anne panted, holding her tight. "We're okay! We're all right. It's over."

And then, somehow, Vince was there, holding them both, and they were safe.

102

"No one was supposed to get hurt," Gina began. "We never meant for that at all. We were trying to do something good, really. It was all supposed to work out for the best for everybody, but most of all for Haley."

"Let's start at the beginning, Gina," Vince said. "Tell us about you and Marissa."

They had gathered in her hospital room—Dixon, Mendez, Hicks, and himself. She was strong enough for it now.

She would be sent home in another day or so, though her ordeal was far from over. Her ankle would require more surgery and physical therapy, and would probably always be a reminder of what she had gone through.

For now, though, the more superficial of her physical injuries had begun to fade from view.

"At the very beginning," she started, "Marissa—she was Melissa then—she and I became friends in the seventh grade. We lived in Reseda. I had a normal family. Marissa grew up in the foster care system.

"Her mother was killed in a car accident when she was eight, and her father became an alcoholic and couldn't take care of her. It was really sad. He died when we were seniors in high school."

"So family was probably really important to Marissa," Vince said.

"Yes. She loved to hang out with my family, and she was always taking care of the other kids in the foster homes she lived in. You didn't know her, but Marissa was the kind of person who would just open up her heart and draw everyone in—especially little kids. She always said she was going to have a big family of her own one day."

Vince offered her a tissue and patted her hand. "I wish I could have met her," he said. "It sounds like she was a very special person."

Who had also perpetrated blackmail and fraud, he knew. But then people were never only one thing.

Gina nodded and struggled for a moment with her emotions.

"So the two of you stayed friends through school and then . . . ?" Mendez prompted.

"We both got jobs, got fired, got other jobs. But we always stuck together. I only had brothers growing up, and Marissa didn't have anybody, so we became each other's sisters."

"And by 1981, where were you?" Dixon asked.

"We were living in Venice near the beach. I was working in downtown LA in the garment district. Marissa was a starving artist. She would sell her paintings at the beach on the weekends, but she worked as a hostess at Morton's steakhouse to pay the rent. That's where she met Bruce Bordain."

"And they got involved . . . romantically?"

"Marissa got involved romantically," she corrected him. "I don't know. Maybe it was because of her not having a dad or whatever. I mean, Bordain is old enough to be her father, but she really liked him. He made her feel special. He bought her gifts, took her places. He gave her the whole song and dance about not being in love with his wife, and how they didn't even live together."

"But it was just a passing thing for him?" Vince said.

Gina nodded. "She was just a toy for him. And then she got pregnant and that was the end for him. She called him and told him, and a few days later she got a check in the mail from him to go get an abortion.

"Can you believe that?" she said, disgusted. " 'Go take care of it,' he said in his note. Like it was nothing. Like, like she was having a wart removed. Then he stopped returning her phone calls."

"Did she have the abortion?" Vince asked.

"It was terrible," Gina said. "She didn't want to. She didn't know what to do. She wanted to keep the baby. She wanted Bruce to love her. The stress literally made her sick. Then she miscarried and everything went wrong. She started hemorrhaging. I thought she was going to die!"

"That's when she had the hysterectomy," Dixon ventured.

Gina nodded. "It was worse than if he had killed her. Having kids was Marissa's biggest goal in life."

"She took it hard," Vince said. Marissa would have been twenty-three years old at the time. Young, with no family to fall back on, working as a hostess, and her knight in shining armor had set off a series of events that had utterly destroyed her fantasy of a perfect life.

"So where does Haley enter into this?" Mendez asked.

"Once a week we both volunteered at a women's shelter in Venice," Gina said. "We met this girl our age. She was pregnant. She called herself Star, but we never knew her real name. She said she came to LA to become a movie star, but changing her name was as close as she ever got."

"And the father of her baby?" Vince asked.

"We never knew. I don't think she knew. One day she'd tell us it was her drug dealer, and the next day she'd say he was a struggling actor or a big-shot director.

"Star would talk about getting rid of the baby, having an abortion. Then she would decide she wanted the baby, and she would talk all this crazy talk about how she would raise the baby and have a really nice apartment and buy the baby everything. But she didn't have any money. I mean, get real. She was a homeless drug-addicted prostitute. She didn't have any way to support herself, let alone a baby.

"It bothered Marissa a lot. She was afraid of what Star would do to the baby, how she might have it and throw it in a Dumpster, or have it and drown it in a toilet. Or maybe she would sell it. Marissa said she had read about people selling babies to pedophiles and sick stuff like that. I didn't even want to know that could happen!"

"So Marissa came up with a plan?" Vince said.

"She said, what if she got the baby and told Bruce Bordain it was his. The timing worked. He has tons of money. What would it be to him to pay for raising a baby? Nothing. And he should have been doing it anyway, for Marissa's baby.

"The baby would be taken care of and so would Marissa. She would be able to concentrate on her art. She would have the child she always wanted. It would be good for everyone."

"Except Bruce Bordain," Mendez pointed out.

"Well . . . neither one of us felt very sorry for him."

"So Star had the baby and what? Marissa just took her?" Hicks asked.

"No, no. It wasn't like that," Gina said. "They made a deal. Marissa would pay for Star's drug rehab and prenatal care for the baby. There would be one payoff when the baby was born, and Star would have the birth certificate made out the way Marissa wanted."

"So it was like a private adoption," Vince said.

"Basically. Marissa sold everything she owned and took a second job to do it. She couldn't let Bordain see her because of course she wasn't pregnant. So she had to quit her job at Morton's. She told her boss she was quitting because she was pregnant, knowing Bruce would ask when she wasn't there. She got a job at a seafood place in Santa Monica and worked days at a boutique.

"She waited until right before Haley was born to call Bordain and tell him she was having the baby. He sent another check, but he told her he didn't want to hear from her again."

"So she moved to Oak Knoll," Mendez said.

"She knew his wife lived here part-time. It was the only place the Bordains had a home that we could afford to move to."

"And what was your part in it, Gina?" Dixon asked.

"It was an adventure, Marissa told me," she said, rolling her eyes at the ultimate understatement. "I thought, why not? We decided we would take some of the money Bordain had given her and money that I had saved, and start the boutique."

"And this is when Marissa changed her name?" Mendez asked. "About the time you moved up here?"

"Right before. She didn't trust Star not to change her mind and show up one day and want Haley back. So we made up the whole story about her being from Rhode Island, and being cut off from her family—like a heroine from a Sidney Sheldon novel or something. It was kind of exciting."

"So, you both moved up here," Dixon said. "Bruce Bordain couldn't ignore Marissa if she was here right under his wife's nose. Did he ever question that he was the baby's father?"

"No," Gina said. "I thought he would. I thought he'd want some kind of blood test or something, and then we'd be sunk. But the money mattered less to him than if Marissa would have made a big public stink about it—or I guess I should say it mattered more to Mrs. Bordain. The whole support-the-artist thing was her idea."

"Let me get this straight," Mendez said. "Marissa went to blackmail Bruce Bordain, and his wife came up with a plan that kept her in their lives?"

"Creepy, huh?" Gina said. "But I guess in a weird way it was a control thing over her husband, you know? And she really got into it.

"She treated Marissa and Haley like they were her pretend family or something, like they were life-size dolls or something. Even though Marissa was an artist, Milo decorated their house the way *she* wanted it. She designed the art studio—how crazy is that? She would tell Marissa what to wear to events, and if Marissa didn't do it Mrs. Bordain would have a fit."

"How did Marissa feel about that?" Vince asked.

"She said that was a small price to pay, and so what if Milo wanted to dress her up? She kind of liked the game playing, seeing what she could get away with—the people she had as friends, the men she chose to date. She would only let Milo have just so much control and no more.

"That had gotten worse lately," she said. "They had started arguing a lot. The more independent Marissa tried to be, the more controlling Milo was."

Which would have made a free spirit like Marissa only try harder to slip free of her owner's hold, Vince thought. It would have been a vicious downward spiral in their relationship that would only have exacerbated Bordain's need for control

In her own way Milo Bordain wasn't so different in her need for order than Zander Zahn had been. The difference was Zahn had exercised his need for order over inanimate objects. Milo Bordain needed to control the people in her life like pieces on a chessboard.

"I told Marissa to put an end to it," Gina said. "Why live like that? It was so sick and twisted. She needed to get away from the Bordains. Her career as an artist had taken off. She was making good money. The boutique is doing well. She didn't need them anymore."

And that, Vince knew, was what had gotten Marissa Fordham killed.

Milo Bordain would never have been able to tolerate Marissa—the daughter she never had—taking Haley—her make-believe grandchild—out of her life. Her real-life dolls were going to walk away from her real-life playhouse, and she would control them no more.

"And was Marissa going to do that?" Mendez asked. "Tell Milo Bordain it was over?"

"She was going to tell the truth, and that should have been the end of it."

"And it was," Dixon said.

"I can't believe Milo was the one who did that to her," Gina said, the tears rising again. "How could one woman do that to another woman? And how could she do that to Haley?"

"She couldn't leave a witness," Mendez said.

"But she loved Haley! How could she hurt her like that?"

"People like Milo Bordain don't love the way the rest of us love, Gina," Vince explained. "They are the center of their universe, and everyone else is just an object that revolves around them. They might think the object is beautiful and that they have to possess it, but in the end it's just a thing to them."

The emotion came over Gina then like a wave she couldn't hold back, and she started to sob, and Vince suspected she was seeing that crime-scene Polaroid he had shown her of her best friend butchered on the kitchen floor.

He wondered if Milo Bordain would replay that same scene in her memory. Probably, but with very different emotions attached.

She was sitting in jail now. ADA Kathryn Worth had made sure there would be no bail. Milo had been caught with knife in hand going after Anne and Haley. No judge was going to dare risk it—no matter how much money the Bordains could throw around.

Milo Bordain would go to prison where she would be the state's doll, where she would be told what to wear and where to sleep and when to eat. Vince wondered if she would even see the irony in that.

103

"Milo Bordain," Mendez said as they walked out of the hospital into the sunshine. "Nobody saw that coming."

"No," Vince admitted. "The brutality of that murder . . . That's usually something women reserve for unfaithful husbands, not each other. In hindsight, all the pieces fit. She felt like Marissa was hers, bought and paid for, literally. And like any spoiled child, if she couldn't keep her toy, nobody else could have it either."

It sounded so straightforward and logical, he thought, when it was one of the most twisted, insane murders he had ever worked. His buddies at the Bureau had already tapped him to come to Quantico and present the case for study.

"The press is already trying to come up with a catchy nickname for her, comparing her to Lizzie Borden," Mendez said.

"Lizzie Borden was never convicted, you know," Vince said. "Milo Bordain is going away forever and ever, amen."

"The Bordains have deep pockets. They'll try to buy an insanity plea."

"I don't care what they try," Vince said, digging his car keys out of his pants pocket. The wind came up and flipped his necktie back over his shoulder. "A jury gets a load of those crime-scene photos—wherever they put her, they'll throw away the key."

"Do you think she's crazy?"

"In the legal sense? No," he said. "Not at all. She killed Marissa out of rage. She thought she had killed Haley, getting rid of the only witness. Why she excised the breasts might have been symbolic initially— destroying what was feminine about Marissa—but sending them to herself in the mail was definitely self-serving."

"Trying to divert attention away from herself as a suspect by portraying herself as a victim," Mendez said. "That's some kind of cold blood running through her veins."

"She's calculating, not crazy," Vince said. "That's why she was so upset when she didn't get custody of Haley. She figured if she had the child in her control, she would have made certain one way or another the girl would never ID her as the killer."

"She's evil," Mendez said. "That should be a legal term. She's guilty of being evil. That's simple."

"We can look at anything and make it simple," Vince said. "Even murder. Every one of them can be boiled down to this: Either somebody didn't get what they wanted, or someone wanted exactly what they got. Disappointment or desire."

"Or both."

And the result was ultimately all the same: lives broken and the death of dreams. Marissa's life had held a wealth of promise, now gone. She would no longer have the chance to make the world a better place by creating art or by raising a wonderful child. Milo Bordain, who had been a driving force in the community and instrumental in raising funds for half a dozen charities, would leave a void in those positions. Mark Foster, a bright light in his field, had given up his future trying to protect a secret. And Darren Bordain, who had known nothing about his lover's attempt on Gina's life or his mother's murder of Marissa, was left emotionally devastated without the two people most important in his life.

Bruce Bordain, who had effectively set this all in motion by cheating on his wife and destroying the dreams of a young woman, would walk away unscathed.

"How's Anne?" Mendez asked.

A smile tugged at one corner of Vince's mouth. "Remarkable. Beat up, cut up, but incredible. But I told her if somebody tries to kill her one more time I'm locking her up for safekeeping."

"She's had a rough few days."

"She's more worried about Haley, but Haley will be all right. Between the two of us, we'll make sure of it."

"You'll adopt her?"

"Absolutely," Vince said. "We'll get a jump start on our family with Haley Leone."

Mendez grinned and clapped him on the back. "Congratulations."

"I'm a lucky man," Vince said. "How about you?"

"I heard Steve Morgan moved out. He told Sara he never had an affair with Marissa. Marissa wouldn't have him because of Sara and Wendy. But he would have done it, and that's what counts."

"And what are you going to do?"

Mendez stuffed his hands in his pockets and shrugged as he leaned back against the car. "Listen when she wants to talk."

"One step at time."

"Yeah," he said ducking his head. "I think maybe I'll go take one now."

104

Anne watched Haley playing in the grass with the kittens that had moved into Casa Leone. There was nothing quite like a near-death experience or two to make one appreciate the simple things in life.

"But why did any of this have to happen?" Wendy asked. "Why do all these bad things have to happen?"

They sat side by side on the patio sofa, Anne with her arm around Wendy's shoulders. Sara had brought her over hoping she could stay for a few hours while Steve moved out of their house.

"I don't know," Anne said honestly. "We don't get to have a nice neat explanation for everything that happens in life—bad or good. I guess that's what life is: Things happen, and how we deal them makes us who we are. We can either choose to learn and rise above, or give up and let the bad things defeat us."

"It's so hard!" Wendy said, tears springing to her eyes.

"I know, honey, but you're not alone, and you'll get through it. You won't let the bad things beat you," Anne said, giving her shoulders a squeeze. "I have something for you. Watch Haley. I'll be right back."

Anne went inside the house and came back out with a small wooden plaque with an inscription engraved on a brass plate.

"Someone gave this to me last year after . . . what happened. And I looked at it every day, and thought about what it means and what it means to me in my life. And now I'm going to give it to you. And I want you to look at it every day, and think about it, and think about what you choose for your life."

Engraved on the plaque was a quote from Ernest Hemingway's *A Farewell to Arms*.

"The world breaks everyone and afterward many are
strong at the broken places."

May you grow strong at the broken places.

"Do you understand what that means?" Anne asked her.

Wendy nodded and hugged her carefully. "I won't let the bad things beat me."

Anne smiled. "Why don't you go help Haley play with those kittens?"

As Wendy went to play with Haley, Vince came out onto the patio and sat down beside Anne, leaning down to kiss her gently.

"How are you feeling, Mrs. Leone?"

Anne looked up into the shining dark eyes of the man she loved. What would the future bring them? Good and bad. The adoption of their first child and the trial of Peter Crane. Their love had been forged in adversity and tempered by another trial by fire. And here they were. Together, a family. Strong at the broken places.

"I feel lucky, Mr. Leone," she said. "I feel lucky."